STATE SLAVE

D. G. VODA

BK
BROWN
& KING

STATE SLAVE

Copyright © 2016 by D. G. Voda

ATTENTION BOOKSELLERS:
Wholesale copies of this book may be ordered from industry distributors Ingram (800-937-8200) and Baker and Taylor (908-541-7000)

ISBN-13: 978-0997570809
ISBN-10: 0997570806

Jacket design and illustration: Tomasz Pudelko
pudelkot@gmail.com

10 9 8 7 6 5 4

A WICKED PIECE OF SCIENCE FICTION SATIRE

The FreeFone on Friendster Boraxo's desk rang. The screen showed that the call was from PeacePerson Investigator Enterprise Green. Boraxo frowned and picked up the instrument.

"Do you control a slave named Differently-Abled Zook?" the investigator asked.

"Why, yes," said Boraxo, taken aback. "He's one of my best workers."

"Do you know anything about his whereabouts last night?"

"Last night? No. The last I saw him was yesterday afternoon, at the Gratitude Day Chastisement. Why? What has he done?"

"Nothing," said the investigator. He asked a few more questions about Zook's work duties and psychological profile and rang off.

Disturbed, Boraxo put down the FreeFone. He knew that Zook must have done something wrong or he wouldn't be the object of an investigation. The State never investigated anyone unless a crime had been committed, and it always turned out a crime had been committed. There were, after all, rules and regulations for everything, with everything recorded, so it was merely a matter of searching to discover which offense best suited the State's need for prosecution.

So Zook was certainly a criminal, or soon to be one.

In an upside-down future where everything is provided but everyone's a slave, one man is about to learn the price of free.

CONTENTS

For Pat Allen. Thanks.

The most totalitarian system is the one where the penetration of the regime into the soul of the individual is complete.

– Vaclav Havel

1.

YOU CAN'T ARGUE WITH FREE

The Shredder was already being prepared for the last chastisement of the day, and Differently-Abled Zook still didn't see any sign of his slave friend Sustainable Bacon.

Zook had been trying for years to get himself sold to AssemblyPerson Harold Wild, and an under-groundskeeper position had just opened up at the palace. Zook was desperate to get the job, and Bacon—a private slave on Wild's staff—had promised to maneuver a personal introduction to Wild immediately following the executions.

It was a beautiful sunny morning, perfect for Gratitude Day, with a cloudless sky and a slight sea breeze stirring the flags at the tops of the bleachers. The stadium was, of course, packed, with the various state slave cohorts arranged in numerical order around the field, each state slave fluttering the little UCC flag they had been given as they entered the event. The banners which Zook's department had designed and painted were prominently displayed on the stadium fence all the way around the field: *"Silence=Perks"*; *"We Have Achieved Beige"*; *"You Can't Argue with Free."* Along the edges of the infield were the white tents shading the Friendsters, with golden-tunicked private slaves carrying canapés to the mingling dignitaries, while in the center, state slaves were hosing the gore out of the giant Shredder in preparation for the morning's next and final event.

But where was Bacon? Zook stole a glance at his FreeFone, hoping for a FreeVid, or at least a FreeText.

Nothing.

"Eyes forward!" barked Zook's Friendster. Not-for-Profit Boraxo was a short man with a shallow chest and stooped shoulders. He stood on the top row of the bleachers where he could keep an eye on his circle of slaves.

Zook pressed his lips together and slipped the FreeFone into his pocket. He didn't like Friendster Boraxo, although of course he would never say so out loud. Boraxo, a state slave himself until his daughter had married into a FriendsterVille family, not only lacked the artistic taste to run a design circle like MDC, but was harsh on the GovMint slaves under his control, writing them up for minor infractions and even sending repeat offenders to Reprimand.

Zook sighed. Hopefully, with Bacon's help, he wouldn't have to put up with Boraxo much longer. Life would be so much easier as a private slave.

Suddenly trumpets blared and the final Ingrate was ushered into the stadium, prodded by two orange-robed PeacePeople holding needler-spears. The Ingrate was an elderly woman with matted gray hair and a slight limp. Her skinny, sun-burnt arms were tied together in front of her, and as the Shredder's blades flashed in the bright CalSobrantes sunlight, a state slave deftly slipped her hands onto the hook and motioned to the crane operator to haul her aloft.

An excited buzz rippled through the stadium as the Ingrate kicked and screamed at the end of the hoisting cable. Zook, in his mid-30s and a veteran of the Flash War, had seen plenty of chastisements—by Shredder and worse. He glanced only momentarily at the condemned Ingrate before he turned his eyes on AssemblyPerson Wild's tent, hoping to see Bacon.

Wild sat in an upholstered chair set upon an elaborately detailed silk rug, hobnobbing with some of Mento's High Friendsters. One of Wild's hands held a fluted glass and the other a stick of Don't, which from time to time he put to his lips and inhaled.

Beside him was a striking red-haired woman in a green sheath dress, her white-gloved hand resting lightly on Wild's thigh. She held no official position in the entourage, but all the slaves knew her as Wild's long-term mistress. She went by a single High Friendster name of Sparklett. Of erect bearing, with cascading ringlets of shining hair, she was taller than Wild and more self-possessed, lithe and fully in her body. From this distance, she appeared to be following the general conversation in a polite manner without really joining in, but Wild's gaze returned to her over and over, always to be met by Sparklett's attentive grave eyes.

To Zook her reserve was both tantalizing and mysterious, and he swallowed down a momentary resentment that she was on Wild's arm and not his own. Zook's currently assigned FreeBuddy, Locally-Sourced Nukiforo, definitely wasn't in Sparklett's league.

At the Shredder, the condemned Ingrate was now fully in position, dangling over the exact center of the glass enclosure around the Shredder blades, and the crowd roared as she struggled and swayed. Wild put his Don't aside and rose, walking up to the microphone at the edge of his tent. He wore the familiar black tee and pony-tailed hair of the High Friendsters, but was shorter and stouter than Zook had remembered.

A state slave, bowing repeatedly as he approached, presented Wild with a card on a silver platter. Wild picked it up and squinted at it, then turned to the microphone.

"Ingrate Eco-Friendly Bauman," he announced to the crowd.

Wild squinted at the card and paused; as Defender of Slaves, he could commute the Ingrate's sentence if he so chose.

Instead he let the card flutter to the ground.

"Two dips," he said. "Illegal swig cup."

A gasp went up from the stadium. The Gratitude crackdown was hitting close to home. Many slaves used oversized swig cups to cut down on the number of trips to the FreeSmoozee machines, which weren't always convenient to an AuthorizedWorkPlace.

"Illegal swig cup. How could she be so stupid?" said Slavicen Sarno, a fellow designer at the Circle, notorious for his literal-minded adherence to every new rule and regulation.

"Yes," agreed Zook dryly. "Very stupid."

Zook had just such a cup himself—locked in the bottom drawer of his desk at the department. After today, however, he would have to destroy it—just as he had previously destroyed his cache of illegal incandescent light bulbs and illegal oil-based plastic bags.

Wild handed off the microphone to a waiting slave and plopped back to his seat. The Ingrate, momentarily exhausted, hung limply from the hook above the Shredder.

"Dip!" came a cry from a state slave the far end of the stadium.

The other state slaves took it up. The chant was part of the ritual and encouraged by the High Friendsters:

"Dip, dip, dip!"

The Ingrate stirred from her stupor and began to writhe and scream.

"Dip, dip, dip!"

Wild waved his fingers breezily in the air, and the crane operator began lowering the woman—who shrieked and twisted quite energetically despite her age—into the Shredder.

The first dip took off the Ingrate's legs up to her knees. She was immediately winched up again, blood dripping from her stumps and shuddering as if from an electric shock.

"Dip! Dip! Dip!" the crowd yelled again, and at a further nod from Wild, the operator threw the winch into reverse, returning the still-struggling woman into the chopper blades. Chunks of muscle and bone splattered against the already bloodied sides of the transparent tank as little by little, the Ingrate was shredded alive—first her thighs, then her hips, then her stringy intestines, until nothing was left but her shoulders and lolling head, which the operator released into the blades with a single bloody *SHRRROP*.

The dignitaries rose to leave and the crowd followed suit, adding lusty cheers now that Chastisement was over. That meant the slaves would have the rest of Gratitude, until sunrise tomorrow, free.

Zook's circle started pushing for the exit, but Boraxo, arms on hips and feet apart, blocked their path.

"Friendsters first," he yelled. "Wait your number."

Zook anxiously scanned the field, where the state slaves were already cleaning up and the dignitaries milling and beginning to exit.

Wild was halfway to the exit, engaged in joking conversation with a tall black woman Zook recognized as Friendster Robineau, Mento's Executive in Charge of Production. Behind him Sparklett chatted with another High Friendster, then followed their retinue of private slaves, none of them Bacon. They disappeared into the exit tunnel and were gone.

Damn! thought Zook, shifting impatiently from foot to foot. He would have lunged past Boraxo if he didn't fear getting a Reprimand on his record.

Finally, their cohort's number was called, and Zook

pushed through the crowd, punching up Bacon on his FreeFone and scanning the crowd for some sign of him.

The call failed to connect and Bacon was nowhere to be seen among the excited throngs of state slaves talking and laughing on the walks.

Weaving around the pedestrians, Zook ran along the stadium wall to where a row of black AtomoLimos waited curbside, then up to the carpeted area where the limos were queuing to load the Friendsters.

There were Wild and Sparklett, not five yards away, waiting for their limousine to pull up. Wild was scowling, looking down the street for the car, while Sparklett fussed with a perfectly-coiffed dog a slave had handed her. Zook was almost close enough to touch the Friendsters, if it hadn't been for the red barricade fences and the phalanx of plops to keep away the state slaves.

Where was Bacon?

Zook leaned against the barricade.

"You. Stand back," shouted an immensely fat PeacePerson.

"I'm waiting for someone," said Zook, standing on his tip toes to see if Bacon were further back, in the exit tunnel. The AtomoLimo was pulling up but there was still time for an introduction if Bacon could be found.

"Stand back," said the fat plop, giving Zook a shove.

Zook stumbled back a step, anxious and frustrated. "Watch how you treat a slavicen," he snapped.

Sparklett, waiting for Wild to climb into the limo, heard the commotion and turned her head sharply, her green eyes quickly taking in Zook and the bullying plop.

Zook felt Sparklett's eyes upon him and reddened in shame.

When the big plop went to shove him again, Zook—completely uncharacteristically—shoved back.

The plop's eyes went wide. He grabbed Zook by the wrist and started to pull a needler from his plop belt.

Sparklett suddenly stepped forward. "Stop!" she commanded the plop.

The plop's needler froze in mid-air and he looked at her questioningly.

Sparklett's grip on her dog loosened and she let the animal spill from her arms.

"My dog!" she said. "Get it!"

"But Friendster," said the plop, "I'm in the process of arresting this unruly hooligan…"

The dog barked and returned to Sparklett, but she gave it a shove with her leg.

What the hell, thought Zook.

"I said get it," Sparklett ordered the plop.

With a malevolent glance at Zook, the PeacePerson let go of his arm and stooped to get the dog, dropping to his knees as it ran past. The animal juked out of the plop's grasp and ran under the barricades into the roadway, where it began running in confusion as a second black AtomoLimo approached.

The fat plop was still on his knees, struggling to get up.

Without thinking, Zook leapt over the barricade and ran after the dog, trying to shoo it out of the path of the oncoming vehicle.

The dog circled around confusedly, running directly into the path of the limo. Zook took a few giant steps into the roadway and made a flying leap for the animal, managing to grab it up by the scruff of its neck just as the limo swerved to a stop, striking Zook a glancing blow.

He spun around and tripped, but managed to hold on to the frightened dog, a wire-haired terrier with a bejeweled collar.

"It's okay, boy," he said to the animal, surprised to find that it smelled faintly of lavender.

He got up and walked back with the dog in his arms.

Sparklett was waiting on the street side of the barricades.

"Thank you," said Sparklett, taking the animal from him. "How brave of you."

He assumed she was putting him on.

"It was nothing, Friendster," Zook said, crouching and averting his gaze.

To his amazement, Sparklett grabbed his chin and turned his face up to hers. Her eyes, a beautiful shade of pale gray-green, bore directly into his, and Zook—whether out of insanity, shock, or boldness—found himself staring back.

"I said it was brave of you," Sparklett insisted. "Do you understand?"

"Yes, Friendster."

"Better," she said. "Your name?"

"Differently-Abled Zook."

"Remember," she murmured, or Zook thought she murmured.

Then she turned and pushed back through the gathered plops to the waiting limo, which pulled away from the curb and was gone.

Zook stood watching, mouth agape, still trying to process what just happened. Did she say "remember"? Remember *what*? He already knew his slave name, and she couldn't possibly have meant remember looking into her eyes—which Zook already knew he would never forget. Probably she meant, remember your place, a phrase which frequently tripped off the tongue of Friendsters everywhere.

In any case, he had missed his chance to meet Wild.

Zook saw the plops staring at him and deemed it prudent to move along, vaguely moving toward the stadium entrance with its big banner, *FreeFood, FreeMed, FreePad*.

He pulled out his FreeFone and was surprised to see he had six messages, five FreeSexts from his FB

Nukiforo and a FreeVid from Bacon. He clicked on the FreeVid.

"Sorry I missed you, Slavicen. They have me working the kitchen," the bobblehead Bacon said. "But Friendster Wild is due here soon. Come to the palace door right away and I'll try to get you in to see him."

Great! thought Zook. He stared at Nukiforo's messages for a moment then guiltily flicked the phone off; he was supposed to be meeting her to celebrate Gratitude Day but she would have to wait.

+ + +

The People's Palace was a long, low, concrete-and-glass structure which sat on the crest of the hill overlooking Mento beach. Before the Great Catastrophe, it had been the private mansion of EvilBizMan No. 114, but now—remodeled, updated, and expanded—it was one of Mento's many free museums. Not, of course, that it was actually open to the public. Shortly after his election, AssemblyPerson Wild declared himself official caretaker of the People's Palace, in order to better protect its rare furnishings and the delicate ecosystem of the extensive gardens. The People's Palace had served as his private residence ever since.

As Zook climbed up the road higher toward the palace gate, he could hear the pounding music from the Gratitude celebrations at the pier, and a glance behind revealed that Sacagawea Square—where he was supposed to be meeting Nukiforo—was jammed with excited slavicens. From this height he could take in the whole stretch of the town from Diversity Point to Friendly Dolphin Lighthouse, including the jumble of neglected wind towers—many missing blades—tilted drunkenly against the horizon, a forlorn reminder of the Flash War.

"State your name," the gate inquired in a pleasant machine voice as he approached.

"Differently-Abled Zook," he said.

Just then a smaller door to the side of the gate swung open. "Welcome, Slavicen. You are on the guest list. You may enter with your hands up."

Zook followed a holo-arrow into a small, empty room and stood with his hands over his head while he was scanned. The scan seemed to take an inordinate amount of time and eventually Zook asked, "Is everything okay?"

"A security lock-down is in progress," said the door. "For your own safety, please keep your hands overhead until the alert is over.

"This conversation is being recorded for training purposes."

Zook stood awkwardly, his arms getting more and more tired. From outside came the whine of what sounded like a hopper landing. When the noise ceased a chime sounded and an interior door slid open.

"Thank you," said the door. "You may now exit to meet your party."

2.

YOUR HOUSE IS OUR HOUSE

There, pacing in the reception courtyard, stood Zook's oldest friend, Sustainable Bacon, resplendent in his purple-and-gold private slave livery.

"It's about time," he said. "What took you so long?"

"Gratitude Day. All the FreeBikes were gone and I had to walk."

Bacon frowned. "Where's your dress tunic? You can't meet the Assemblyperson like *that*."

"I came straight from the stadium."

"You're kidding, right? This isn't some little state slave Friendster from down the hill. This is AssemblyPerson Wild. There are a lot of people who want this position. You've got to be presentable."

"I thought I *was* presentable," protested Zook. "Besides, it's only a groundskeeper position, isn't it?"

"You don't get it. Everything's got to be perfect for Friendster. Besides, you'll make me look bad."

"I could run back," Zook offered.

"No, there's not enough time," said Bacon. He continued to look at Zook appraisingly, then sighed. "All right, Slavicen, I guess we can make it work. I'll dig you up a spare tunic, and you can wash in the prep room."

"Thanks," said Zook, miffed at Bacon's attitude but willing to swallow a lot of guff for a chance to become a private slave.

"We've got to get going. Friendster's hopper is here and he's going back to the capital early."

"Lead on," said Zook.

+ + +

They jumped into Bacon's FreeCart and scooted off along the perimeter of a huge lawn of lush green grass that gently led up to the house, navigating to avoid the sprinklers. Zook was agog, since watering a lawn— *having* a lawn—was nominally a crime punishable by Shredder. The house itself—low, with huge windows, and faced with a rose-colored marble—was almost as long as the field at Gratitude Stadium.

"The hopper pad is around back," said Bacon, happy now that they were underway. Zook had known Bacon all his life, since they had played together in the rubble of Geranium Street. Zook was amazed to see how Bacon's life had blossomed in the UCC, where he had successively been first a star athlete in Co-Op-Ball, then a sought-after quartermaster during the Flash War, and now a private slave for one of the most powerful personages in the UCC. "Go along to get along," Bacon always said, and he seemed a walking embodiment of the wisdom of that position.

"You'll love it at the palace," he was saying now. "It's only busy when the AssemblyPerson's here, which is hardly ever, and the food is the best, and your FreePad has a private bath, and there's a club room for us private slaves where we're allowed to play cards and watch FreeVid, even after curfew."

"Wow, sounds great," said Zook. His own FreePad had a shared bathroom and his electricity switched off promptly at 2100, leaving him bored and awake in the dark.

"Oh, and I'm a captain in the bowling league. We have permission to use the old bowling alley."

"What's a bowling alley?" asked Zook.

Bacon laughed. "Pre-Zero recreation," he said. "There's a lot of that old stuff still in place here. I'll

12

show you later, if Friendster takes you on."

Bacon zigzagged through the topiary garden and around the corner of the house, its huge, gold-tinted windows reflecting the manicured grounds. Zook, who until now felt reasonably sure that he would make a good showing in his interview with Wild, felt his confidence beginning to crumble. He turned to Bacon.

"What kind of questions do you think he'll ask?" said Zook.

"Don't worry about it."

"I mean, is he going to want to know about my education? My job background? My gardening experience?"

Bacon laughed again. "No, he doesn't care about any of that."

"He doesn't?"

"He probably won't even talk to you. I'll introduce you and tell him why you're here, then you keep your mouth shut and just S and B."

"S and B?"

"You know—smile and bow. I'll point out that you've been a devoted constituent since Year Zero and remind him how hard you slaved last year to help get him re-elected."

"But I never slaved to get him re-elected," said Zook.

"Sure you did," said Bacon. Didn't you march with all the other state slaves in the big get-out-and-vote campaign? He was the only one on the ballot so you were working for him."

"But what if he asks…"

"I told you, just S and B. This is the way that it's done, Slavicen, trust me."

They came to a broad concrete pad where a private slave was polishing the AtomoLimo Zook had seen earlier that day. Behind him, in the shade of the garage, several more limos were lined up. Bacon swerved the

FreeCart into the garage and stopped.

"Come on," said Bacon.

Zook followed Bacon through a door that led to a room full of shop machinery. A private slave in safety glasses and purple overalls was turning a small part on the lathe at the far end of the room. Bacon acknowledged him with a nod and waved Zook to follow him. They passed into a carpeted hallway (Zook had never walked on such plush carpet before—very soft), turned a corner and finally pushed through a large door into a store room packed with boxes and old picture frames. There was a huge, draped window and, across from that, a utility sink in the corner.

Bacon drew back the curtain and checked outside.

"The hopper's still here so we're good. I'll try to introduce you as Friendster is leaving. Meanwhile you can clean up."

"Where do you want me to meet you?"

"Right here. Wait until I come for you. No wandering about or the guards are liable to cut off your head."

"That would certainly ruin my day," Zook said dryly.

"Seriously. Remember, let me do all the talking and don't look the Friendster in the eye, okay?"

"Okay, I'll just S and B," said Zook. Years of conditioning had drilled in him that slaves had to be obsequious before Friendsters, but for some reason it still bothered him.

Bacon saw the expression on Zook's face and mistook it for anxiety. "Don't worry," he said. "It's all who you know, and you know me—the best, if I do say so myself."

Zook laughed. "Thanks, Slavicen."

"I'll bring you a fresh tunic."

Bacon disappeared behind a padded door and Zook found himself alone in the store room. From outside came the steady throb of the hopper's engines, and Zook pulled back the curtain for a look. There, on a huge stone deck encircled with balustrades, sat the sub-orbital hopper, the turbines in each of the four corners pointing downward and blowing billowing waves of heat across the patio. Zook had seen hoppers flying overhead in the Flash War, but had never been this near, and had certainly never ridden in one. Two private slaves, in dark purple livery and wearing hazers on their hips, stood on either side of the launch pad. Protecting the AssemblyPerson, Zook presumed, though from what he couldn't guess. When one of the guards turned his gaze toward the store room window, Zook let the curtain fall back into place and shrunk back.

Zook stepped to the sink and splashed a little water on his face. He found some paper towels, but couldn't believe that he was meant to waste a tree simply to dry his face and looked around the room for a slave rag. There were metal shelves near the door holding frames, canvas, and mats, and against the far-wall, a jumble of pre-Zero art frames. A workbench held knives, rulers and t-squares. It strangely resembled the back room of the Mento Design Circle where he worked, and he realized he must be in the anteroom of some kind of art gallery.

Curiosity aroused, Zook turned the knob of a massive door to his left, pulling it open an inch. A half-dozen canvases of various sizes hung on the long white wall, illuminated by the muted light filtering in from the draped windows opposite. Any display of pre-Zero art was, of course, strictly prohibited, but Zook's job as a Colorist for the MDC gave him access to otherwise forbidden reference materials. Over the years, Zook had surreptitiously examined many of the huge art books in the reference room, and had put together in his mind a tentative history of art before the Flash War and the rise of the UCC. On Wild's gallery wall hung a Madonna and child at least 500 years old, and beside that a small vertical scroll depicting a bare tree against a distant mountain that Zook guessed was FarEastern. Alongside the scroll were two posters advertising pre-Zero gasoline vehicles, then an oddly-painted portrait of a woman that Zook recognized as the work of the artist called Picasso.

All pre-Zero, all illegal, and thus all subject to destruction. But there they were.

The distortions in the Picasso were bizarre, and Zook cracked the door open a bit wider for a closer look.

In the process, he caught a glimpse of an adjacent painting that was even *more* extraordinary. It was framed in an elaborately carved and gold-gilded frame, but what really caught Zook's eye was the subject.

A clown painting.

On velvet.

A Pedro?

It had to be a Pedro.

Just like *his* Pedro. The one he had rescued from the dumpster.

He took a deep breath.

It certainly *looked* like a Pedro.

He pushed the door open wider, just to be sure.

It was very similar to *his* painting—the same size, the same rectangular shape, the same rich black velvet background that made the subject pop. The clown was like *his* clown, except that this clown appeared to be extremely happy, and was leaning against the light post instead of lying slumped in the gutter. He wore the same tall EvilBizMan top-hat, but un-smashed, and with live flowers stuffed in the rim. Red hair puffed out from under the clown's hat, just as in *his* painting, but instead of frowning the clown was smiling a huge smile with big red smeary lips. His left hand, gloved in white, held a cigar, a thin wisp of white smoke curling from its glowing tip. And—yes!—there was the bottle of forbidden alcohol, labeled "XXX," sticking out of the clown's side pocket.

The clown looked happy, confident, complete, as if he were sitting on top of the world.

But to Zook there appeared to be something amiss. What? He stared and stared but couldn't put his finger on the source of his unease.

Maybe it wasn't a Pedro after all?

From his vantage place in the storeroom, Zook could see a signature in the painting's lower-left corner, but small. Zook squinted but still couldn't make it out.

He had to know. There was no one in the gallery, and the curtains were drawn on the huge windows, so Zook decided to take a chance.

He scurried up to the painting. Yes, just as Zook thought: the signature *was* "Pedro." He should have known from the magnificent technique—the values of light and dark, the deft brush work.

Up close, though, Zook noticed an incongruity that had escaped him from the distance. In the corner of the clown's right eye, a tiny tear was forming, small and wet and glistening. It looked so real that Zook reached out and touched it, just to make sure it was actually painted.

A smile *and* a tear? Odd. It seemed odd.

Zook heard a soft click behind him and turned. A draft had blown shut the door he had come through, and there was no knob on this side. With a glance toward the curtains to make sure the guards couldn't see him, Zook approached the wall and began feeling along the crack of the door's outline for a latch.

Nothing.

"Open," he commanded, thinking maybe it was a talking door. But if it were, it wasn't talking to him.

Outside, Zook heard voices shouting over the rev of the hopper engines. He parted the curtains and saw four more private slaves fussing about, unloading a half-dozen large leather cases (leather!) from a metal trolley and lugging them up stairs that had been lowered from the hopper's side.

The hopper would be loaded soon. Where was Bacon? Zook *had* to get an introduction to Wild.

Just then, from beyond the door at the other end of the gallery came another muffled voice—but louder, purposeful, gruff in tone.

Zook quickly crossed and pulled the door open a crack. It was Wild, talking into an elegant white Friendster FreeFone while simultaneously rooting for some papers in a briefcase (more leather!) held open by a private slave. Another private slave stood with a clipboard at a respectful distance, taking down Wild's shouted, snarled notes. Smoke wafted from a burning stub Wild juggled between hands, and Zook was shocked to realize it wasn't a stick of Don't, but a pre-Zero cigar of wrapped tobacco. Everyone knew that tobacco was a health risk and grounds for the Shredder, but neither of the slaves seemed the least bit alarmed, and Wild himself was so nonchalant that it was if he smoked tobacco every day.

Zook would have to ask Bacon about it, if Bacon ever got here. Clearly, the AssemblyPerson would be leaving at any moment. Zook retreated into the gallery and sent Bacon a quick FreeText. He waited a full minute for a response, then pocketed the FreeFone and cracked the door open again.

Wild was still engrossed in his phone conversation, but now he was pacing, and another pair of private slaves had appeared and positioned themselves on either side of the huge gold-and-glass doors leading to the hopper pad, their hands on the slider handles.

Suddenly, Wild punched off his fone, deposited a few papers in his briefcase, and motioned for the slave holding it to snap the case shut. He gave a few final instructions to the slave with the clipboard, then turned. The two slaves slid the doors open, admitting the roar of the hopper and gust of kerosene-laden air, and Wild headed for the exit.

Zook only had a moment to make up his mind. Bacon was nowhere to be found, and Zook might never get another chance to talk to Wild in person.

If he ever wanted to be a private slave, *now* was the time to act, and he must act boldly.

Zook stepped out from the gallery and ran up to Wild's retinue. "AssemblyPerson? AssemblyPerson?"

Wild's eyes opened wide at Zook's approach and he took a quick step back behind his slaves.

"Who the hell are you?" he said.

"A state slave, Friendster. One of your charges."

Zook took another step forward, and Wild another step back, holding the slave with the briefcase in front of him like a shield.

"Guards!" shouted Wild.

"No, no," said Zook. "I'm not going to hurt you. I'm a true follower! A slave in the commune! I've come to ask a boon! A small favor."

At the word "favor," a look of relief flooded Wild's face, and the fear of a moment before was replaced with contempt.

"Who do you think you are, accosting me like this?" Wild demanded.

Zook realized that—in his excitement of actually reaching the AssemblyPerson—he had forgotten Bacon's admonishments to smile and bow. Zook made up for it now, bending from the waist repeatedly and looking only at Wild's shoes, which were not hemp thongs like the state slaves wore, but actual pre-Zero sandals, intricately woven of—yes!—more leather.

"Friendster, forgive the intrusion," Zook said to the shoes. "I am merely one of the many minions who

19

helped get out the vote in the last election and I've come to ask…"

"How dare you approach me in the People's Palace!" Wild said, as three guards came running in from three different directions. "Throw this slave out," said Wild.

Zook stood up, just in time to see Wild turn his back to him and make for the exit.

"But Friendster!" Zook shouted, as all three guards descended on him, one twisting his arm, another knocking his feet out from under him, the third pulling him down and climbing onto his back.

In a flash, Zook was lying flat on the floor with his face crushed into the cold white marble.

Outside, the intensity of the hopper turbines grew to an unbearable pitch, and then with a roar it popped itself into the sky.

Wild was gone

"Slavicens! Let me up!" said Zook.

"Stop struggling," said the beefy man sitting on Zook's back, twisting Zook's arm up further behind his shoulders.

"I… can't… breathe…" Zook said, as the guard pressed down with his full weight. The man's hairy hand rested on the marble floor beside Zook's face, so Zook bit it, hard.

The guard yowled and tore his arm away. "You dirty Ingrate!" he screamed, and from the corner of his eye, Zook saw the man withdraw a silvery cylinder from his tunic—a needler.

Zook started to squirm madly, and began to bellow even before his tormentor jabbed the electrodes into the back of his neck. A white shower of pain jolted through him, as every nerve of his body felt as if it were being pierced with a red-hot needle. His scream—before of fright and now of excruciating pain—increased in volume and echoed through the marble room.

"Slavicen, stop, I'm complying," Zook managed to gasp out, between stabs of pain.

"Then stop struggling," the guard demanded, needling him again, at a higher level.

Zook's body shook convulsively while stars began to burst in his eyes, dancing and filling up his field of vision as the pain increased.

Suddenly a woman's voice cut through his screams.

"Stop that! What are you doing? Get off that man immediately!"

The men froze and Zook heard the one on his back say, "But Friendster Sparklett, the AssemblyPerson ordered this man off the property."

Sparklett's voice rose in imperious anger. "Release him immediately."

Zook felt the weight slowly lift off his back.

"Help him to his feet," Sparklett ordered. "This man is my guest."

"Your guest?" one of the men gasped.

"Yes. Do you have any objection?"

"No, Friendster."

"Then put that needler away. Help him up."

Reluctantly, Zook's attackers hauled him to his feet and held him until he got his balance. Through watery eyes, Zook could see Sparklett watching and he and straightened his tunic.

"Good. And now all of you out."

The three guards turned and disappeared into a side corridor like rabbits running for their hole. Zook started to join them.

"Not you, Zook. Stay awhile."

3.

SILENCE=PERKS

"Are you okay?" Sparklett said.

Zook rubbed the back of his neck where the needler had made contact and winced. His ears rang with a high-pitched squeal and long tingles of fire arced up and down his body like shorted wires.

"I'm fine," he said. "I think."

But Zook knew he wasn't fine. After all, he was only a state slave, yet here he was, unable to tear his eyes off Sparklett. And that could be dangerous. He began to wonder if the needler had left him loopy, temporarily shutting down the slave filters.

"Better have a seat," she said, leading him to a nearby couch.

Her eyes were huge bowls of deep green that held him as if hypnotized. With her perfect skin, cascading ringlets of reddish hair and erect bearing, she seemed to come from an altogether different country than the rest of woman-hood.

Maybe it wasn't the needler. Maybe it was Sparklett herself, so different from the scores of drab, colorless FBs he had known.

"What?" she said, her gaze meeting his. Behind it

Zook perceived a gentleness and a vulnerability which both intrigued and emboldened him.

Then and there, against all reason, he decided that he *had* to have her—to hold her, to kiss her, to help and comfort her.

"You are *really* beautiful," Zook exclaimed.

"That's interesting," she said, plopping down on the opposite edge of the sofa. "What makes you say that?"

"It's true," said Zook.

"Perhaps," said Sparklett, "But what makes you *say* that. Most slaves can't even look at me."

"I could look at you all day."

"That's very bold," she said. "You know I belong to AssemblyPerson Wild."

Retreat, retreat, Zook thought. Slaves had been shredded for lesser offenses than stealing a glance at a Friendster's woman.

But Wild didn't deserve Sparklett. She was too good for Wild, and he didn't make her happy. He had sensed that when he saw her in the morning, and now he was sure.

Zook could not believe it as he felt himself step forward and closer. Was he really going to try to kiss her?

Yes, he thought, disbelieving even as he thought it, he was!

His eyes held hers and—when she didn't call the guards—he kissed her.

Sparklett hesitated, her mouth closed.

Then he felt her body relax and open to him. She threw her arms around him and kissed as if Zook were the last man on earth.

Sparklett's unexpected fervor shot an ecstatic thrill through Zook's body. Suddenly he felt free and light, as if the weight of the slave chains he had been carrying all of his life had suddenly dropped from him. He couldn't believe he was *here*, on this couch, kissing this absolutely stunning, passionate woman.

"Zook," she said, "Oh, Zook."

There was something vulnerable and sad in her voice. Zook could only respond by holding her tighter.

They fell over onto the couch, wrapped in each other's arms, tongues intertwined. Sparklett was no longer a cold and distant fantasy figure, but real and warm and in his arms—soft, present. Her lustrous hair fell across his face, her hand found its way through his tunic to rest on his chest.

"Wow," Zook said, when they broke for a moment, breathless.

A shadow passed over Sparklett's face. "Don't fail me, Zook," Sparklett said.

He had no idea what she was talking about. "I won't," he said.

She held herself back from him, looking at him searchingly. "If you strike at a king, you must kill him. If you fail me, Zook, we'll die."

"No problem," said Zook, still mystified. "I don't want to die."

Sparklett disentangled herself from Zook and sat up. "What am I doing," she said. "This is madness."

"But it's *fun* madness," he said.

"No," she said. "Stop. First I need to ask you some questions." She stood and moved to a nearby arm chair.

Reluctantly, Zook sat upright. Without Sparklett in his arms, the palace room seemed large, empty and cold. But Zook sensed that something important had passed between them, that they could never be separated now. They belonged to each other. He didn't know why or how, but he *felt* it. And he knew she felt it too.

He waited as she studied him.

"You're different, Zook."

"'Diversity is Our Strength,'" Zook joked.

"It's not funny," she snapped. "Real difference is dangerous. Haven't you figured that out yet?"

She pulled out her FreeFone—the Friendster model with The Bob's profile on back—and thumbed the screen. "Born and raised in the Mento commune... graduated in the 50% of your class with honors... UCC slave regiment Year Zero... lifelong member of the Awesome Peoples Party..." She looked up, perplexed. "Hmmm. Based on your life profile, you seem to be a nobody."

"I wouldn't say that," said Zook, miffed at hearing his life accomplishments dismissed so blithely.

She studied the screen some more.

"How long have you been a hairdresser?"

"Hairdresser? I'm not a hairdresser."

"It says you're a Colorist for the Mento Design Circle."

"I choose colors for GovMint buildings."

"Mmmm."

"It's important work," said Zook, starting to feel defensive.

"I'm sure," she said.

She continued scrolling through his slave profile, then suddenly stopped.

"You served on the Sierra line during the Flash War?"

"I was Hazer Fire Support—cryogenic liquids, chemical reactants, that sort of thing."

"Ever see combat?" Sparklett asked.

"I fought in the battle of FresNot," Zook said.

She put away the FreeFone and looked at him again. Zook had the uncomfortable feeling she was sizing him up.

"I suppose you used codes," she said.

Codes? Of course they used codes. "Orders from headquarters arrived ciphered. We had decrypt guys, but sometimes I had to work them manually."

"Oh?" she said. "How did you do that?"

"If you didn't have the chip, there were long pages of symbols to enter into the scanner. Once during an attack the decrypter was destroyed and I had to memorize an entire symbol sequence to take back to a machine at headquarters."

She nodded. Whatever test she was giving him, he seemed to have passed, for finally she sighed and sat back. "What am I going to do with you, Zook?" she said.

"I could think of a few things," Zook suggested. In truth, his élan was beginning to fray but he had gone too far to step back.

"Get serious," Sparklett snapped, shooting him an annoyed look. "What's this nonsense about wanting to become a private slave?"

Zook was thrown off balance. Only a Friendster could ask a question like that.

"Why is it nonsense?" Zook said. "It's Steady Work. And you get Good Perks."

"You already have Steady Work and Good Perks. That's guaranteed by the State."

"But I'd get to live in the palace. And wear a purple coat."

"You're kidding, right?"

"Why is that so hard to believe? Everyone wants to better themselves."

She mulled his answer over, frowning "You're not very politically advanced."

Zook assumed she was talking about the kind of patronage that thrived in the UCC. "Are you suggesting you could help advance me politically?" he said.

She laughed. "Zook, you are a riot," she said. "Let me show you something."

Sparklett rang the little brass bell on the table beside her and instantly Sustainable Bacon ran in from the far

26

hallway.

"Yes, Friendster Sparklett?"

Sparklett drew herself erect and addressed Bacon in a frosty, angry tone. "How *dare* you bring this slave into my house without my permission," she said. "What could you possibly have been thinking?"

"A thousand apologies, Friendster," he said bowing. "I..."

Sparklett raised her hand. "No. No excuses from a traitor."

"Traitor?" said Bacon, bowing even lower. "I assure you, Friendster, that..."

"You were the mastermind behind this conspiracy to assault the AssemblyPerson, were you not?"

Bacon looked as if he had been hit between the eyes with a two-by-four. "Conspiracy? Assault? Friendster, believe me, I swear I know nothing of what you're talking about..."

"Silence!" shouted Sparklett.

Bacon crouched on the floor, quivering abjectly like some whipped dog.

"That will be all," Sparklett said to Bacon. "For now."

"Yes, Friendster," said Bacon, backing away. "Thank you, Friendster." The color began to return to his face as he S and B'd out of the room.

When he had gone, Sparklett looked at Zook with arched eyebrow. "Well?"

"Well what?" Throughout his life Zook had witnessed hundreds of slaves being reprimanded by their Betters.

"Do you want to be like that? An impotent, groveling moron?"

"Sustainable Bacon's no moron," said Zook. "He's a private slave for an important AssemblyPerson. I'd trade places in an instant."

Sparklett stared at him as if he were from another planet.

"And yet you saved my dog," she finally said. "Why did you do that?"

Zook was puzzled.

"The plop was slow," he said. "Any slave would have done the same thing."

"They would not," she said emphatically. "Most slaves would be too insecure to take the initiative. But you did. Why? To gain my favor?"

"No," Zook blurted out. "Because you're *you.*"

Sparklett seemed to consider, then smiled. "You're a charmer," she said. "Let's go for a ride."

"A ride?" said Zook. "Where?"

"It's a surprise," she said. "Come on."

+ + +

A few minutes later, Zook and Sparklett were seated in the plush rear seat of a huge AtomoLimo, gliding down the back route from the palace. A glass divider sealed off the passenger compartment from the driver, who was a middle-aged slave wearing a cap like the commander of a ship. When they were out of sight of the palace, Sparklett pushed a button on the armrest and said, "South along the beach road until I tell you to stop."

"Yes, Friendster, at your service," came the tinny voice from the front. Sparklett cut off the intercom and turned the dividing window a silvery opaque. The big limo glided down a landscaped road, exited the compound through sliding gates, and wended its way through the crowded town until it passed through the checkpoint (unmanned today until after dusk) and reached the road along the ocean.

"Okay, now we can talk."

They had *already* been talking, but Zook knew what she meant. Guiltily, he drew out his FreeFone and held it

28

up for Sparklett to see.

She laughed. "That's been disabled since you entered the palace grounds."

"Really?"

"Really. Do you think Friendsters want slaves spying on them?"

"I never thought of that."

She gave him another appraising look

"You need to think a lot more, Zook. Realize the mess we're in."

"What do you mean?"

"Take your FreeFone, for example. Why do you think your FreeFone is free?"

"It's a basic Perk," said Zook, "Guaranteed by the GovMint for the betterment of slavicens."

"It's a chain. A golden slave chain to keep you under control."

Sparklett's outrageous opinions began to make Zook feel uneasy. Was she expecting him to object? His FreeFone wasn't a chain, it was identification, entertainment, a way to keep in touch with his slavicen buddies and a way to receive Friendster orders. He was so Grateful to have it. Every slave was. What was she talking about?

"Never mind," she said. She indicated his FreeFone. "Give it to me."

He handed it to her. She rolled down the window— and in one quick movement tossed it out.

Zook, astonished, watched through the back window as the device hit the road and broke into a half-dozen pieces. He lunged for the door handle but found it locked.

"Why did you do that?"

"I'm setting you free, Zook."

"You're going to get me shredded!" State slaves had to carry their FreeFones at all times.

"You're already going to get shredded," she said, "For attacking the AssemblyPerson."

"I *didn't* attack the AssemblyPerson."

"You did if he says you did."

"But I didn't. I swear."

"Oh, stop groveling. You're beginning to sound like Bacon."

Zook sat back and crossed his arms in anger, the warm feeling that had been building between them now thoroughly destroyed. Anyone who would destroy a state slave's FreeFone was crazy or worse.

"Anyway, you had no right to do that," Zook said.

"I had every right," Sparklett said. "I'm a Friendster, aren't I? Can't Friendsters do anything?"

The logic was unassailable, but she had still left him in a lurch. When he got back, he should go straight to the plops and report the whole incident. But what possible story could explain his being alone in a limo with the AssemblyPerson's mistress? Especially if they were about to do what he thought they were about to do.

Sparklett must have read the misery on his face for suddenly her look softened. "Relax," she said. "I'm just trying to show you how things really are. I'll see that there's a duplicate FreeFone in your room when you get home tonight. Your whereabouts will show unreadable."

"You can do that?"

"Not me, personally. But friends. We're all going to need a lot of friends pretty soon."

There it was again—the sly hint that big things were in the air. But the incident with the FreeFone made him wary. He sat back.

"I'm not sure this is a good idea."

"Why not?" said Sparklett, curling her long legs up underneath her on the seat. "I thought I was beautiful."

"You *are* beautiful. It's just that…"

"Let me guess. You're afraid."

30

She seemed to be reading his mind. Now that the needler blast was wearing off, he was beginning to come to his senses. He didn't really think the scuffle with Wild or the temporary loss of the FreeFone would lead to his shredding, but if slept with Sparklett...

"Don't I have reason to be afraid?" Zook said.

"Don't we both?" said Sparklett.

Betrayal was always the problem with non-permitted FreeLove. Could you trust your partner not to report you to the authorities, now or in the future? Sparklett had as much to fear as he did—maybe more.

"What about the driver?" said Zook.

"Don't worry about him. He's safe."

She must have read the skepticism on his face.

"He can't hear us and even if he did he knows to keep his mouth shut," she said.

She un-opaqued the window and shouted at the driver. "You miserable slave, if you ever leak a word about anything you see I'll send your balls to the Shredder!"

The driver jumped and signaled for Sparklett to press her intercom button.

"Sorry, Friendster," the driver said mildly. "I can't hear you through the glass."

"I said, take us to Ecology Point."

She released the intercom button and opaqued the glass. "See?" she said to Zook. "It's just us."

That sounded good to Zook. For the first time since getting in the vehicle, he began to relax.

"What's your opinion of the UCC?" Sparklett suddenly asked.

"Opinion? What do you mean?" said Zook. The question not only was unexpected, he had never known that you could *have* an opinion about the UCC.

"Is it good? Is it just?"

"It's not perfect, I suppose," said Zook. "But it's a lot

better than the old system, with runaway pollution destroying the planet, and women pregnant because the State wouldn't give them birth control, and EvilBizMen oppressing all the pwns."

"So you prefer the current structure?"

"Current structure?"

"The UCC."

"Of course," said Zook. "Who wouldn't? FreeFood, FreeMed, FreePad—even FreeFone and FreeSex. The State takes care of us from FreeBirth to FreeDeath. And like The Bob says, you can't argue with free."

"Some people do," Sparklett said.

"You mean, like, Two Brothers?" The Two Brothers was a illegal anarchist organization demanding a return to FreeFall. "They just don't understand the Social Contract."

"How so?" said Sparklett.

"You know. Like we learned in FreePod—everyone's a state slave, and everything is free."

"'Together we are beige,'" quoted Sparklett.

"That's it," said Zook.

"And do you like beige, Zook?" Sparklett asked.

"Everyone does."

"Not everyone—you."

"Well," Zook admitted, "I'd probably choose something different. If I had a choice."

"The Two Brothers offers a choice."

Shocked, Zook was silent for a moment. Then—haltingly—he spoke. "I'm not interested in the Two Brothers. But I like choices. And I like you."

"That's what I like to hear," said Sparklett. She uncurled her long legs and stretched them languorously.

Zook had never had a serious discussion about color with any woman he had been with, and the cozy mood was returning. Zook couldn't resist. He leaned over and kissed her.

She didn't move away. Her lips were soft and yielding, and she put her arm around him and pulled him close.

"Zookie," she said. "I'm beginning to like you."

"Friendster."

She pulled back and put her hand over his mouth. "Don't call me that. I'm just Sparklett."

"Sparklett."

Zook had never called a Friendster by a first name. It felt dangerous, and freeing. In the UCC, only Friendsters had real first names; slaves were assigned slave names when they first entered FreePod.

Just then the limo pulled off the asphalt and bounced to a halt on a grassy promontory overlooking the sea.

"We're here," said Sparklett, disentangling herself. "Are you positive you want to seal the deal?"

"That's a funny way of talking," said Zook, brushing a lock of hair from her forehead.

"I'm just asking."

Her concern was endearing. But he had already decided to accept the danger, crazy as it was.

He kissed her again.

"There's a blanket in the trunk," she said, pushing a button on her hand rest to pop open the lid. "I'll send the driver away."

4.

LET 183 FLOWERS BLOOM

Dusk found them lying side-by-side on the slope of a grassy hillock overlooking the sea. Zook had seldom been so excited in his life, and their love-making had proceeded in fury and languor by turns, until, now spent, they clung to each other atop the blanket, draped in Zook's tunic. Waves crashed on the rocks a hundred feet below, throwing up fountains of foam which glistened white against the darkening sea. Far up the shore, the lights of the town of Mento twinkled.

Zook propped himself on an elbow so he could gaze on Sparklett's beauty.

"What are you looking at?" she said.

"You." He pulled down the tunic covering her to reveal her bare shoulders.

On the horizon, past the broken windmills, a solitary ship moved north along the coast, its dark hulk steered by the autonomous Machines.

"Do you know where that ship out there is going, Zook?"

"Nobody knows," he said.

"I do," said Sparklett. "It's going to Palaska."

Palaska had been the last place on earth where other humans had existed before being wiped out by the Machines. That had happened during the last Flash War, when all contact had been lost with that remote northern area. Now "Palaska" was spoken of as a mythical place of peace and happiness, like Atlantis, or Camelot.

"That's a good one," said Zook. "Everyone knows that Palaska doesn't exist."

"It exists all right. I lived there."

"That's pretty funny," said Zook. "You lived on a plain of radioactive slag?"

"It's not slag," said Sparklett. "It's a functioning country with thousands of people."

She seemed dead serious.

"That can't be true," Zook said. "Even in FreePod we learned that Palaska was destroyed."

"That's just propaganda The Bob cooked up."

The idea was absurd. Zook, dismayed, tried to see Sparklett's face in the gathering darkness. Zook had heard such talk before, but always from low-level slaves with an inadequate appreciation of the how well they were being taken care of. She had to be testing him.

"The Bob would never lie," said Zook.

"He would and he does."

"But why?"

"He's building a secret army to attack Palaska."

"That's ridiculous."

"Is it? Why do you think he's pouring all that booty into the army?

It was true that every commune had had their Booty Call doubled, and that the People's Army was getting bigger.

"But that's to help the younger slaves get education and training," Zook said.

"Right, training. Training to take over Sand Francisco."

"The Machines control Sand Francisco. You can't defeat Machines."

"The Bob thinks he can. And he might be right."

Zook gave a little laugh, to show that he knew she was kidding. But was she?

In the lead-up to the big war, both the Red and the

Green factions had created war-fighting robots endowed with intelligence and programmed to seek out and destroy enemy assets. The Machines, with their adaptive autonomous programming, proved highly adept at their job, quickly reducing huge swaths of civilization to rubble, and destroying 99% of the world's population in the process.

That was the Great Catastrophe. It had been followed by five years of relative peace, as the Machines regrouped and the focus of the war switched to other parts of the globe. In North America, the former United States was replaced by the squabbling UnTied States, which each separately tried to reorganize defenses. In the west, the United Care Communities, with The Bob as Chief Controller, pulled together a sizable army of state slaves to dig in against future Machine attack.

When the dreaded attack finally came—the Flash War—six weeks of fighting took out all the fiefdoms to the east and north of CalSobrantes, leaving the slaves of the United Care Communities, the UCC, as the last humans on earth. Had the Machines not abruptly ceased fire, for reasons no one really understood, there is little doubt that even the UCC would have succumbed. Humanity would have been wiped from the earth... extinguished to the last man.

"Another war would mean our extermination," said Zook. "No one would pick a fight with the Machines."

"The Bob will. Unless we stop him."

"No way," said Zook. "The two of us?"

"Not just us. With others."

"What others?"

"The Two Brothers."

Now she really was talking treason. A cold chill swept over him.

"Count me out," said Zook. Politics at the level of the High Friendsters was far beyond anything he would dream of contemplating, especially if it involved the Two Brothers.

"You're already in."

"What are you talking about?" said Zook.

"You slept with me, didn't you. That makes you a conspirator."

"A conspirator? I slept with you because... because... well, any man would want to sleep with you!"

"'Want to,' maybe. But you did."

"But you wanted me to."

"Yes, I did," said Sparklett. "And I'm glad I did. But I'm a Friendster and you're a state slave. You know the penalty."

"What?" said Zook, unable to believe the turn the conversation was taking. "You're going to have me shredded?"

"No," said Sparklett. "But you *will* be shredded if Harold ever finds out. That's why you're already in, like it or not."

"But I'm not political. I don't want to join the Two Brothers."

Sparklett laughed. "You don't *join* the Two Brothers. They join you."

"What do you mean, 'join you'?"

"We look for exceptional people. Slaves that somehow manage to think thoughts outside the system."

"So?" said Zook.

"Slaves like *you*, Zook. I said you were different."

"Oh," said Zook. "But I can't. I'm a Loyal Slavicen. I voted for The Bob. I'm not going to get caught up in anything like this."

"Even if it means saving the world?"

Zook had been hearing about "saving the world" every day since he was a kid. Everything was "saving the world": turning out FreeLights, taking the FreeBus, even reusing his FreeFork.

"I've done my bit saving the world," Zook said.

Sparklett sat back in silence.

Zook could feel the waves of disappointment. "What could I possibly do, anyway?"

"I don't know, yet," said Sparklett. "Maybe you could instigate riots…"

"Riots!"

"Or maybe perform sabotage…"

"Sabotage!"

"Or maybe just something simple, like informing. I'm just asking you to think about it. If not to save the world, then as a personal favor to me."

It was Zook's turn to be silent. He certainly wanted to help Sparklett with any personal favors he could offer. But was it worth the risk of getting shredded?

She was looking at him with a neutral expression, waiting for an answer.

"All right," he said. "I'll think about it."

She smiled and put her hand on his. "I knew I could count on you," she said.

"I only said I'll *think* about it."

"When the time comes, you'll do the right thing."

Sparklett's faith in him was touching but disconcerting. But if she wanted to believe he was some sort of an underground hero, now—when she was here so close beside him—did not seem to be the time to disabuse her of her notions.

He rolled over and embraced her. They kissed.

Pretty soon Zook wasn't thinking about anything but Sparklett.

+ + +

Flying into the UCC capital, AssemblyPerson Harold Wild loosened the safety belt around his big stomach just enough to allow himself to float gently in the hopper's zero G. From this height, Wild could see the jagged slash of the Sierras, the glassy floor of the flat

Mojave where the desert had been melted during the Flash War and, in the distance, the illuminated towers of FriendsterVille surrounded by the trickling ribbon of Mead Moat.

With his belly floating weightless, Wild felt a comfortable torpor. He patted his coat pocket for another cigar, but found he had consumed his last. Cigars, although forbidden for the general populace, were widely available for the GovMint elites, but of course were expensive since the tobacco had to come from pre-Zero stock or be grown surreptitiously with private slave labor.

Wild—one of the 183 Friendsters who made up the People's Advisory Assembly—chaired the committee that attempted to coordinate intelligence about the Machines, and The Bob was demanding answers. Aerial photos proved that the Machines had repaired a large swath of Sand Francisco, with huge square structures emerging from the city's rubble and a system of smooth roads radiating north from a newly-dredged harbor.

The Bob was apoplectic. He wanted to know what the Machines were up to and where the roads were going, putting great pressure on Wild's committee to come up with new intelligence. But reconnaissance of the Machines was proving impossible. Intercepted transmissions were indecipherable and human missions inserted into the Sand Francisco area never returned. Even UCC cameras had to be lofted by toy balloons, since the Machines routinely shot down human skysters.

The Machines did what they wanted to do for reasons only they knew, and that was a problem. Humanity had almost been wiped out in the Flash War, and no one knew why the Machines had stopped short of finishing the job. Was their recent activity at Sand Francisco a sign that the Machines were now pursuing peaceful activities? Or was it preparation for resumption of hostilities?

The Bob seemed to believe the latter, and—under the moniker of Operation Save Our Bay—had been feverishly amassing war materiel and building up the military for an armed clash. Since any attack on the all-powerful Machines would be suicidal, Wild was forced to believe The Bob had another card up his sleeve. But no intelligence Wild's committee had unearthed was solid enough to account for The Bob's precipitous actions. That meant the Chief Controller must be acting on independent information.

Wild couldn't permit that. Independent intelligence not only undermined his power base, but might interfere with his plans for the coup.

The Bob's hold on the various factions making up the UCC had been slipping as the economy faltered and his voracious demand for booty grew. With the Machines controlling almost the entirety of the continent, opportunities for booty had grown strained. The fabulous cities of the EvilBizMen had been systematically plundered and stripped, to the point there was little of value left.

Wild thought about those cities—Lost Angeles, Sand Diego, PhoeNix, and the fabulous-but-Machine-controlled Sand Francisco—with wonder and resentment. Knowing what he knew of Elysium Economics, such magnificent wealth could only have been built through the grossest exploitation of the workers, on a scale far beyond anything the UCC could ever hope to achieve while laboring under the burden of supporting over a million state slaves. UCC regulations, after all, limited slavicens to an 84 hours work week, and children under 8 were totally excluded from the workforce.

In the decade following Year Zero, The Bob had launched the Wonderful Reorganization. Under the guidance of the Betters, the slaves had made rapid progress repurposing the rubble of the Flash War—replacing freeways with wind farms, destroying the few remaining petro refineries, and restoring the ruined habitat of the delta smelt. (The latter project had run into trouble when FreeFood ran short and the slaves discovered the smelt to be exceptionally tasty; but mass Shredder activity, systematically applied, had saved the precious fish from extinction.)

But even with these epic advances (and contrary to the predictions of the experts), the economy had continued to contract rather than grow. Doubling the minimum FreePerks just seemed to make everything more expensive, and putting several hundred thousand state slaves on extended work furlough depleted, rather than expanded, the treasury. In desperation, The Bob had increased Booty Calls on the People's AssemblyPersons—not once but several times—until the increased workload and decreased FreePerks began to spark resentment in the state slaves. In the past few years, Wild's own district had paid-over 1,200 SquareTons of gold, silver and electronic waste mined from cratered district cities, straining the resources of the local apparatus to the breaking point.

And now The Bob was gearing up to attack Sand Francisco. The Bob's insistence on this ruinous course of action was what finally enabled Wild to convince his fellow conspirators that it was time for a regime change. If their plans went well, The Bob would be out of the picture very soon and Wild would be in control.

Just then, a beautiful young slave with a blond hair floated down the aisle to him, her uniform (which Wild had himself approved) revealing deep cleavage.

"Shall I buckle you in, Friendster?" the girl asked. "We're about to start reentry."

"Yes, go to it," said Wild. With his belly floating

weightlessly, Wild felt years younger.

The girl floated closer, pushed Wild gently back into his seat, and cinched his seatbelt, all the while smiling as trained.

"Does that feel more comfortable, Friendster?"

Wild put his hand on her curvaceous buttocks. "It would feel a lot more comfortable if you were strapped in here with me."

The girl cast down her eyes. "Yes Friendster. Whatever you want." She began jiggling the latch of the safety belt again to get it open, but Wild put his hand on hers and stopped her.

"I was only joking," Wild said. The truth was, Sparklett had practically wore him out that very morning, and he was entirely sexually sated. "Not today, Princess. But why don't you come up to the rooftop pool tomorrow afternoon?"

"Yes, Friendster, tomorrow afternoon at the pool."

"It's a date then," said Wild. "It *is* 'Princess,' isn't it?" Even though it forbidden, all of Wild's servants had pet names since he didn't want to be bothered with their nonsensical State names.

"Yes, Friendster, they call me Princess."

Wild felt weight returning and released her hand. "Okay, Princess. Scoot."

She found her footing in the growing gravity and scurried back behind the curtain. Wild watched her. Yes, by tomorrow he would be ready.

He thought back to the strange young man, Zook, who had accosted him at the palace. How did a state slave get onto his private grounds, and where did he get the temerity to approach a Friendster without permission?

Zook might be the harmless peon he claimed, but it was just as likely that he was a plant from The Bob. In any case, Wild decided he had better handle him now.

Wild pulled out his FreeFone and connected to his private secretary.

"Send a note to Mento Peace Center," Wild ordered, skipping the niceties. "Have them see what they can find out about the slave who attempted to speak with me at the People's Palace this afternoon," said Wild. "Information and surveillance for now. Got that?"

"Yes, Friendster," said the secretary.

Wild could see they were landing and flicked off the FreeFone. He clasped his hands across his belly and watched as the flight descended into the canyon of towers of the capital. In FriendsterVille the dangers were largely political, and Wild felt secure here. If this slave Zook were an actual threat, Wild would soon know, and he would have no problem taking him out.

+ + +

After a last, lingering kiss, Zook stepped out of Sparklett's AtomoLimo and back into the squalid reality of Mento. The broken path where she dropped him was in a dark, obscure corner of town, far from the Gratitude Day party in the commune center. Zook watched with a sigh as the limo carried Sparklett up the hill and away to the Palace, leaving him alone but full of joy.

He didn't know what Sparklett saw in him, but for the first time in his life, he was in love. *Real* love, not the dull simulacrum of love he was used to experiencing at the Circle of Human Services FreeLove parties. Regaining the paved streets, he half-ran, half-skipped toward his FreePad, oblivious about the impression he was making.

After their love-making, there had been no more talk about the Two Brothers, and Sparklett had promised to help Zook get bought into Wild's private slave retinue. All Zook had to do was apply for the position at the AssemblyPerson's district office and Sparklett would see to it that his application received special attention. Once

Zook had a slave cubby at the Palace, they would be able to see each other as much as discretion allowed.

Sparklett *and* a private slave position. It was more than Zook had ever dared hope for. His mind spinning with visions of palace life, Zook made his way through the thinning holiday crowds until at last he was back at his slave warren on Living Wage Drive.

Some overzealous partiers had ripped down the metal sign warning of carcinogenic chemicals in the building, and Zook stepped over it through the propped-open front door. His FreePad was in a divided pre-Zero apartment, and he crept through his Pad mate's room to reach his own cubbie.

He had barely pushed open the plywood door when heard the angry buzzing of a FreeFone. It took a moment for Zook to realize it was *his* FreeFone, the replacement Sparklett had promised, placed in his room by some unknown person.

He snatched it up just as the ringing stopped. The new FreeFone looked exactly the same as the FreeFone it replaced, right down to his biometric photo. When he thumbed in, he discovered the source of the angry buzzing: 14 FreeSext messages and four FreeVids from Locally-Sourced Nukiforo, his FB.

Zook signed heavily and plopped himself down on his FreeMat. In the excitement of his evening with Sparklett, he had entirely forgotten that this was his night for FreeSex with Nukiforo. He punched one of the FreeVids at random, and Nukiforo's angry face appeared in the air above the screen.

"Where are you?" she said in a whiny voice. "You were supposed to meet me here." The music in the background reminded Zook that "here" was the festival in Sacajawea Square.

One of the FreeSext was more succinct: "I'm going home. You had better show up."

"Shit," said Zook. It was every slavicen's duty to help repopulate the State, and Nukiforo had already cost him six dePerks for his last missed session.

"On my way," Zook FreeSexted with a sigh. Before he left, he splashed himself with some FreeSpice, even swishing some around in his mouth.

5.

ALL YOU NEED IS LOVE

Locally-Sourced Nukiforo lived in MacArthur Park, a huge cluster of identical tiny-home buildings built of stacked storage containers from old Lost Angeles harbor. The desert landscaping around the units consisted of scraggly spiked plants and a sprinkling of pea gravel atop dust—the whole scene cast into sharp contrast by pole-mounted spotlights. A few knots of Gratitude partiers hung around concrete benches chatting and smoking illegal Don't. The park was reserved for female state slaves of child-bearing age, and Nukiforo had a tiny-house container all to herself since her former FreePad-mate had gotten pregnant and been moved to upgraded Breeder housing.

Zook found Nukiforo at home in her container, though she wouldn't open the door.

"Come on, Nuki, it's me."

"Go away."

"I can explain everything."

"Screw off."

"Just open up," said Zook. "I'm sorry I'm late. I was detained."

The door opened a crack but the chain stayed on. Nukiforo was ready for bed, draped in standard 18% gray FreeJs, but her eyes were red and swollen. She had obviously been crying, and Zook felt genuine remorse.

"Detained by the plops?" she asked.

"I had to go up to the palace to see about a private slave position."

"Oh," she said. "That."

Nukiforo disapproved of Zook's ambition to become a private slave, even though in principle it would mean more FreePerks and a higher PerkGrade for her if they successfully manufactured any babies. The reality was, she didn't really believe Zook was good enough to get bought by a High Friendster.

"I came here as soon as I could. Honest," said Zook.

"What happened to your face? Did you get that at the palace?"

There was a large scrape on his forehead where the guards had pounded his face to the floor.

"I, uh, tripped on the curb."

The chain came off.

"All right," she said. "Come in."

In the absence of her roommate, Nukiforo had pushed aside the curtain normally dividing the space, revealing the entire length of the living container. There were bedroom areas at either end and a shared kitchen/bath along the wall in the center. Nukiforo had, apparently, recently taken a bath in the single galvanized metal tub, which cleverly doubled as a table when covered with its plywood top. In the bedrooms, a poster hung above each FreeMat as a decoration. "Don't Interrupt Friendster" said the one closest to the entrance; the other, a rare two-color in red and green, hung directly above Nukiforo's FreeMat. "Live, Love, Breed," it counseled.

Zook stepped over the threshold with his customary feeling of dread. With other women he had already fathered (or believed he had fathered, since he lacked access to his paternity records) three of the four required slavettes, but production with Nukiforo was proving far more difficult, despite their high biological compatibility index.

Nukiforo put the lantern on a shelf and flopped onto her FreeMat indifferently, brushing aside discarded wrappings from the BobBits she had evidently picked up at the festival. She was attractive enough, with large brown eyes and dark hair a bit longer than required. But she always seemed to have a reason to be angry with him, making their encounters difficult. Zook took a seat on the edge of the FreeMat, not daring yet to come too close.

"You look really pretty tonight," he said.

"As if you cared. I waited for you two hours at the statue."

"I told you, I got detained. My friend Bacon promised to introduce me to AssemblyPerson Wild."

"Oh, right. You are such a bullshitter."

"You won't say that when I become his private slave."

"Like that's ever going to happen."

"You might be surprised."

She sat a moment, searching Zook's face to determine if he were serious.

"You could have messaged at least," she finally said.

"That's the funny thing. FreeFones are blocked in the palace."

"Really?"

"The Friendsters don't like them. They don't want anyone to know where they are or what they're doing."

"AssemblyPerson Wild told you that?" she asked suspiciously.

Better to leave Sparklett out of it. "Yeah," Zook said. "Though we only talked for a minute."

"Then why were you there so long?" she said craftily, hoping to trap him in a lie.

"You can't just walk in and demand to see the AssemblyPerson. I had to wait a long time. That's the way it is. Oh, and guess what?"

"What?"

"You know my clown painting that you hate? Well,

Wild owns one, too."

"Why would he own a clown painting?"

"*Because*, as I told you, it's an important work of art."

"An AssemblyPerson would never have illegal artwork. Besides, that dumb thing is going to get you shredded. Why do you have to be so different? No one else has a clown painting, or thinks they're so high and mighty they deserve to be a private slave. Why can't you be normal, Zook, like everyone else?"

"I *am* normal," Zook said.

"No you're not," said Nukiforo. "If you were I'd be pregnant by now. But you can't even show up for our FreeLove appointments. And if you don't make me pregnant soon I'll lose all my MomPerks."

Zook could see she was about to pitch a fit again so he tried to calm her. "It will be okay," he said. "If I get to be a private slave you'll get *extra* MomPerks.

"And you really talked to the AssemblyPerson?"

"Only for a minute. He had to get on a hopper to return to FriendsterVille."

"All right," Nukiforo said. "I guess I forgive you."

She unbuttoned her FreeJs, threw them aside, and leaned back on a pillow. "I'm ready," she announced. "Let's go."

Zook unbuttoned his own tunic with a bit less haste.

"What's wrong," she demanded, as she saw his hesitation.

"Nothing," said Zook. "It's a little cold in here."

"You'll warm up," Nukiforo said.

Zook certainly hoped so. "Mind if I turn down the lantern?"

"No, go ahead," she said. "Save some fuel."

Zook turned down the lamp as low as it would go, then dropped his tunic to join Nukiforo on the FreeMat.

+ + +

A futile half-hour later, Nukiforo pushed Zook off.

"That's enough," she declared. "You sicken me."

"I don't know what's wrong," Zook said. "We've never had a problem before."

"Ha!" said Nukiforo. "*You* always have a problem. You were never at the palace. You were out having FreeSex somewhere, weren't you?"

"No, I swear!" said Zook.

"Liar! I should have known!"

She turned her face to the wall. Zook put an arm around her and attempted to snuggle.

"Don't touch me," Nukiforo said. "You're a terrible FB. You're going to cost me my MomPerks."

Zook could see she was crying again and once again tried to embrace her.

"I said, don't touch me!"

"All right, all right," said Zook. "But if I don't touch you, you'll *never* go into production."

"I'm through with you. I'm going to request another inseminator."

Zook already had five dePerks. Any more and he'd have a hundred extra hours of community service. "Nuki, please. Don't be like that."

"You were with some FreeSlut, weren't you?"

"I swear, I wasn't!"

"Then why can't you get it up?"

"We'll work it out. Give me a chance."

"You don't care about me. If they take me out of rotation, I'll lose my FreeSwimercize classes, my FreeFood increases, my priority FreeBus pass…"

Zook tried to interrupt: "They're not going to take you out of rotation."

"Yes they will! I've been waiting months to get pregnant so that I can get my housing upPerk, and you don't even care."

"Nuki, we'll do it, I swear, just rest a few minutes."

"And I'll never get to go to Domo!"

Domo was the special seaside hotel set aside for bearing State mothers.

"Yes you will. Just relax and give me a minute. There's no curfew tonight."

"No. Go away. I wouldn't want your filthy slavette even if you could give me one. Get out of here and go back to your FreeSlut."

"Nuki…"

"Go!"

A few minutes later, Zook stumbled out the MacArthur Park gate and made his way through the dark Mento streets toward his FreePad. His head was splitting. He didn't really blame Nukiforo for being angry with him—she was approaching the end of her use-cycle and would be put up for sale in Newvember if she didn't enter production—but he resented being chosen to her and felt trapped by his disinterest in her charms.

FreeSex was one of the key Health Benefits of FreeMed, and Zook had never had any problems with previously assigned FBs. These had been an assortment of fun and juicy girls of child-bearing age who, as instructed in class, "left their hang-ups at the bedroom door" and never had any complaints about Zook's performance.

Nukiforo could cause a lot of trouble if she carried through her threat to dump him for another FB. It wasn't just the dePerks he'd receive and the accompanying community service. He'd also have to recertify before the Board of Sexaminers, which meant going through the whole paperwork process again and meeting with a State Sexologist. Then he'd have to be poked and prodded at the FreeClinic to determine his disease status and get graded for a new hookup card. Finally, there would be 12 hours of sexual-function testing at Central

Station, where he would be observed and graded through a one-way mirror. Zook hated that. The sex surrogates were all so experienced and encouraging that he felt intimidated, and he dreaded the follow-up observations and recommendations from the State examiners.

Zook sighed. It would be far better, he decided, to try to patch things up with Nukiforo before she could act on her threat. He paused and direct FreeSexted her: "I'm sorry for everything. My fault. Let's talk tomorrow." In the morning he would FreeVid her a cute cat VidYo and then call her at lunch to chit-chat as if nothing had happened.

Curfew had been cancelled for Gratitude Day and it was very very late. At last he climbed the stairs to his FreePad and crept past the sleeping slavicens in the front bedroom. Slipping into his room, he threw himself on the FreeMat, exhausted. He was very tired and had to be at his circle in just a few hours.

He turned on his side and tried to sleep, but the moon cast a pale glow across the room, illuminating the clown painting—the Pedro he loved—hanging on the door frame where it had been tacked for two years.

Zook examined it. Even in the weak moonlight, the image seemed to jump out from the background, vibrant and alive. Painted in acrylic on black velvet cloth, it depicted a drunken clown passed-out against a lamp post and slumped into the gutter. The clown held a dead cigar in one hand and an empty alcohol bottle in the other. The clown's eyes were Xs and his greasepaint was smeared into a weary frown across his unconscious face. His top hat, half-crushed, bore wilted flowers on the brim.

Zook could see immediately that his painting and Wild's must constitute a pair, meant to hang side-by-side. In Wild's version, the clown was laughing and ebullient; in Zook's, defeated and debauched.

Zook sat up. He suddenly realized why Wild's

painting had seemed to him incomplete. The stag. Wild's painting was entirely missing the magnificent stag that stood off in the background of his painting, to the left of the drunken clown. The animal was posed holding high a huge rack of antlers and gazing down on the fallen man—sadly, it seemed to Zook, though how the artist had achieved that effect was a mystery.

He looked more closely. There was something in the stag's right eye, almost as if...

Zook retrieved his FreeFone from under the pillow and shined its light of its face on the velvet.

Yes. A tiny highlight of paint, which Zook had at first taken to be a slip of the artist's brush, adorned the corner of the stag's eye.

The hint of a tear, which in Wild's painting emanated from the eye of the clown, had somehow, in this painting, transferred to the animal.

The stag was crying.

And that made Zook sad, too. The clown's unconscious stupor and degraded state somehow caused something in his heart to resonate.

It was, Zook realized, a vibration of the same resonance he felt when he lay with Sparklett.

Pedro was a genius.

+ + +

Zook thought back to how he had acquired the clown painting in the first place.

Some state slaves renovating a decrepit old cottage not far from the Mento Design Circle had ripped open a wall to find it stuffed with old photographs, posters and paintings, apparently hidden during the Flash War. Since only approved pre-Zero images were allowed, the slaves had treated the haul as if it were radioactive and dumped the material at the MDC for processing.

Friendster Boraxo, Zook's boss, had decided that he would go through the material himself to determine what was forbidden and what could be put in the Circle's design library. Zook (who was fascinated by pre-Zero art and didn't understand why it was forbidden in the first place) had jumped at the chance to organize the mess of materials, sorting photographs by subject, peeling apart water-damaged posters and flattening out the scrolled artwork—including the velvet clown painting.

Zook cringed as Boraxo proceeded to discard 90% of the material he had carefully arranged on the view table.

"Trash, trash, destroy it all," Boraxo proclaimed, barely looking through the piles.

"But what about this clown painting?" Zook said. He had never seen a painting on velvet before and thought it ingenious.

"Trash like the rest of it," said Boraxo, holding it at arms' length with distaste.

"Pardon, Friendster, but if I may ask—*why* is it trash?"

"Because it is," said Boraxo, pushing it off the edge of the desk into the discard pile. "Now *here* is something we can use," he said, holding up a poster of an orange rectangular blob. It appeared to be an advertisement for an art show, but the bottom part of the poster was ripped and the artist's name missing.

"Sublime," said Boraxo.

Zook thought the colors were beautiful, but he knew that wasn't why his Friendster liked the image. Boraxo liked it because it had no recognizable subject and was, therefore, completely safe.

Zook was surprised by the thought, which welled up from his subconscious unbidden, like oil seeping to the surface from subterranean pressure. He looked at the orange rectangle and then at the velvet clown painting in the trash and suddenly knew that Boraxo was a fool.

That evening, on his way home to his FreePad, Zook had detoured past the trash dumpster and rescued the clown painting from destruction. He brought it home under cover of night and tacked it up on the back of the door to his FreePad, where no one would ever see it but him.

Zook had never deliberately disobeyed a Friendster order before, and he was afraid of what Boraxo might do if he ever found out. From his first day in FreePod, Zook had been taught that everything valuable belonged to the State, and he felt a tinge of guilt for treating the Pedro as if it were his own.

But as he admired the painting which Boraxo had condemned, a stubborn resistance arose in his breast, and he suddenly felt certain he had done the right thing.

"No," he told himself. "It's mine. They had a chance to keep it and they threw it out."

The world needed clown paintings.

Or maybe just his world?

He would figure it out in the morning. For now, he had to sleep.

6.

YOUR BETTERS KNOW BEST

Not-for-Profit Boraxo stood in his office looking through the mirrored-glass down onto the creative floor of the Mento Design Circle. He had more than thirty designers working for him now, each slave hunched over a desk and each working busily, if not happily, at their assigned tasks. By appointment to The Bob, the MDC designed and produced the banners, posters, leaflets and declarations found everywhere in the UCC, and under Boraxo's leadership was moving into interior furnishings and civic crafting as well. Boraxo's father-in-law had promised him a position in the Fair Distribution Department if Boraxo met and exceeded production quotas three years in a row. The promotion would mean more FreePerks and a chance to move from the stix to the capital at FriendsterVille. So far, everything was on track.

Just then the FreeFone on his desk rang. The screen showed that the call was from PeacePerson Investigator Enterprise Green. Boraxo frowned and picked up the instrument.

"Do you control a slave named Differently-Abled Zook?" the investigator asked.

"Why, yes," said Boraxo, taken aback. "He's one of my best workers."

"Do you know anything about his whereabouts last night?"

"Last night? No. The last I saw him was yesterday afternoon, at the Gratitude Day Chastisement. Why?

What has he done?"

"Nothing," said the investigator. He asked a few more questions about Zook's work duties and psychological profile and rang off.

Disturbed, Boraxo put down the FreeFone. He knew that Zook must have done something wrong or he wouldn't be the object of an investigation. The State never investigated anyone unless a crime had been committed, and it always turned out a crime had been committed. There were, after all, rules and regulations for everything, with everything recorded, so it was merely a matter of searching to discover which offense best suited the State's need for prosecution. So Zook was certainly a criminal, or soon to be one.

Boraxo went to the one-way mirror. Zook was shuffling papers at his cluttered desk. He did not appear to be acting suspiciously. In fact, he looked a lot more focused than his co-slaves on either side, who appeared to still be suffering the effects of last night's Gratitude festivities. Zook did, however, have a serious scrape on his forehead that could have been the result of some unauthorized activity.

Boraxo suddenly wondered if the plop had been testing his loyalty by asking him what he knew about Zook's whereabouts. After all, the town was peppered with cameras and Zook carried a FreeFone like everyone else, so the authorities could quickly look up any slave's whereabouts if they wanted. But as Zook's Friendster, Boraxo also had access to all of Zook's movements. Were they waiting to see if he, Boraxo, were concealing something?

Quickly, Boraxo slid a few tabs on his desktop, calling up the location records of all of the slaves he controlled. However—and Boraxo had never seen this before—the records of Zook's whereabouts the previous day were missing, replaced by a comment, "Location

Module Error."

What the…?

Was Zook's FreeFone broken? Had he strayed Off the Map? No. Different error messages would have been generated in those cases. Where on earth had Zook been?

Wherever it was, the lack of strict records of Zook's whereabouts reflected poorly on the Circle, and Boraxo regretted remarking to the plop that Zook was a good worker. That might come back to haunt him. He would have to act decisively, but carefully, to make sure his own reputation remained untainted.

He buzzed Zook's desk. "Get all your materials together and see me in my office."

"Yes Friendster," said Zook. "When?"

"Now."

"Now? But…?"

"Now," said Boraxo, his temper flaring.

"Yes, Friendster," said Zook, jumping at the tone of Boraxo's voice and scrambling to get his work together.

Slow response, Boraxo wrote on Zook's personnel file. That was a start.

+ + +

Zook knocked on Friendster Boraxo's door, not quite sure what he was in for, but certain that it wasn't good. So far as Zook knew, he hadn't done anything to anger Friendster so he assumed that there had been another irrational policy change or regulation that had put Friendster in a bad mood. It was clear that Boraxo meant to dress him down, and it was a state slave's job to take it.

He gave the door a knock, and entered when acknowledged. Inside, the office air was frigid. To Save the World and Because Global Warming, air-conditioning was prohibited in all work and manufacturing areas, except for the offices of

Friendsters, where superior thinking skills required comfort.

"Zook, I've come to a decision," Boraxo said. "I'm selling you."

"Selling me?" Zook said, startled.

"There's a requisition for a Colorist at Salt Point, in East Desert," Boraxo said. "I can get a very good price."

"But why, Friendster?" said Zook. "I've been working here for years. My reviews have all been good. And you even named me State Slave of the Month last Bobuary."

"Well, you're not State Slave of the Month now," said Boraxo. "Look at you. Your appearance is slovenly. And what happened to your face? What were you doing last night?"

"Last night?" said Zook. The question threw Zook. Had Boraxo somehow heard about his fight with the guards at the palace? "It was Gratitude. I was visiting friends."

"Come on, slave—you don't expect me to believe that, do you? I happen to know you are under suspicion."

"Under suspicion?" said Zook. "What makes you say that?"

"Don't play innocent," said Boraxo. "An investigator from the PeacePersons called me this morning."

Zook stirred uneasily. So that explained Boraxo's sudden displeasure. But why would the plops be investigating him? Had Nukiforo followed through on her threat to report him?

Or was it about Sparklett?

"What kind of inquiries?" Zook said at last.

"What kind do you think?" countered Boraxo. "They wanted to know about your job performance and character," said Boraxo. "What do you suppose I told them?"

"I have no idea, Friendster."

"That's right! You have no idea!" fumed Boraxo. "You slaves have no idea how much trouble you put me through. Now—where were you *really* last night? Your FreeFone data is garbled."

"I was with Locally-Sourced Nukiforo. My FB."

"Did she give you that bruise?"

"No. I fell." Zook knew it was a flimsy excuse, but the less he said the better until he could get some grip on what was happening.

Boraxo sat back, drumming his fingers on the desk. "You're not making this any easier," he said. "As to your performance—let me see those projects."

Zook placed his materials on Boraxo's desk. Zook was proud of the job he was doing for the department and hoped that reviewing his excellent work would calm his Friendster down and bring him to his senses.

Boraxo opened the first folder, which contained photographs and swatches of the various paint colors Zook was considering for the 7th Street wall. Zook's job title, "Colorist," was a bit of a misnomer since the only colors he was allowed to work with were shades of gray. Solvents for the pigments of brighter colors gave off the unacceptable levels of VOCs, and gray was a renewable resource. On the project board, Zook had circled his favorite shade, a light gray with the maximum amount of yellow allowed by regulation.

"Is this your final choice?" asked Boraxo, pointing to the circled swath.

"Yes, Friendster. It blends well with the buildings on either side, see?"

"Wrong," said Boraxo. He drew a big X through Zook's choice and circled another swath in a dark, almost black, gray. "Use this one."

"But that's going to emphasize the mass of the wall," said Zook. "Slavestrians will feel overwhelmed."

"I didn't ask your opinion," said Boraxo. He made a

note in Zook's file and turned to the next folder, the interior colors for the booty audit office. More swaths with more shades of gray. Zook had circled two of them, slightly contrasting versions of gray, this time with a touch of blue.

"Why are there two samples circled? Can't you decide?"

"I thought we could paint the long wall here in the dark shade and use the lighter shade on the wall opposite the window."

"Too expensive," said Boraxo. "You slaves know nothing about budgeting. It's always spend spend spend the State's money."

He Xed out both of Zook's choices and circled another. "Use this," he said.

"But that's—ugly," Zook blurted, surprised at himself even as he said it.

"Are you questioning my orders?" said Boraxo. He almost seemed to be daring Zook.

"No, Friendster," Zook said.

"Good," said Boraxo. He made another note in Zook's file and picked up the third folder, carpeting for the Knights of Bob guild hall. Zook had carefully assembled a grid of six swatches of carpet, all, of course, a shade of gray, but each with different and interesting texture.

"Where did you get these swatches?" Boraxo said.

"From the reference files," Zook said.

"Did I give you permission to access the reference files?"

"Why, no Friendster. But everyone uses the reference files all the time."

"I'm not interested in what everyone does, Slavicen Zook. I'm interested in what you do."

The Friendster made a third note in Zook's personnel file, closed it, and pushed the files back to Zook. Far from being impressed with Zook's work, he seemed more disapproving than ever.

"That will be all," Boraxo said. "Go correct your work. You will be notified when the sales arrangement is completed."

Zook realized that Boraxo's review had all been a game, intended to document Boraxo's displeasure with Zook in the wake of the plop inquiry.

"Dismissed," said Boraxo.

Zook bowed and left. But he wasn't smiling

+ + +

Back at his desk, Zook spent the rest of the morning in unsettled silence. Boraxo's abrupt decision to sell him had obviously been triggered by the PeacePerson's investigation—but why were the plops investigating him?

Now that he had time to think, Zook dismissed the idea that he had been spotted with Sparklett. Zook reasoned that, had that been the case, he would already have been arrested. More likely the plop investigation had to do with Zook's scuffle with Wild's guards. Could the AssemblyPerson be checking up on him to see if he were any threat?

The possibility depressed Zook. It had taken him to years to actually get close enough to Wild to speak to him, and his private slave ambitions would be dashed if the AssemblyPerson felt he wasn't trustworthy. It didn't matter that Zook's eagerness to meet Wild was innocent, and that there was nothing for any investigation to reveal. Zook had made a bad first impression which he would have to work hard to counter.

Sparklett had instructed Zook to apply at Wild's district office today, before the AssemblyPerson awarded the position to someone else. Zook had planned to discreetly disappear from his desk that afternoon under the cover of visiting a job site, but Boraxo would never let him go now. In fact, the Friendster's sudden decision to sell Zook into slavery in East Desert would be catastrophic to Zook's plans.

A desperate idea formed in Zook's mind. He *had* to get to the District Office today—not only before the private slave position was filled, but before the plops made further inquiries that could get back to the AssemblyPerson and taint his chances. But since Boraxo would never voluntarily allow Zook out of his sight, Zook had only one option.

He would have to fake illness. Even a Friendster would hesitate to interfere with a slavicen's right to FreeMed.

Zook would have to make it convincing, though.

He pushed the buzzer for Boraxo's office.

Boraxo's voice came from a speaker at Zook's desk: "Yes, Zook, what is it now?"

"May I be excused, Friendster? I feel sick."

Out of the corner of his eye, Zook saw Boraxo un-opaqued his office mirror to get a better look at him. Zook did his best to look suitably ill. Then the mirror was opaque again.

"You'll live," said Boraxo.

"But Friendster…" said Zook.

"I said you'll live," said Boraxo. "Get back to work."

Boraxo's reaction was what Zook had expected, but Zook was only laying the groundwork for what was to come. He sat at his desk, willing himself to look progressively more ill, breathing erratically and emitting little groans.

Bong and Sarno, the slaves on either side of Zook, eyed him covertly before burying their heads in their work, unwilling to get involved.

After another quarter-hour, Zook buzzed Boraxo again.

"Friendster, I'm sick," Zook asserted.

"You're faking," said Boraxo.

"I really must insist on my right to FreeMed," said Zook.

Before Boraxo could answer, Zook rose suddenly from his seat, then dramatically let himself fall to the floor (a little harder than he had planned since he was still sore from yesterday's beating). Half-curled in a ball, he spasmed his body in a passable imitation of an epileptic fit.

Slavicen Sarno, horrified, jumped from his seat to help, cradling Zook's torso in his arms even as Friendster Boraxo emerged from his office.

"He's having a seizure, Friendster," said Sarno. Zook's body was shaking and his eyes rolled up into their sockets

Boraxo looked at Zook suspiciously, then bent and slapped him hard. "Snap out of it," he said.

Zook let a great string of drool escape from his mouth and continued to contort and writhe.

"I don't think he can breath," Bong observed. All of the slaves in the office had gathered around, watching the spectacle unfold and waiting to see what the Friendster would do.

Boraxo stood up.

"*You* and *you*, get him to the FreeClinic," Boraxo commanded. "Everyone else—back to work."

+ + +

An hour later, Zook sat on the edge of an examining room table, looking remarkably better. His seizure symptoms had begun to abate as soon as he had been escorted into the clinic's waiting room, and disappeared altogether by the time his escorts had left. A pimply-faced girl in a white smock—Zook assumed she was a trainee of some sort—took his temperature and drew blood, then left him alone in the room "for observation," though no one came by to observe.

Zook, bored, leafed through the various State pamphlets on healthy eating ("Always finish eating the variety of pure fruits and vegetables provided to you by your Friendster") and disease control ("Mosquitoes and other disease-vector insects should be controlled by the burning of incense, never by toxic chemicals"). He was just about to wander out of the room in search of a doctor when the pimply-faced girl returned.

"Your blood work and vitals are normal," she said. "When did this episode occur?"

"About an hour ago," said Zook.

"Probably just something you ate," she said. "I'll release you so you can return to work."

Zook did not want to return to work.

"How long before the real doctor arrives?" he asked.

"I *am* the real doctor," the young girl said. "Or rather, I'm the FreeDoctorAssistant, which is all that's required at this location."

"But I can't go back to work this afternoon," Zook said.

"Why not?" said the girl.

"I… I…" He tried to think of something that would appeal to her. Finally, leaning close he blurted out, "Doctor, I just found out my FB is pregnant," whispered Zook. "We want to celebrate. Do you understand?"

"You need a day pass," said the girl, flatly.

Zook nodded.

"I should have known," the girl said. "Why does every state slave come here when they want to get out of work?"

"It's not that," said Zook. "She really is pregnant and we really do want to celebrate."

"Oh, stop with the sob story," said the pimply girl. "Do I look like I was born yesterday?"

Actually, she did, but Zook kept his mouth shut.

"Maybe we can work something out," he finally said.

65

"Like what?" said the girl, interested. Barter was a way of life in the UCC. State slaves, after all, had to look out for one another.

Zook thought. "I work as a colorist for the commune," he said. "Maybe you can use a gallon of paint for your FreePad?"

"White?" she asked, pulling out a pad of passes.

"Will light gray do?"

She considered, her pen hovering above the pass.

"Shall we say, *two* gallons?"

It was highway robbery but Zook nodded. "I'll drop it by tomorrow."

She signed the day pass and handed it to him.

"One afternoon for two gallons," she said. "Get well soon."

7.

BETTER A STATE SLAVE THAN A BIZMAN PWN

AssemblyPerson Wild's District Office was located in one of the nondescript GovMint buildings that fronted the water, blocking the harbor view from the sight of smaller, less-important buildings further inland. Wild entered near a small FRestaurant for GovMintal functionaries and then took the elevator to the ninth floor, where he quickly found the door.

Inside, a half-dozen state slaves sat in folding chairs lined up in rows along the walls. A huge banner proclaimed *"Better a State Slave than a BizMan Pwn,"* while a smaller sign advised *"Keep Your Hands Visible."* The chairs faced a window opposite the door, where an extremely large woman with jet black hair sat at a reception desk behind bulletproof glass. Hemp rope, arranged in a corral sufficient to hold at least fifty supplicants, led up to the window in a maze. Since it was empty, Zook walked around the ropes and approached the woman directly.

She sat behind the glass at a desk with an AuthorizedWorkFone on one side and a computer monitor on the other. In between, she had shoved her keyboard out of the way and was playing PluckyDucky on her FreeFone. Even though Zook was standing right in front of her, the woman ignored him, intent on herding 3-D VidYo ducks into their nests while avoiding EvilBizMen kicking the ducks out of the way.

"Excuse me," Zook said.

The receptionist looked up, annoyed. "Did I call you? Wait in line until I call you," she said.

"Line? There is no line," said Zook.

"There's the line right there," she said, pointed to the roped-off maze.

"But there's no one there," Zook said.

"Don't you smart-mouth me," the woman said. "Get in line and wait until you're called."

Zook stepped back into place between the two stanchions.

"And no jumping the line," the woman said. "The maze starts near the door."

Zook got out of line, walked around to the entrance of the empty maze, and began weaving through it back-and-forth under the glaring eye of the woman behind the counter. When he once more neared the front, she abruptly drew a curtain across the heavy BuzzOffGlass.

The curtain was open a crack and Zook could see the woman's hands as she continued to play the game.

A gray-whiskered man sitting nearby observed Zook's impatience and chuckled.

"You have to wait, Slavicen," said the man. "This is my third day."

"Third day?" said Zook.

"Yes, sir, I been here three whole days trying to see someone. I need a Form Blue 19 before Friendster can send me north to Lost Angeles. You ever been to Lost Angeles?"

"No," said Zook, still mulling over the man's three day wait.

"Well I ain't never been to Lost Angeles either," the

man said. "But you need a Form Blue 19 to get past the checkpoints, see? My Friendster, he sell brick. Plenty brick up there I hear, but I never been there. What your Friendster do?"

"My Friendster? He doesn't do anything but boss us around," said Zook.

His companion laughed. "Ain't that the truth?" he said. "My Friendster is plenty mad that I wasted three days waiting here, but me, I don' mind. I got nothing else to do. Might as well sit here in this nice GovMint room as sit on a smelly old FreeBus travelling to Lost Angeles."

"Excuse me," Zook said. He couldn't afford to wait three days to see someone. He stepped up to the curtained window and tapped.

The curtain came back.

"I told you to wait," the receptionist said.

"Can't I at least leave my name?" Zook asked. "They're expecting me," he added.

The woman looked at him suspiciously. "Who's expecting you?"

"Well, I'm not sure exactly," Zook said. "It's about the private slave position at the People's Palace."

"Private slave position?" the woman said. "Who told you there was a private slave position?"

"Well, I have a friend at the palace, you see? And she said..."

"You have a friend? Why didn't you say that when you came up? What's your name?"

"Differently-Abled Zook," he said.

"Zook," she said. "How do you spell that?"

Zook spelled his name for her and she typed it into a machine on her desk.

"Okay," she said at last. "You're in the system. I'll call you when they want you."

The curtains snapped shut again.

Zook sat.

"Yes, sir, it take a lot of brick to build a wall," his new Slavicen friend resumed, continuing as if Zook had never left. "Right now we're putting up big new GovMint offices where the old harbor park used to be," he said. "Them offices five-story high and they brick from top to bottom. That's a lot of brick," he said.

"Fascinating," Zook said.

"I'm a hod-carrier myself. That's my specialty. You ever carry hod?"

"I haven't had the pleasure," he said, fidgeting in the uncomfortable seat. Maybe a hod-carrier could afford to sit here three days, but Zook only had a single afternoon. He decided to play his trump card.

Zook rose and went back to the window, knocking on it sharply with his knuckles.

The curtain slid open angrily and the woman glared.

"Can't you see I'm busy?" the receptionist snapped, pausing her FreeVid game. "What?"

"Make sure you tell them Sparklett sent me," Zook said.

The woman blinked and sat back. "Sparklett? Your friend is *Sparklett*?"

"That's right," said Zook.

"I am *so* sorry, Slavicen," said the woman, sitting up straight and whisking the VidYo game out of sight. "I'll let the Friendster know right away."

While Zook watched, the receptionist picked up the AWT handset and punched a button. "Regarding number 22880? He says Sparklett sent him... Yes, Sparklett... That's what he said."

She listened for a moment, then put the fone down and looked up at him brightly.

"Friendster Jowry will see you immediately," she announced. She rose and opened a big metal door. "Right this way," she said, smiling.

A minute later Zook was ushered into a large corner office with a view of the ocean. The woman behind the desk stood. She was frail and slender and her face was deeply etched. She wore a bright green scarf and a short open jacket. "Pleased to meet you, Slavicen Zook," the woman said, extending a hand. "I'm Judy Jowry, the Social Risk Mitigation Manager. Please, have a seat."

Zook was impressed. Jowry must be a High Friendster to have a non-slave name like "Judy." He suddenly felt shabby in his regulation state slave tunic.

"Would you like some FrEau? FreeCaffe?"

"No, I'm fine," Zook said, sitting down.

"After we've kept you waiting you must let us do *some*thing," Jowry said. She turned to the receptionist, who had been hovering near the door, and commanded, "Run down to catering for some patisseries," she commanded. The state slave bowed and left, closing the door behind her.

Jowry settled into her chair behind the desk and clasped her hands in front of her. "Now, Slavicen, what can I do for you?"

"I want to be a private slave for AssemblyPerson Wild," Zook blurted out.

Jowry's face was a neutral mask, betraying no emotion. "I see," she said. "And who is your current Friendster?"

"Not-for-Profit Boraxo," Zook said, "at the Mento Design Circle. I'm a Colorist for the commune," Zook said. "I pick colors. Whenever there's something to be colored, I mean."

"Yes," said Jowry, "It sounds very demanding. I'm sure you're a fine slave. But your Friendster, Friendster Boraxo, how would he feel if the AssemblyPerson bought you away from him?"

Zook could hardly tell her Boraxo already had him on the block. He chose his words carefully. "I don't believe he would stand in the way of AssemblyPerson Wild's wishes."

"Very gracious," said Jowry.

There was a gentle knock on the door, and the receptionist re-entered, out-of-breath, carrying a polished wood tray elaborately arrayed with a selection of pastries such as Zook had never before seen. She set the tray on the edge of Jowry's desk and backed out of the room, closing the door behind her.

"Please," said Jowry, pushing the tray an inch toward Zook. "Help yourself."

The patisseries looked delicious, far more elaborate and beautifully-made than the misshapen FreeGluten-FreeCookies sometimes served in the FreeAteria. There were little torts of strawberries and cream, squares of white marzipan topped with nuts, and small square cakes frosted with chocolate.

Zook reached for one of the latter. "Thanks," he said, stuffing it in his mouth.

"Have another," Jowry urged. "We wouldn't want anyone at the palace to get the impression that we didn't treat you well."

Zook scarfed down a second cake.

"Delicious," he said.

She sat back and watched him eat.

"Slavicen Zook, I don't want to disappoint you," she said as the pastry disappeared. "You *do* realize that the AssemblyPerson already has a full staff of Colorists? The new position will be a groundskeeping position. *Under*-groundskeeping. Planting flowers. Pulling weeds. Would that still interest you?"

"Oh yes," said Zook. "Anything to get onto the staff."

Jowry hesitated. "I'm sorry to have to ask you this, Slavicen Zook, but normally... Well—do you *have* any groundskeeping experience?"

Zook saw what she was driving at.

"No, not exactly," he said, switching into sales mode. "But I am an excellent learner. I was the only one to notice that the fern in the corner of our office was dying, and I gave it water and nursed it back to health. And in the Flash War, I was often sent to gather firewood and cut brush."

"I see," said Jowry.

"Plus," said Zook, pressing his point, "I voted for AssemblyPerson Wild in every election, you know."

This was certainly true, as Bacon had pointed out.

"Yes," said Jowry. "I saw that on your record."

"I'm a great admirer of AssemblyPerson Wild's work."

"Your qualifications seem to be in order," Jowry said at last. "However…"

"What?"

"Again, forgive me, Slavicen Zook, but, if I may…"

She slid open a shallow drawer and took out some papers.

"According to this report, you were involved in an altercation with the palace guards yesterday," she said.

"That was a mistake," he said.

"You weren't involved in a fight with the palace guards?"

"Well, yes," said Zook. "But it was all a misunderstanding. I was just trying to talk with the AssemblyPerson."

"It says they had to use a needler."

"A mistake, I said."

"I see," said Jowry. She closed the file, then sat back.

"I trust you understand that I'm in a very delicate position here," Jowry said at last. "Many people would like to be a private slave for the AssemblyPerson, but I must choose the best from among the candidates. You mentioned, I believe, a certain name to my receptionist as a reference. A Friendster, you said, named Sparklett. Is that correct?"

"Yes," said Zook.

Jowry shifted uneasily in her chair. "This is very awkward, Slavicen Zook, but, may I ask, *how* do you know Sparklett?"

"From the palace," Zook said. "Slavicen Bacon introduced us."

"Of course, of course," said Jowry. "His name appears in the file. But Sparklett—she is, you say, a friend of yours?"

"Yes, she's a friend," Zook said.

"And she sent you here, personally, to apply for this position?"

Zook heard the note of skepticism in Jowry's voice. It was becoming tiring, despite the kid gloves treatment so far.

"What? You don't believe me?" said Zook.

"The name 'Sparklett' is widely known," said Jowry carefully. "Many people claim to be a friend of Sparklett."

"Well, I *am* a friend of Sparklett. A very good friend."

"Yes, yes, of course," said Jowry, backtracking quickly. She picked up the file on her desk, tidied it neatly, and slipped it back into the drawer. When she looked up, her frown of concern had been replaced with a smile.

"There are multiple candidates for this position," she said. "But for a friend of Sparklett, I don't foresee any problem."

"Great," exclaimed Zook, hardly believing his ears. He had waited so long for this moment.

"Just bring me a written reference from Sparklett and the position will be yours."

Zook hadn't been expecting to be asked for a

reference. The smile fell from his face.

Jowry saw his look and went on in a reassuring manner: "It doesn't have to be anything formal. A note will do. Just so I can make my file complete. Your friend will do that for you, won't she?"

Zook felt sure Sparklett would write a reference, but Sparklett had specifically warned him not to contact her again until he was assigned to the palace. He'd have to figure out some way around that.

"I suppose it can be arranged," said Zook.

"Okay then, Slavicen" said Jowry, standing up and offering her hand in the State salute. "The job is as good as yours."

+ + +

PeacePerson Investigator Enterprise Green sat in a parked FreeCar and waited for Zook to emerge from the building. Green's orders—which had originated with the palace itself according to the priority code—was for information and surveillance on one Differently-Abled Zook, the subject now upstairs in the AssemblyPerson's District Office.

It hadn't been any trouble finding him. A FreeText from an informer had alerted the Peace Center to the subject's departure from the FreeClinic, and Green had simply pinged Zook's FreeFone to follow him here. Cameras provided several good pictures of the subject in the elevator, which the receptionist slave positively identified as Zook.

The paperwork from the palace was scanty. Apparently seeking a private slave position, Zook had attempted an unauthorized approach of AssemblyPerson Wild, leading to a scuffle with the palace guards. He had been released on the command of an unnamed Friendster and removed from the palace. The orders for information and surveillance had come down later that afternoon—probably, Green guessed, from AssemblyPerson Wild himself. Wild was of an extremely suspicious nature (he kept a personal FreeMail server in his bathroom) and frequently relied on Mento Peace Center officers to keep tabs on political antagonists.

Green could see why Wild might be wary of Zook. Between the subject's altercation with the AssemblyPerson, and the feigned illness and the secret meeting with Jowry, Zook was certainly acting suspiciously. Furthermore, a search of the slave's FreePad had revealed an odd pre-Zero painting of an intoxicated clown, proof that the subject harbored unsavory non-authorized sentiments.

If Zook were a dangerous radical, however, he must be under deep cover, for Green found little of consequence in Zook's historical record. Zook's file recorded only minor de-perks, some from years back, and he was a steady, though apparently uninspired, laborer at the MDC. On the surface at least, Zook appeared to be exactly what he claimed: a boon-seeking slave who didn't understand how the system really worked.

But if that were the case, why the painting? He would be sure to mention this anomaly in his report. It was well known that the AssemblyPerson himself had a strong interest in pre-Zero images.

Another aspect: For months, vague rumors of discontent among the High Friendsters had been filtering down, ever since The Bob had increased Booty Call assessments and started mobilizing the army. Green's sources in the capital had hinted that more money than usual was being embezzled from the People's Lockbox, even as criminal activities by the Two Brothers intensified. Several UnderAssemblyPersons were incarcerated at SuperPAC, and at least one member of the People's Advisory Assembly had committed suicide by self-strangulation, an obvious warning.

But what was being warned against and by whom? Wild had been a close associate of the suicided man, though he remained untainted by the scandal.

Could Zook be involved in a palace intrigue?

Green closed the file with a sigh.

Just then, the subject emerged from the building. He stumbled on his way out of the revolving door, then stood on the sidewalk squinting at the signposts and looking about indecisively.

The subject certainly *seemed* clueless—until he caught sight of Green's plop car. Then Zook turned and scurried guiltily down Duranty Street. Not only was Duranty Street a different route than the one the subject had arrived by, but it led to a deserted quarter of town where the deteriorating buildings had not yet undergone Civic Improvement.

That was strange.

Green took manual control of the FreeCar and eased the vehicle down the main thoroughfare, turning on Duranty to follow Zook.

8.

OBEY HERE NOW

Zook was a block ahead, walking at a brisk rate past a series of abandoned storefronts, and Green crept behind him, keeping his distance so as not to be seen.

When Zook turned again—this time north along the edge of the crumbly cliffs on the edge of town—he stopped and looked behind him, apparently to see if he were being followed.

Green pulled the FreeCar to a stop, but the subject hastened his pace and darted into into a narrow alley.

What *was* Zook up to? Afraid of losing him, Green tapped the accelerator on the car and followed, turning just in time to see Zook running through a weedy lot toward an abandoned garage in the distance.

Green had been here before, and knew that this particular row of buildings backed on to the concrete ravine of a pre-Zero storm drain. He turned the FreeCar off the pavement and bumped over an ancient crumbling parking lot to the alley behind. Sure enough, there was Zook, attempting to climb a rusted fence into the ravine beyond.

Green's instructions were for surveillance, but there was a limit to how much suspicious behavior he could put up with. It was time to rattle this slave's cage.

Green gunned his FreeCar toward the subject and keyed the mike. "Slave! Off the fence! Now!" he bellowed over the exterior loudspeaker.

Zook, half way up the fence, froze in indecision.

"Down!" Green barked. "Put your hands in the air."

Zook climbed from the fence and held his hands above his head.

"Turn around. Hands on the fence. I'm going to frisk you."

"But what did I *do*," the subject whined.

"Evading a PeacePerson, for a start," said Green. "We'll figure the rest out later. Now turn around."

Zook turned and put his hands on the fence, while Green gave him a thorough search. The slave had no weapons on him, only a plastic key, two sticks of hemp chewing gum, and a wadded up piece of paper.

Not much but at least it provided a pretext to ask a few questions, gather some info that he could put in his report to the AssemblyPerson.

Green unwadded the paper. "On a FreePass are you? I suppose you think this gives you run-of-the-town."

"I'm sick," the slave claimed. "I was at FreeClinic."

"FreeClinic 9. That's on the far side of Mento. What are you doing here?"

"I… I decided to take a walk. That's not against the law, is it?"

"It is if you're using a fraudulent FreePass."

"But there's the doctor's signature," said Zook, pointing. "It's real."

Green folded the pass and slipped it in his own pocket.

"Maybe," said Green.

Zook was beginning to irritate him. Like many of the small fry Green dealt with, Zook was insufficiently deferential. It burned him up to see what these state slaves thought they could get away with. What part of "slave" didn't they understand?

"What were you doing at the AssemblyPerson's office?"

That seemed to throw the subject. Green could almost see the gears turning in Zook's head as he tried to cook up some appropriate lie.

"And don't piss me off," said Green. "I get nasty when I'm pissed off."

"I was applying for a position, okay?" the man said at last. "A slave position at the palace."

The statement was consistent with what had been written in the palace report but still ridiculous. "Slaves don't apply for positions. They get bought and sold."

"This is a special position. A private slave position that only goes to certain people. A slavicen at the palace told me about it."

"What slavicen?"

Zook hesitated.

"Come on," said Green. "Who was this person?"

"Sustainable Bacon," Zook finally said. "He's works in the palace for the AssemblyPerson."

Green already had this information but he pulled out a pad and made a show of scribbling some notes. "And how do *you* know this slavicen who works at the palace?"

"Bacon and I, we grew up together in the same neighborhood, Pre-Zero, when we were kids," Zook said. "He told me about the position and, well, I was sick and I had the FreePass so I went over to the office to apply."

Green wrote more notes while covertly watching the subject. Was Zook actually stupid enough to think that Green was buying this mix of half-truths and lies? He decided to turn up the heat.

"Why did you assault the AssemblyPerson?" he

asked abruptly.

Zook blinked. "I don't know what you mean," he said.

"Yes you do. My sources tell me that you rushed AssemblyPerson Wild from the shadows as he attempted to board his hopper."

"That's all a misunderstanding. I merely tried to approach him to ask about the job opening."

"By threatening his life? My sources say it took three men to restrain you."

"Then you're sources are wrong," Zook said. "I was waiting where Bacon put me and politely approached my AssemblyPerson for a boon, as is the slavicen's right."

Slavicen rights. Normally when slaves started blabbing about rights, Green took them down to detention to give them a lesson about how rights really worked. He'd love to put this guy in the slammer but his orders were information and surveillance.

"Okay," said Green, handing him back his pass. "You're free to go."

"I'm free to go?" said Zook, startled.

"Didn't I just say that?"

"Thank you, PeacePerson, thank you," said Zook, smiling and bowing.

"Get going," said Green.

He watched, hands on hips, until the subject scurried out of sight up the roadway and around the corner. Then Green climbed back into the GovMint FreeCar and buckled his six-point safety harness.

He had more than enough new information. He'd write Zook up and send the report upstairs.

+ + +

Zook spent the rest of the day at home in bed, pretending to be sick to better establish his alibi after the brush with the plop. With all the excitement and nervous tension of the day, in fact he *did* feel a little sick, and dozed fitfully between bouts of watching State FreeVids on the Peoples Broadcasting Server. He was in the middle of a compelling documentary about drowning polar bears when the program cut off and all the lights went out.

It was 2100 hours, curfew.

Zook rose restlessly and looked out the window. With the street lights off, the blackness of the sky seemed to reach oppressively down from above and join with the blackness of the ocean beyond the town in the distance.

If his FreePad had been on the other side of the building, he would have been able to see the still-lit lights of the People's Palace far up on the mountainside. Zook suddenly felt intensely lonely. He tried to imagine what Sparklett would be doing at this hour. Holding long erudite conversations with other High Friendsters? Watching some amazing live acrobats in a private palace theatre? Lying naked in a candle-lit spa, her perfumed body covered with warm stones?

Or wiring explosives to blow up some GovMint building?

Had Sparklett *really* invited him to join the Two Brothers conspiracy? "Think about it," she had said. But Zook didn't need to think. He liked his arms and legs and didn't want to see them disappear down a Shredder. Maybe the invitation was some kind of test, to see if Zook were really loyal to The Bob? SecretPoliceShoppers among the slaves were always posing innocent-sounding questions, intended to ferret out any hints of political incorrectness. Or maybe the invitation had been a joke? Sparklett seemed to have a sly sense of humor. But she had seemed deadly serious.

Zook just couldn't square his image of Sparklett as a beautiful, elegant High Friendster with the bomb-throwing radicals that sought to send the UCC back to

FreeFall—a time when the EvilBizMen pwned the populace and BigBanks locked all their money away in steel vaults while the poor suffered without even FreeFones.

"Think about it." How could he *not* think about it? Why would anyone in Sparklett's position want to risk getting shredded by dabbling in anti-State subversion? It didn't make sense.

But then again—why would someone in Sparklett's position deign to have sex with a lowly state slave like himself? That was an occurrence just as incredible.

Obviously there was more to Sparklett than he understood. She was involved in activities clearly not sanctioned by the State.

What had he gotten himself into? All he wanted was a private slave job.

Zook stepped back from the window and threw himself onto the FreeMat. The room was unventilated and stifling, so that he pushed aside even his threadbare sheet. How was he going to get the written recommendation Jowry wanted from Sparklett? Not only was he not supposed to contact her until he had secured a position inside the palace, the plops were now probably monitoring his conversations. Friendster Boraxo had indicated that Zook was under suspicion, and certainly it was no coincidence that the plop had followed him that afternoon.

The plop had asked specific questions about Zook's scuffle with the palace guards, proving the incident was part of his Permanent Record. The mishap must have prompted an investigation, even if the whole thing were an innocent mistake.

The thing he feared most was that the plops would find out about his tryst with Sparklett. But if anyone knew about that, surely he would have been shredded by now. *Ergo*, no one knew. *Ergo*, he was safe, for the moment. The most the plops could discover was that he had claimed to be a friend of Sparklett's at the District Office. And as Jowry had said, many people claimed to be a friend of Sparklett.

He smiled when he thought back to the interview with Jowry. The deference he had received, the welcome, the delightful little cakes—all seemed to prefigure the luxury of private slave life at the palace. Zook could see himself there now, bowling in the People's bowling alley, stuffing his face at the People's banquet, hanging out with his private slave friends around the People's pool while his Friendster was a thousand miles away in FriendsterVille.

He could hardly wait.

All he had to do was get a note from Sparklett. While it was true she had told him not to contact her, she hadn't said anything about Slavicen Bacon. After Bacon's humiliation at Sparklett's hands, he probably would prefer to stay out of her sight, but surely he wouldn't refuse a direct request from his old friend Zook for assistance? He and Bacon had grown up together on Geranium Street, almost as brothers. They played soldier together in the rubble of the Great Catastrophe, set traps in the radioactive creek for odd-shaped fish, and were both drafted into FreePod together when the UCC took over.

Bacon would help him get Sparklett's note, Zook was sure.

He finally felt his body relax and his mind begin to calm. He turned on his side and began to drift off. He would get the note for Jowry, the cops would go away, and he would soon be working at the palace within sight of Sparklett. Everything was finally falling into place.

He was almost asleep when he remembered Nukiforo. He had a FreeSex date with her hours earlier but had completely forgotten.

She was not going to be happy.

+++

The next day, in the GovMint seat of FriendsterVille, Assemblyperson Harold Wild gave a quick kiss to the slave girl he had rented the previous night and shooed her out of his limo to her FreeSexCoop.

Time to get back to business. Wild had a lunch meeting with The Bob across town in thirty minutes and he would need every minute of that time to compose himself. Plans for Wild's coup were advancing rapidly and The Bob's assassination was scheduled to take place the following week.

During the luncheon, Wild would have to be extra careful to give an impression of total normality.

"The Bob-O-Sphere," he ordered his driver. That was the informal name of the People's Love Tower, a surviving casino from before the war which now housed The Bob's living quarters and offices. The meeting would take place on the Bob-O-Sphere's rooftop deck, with its panoramic view of FriendsterVille.

Situated halfway between the provinces of CalSobrantes and mineral-rich stretches of GoneTana and HellBerta, FriendsterVille was the logical capital of the United Care Communities, a strategic link between north and south. Its capture during the Flash War had been one of The Bob's earliest military priorities. For reasons unknown, the Machines had primarily attacked the city with yeti-rays, mummifying the inhabitants but leaving the bulk of the city's structures intact. The Bob's army took control as soon as the Machines had gone and it quickly became the Awesome People Party's stronghold.

After clearing out over a million mummified bodies and restoring electrical generation from the Soros Gorge Power Complex, The Bob had parceled out the old hotels and casinos to his political allies and loyal lieutenants, and FriendsterVille had become the wealthiest and most prosperous city in the UCC—the jewel in the crown of the UCC's achievements. As the seat of the GovMint and the home of the People's Advisory Assembly, it was a city of hedonistic delights: fine restaurants with delicacies of sea and field; nightclubs reeking of forbidden tobacco, with conversation lubricated by copious amounts of forbidden alcohol and billowing clouds of forbidden Don't; private antiquaries stuffed with fine furnishings and textiles seized from the eStates of EvilBizMen; and, of course, numerous FreeSexCoops, where the most beautiful state slaves from the entire country were made available to anyone in the Players Club.

And FriendsterVille, as reconstructed by The Bob, was *only* a city for those in the Players Club. The High Friendsters needed much time and leisure to be able to remake UCC society along the lines of Super Social Justice and Elysium Economics. Because their work was so important, The Bob had thought it wise to conceal from the slavicens the exact nature and scope of the High Friendsters' doings. If The Little People ever accidently mistook the Players' hard-earned relaxation for raw debauchery, they were apt to lose Gratitude for the FreePerks conferred upon them by their Betters. So far as The Little People knew, FriendsterVille was just another ring of pre-fabs around a crater where a city once had stood, and no one in the Players Club would ever admit to anything different.

Wild was jolted out his reverie as the AtomoLimo pulled up the base of the Bob-O-Sphere and glided to a stop.

"Welcome to the Bob-O-Sphere!" one of The Bob's private slaves said jauntily, opening the door. Wild grunted and walked into the lobby, where he presented his ID and was scanned and frisked by silent and thorough HomeLove Security plops. Another enthusiastic private slave welcomed him to the elevator, this time by name, and punched the button which would whisk him to the roof deck, where the lunch was to be held.

As the doors closed and the elevator began to ascend, Wild's heart rate also began to rise. *Keep cool*, Wild reminded himself. *In a few weeks you will be master of all.*

Only a select few knew of Wild's plot to assassinate The Bob, and they were tightly bound to Wild with golden ropes he had spent years securing.

In a land where everything was free, it was incredibly expensive to maintain the infrastructure required to keep a pleasure city like FriendsterVille going. By the laws of Elysium Economics, nothing was actually produced in the UCC, and all wealth flowed from reusing, repurposing and recycling the wasteful extravagance of the EvilBizMan, pre-Zero civilization.

And with the country gearing up for war under the Save Our Bay initiative, the expenses were piling up astronomically. Already in the past year The Bob had twice levied huge new Booty Calls on the slavicens' representatives. In his district alone, Wild had been forced to double the number of state slaves dedicated to mining the local ruins, and to raise their hours by 20%.

The other AssemblyPersons were in the same position or worse, and Wild had for some time been subtly exploiting their dissatisfaction to build a foundation of support for his plans. Even better from Wild's point of view was the Assembly's growing dismay with Operation Save Our Bay. This was no mere pushing into an area already deserted by the Machines, but was rather an attempted annexation of Sand Francisco, an area where Machine activity had been constant for years.

Most AssemblyPersons looked upon The Bob's war plans as utter madness. War with the Machines was a proven guaranteed loss. Between the Great Catastrophe and Flash War, the Machines had extinguished humanity from almost the entire globe. No one knew why they had spared the territory of the UCC, but it certainly wasn't The Bob's Glorious Offensive, as the party line declared. If the Machines hadn't unexpectedly ceased fire, there would be no UCC at all.

At first the lull in the fighting was thought to be a retreat while Machine forces regrouped, but as years passed and the peace held, it was generally understood that the Machines had granted human beings a reprieve. The reason for the hiatus was unclear and gave rise to various theories. Some believed the Machines had decided humans were too weak to bother with; others that they were keeping people alive to study, like germs in a petri dish. In the end, no one had a clear explanation and just accepted the cessation of hostilities as a given.

Although Wild understood that Sand Francisco was a tempting target, he saw no way for The Bob's attack to succeed. The city had been a Machine stronghold for decades, and The Bob's plans were wildly optimistic. Since Year Zero, Chief Controller Bob had been the UCC's supreme strategist, gradually eliminating his opponents and tightening his grip on the world's wealth. But now even the Assembly saw that The Bob was overreaching himself. The Players wanted to remain in the Players Club as long as they could, and war might deprive them of their pleasures.

Which was why *now* was the time for Wild to push his coup forward. Wild's control of key Friendstercratic posts was almost complete, and a cadre of General Lowe's officers stood poised to take over the army. When the assassination was accomplished and the army take-over a fact, the Assembly would—Wild felt certain—loudly welcome him as the new Chief Controller.

Wild ears popped as the elevator swiftly rode to the top of the tower.

Just keep cool, Wild reminded himself. *The Bob knows nothing. Just act completely normal until it's time to strike.*

9.

YOU GET WHAT YOU GIVE

A moment later, the elevator doors slid open and Wild stepped directly onto the Bob-O-Sphere's sunny roof deck.

Under a festive yellow awning, a rectangular banquet table had been set, where a half-dozen members of the Assembly were already seated—all members, Wild noted, who had expressed reservations about the Bob's recent policies. Behind the serving station and at strategic locations along the edges of the deck were arrayed fully-armed troops from The Bob's HomeLove Security Department. The Bob himself had not yet entered.

"If you please, AssemblyPerson, follow me," said a private slave, leading Wild to a seat at the table. On his right sat AssemblyPerson Toth and on his left AssemblyPerson Cossaboom, from Sand Diego and Central Valley respectively. The others present were legislators from smaller, poorer northern districts, along with a woman, her graying hair braided in the severe style of a mid-level staffer, whom Wild didn't recognize. The table was exquisitely set with fine pre-Zero dishes and silverware, and Wild was barely seated before a pair of tall slave girls arrived, one to pour wine, the other offering a tray with an array of various appetizers.

Wild was just picking out a few brandied mushrooms and pecan-dusted shrimp purses when The Bob stepped onto the deck from a private entrance near the spire. All

90

conversation at the table stopped as the guests watched the Chief Controller momentarily pause to examine the offerings in the kitchen before striding across the outdoor carpet to take a seat at the head of the table, frowning as usual.

He was not a tall man, but his striking gray eyes seemed to glow supernaturally, and his coarse beard was perfectly manicured although peppered with gray. In his public appearances, The Bob wore the same drab slave tunic as everyone else, but in FriendsterVille, he wore only sports jackets stitched of the finest pre-Zero materials available. His style of dress, of course, had sparked a new fashion within the Players Club. Now, throughout FriendsterVille, only slaves wore traditional tunics or robes, while GovMintal officials sported well-cut jackets in pre-Zero fabrics bought at great expense from The Bob's personal warehouse.

"Let's start," The Bob said abruptly, as soon as he was seated, snapping his fingers at the head waiter. Instantly, a half-dozen slaves, dressed in The Bob's private livery of royal purple, descended on the table with scores of dishes. Everyone knew the real business of the luncheon wouldn't begin until the meal was over, and the food served was, of course, of the finest quality. Wild started with the smoked delta smelt and dolphin-filled raviolo, skipping the rum-soaked brioche but not the ripe panda-milk cheese. Between courses, The Bob grunted pleasantries about progress in electrical generation and the creation of a new wet-lands on the edge of FriendsterVille which he was currently stocking with eagles for hunting. On The Bob's recommendation, everyone tried a floral Highfield sauvignon blanc from pre-Zero Zealandia—a vintage, Wild knew, the value of which had greatly increased since that island's unfortunate eradication.

Wild privately thought the wine a passable selection

but not as exceptional as The Bob seemed to believe.

As the last dishes were cleared, the cigars and the Don't came out and Chief Controller got down to business.

"Friendsters, thank you for coming," said The Bob, as if any of them had a choice.

The servers, sensing the change in mood, quickly withdrew and the guests sat quietly, waiting for the shoe to drop.

"As I'm sure you realize," he said, "Momentous things are happening here in FriendsterVille. The army is growing rapidly and Operation Save Our Bay is quickly gaining momentum. And The Little People, our dear little slavicens, have responded magnificently to our call for increased productivity."

His brow furrowed and his face grew dark. "But a few legislators in the People's Advisory Assembly have chosen to drag their feet," he continued. "You know who you are. That is why I have decided to move elections forward to the 7th of Sustaina."

It didn't take a genius to perceive his meaning. While the members of the assembly were ostensibly elected by the slavicens, the only slate was that of the APP (the Awesome Peoples Party), and The Bob controlled who would be on that slate. In effect, by moving the elections forward, he was threatening to depose Wild and the other AssemblyPersons present.

But if it were a real threat, Wild thought, there would have been no luncheon and no warning. Therefore it was the opening ploy of a negotiation.

"How so?" said Wild mildly, taking a puff on his cigar. "Haven't we served you admirably?"

"No you have not!" said The Bob, slamming his fist on the table hard enough to cause his drink to spill over. Three slaves rushed to clean up the mess and Bob waited for them to disappear before he continued.

"The six of you are far behind in your voluntary donations," said The Bob. "And you, Harold, most of all."

Since only those in the Players Club had RealNames, it was a mark both of refinement and politesse to use them in formal conversations.

"Not so, Robert," said Wild. "My district is and has always been among your largest contributors, and 70% of our productivity already is attributed to you."

"Attributed but not delivered. UnderComptroller Mutz" –he nodded toward the braided-haired woman to his right—"has called to my attention certain irregularities in the payment schedule."

Mutz produced a folder from a pre-Zero leather briefcase and handed out a one-page summary detailing expected revenues and shortfalls from each of the gathered AssemblyPersons. Wild's colleagues up and down the table looked at the sheet with dismay, but Wild merely glanced at the page and pushed it aside. "A matter of accounting, Robert," said Wild. "Most of the materials we mine from around my district have to be sorted, cleaned and evaluated before a value can be fixed. This takes time. I am doing everything in my power to speed up the process as I'm sure are my colleagues."

"You're stalling," said The Bob, bluntly. "The embargo of your Voluntary Donations are beginning to impair the Save Our Bay effort."

"'Embargo' may be a mischaracterization," said Wild, coolly. It was like playing a pre-Zero card game against a very crafty opponent.

"If you will look closely at the summary I have prepared," said Mutz, "you will see that the rate of booty contributions have steadily slowed."

"I also note that the absolute amount of booty contributions has increased," said Wild.

He turned to The Bob. "Is your concern over the booty rate really so great as to warrant early elections?" asked Wild.

"We must all pull in the same direction," said The Bob loftily.

"But can you be sure that new AssemblyPersons elected in our place will actually be more capable of delivering to you the revenues you seek?" As he said this, he stared steadily at UnderComptroller Mutz, whose face began to flush a bright red.

The Bob saw her discomfort and laughed. "The Save Our Bay effort costs booty, Harold," he said. "What do you suggest?"

"We have been settling our books with your people here in the capital at the end of each quarter. Perhaps we could speed up the cycle and transfer payments every two months instead," Wild said.

He looked to his colleagues for assent and then continued. "Would that be satisfactory, Robert?"

"Do you think that this, uh, increase in efficiency could be effected monthly?"

"I am sure, Robert," said Wild, "if that is what you wish."

The Bob smiled. "Let it be done then."

"But speeding up payments doesn't mean you will get all the revenue coming to you," the UnderComptroller interjected.

The Bob glanced at the phalanx of soldiers rimming the perimeter of the roof, and then at the invited AssemblyPersons. "Oh," he said. "I'm sure I'll get all of the donations coming to me."

"But, Robert…" said Mutz.

"Who gave you leave to call me by my name?" The Bob thundered. "You are not yet an AssemblyPerson, and you may never yet be one."

Mutz, startled by the outburst, immediately shrank

back and fell silent.

"That will be all," said The Bob, suddenly losing patience with the whole lot of them. "We will forget early elections for now and see how the new arrangements work out. You may go."

The AssemblyPersons rose and bowed to go, Wild with them.

"Thank you, Robert," he said.

"Harold, stay a while," said The Bob. "You others, out."

When the deck was clear of all the guests but Wild, The Bob motioned him to the railing. Wild approached warily. He wouldn't put it past The Bob to have him thrown over the side, but the soldiers were too far back to assist and The Bob's mind seemed to be elsewhere.

"Look at it," said The Bob, gesturing at the jumble of roads and buildings which reached out at their feet toward the horizon. "Did you ever wonder how all this got here?"

"Most of the materials were brought in from the coast, I imagine," said Wild, "before the Great Catastrophe."

"Of course," said The Bob. "But where did the wealth come from to build all of this magnificence?"

The question seemed genuine, but where was he going with this? "The EvilBizMen built it," said Wild, giving the standard answer.

The Bob still seemed dissatisfied.

"Do you know, Harold, that the UCC controls more slaves than any EvilBizMan of the past? And yet, where are *our* cities?"

"The UCC has hundreds of communes."

"Communes, yes. But no *cities*. Nothing to rival this. And do you know why?"

Wild had never thought about it, and he certainly didn't want to be caught up in a disagreement with the

Chief Controller. But he saw that The Bob was expecting an answer. "Not enough slaves?" Wild ventured.

"No!" said The Bob, adamantly. "We already have too many slaves. They're nothing but leeches, sucking wealth from my State.

"But I've been thinking," The Bob said, tapping the side of his head to indicate his great brain-power, "and I've finally figured out what the problem is.

"There's nothing left to pillage."

The Bob looked at Wild with shining eyes, clearly expecting him to be knocked over by the profundity of this pronouncement.

"I'm, ah, not sure I understand," said Wild.

"Don't you see?" said The Bob. "How do you think the EvilBizMen got all their money? Through exploitation of their pwn workers! What is wealth-creation but economic rape?

"But now there is no one left to steal from. If we want the UCC to continue to grow and prosper, we need new victims to subjugate—to rape. In other words—we need war."

So *that*, Wild thought, was why The Bob had brought him here—to gain his support for the war. Wild had been careful to say nothing against Operation Save Our Bay in public, but his opinions were well known in the assembly, and to The Bob's spies as well. Wild would have to walk a fine line in mollifying him.

"If you are referring to the Save Our Bay initiative, I hardly think the Machines will be an easy victims." said Wild.

"They might be easier to conquer than you know," said The Bob.

Wild could hardly believe his ears. The Bob's confidence bordered on the psychopathic. "The Machines are formidable," Wild pointed out. "They are more likely to conquer us than for we to conquer them."

"Perhaps there is a weakness in their defenses," said The Bob.

"Weakness? What weakness?" Wild said. "If the Machines hadn't stopped attacking at the end of the Flash War we would all be dead."

"But they did stop attacking."

"Your Glorious Offensive?" said Wild, unable to keep the incredulity out of his voice.

The Bob made a dismissive gesture. "That explanation is for The Little People. But I *do* know that at the end of the Flash War, the Red and Green Machines were engaged in the final, decisive battle. After fighting for a generation, it doesn't make any sense for them to suddenly stop fighting humanity when on the brink of their final victory. Unless they allied with a third party."

That was a novel idea, thought Wild, especially since there could be no third party. But he only said, "And who would that be?"

"Let me point out that the Machines at Sand Francisco seem mostly to concentrate on dismantling the usable factories and moving them offshore by ship."

This was news to Wild. "By ship?" he said. "To where?"

"The ships travel north. What does that suggest?"

"Palaska," said Wild. "But Palaska is destroyed."

"I think not," said The Bob. "We only know that we have no radio contact."

Wild was aware of the persistent rumors of life in Palaska but had dismissed them for lack of evidence. The UCC's lone submarine, the *Starfish Enterprise*, had visited the Palaskan coast and found the mountains melted into the ocean for hundreds of miles. "No one could have survived in Palaska," said Wild.

"Not along the coast, but further inland," said The

Bob. "I think the Machines are even now allied with another remnant of humanity in the Palaskan interior who will make war on us and find us perilously weak."

Survivors in the interior of Palaska seemed barely possible, but an alliance between Palaska and the Machines? The Machines didn't need anyone's help to destroy the UCC. And an impending attack? Crazy.

"What proof do you have of this alliance?" Wild asked.

"Sand Francisco itself. The ships, the hoppers, the roads, all pointing north. The Machines are sending thousands of SquareTons of war materials north, and for what purpose if not to attack us?

The Bob was losing it, thought Wild. You bring materials to the front, not the rear, blowing his whole theory out of the water.

"I see," Wild said mildly.

"Sand Francisco is a nest of vipers," said The Bob. "We must wipe it out before Palaska and the Machines attack.

The Bob sighed and put a hand on Wild's shoulder. "I know you are behind the opposition," The Bob continued. "But now you understand why Operation Save Our Bay is so important. I want your support."

Wild leaned against the railing and pretended to contemplate the street scene below. Lack of contact with Palaska and ships heading north didn't seem to be very good evidence of an impending attack, but at least it began to explain The Bob's headlong rush to arm the country.

"What makes you think an attack on Sand Francisco can succeed?" said Wild. "The Machines will annihilate our troops."

"I told you. The Machines have a weakness. The Creator code."

Creators were the long-dead scientists who, over a

hundred years earlier, had programmed the first war Machines, precipitating the Great Catastrophe and subsequent Flash War. Originally, they had created code keys which could turn the Machines on and off, allowing them to be controlled and reprogrammed by humans. But the intense fighting during the Great Catastrophe had leveled all known repositories of the Creator codes, and decades of subsequent searches had found nothing.

"You've recovered the Creator code? You actually have this code in your possession?"

"Yes," said The Bob. "And no. It's in a truck load of documents which was found underground at a research lab. Unfortunately, the enemy managed to destroy most of the documents before they were killed. Shredded, into millions of pieces of confetti."

"Then how do you expect…"

"I've had people working for the past ten years, reassembling the documents bit-by-bit. We are almost through. Soon, very soon, I will have that code."

For the first time, Wild understood the reach and strategy of The Bob's plans. With the code he could control the Machines, and with control of the Machines, the riches of the entire world would be his. Sand Francisco would just be an appetizer, and Palaska—if a threat at all—would be instantly neutralized.

Wild looked up at The Bob with new admiration. "This changes everything," said Wild.

The Bob's eyes glowed and he put a hand on Wild's shoulder. "Big changes are coming, Harold. I'm going to need a right-hand man."

But Wild was already thinking several steps ahead. Whoever possessed the Creator code would not only be the Chief Controller of the UCC, he would, in effect, become emperor of the entire world. And if all went well with Wild's plans, in a few days The Bob would be an incinerated pile of black ash.

Wild's heart once more began to beat out of his chest. *Patience*, he counseled himself.

He turned to The Bob and smiled. "What can I do to help?"

10.

JUST WAIT

Zook, anxious and frightened, sat alone in the Peace Center interrogation room, waiting to see if the plops were going to keep him or let him go.

He sat quietly, trying to project innocence, knowing that his interrogators—Investigator Green and another plop, a bald behemoth named Flowers—were watching through the one-way mirror. They had already stripped Zook of his possessions and garbed him in the lime green jumpsuit of a criminal Ingrate, which he most certainly was not.

So far, no reason had been given for his arrest, if arrest it was. He had been peacefully sleeping in his FreePad when suddenly his door was shouldered open and a half-dozen armed plops had burst into his room, pulled a sack over his head and dragged him away in an eMob.

That had been in the middle of the night. He was brought to this interrogation room, where the two plops had spent hours asking Zook endless questions about his activities of the last few days. Why had he approached Wild at the palace? What did he say to Jowry at the District Office? Why did he run from the peace investigator the previous afternoon? How did he know Sparklett?

Zook had told the truth as much as possible. He had gone to the palace to pursue the private slave position that Slavicen Bacon had told him about; he had never laid a finger on AssemblyPerson Wild; he had left the

101

palace soon afterwards and viewed some Gratitude activities in Sacagawea Square; it was his own idea to approach the District Office.

Only the questions about Sparklett scared him. He recalled all too well her admonition that if he failed her, they both could die. He had no idea why Sparklett had intervened in his beating, he told the plops; he had only dropped Sparklett's name in order to obtain the job interview; it was only coincidence that he had rescued her dog the previous morning; he couldn't make out any of the faces of the people in the photo of the AtomoLimo and had never ridden in one in his entire life.

That was his story and he stuck to it. Somewhere around dawn the questions let up and the two interrogating plops disappeared from the room. The longer they stayed away, the more Zook began to believe that they would let him go. He would be late for work, of course, but he would worry later about smoothing things out with Friendster Boraxo.

The door buzzed open and Green and Flowers reentered the room and sat down. Flowers was carrying a large cardboard tube.

Green pulled a written report from inside his tunic. "Your story appears consistent with the facts you have given us," he said. "Friendsters Boraxo and Jowry have each confirmed your story, and your FreeFone data, although corrupt, collaborates your movements."

"Then I can go?" Zook asked.

Green sat back and steepled his fingers. "Your statements about your relationship with Friendster Sparklett seem highly suspicious, but naturally, we don't like to disturb a High Friendster unless absolutely necessary. And I am happy to report that in your case, we have decided it won't be necessary."

Zook breathed a sigh of relief. "Thank you, Friendsters," he said, smiling at each in turn and rising.

"I guarantee that your faith in me will not prove misplaced."

"Not so fast," said Green, roughly. "Sit down."

Zook sat, and Green nodded to his companion at the other side of the table.

Flowers pulled the cap off the cardboard tube, spilling a piece of black cloth onto the tabletop.

"We found this on the wall of your room," he said, unfurling the cloth.

The Pedro.

It was a shock to see the clown painting under the bright lights of the peace office, and Zook watched with anger as the clumsy plop smoothed out the delicate velvet with his big meaty hands, brushing off bits of loose acrylic paint as if they were crumbs on a tablecloth.

Zook's first thought was, *they have no right to take my painting.* But of course possessing pre-Zero art was technically a crime, although Zook had never heard of anyone being prosecuted for it. Many slaves had unlicensed images tacked to their walls. If this was the most the plops had on him, he was home free.

"So?" he said, feeling defiant.

"Why do you have it?"

"It's a decoration," Zook said, stating the obvious.

"It's pretty ugly for a decoration, isn't it?" said Green.

"It's beautiful in its own way," said Zook. "I like it."

"Really?" said Green. He and Flowers exchanged a look and Flowers brought out a notepad. "Fill me in. What do you like about it?"

"The composition," said Zook. "The inventive media. The chiaroscuro."

Flowers pen stopped. "The what?"

"The chiaroscuro. The treatment of light and dark. The black velvet really makes the highlights pop. It's a masterpiece."

Green turned the painting, looked at it skeptically, then rotated it back to Zook. "And what about the subject matter? Do you like that, too?"

"I think it's brilliant," said Zook. "Look at the way the clown is slumped. His crushed hat. His sad expression. I've never seen anything like it. This is the work of a very talented artist."

"This man appears to be deeply intoxicated on illegal alcohol," said Investigator Green. "Is that an example of 'talent?"

"His world is sad and he's escaping. And here"–Zook touched the painting, the face of the stag–"There's a tear here. The stag is crying."

"Interesting," said Green, giving the Pedro a cursory glance.

Green had hardly looked at the painting. "Did you hear what I said?" Zook cried out. "*The stag is crying.*"

Green looked again. "Yeah? So?"

"Doesn't it touch anything in you? Make you *feel* something?"

"Not particularly," said Green. "Is it some kind of a joke?"

Zook was flabbergasted. Could a PeacePerson really be so aesthetically obtuse?

Investigator Flowers jumped in. "You are right," he said. "It's very unusual. How old is it?"

"A few decades," Zook said, sensing a trap.

"So it's not pre-Zero."

"Er, definitely not," said Zook. He doubted the plops could date the painting but had to watch his words.

"You're absolutely certain?"

"I'm a Colorist," said Zook. "I know these things."

"And, tell me again, how did you end up with it?"

"As I said, my boss, Friendster Boraxo, threw it away."

"So it's Friendster Boraxo's work?"

"No, he could never create anything like this. He can't even draw," said Zook.

"Where did he get it then?" said Investigator Green.

"Some workmen brought it," explained Zook. "They were demolishing a building on the edge of town and found a number of posters and other images hidden behind a wall. They brought them to the design circle to see whether they could be of any use."

"So it *does* come from a cache of pre-Zero images?" said Investigator Flowers.

"I only know that Friendster Boraxo reviewed the materials, saved one or two images for our reference library, and discarded the rest."

"When was this?"

"I don't remember exactly," said Zook. "A few years ago. In the summer."

"Did you steal any other paintings?"

"I didn't steal anything," said Zook. "I told you, Freindster Boraxo threw it in the dumpster. It would've been destroyed."

"Did it ever occur to you that destroying unauthorized images was exactly what your Friendster intended?"

Zook was beginning to sweat now. "I liked the clown painting and it seemed a shame to throw it away."

"So you took it without permission," said Flowers.

"I didn't need permission," said Zook. "It was just sitting there in the top of the dumpster."

"Did you show the stolen painting to anyone else?" asked Green.

They were taking turns now, trying to get him to admit guilt for something he didn't feel guilty about. He tugged on the collar of his criminal jumpsuit, which seemed to be shrinking. "No," Zook said.

"Not even to a woman named—" Flowers looked at

his notes—"Locally-Sourced Nukiforo?"

"No," said Zook. Why were they dragging in his FB?

"How long have you two been together?" Flowers asked.

"Almost a year," said Zook.

"A year? Not longer?" said Green.

"Look," said Zook. "I'm a Loyal Slavicen of the UCC. Am I being charged with something? What is the purpose of all these questions?"

"Do you have anything to hide?" asked Green.

"Of course not," said Zook.

"Then why do you object to answering a few questions?" he said.

"I should be getting ready for work. You're going to cause problems with my Friendster."

"Is that why you lied to us about the clown painting?" said Green. "You said you never showed it to anyone. But Nukiforo says you showed it to her, and she told you to get rid of it."

"That might have happened," admitted Zook. "I… can't remember."

"Omitting information when questioned by authority—you can be Shredded for that."

"Look, all these accusations and more accusations are ridiculous," said Zook. "I haven't done a damned thing wrong."

"But you have. You've assaulted an AssemblyPerson, obtained a false medical pass, lied about your whereabouts, and stolen a painting."

"You guys are crazy," Zook said. And to his surprise, he realized that he really meant it—they *were* crazy, persecuting a Loyal Slavicen for a series of infractions that, in a sane world, wouldn't add up to anything.

All Zook wanted was to move from being a state slave to being a private slave. His life felt static, an amorphous gray grind. He wanted some of the sparkle and excitement that he saw in the life of the High Friendsters—the color that rubbed off on their private slaves. Zook knew he could never become a High Friendster himself, but it didn't seem beyond him to live life in their afterglow.

Bacon did. Why not himself?

Zook believed in the UCC, had fought for it during the Flash War, and always did exactly what he was told. He dutifully separated compostables from recyclables, avoided gluten and dressed cruelty-free. He Saved the Earth by keeping his heat at 62, reduced his carbon footprint at work, and always Questioned Authority except when it was authority coming from the lawful State.

Every Gratitude Day he held his hand over his heart and happily recited the three freedoms ("Freedom from Want, Freedom from Fear, Freedom from Religion"). He didn't complain when the chipboard furnishings of his FreePad fell apart or his work hours were adjusted upward to Spread the Wealth. He supported Operation Save Our Bay and waited patiently to see what it was. He thought of cows fondly, and wouldn't have eaten an endangered beefsteak even if it were free-range. It wasn't his fault that Nukiforo wasn't pregnant and the only thing he had to himself was his clown painting.

He would be damned if he would let the plops or anyone take it from him. It was a flagrant violation of his rights as a slavicen.

He stood and began rolling up the painting.

"I'm going," said Zook. "And I'm taking my painting with me."

"Sit down," said Green.

"You can't question me like this," said Zook. "You have to bring charges." He quoted from the UCC constitution, which all school children were forced to memorize: "'Slavicens of the UCC are guaranteed inviolability of the person and may not be arrested except by warrant.'"

"I said, sit," Green repeated.

"If you have anything more to say to me, I will apply for a FreeLawyer.

"Good day, PeacePeople."

Zook turned his back to the plops and twisted the door knob. Swinging the door open, hee took a step into the hallway.

That was as far as he made it before he felt the prick of the needler in his left buttocks. Scorching pain shot through Zook's body and the world turned red as all the neurons in his body fired and every muscle in his body simultaneously went rigid.

He fell forward like a sack of laundry tossed from the back of a truck, and the painting flew from his hands and unscrolled before him on the ground. Before the needler convulsions ceased, the two plops were upon him, kicking him repeatedly with their heavy hemp boots until Zook let out a long, anguished cry—the cry of a wounded animal who realizes with certainty he is about to be killed.

Then, his body convulsing and his brain completely overwhelmed with pain, Zook passed dead out.

+ + +

FreeLawyer Civic Poundsand reluctantly entered the Mento Peoples Building, automatically throwing his briefcase on the X-ray belt and holding his hands over his head so that he could be patted down by the lobby plop. The pat-down revealed nothing, but Poundsand saw the x-ray tech and a second, inside, guard peering at the image of his bag on the screen in huddled confusion.

"You got pens in the bag," said the inside guard as Poundsand went to retrieve it. "No pens allowed."

Poundsand had forgotten that pens had been forbidden ever since a prisoner had used a pen to scrawl

Two Brother slogans on a wall. He watched helplessly as the plop expertly extracted all three of his pens from his briefcase and threw them in into a waste can already overflowing with contraband writing instruments.

"I'm an attorney," said Poundsand. "How am I supposed to take notes?"

"Above my PerkGrade, Slavicen," said the guard plop. "All I know is, pens are forbidden."

Poundsand picked up his briefcase, now three pens lighter, and headed down the corridor door to meet this Zook character.

Zook's file had landed on his desk the day before, but the long list of charges made no sense on the basis of what he read in the record. Only after a friendly call to Investigator Green did Poundsand come to understand that Zook had been harboring an unauthorized painting in his FreePad. That explained the presence in the file of a photo of a clown painting—an illustration of a drunken miscreant on a tar-black background. Poundsand knew nothing about art, but he knew that the State laid claim to all pre-Zero imagery and that state slaves had no need to own anything since everything they needed was provided by the State for free.

Including, Poundsand thought wearily, a FreeLawyer for just such cases as this.

It was a grave matter for an individual slave to be accused by the State of a crime, and it was Poundsand's job, as the prisoner's Apologist, to make sure his ward understood the stakes and made choices that would prove the least-painful for him while satisfying the needs of the authorities. Poundsand prided himself on being able to walk this narrow pathway well, and only three of his clients had ever ended up in the Shredder.

Poundsand met the prisoner in the small sparsely-furnished room reserved for such interviews. From the Investigator's notes, Poundsand was expecting a fierce, gruff-looking Don't addict, but Zook was unprepossessing: medium build, average height, with fine thin hair already receding from his forehead despite his relatively young age. Zook—unshaven, with bags under his eyes and dressed in crumpled prison fatigues— did, however, have the same guilty look as all of Poundsand's clients.

"Slavicen Zook? I'm your FreeLawyer, Civic Poundsand. I'm here to help process your case," he said.

"Thank be to The Bob," said Zook, rubbing his wrists where the cuffs had been removed. "You will not believe what's been going on here. They interrogated me, needled me, took my painting and kept me overnight, with only FreeGlutenFreeBread and water."

"Quite normal," said Poundsand.

"Normal?" said Zook. "I haven't even been charged."

"Oh, but you have. There's a whole menu of charges. The Demonizer will pick the ones he likes after your hearing is over."

"Huh?"

"It's all according to procedure," Poundsand reassured him. "Swift and certain justice and all that." He looked down at the plops' notes. "The main charge seems to be illegal conversion of State property." He saw the look on Zook's face. "The unauthorized clown painting," Poundsand explained.

"But that was *my* clown painting. The plops stole it."

"'Steal' is a strong word to use about duly authorized PolicePersons. I wouldn't advise you to repeat that in court."

"They stole it off my wall and they needled me besides. I demand to be released immediately. *And* I want my clown painting back."

Poundsand sighed and leaned back in his chair. This wasn't going to be as easy as he had hoped.

"That's not the way it works," said Poundsand.

"There's going to be a hearing first where the Demonizer will present evidence against you."

"But there isn't any evidence against me. I didn't do anything."

"That's up to the Administrator to say. I'm just here to assist with the procedures."

"Then what good are you?" Zook exclaimed. "I thought you were my lawyer."

"No, I'm your *Free*Lawyer," Poundsand said, setting him straight. "The State pays my Perks. And if you want any chance at all of getting out of here, I advise you to cooperate."

The prisoner looked as though Poundsand had thrown a bucket of water in his face. "All right," he said at last, looking up in resignation.

"Good," said Poundsand, feeling like he was making some progress. "Now here's what's going to happen: your hearing date is Augusta 13, which gives us four days to prepare our case..."

"Four days!"

"... which should, I believe, be ample for a case of this level of complexity."

"How will we even have time to choose a jury?" asked Zook.

"Jury?" said Poundsand. "This is not a formal civil trial," said Poundsand. "This is an administrative hearing. Everything will take place here in the People's Circle. The Administrator will preside. He'll rely extensively on the evidence in the interrogations the PeacePersons provided."

"What?" Zook exclaimed.

"Don't worry," said Poundsand. "The Administrator has a fine background. He's certified in critical race theory, postcolonial and decolonizing theories, intersectionality, queer studies, sexual microaggression nomenclature and rankism."

Zook didn't look impressed. "Can't I demand a jury?"

"Might I remind you," said Poundsand, leaning back and looking at the prisoner appraisingly, "that you're not in a position to demand anything. Frankly, the only chance you have at the hearing would be to prove your innocence, and, after reading the Investigator's notes, I don't see how that's possible."

"But I *am* innocent," said Zook. "If we can prove that, they'll have to let me go—right?"

"Hypothetically," said Poundsand. "But you've already incriminated yourself by possessing the illegal clown painting. That is clearly State property."

"I pulled it from a dumpster," said Zook. "How can it be State property if it was thrown away?"

"You don't understand the law. Everything you have is a gift from the State, to use only as long as you are productive slavicen and not an Agitator or Ingrate. Therefore it doesn't matter where you got the painting. It can't possibly belong to you."

Zook looked glum. "That's not much help," he said.

"I'm an Apologist, not a magician," Poundsand said. "Your case, I'm afraid, is open-and-shut."

The prisoner sat in sullen silence, but Poundsand suddenly had an inspired thought. "Unless, of course, you can prove that the painting was never in your possession?"

"How would I do that? I had it hanging on my wall."

"Well, perhaps you didn't put it there. Maybe a PadMate was trying to frame you? Or some enemy at work?"

"No, nothing like that," said Zook.

Poundsand frowned, his hope for an amusing Apology dashed. "Well then," he finally said, "Under the circumstances I suggest that you throw yourself on the mercy of the court. If you agree, I may be able to strike a deal with the Demonizer before your hearing date."

After a long moment, Zook said: "What kind of deal?"

"You plead guilty and agree to pay the costs of your Vilification. That might sound daunting, but I can get the court to accept garnishment of your food and housing Perks over the next seven years. Once out you would be on probation, subject to random brainial inspections, but if you keep your nose clean..."

"But what about my painting?"

"The stolen goods have already been recovered, so that's a moot point," said Poundsand. "But as you say, the painting was just a piece of rubbish anyway."

"But I *liked* it," whined Zook. "I want it back."

"You can forget that. Your personal preferences are not at issue here," said Poundsand.

Zook sat a moment, considering. "No, I guess not," he conceded.

Poundsand stood up and began gathering his papers. "Good," he said. "I'm glad I was able to clear up the situation. I'll talk to the Demonizer this afternoon and see what I can negotiate. Believe me, this is the best for all. I'll get back to you as soon as I have news."

He snapped the briefcase closed and headed for the door, but before he could press the buzzer to call for the guard, the prisoner spoke up behind him.

"No. I don't want a plea deal."

Poundsand turned. "It won't take long," he said. "I might even be able to get it recorded this week, in which case you can be back at your FreePad on Monday."

"I want a hearing," Zook said.

Poundsand felt himself getting irritated. What was this obstinacy?

"I've already explained to you that you don't have a case," he said. "In a hearing, the outcome could be much worse."

Not to mention, Poundsand thought to himself, the

amount of work and aggravation he would have to go through to prepare a formal case for such a hopeless cause.

"I'm innocent," said Zook. "They can't get away with this."

"*'They'* are *us*," said Poundsand. "It's '*The People* v. Zook.' What chance do you think you have against *The People*?"

"I don't care," said Zook. "I'm tired of being shoved around. I'm a slavecin and I have rights."

"Rights!" said Poundsand.

"Well, don't I?" said Zook. "Doesn't it say in the constitution that all slaves are entitled to due process?"

"You don't seem to understand your position. If you take that line at the hearing you'll be laughed out of the room. I'm telling you this plea bargain is the best you can do. If you insist on a hearing, *any*thing could happen—even the Shredder."

"I'm entitled to a hearing and I want it," said the prisoner, digging in his heels.

What a imbecile! thought Poundsand. He hated it when his clients failed to heed his good advice.

"Suit yourself," said Poundsand, shaking his head in disapproval. "I'll inform the Demonizer."

He turned back to the door and pushed the buzzer for the guard. It was his professional opinion that prisoners who demanded justice deserved what they got.

114

11.

LAWS ARE FOR THE LITTLE PEOPLE

The hearing (an "administrative matter" Zook had been warned, not a full-blown trial), was held in a courtroom at the Mento Peoples Center, a bland beige box with an elevated desk for the judge.

Zook sat anxiously at the table provided for the Accursed, waiting for his attorney. On the wall to his right hung a golden banner with the gifts of the UCC:

THE FOUR GIFTS
- FreeFood
- FreePad
- FreeMed
- FreeWork

On the left hung another banner with the complementary attitudes:

THE FOUR ATTITUDES
- Gratitude
- Respect
- Solidarity
- Selflessness

FreeLawyer Poundsand arrived, grunted a welcome to Zook, and sat beside him at the rickety folding table provided for the Accursed.

"Finally," said Zook. "A chance to defend myself."

Poundsand, who would be playing the role of Zook's Apologist, looked at him with a raised eyebrow. "We'll see."

"I don't see how we can lose," said Zook.

Poundsand shrugged.

Just then Investigator Enterprise Green entered from the rear of the courtroom, followed by a line of colorless state slaves carrying boxes of trial materials. He took a seat at the long, heavy State table, glanced at Zook, and donned an impressive tri-cornered hat.

"What's *he* doing here?" Zook asked.

"He's the Demonizer."

The Demonizer, Zook knew, was the person who prosecuted the case for the State. "The Demonizer? How can he be Demonizer if he was the plop gathering evidence."

"The Greens are born lucky," said Poundsand. "His family has lots of pull in FriendsterVille."

Zook watched with dismay as Green arranged the mountain of folders and paperwork his slaves had unpacked.

Poundsand saw the look on Zook's face. "It's not too late to enter a plea," Poundsand said. "I can talk to the Demonizer before we start."

Zook shook his head emphatically "no." He had come this far and now he would make his case.

A slave who had been standing to the right of the dias suddenly knocked his ceremonial lance against the floor three times. "All rise," he proclaimed.

The Hearing Administrator entered the courtroom through a curtain and took a seat at the huge desk front and center. He was a thick-set man dressed in robes of State purple, and his resemblance to the Demonizer was striking. Both had thick gray hair, unruly eyebrows and a growing heaviness around the waist. After briefly consulting some paperwork, the Administrator motioned to the Demonizer, who strode up to the dias. The two men traded greetings and smiles and immediately entered into whispered conversation.

Zook looked on suspiciously. "They seem awfully chummy," he said.

"They're brothers," said Poundsand.

"*Brothers!*" said Zook.

"I told you the Greens are lucky."

"How am I going to get a fair hearing if the Administrator and Demonizer are brothers?" Zook moaned.

"Careful!" Poundsand hissed. "Impugning the reputation of a court officer is an offense in itself."

Zook felt his heart sink. The brothers concluded their whispering and the one behind the desk pounded his gavel and signaled the slave with the lance.

"*'The People vs. Differently-Abled Zook,'* the slave intoned. "Administrator Non-GMO Green presiding."

"My time is extremely limited here today so let's get to it," said Administrator Green, pushing aside the case file. He looked directly at Zook. "The prisoner will stand. Charges to be determined. How do you plea?"

Zook stood, and Poundsand stood with him. "Last chance," Poundsand whispered. "Plea 'guilty,' damn it. You're a fool if you don't."

Zook took a half-step away from Poundsand, stood tall, looked at Administrator Green directly and announced, "Not guilty, your Honor."

Out of the corner of his eye, he saw Poundsand frown, but it was Demonizer Green who seemed the most surprised.

"Not guilty, Slavicen Zook?" Demonizer Green said, scratching his head under his tri-cornered hat. "The Administrator and I were led to believe that you would be entering a guilty plea."

"Not guilty," Zook said again, firmly.

"I have repeatedly advised the prisoner to enter a guilty plea," explained Poundsand, "But he has chosen to ignore my advice."

The Administrator looked displeased. "Regrettable," he said, "especially in view of my time constraints.

However, in accordance with UCC General Administrative Guidelines, I am entering a plea of 'not guilty.' You may be seated. First witness."

"You're making my job *very* difficult," Poundsand said to Zook once they were seated.

"Whose side are you on, anyway?" snapped Zook. "You're here to defend me."

"Not exactly."

"What?"

"I'm here to make sure you follow the proper State procedure. Your defense is just incidental."

"But…"

Just then the door in the back of the courtroom opened and a court slave led Not-for-Profit Boraxo to the witness stand. Zook, who knew his Friendster's moods intimately, could tell that Boraxo was very angry and when he looked at Zook, it was with a glare.

The court slave swore him in: "By the power invested in me by the United Care Communities and through its chosen instrument, the Awesome Peoples Party, I order you to tell the story, the whole story, and nothing but the story, as previously arranged. Do you so agree?"

"I do," said Boraxo.

At a signal from the Demonizer, a photograph of Zook's clown painting was projected on a screen.

"Do you recognize this painting?" said Demonizer Green.

"Yes," said Boraxo. "Some workmen found a batch of pre-Zero images when they were renovating an old building. They brought the batch to the MDC. That's one of them."

"The MDC, that's Mento Design Circle, right? And you are its head?"

"Yes, for the past six years," said Boraxo.

"And as head of the MDC what, in your opinion, is the artistic merit of this painting?"

"Zero," said Boraxo. "No artistic merit whatsoever."

Boraxo was an artistic illiterate, in Zook's opinion. The Pedro composition was a classic triangle, perfectly proportioned, with exemplary brushwork—far more interesting that the State motivational posters the MDC churned out.

"'No artistic merit,'" repeated Demonizer Green. "Is that why you decided not to acquire the image for the design circle library?"

"The subject is grotesque," said Boraxo. "I deemed it a moral hazard and ordered it destroyed."

Demonizer Green continued: "And the prisoner there, Differently-Abled Zook—he is one of your slaves is he not?"

"For now," said Boraxo. "Although I'm in the process of trying to sell him to Salt Point."

"Really?" asked Demonizer Green with a look of interest. "Why is that?"

"Thievery," said Boraxo. "It has come to my attention that Zook has been stealing State property."

"That's a lie," Zook blurted to Poundsand, loud enough to be heard by the bench.

Administrator Green leaned forward and pointed at Poundsand. "The Apologist will keep control of his client," he said.

"Quiet," said Poundsand to Zook. "You'll have a chance to speak later."

Zook, somewhat mollified, shifted his weight and crossed his arms.

The Demonizer continued: "Friendster Boraxo, did you ever give this painting to the Accursed, either as a gift or for a legitimate research purpose?"

"I most certainly did not," said Boraxo. "It was clearly a dangerous image."

"And that is why you threw it in a dumpster for destruction?"

"Yes."

"This is getting tedious," said the Administrator from the bench. "Wrap it up."

"One last question," said Demonizer Green. "How would you describe the prisoner's performance at work?"

"Indifferent," said Boraxo. "His mind always seemed to be wandering. Needs constant supervision."

"Thank you, Friendster Boraxo, you may step down."

As Boraxo exited the witness stand, Zook turned to his FreeLawyer in dismay.

"Step down? When do we cross-examine him?"

"You don't cross-examine at an administrative hearing," Poundsand said. "I told you, you'll have a chance to present later," said Poundsand.

It was Zook's turn to glare at Boraxo as the Friendster walked down the aisle. Zook made a note to remind the Administrator that Boraxo had entered many glowing recommendations into Zook's personnel file.

"Move it along, people," said the Administrator. "Let's get this over with."

Demonizer Green waved his tri-cornered hat at a slave in the back of the courtroom. The slave exited and returned a minute later from the witness room, leading in Sustainable Bacon.

Zook sat up, happy to see a friendly face. But Bacon looked nervous and uncomfortable as he was sworn in, and when Zook caught his eye, Bacon looked away.

Demonizer Green approached Bacon on the witness stand and pointed to the projected photo.

"Have you ever seen this clown painting before?"

Bacon glanced at the painting, then back at the Demonizer, avoiding Zook's gaze. "Yes."

"And *where* did you see this painting."

"At Zook's FreePad. It was hanging on the back of his door."

"And did the Accursed tell you how he had acquired

the painting?"

"Yes. 'Rescued from work,' I believe he said."

"And did he ever express knowledge that the painting was not a legal image?"

"Yes."

"What did he say?"

Bacon looked down at an index card he was holding in his hand and read. "He said, 'The painting is pre-Zero and therefore illegal.'"

Until this point, Zook had forgiven his friend for his canned testimony, but this last statement was an outright lie. "I said no such thing!" he blurted.

The Administrator crashed down his gavel. "Silence!

"You heard the judge," Poundsand said to Zook. "Keep your mouth shut."

Zook sat back, seething.

"If I may continue," the Demonizer said mildly.

"Go on," said Administrator Green.

"Slavicen Bacon, when was the last time you saw the Accursed?"

"On Gratitude Day, at the People's Palace."

"And what was this slave doing at the People's Palace?"

"Ah... visiting me."

"On your invitation?"

Bacon fidgeted. "Yes, but it was his idea. I had mentioned an opening on AssemblyPerson Wild's private slave staff and he wanted my help in approaching the AssemblyPerson."

"And did you give him that help?"

"I didn't get a chance."

"Why not?"

"He attempted to approach the AssemblyPerson on his own, without my assistance or knowledge."

"And what happened?"

"I don't know exactly but the guards restrained him.

When I came in Zook was being needled on the floor."

"Needled on the floor for assaulting the AssemblyPerson," Demonizer Green repeated for emphasis.

"Yes," said Bacon.

Zook sat in frustration. He did *not* assault the AssemblyPerson—but his FreeLawyer gave him a warning glance and Zook bit his tongue.

The Demonizer was checking his notes, then took the questioning in an entirely different direction. "You're familiar with the Four Gifts?" he asked Bacon.

"Of course," said Bacon. He nodded toward the golden banner to his side. "They're right there on the wall."

"Can you read them please?"

"FreeFood, FreePad, FreeMed, FreeWork," said Bacon.

"And how long have you known the prisoner?"

"All my life," Bacon said. "Almost thirty years."

"Now," the Demonizer said, "In the entire thirty years you've known the Accursed, do you ever recall any spontaneous expression of gratitude for any of the benefits bestowed upon him by the State?"

"No," said Bacon. "He never wanted to talk about such things."

"So in all the years you've known him, the Accursed never expressed gratitude for the gifts of the State?"

"No, never," said Bacon.

"Did the prisoner ever express admiration for The Bob?"

"No."

"Or for the United Care Communities as a whole?"

"No."

"And was he satisfied with his FreeWork?"

"No. He wanted to work at the palace."

"So you would say the Accursed is someone who

doesn't really appreciate the gifts of the State—correct?"

"Yes," said Bacon.

"In other words, he's an Ingrate, correct?"

"Yes," said Bacon. "I mean, that's what an Ingrate is."

"Point taken," said the Administrator. "Let's move to the next witness."

"As you wish," the Demonizer said. Bacon was excused, and Demonizer Green snapped a finger at a slave who scurried out to the witness room. He returned a minute later leading Nukiforo to the stand.

"What's she doing here?" Zook asked Poundsand.

"We'll soon find out," said the FreeLawyer.

Nukiforo was sworn in. Under the harsh fluorescent light, she looked older than Zook remembered, and he noticed for the first time a wisp of gray hair at her temple. Her FreeMakeup was smudged and Zook realized she had been crying.

Demonizer Green, carefully balancing his tri-cornered hat, rose and approached Nukiforo.

"State your name," he said.

"Locally-Sourced Nukiforo."

"Do you recognize the prisoner sitting at the Apologist table?" he asked.

Nukiforo glanced at Zook as if he were an insect, then turned back to the Demonizer.

"Yes," she said. "That's Differently-Abled Zook."

"He's your FreeBuddy?, is that correct?"

"Unfortunately," she said.

"Is that a 'yes' or a 'no'?" interjected Administrator Green.

"A 'yes,' your Honor," said Nukiforo.

The Demonizer gestured at the clown painting projected on the wall. "Do you recognize this image?"

Nukiforo looked at the photograph with disgust. "It's that horrible thing he brought over to show me one

FreeTime."

"And this 'horrible thing'—did he say where he got it?"

"Yes," she said. "He said that he had stolen it from work."

"I never said that," Zook whispered to Poundsand.

"Were those the words he used? That he had 'stolen' it'?" asked the Demonizer.

Nukiforo looked at Zook with darts in her eyes.

"Yes," said Nukiforo.

"Can't you make an objection or something?" Zook whispered to his FreeLawyer.

"Not in an administrative hearing," said Poundsand.

Zook jumped up from his seat. "That's not true," said Zook. "I never said that!"

The Administrator pointed at Poundsand. "One more remark from your client and I will order sanctions. Do you understand?"

"Yes, Administrator," said Poundsand.

He pulled Zook back in his seat. "Are you *trying* to lose this case?"

Zook sat, sullenly.

"Demonizer Green, please proceed."

"Slavicen Nukiforo, you've known the defendant for 18 months now, is that correct?"

"Just about," Nukiforo replied.

"And are you pregnant?"

Nukiforo hesitated and looked like she was about to burst into tears.

"No," she said, her voice heavy with shame.

"Weren't you each tested?"

"Yes."

"And you are both certified to be physically capable of conceiving?"

"Yes."

"Then why aren't you pregnant?"

Now she actually did burst into tears. "I'm not the problem. *He* is. He doesn't know how to make love to a woman. He misses appointments, doesn't call or text, forgets the paperwork..."

"Did you ever express concern to the prisoner about his behavior?"

"I tried to show him the State Parenting Manual but he just laughed," she said, blubbering.

Zook remembered the evening when she had brought out the FreeSex manual, *The Duty of Sex.* The illustrations were instructive, but each page was accompanied by a second page of mood-killing GovMintal cautions, ranging from warnings about lower back pain to required disclosures about known-carcinogens in sexual lubricants.

"Not only that," Nukiforo continued, "Half the time he didn't even finish."

"What do you mean?" the Prosecutor pressed.

"He would release himself manually," Nukiforo said. "Without my help. Wasting my chance to get my MomPerks."

"And did you encourage this behavior?"

"No. Why would I?"

"So the prisoner here failed to get you pregnant by illegally engaging in *coitus interruptus?*

"What?"

"He purposely failed to produce a state slave?"

The sobs were coming again. "Yes," she choked out.

Zook sprang to his feet. "Check the records," he demanded. "I've already sired three state slaves."

The Administrator smacked down his gavel again. "100 DePerks sanction," he said to Poundsand. "And *you*," he said, pointing his gavel at Zook. "You are not helping your case."

Poundsand pushed his face into Zook's and whispered furiously, "One more eruption from you and I will concede the case to the Demonizer."

"You can't do that," said Zook.

"The hell I can't," warmed Poundsand. "It's in the constitution."

Zook squirmed. He had been expecting a far more vigorous defense from his FreeLawyer, but maybe the best was yet to come. After all, none of their own witnesses had been called, and Poundsand said they would have a chance to rebut the Demonizer's specious lies. Maybe he *was* out of line.

"Sorry," said Zook. "I guess I don't understand the legal system quite as well as I thought."

"Can't you be like everyone else?" Poundsand said, exasperated. "Trust me."

12.

JUSTICE, SOCIAL JUSTICE, SUPER SOCIAL JUSTICE

Nukiforo, racked with sobs, was led away from the witness stand.

Administrator Green waited until she was out of the courtroom and then turned to Poundsand. "Does the Accursed have any witnesses?" the Administrator asked.

Relief flooded Zook as he realized he was finally going to get his day in court.

Poundsand looked up. "No, your Honor."

"What do you mean, no witnesses?" said Zook. "I gave you a list."

"They declined to testify for you."

"All of them?"

Poundsand shrugged. "It's a FreeCountry.

"What about Sparklett? She'd testify in my behalf."

"Out of the question," said Poundsand. "You don't subpoena witnesses like that."

"Why not?"

"There are worst things to be charged with than possessing an illegal image," said Poundsand. "'Sparklett' is a name you best not mention."

Zook felt smothered, as if the oxygen were gradually being withdrawn from the room. They had to do *some*thing.

"Well, what about cross-examining the Demonizer's witnesses?"

"You've been watching too many FreeVids. I've already told you there is no right to cross examine in an administrative hearing."

"But you said we could rebut," Zook exclaimed.

"You misunderstood. I said you could present, not rebut."

"And when is that going to occur?"

"Now," said Poundsand. "If you would just let me do my job..."

The Administrator looked irritated at Zook and Poundsand's lengthy process. "Time is wasting," he said. "If the Accursed has something to say, get on with it."

Poundsand stepped out from behind the table and took a step towards the dias. "Thank you, your Honor. This has been a trying case and I'm sure we can wrap it up quickly.

Zook watched him narrowly, anxious to hear the defense his FreeLawyer had crafted for him.

"The Apologist finds himself in the unusual position of defending an Accursed who has repeatedly ignored best advice of counsel.

"There is little doubt that the Accursed did, in fact, surreptitiously obtain the painting in question. Testimony of Friendster Not-for-Profit Boraxo shows that the property was indeed pre-Zero and was obtained without proper permission or authority. Testimony of state slave Sustainable Bacon proved that the Accursed was aware of the illegality of the image. Testimony of state slave Locally-Sourced Nukiforo establishes direct admission of the Accursed's guilt.

"Furthermore, the painting in question was aesthetically displeasing and therefore a purposeful affront to community norms. Slavicen Zook was a slovenly worker, a danger to our elected AssemblyPerson and an inadequate reproducer. Taken as a whole, the Accursed's actions show a recalcitrant attitude and insufficient gratitude for State-conferred benefits.

"The Apologist therefore finds himself in a quandary,

and it is hoped that the Honorable Administrator realizes the difficult and delicate position of this counselor."

"I understand," said the Administrator.

Zook frowned. Poundsand's preliminary remarks seemed unnecessarily accommodating but perhaps it was the custom to begin a defense by smoothing the way with deference.

The Administrator checked some papers and glanced at the courtroom clock. "It is nearing noon and I have an extremely urgent appointment. Does the Apologist have anything more to add?"

"Nothing, your Honor, except that Accursed throws himself upon the mercy of this court."

Zook looked up sharply at his FreeLawyer. Did he just hear what he thought he heard?

"Whoa, whoa, whoa!" Zook said, jumping up from his seat. "That's not a defense!"

"You see what I'm dealing with here, your Honor," said Poundsand.

The Administrator banged his gavel. "Another 100 DePerks sanction and the Accursed will be seated," he said.

"I want to speak in my own defense," said Zook.

"You have a FreeLawyer to speak for you," said Administrator Green.

"'Every slavicin shall have the right to confront his accuser,'" said Zook. "It's right there in the Bill of Gifts."

Demonizer Green was on his feet. "Except when the accuser is the State, as in the present instance," he said. "*The People v. Global Warming Glenwop.*"

Administrator Green frowned and turned to Zook. "Are you contending that FreeLawyer Poundsand has failed to mount a proper Apology?"

"That's exactly what I'm contending," said Zook.

"But your Honor!" said Poundsand. "I have been on

this case since the beginning. I have spent countless hours representing this man and given him a most vigorous Apology, if I do say so myself."

"You've given me nothing at all," said Zook. "I dismiss you."

"You can't dismiss me," said Poundsand. "I'm a FreeLawyer."

"That's not true!" said Zook.

"He's correct," said the Administrator, rubbing his temple as if Zook were giving him a headache. "An Accursed may, with permission, dismiss State appointed counsel and appear *nudus ante iudicium*, 'naked before the court.'"

He turned to Zook. "May I take it you wish to appear *nudus ante iudicium*?"

"Absolutely I do," said Zook.

"It's a serious step that displeases the State. I advise against it," said the Administrator. "However, if that is what you wish..."

"Will I get to speak freely?"

"As freely as the law permits."

"Then that's what I wish."

Administrator Green sighed and made a decision. "FreeLawyer Poundsand, you are released from the case. The Accursed may make his own Apology."

Poundsand returned to the Apologist table and gathered up his papers in a huff. He seemed to take the ruling as a personal affront. "I hope you get the Shredder," he hissed at Zook before marching out of the courtroom, letting the door slam with a bang.

"All right," Administrator Green said. "What have you got to say for yourself?"

The minute the Administrator addressed him, Zook swallowed hard. He had no legal training and had barely even understood the proceedings. On the other hand, he could hardly do a worse job of defending himself than

Poundsand had done. He gathered up his courage and stepped out from behind the desk.

"Administrator, I am but a state slave and not a skilled FreeLawyer, so please forgive me if I prove unfamiliar with court etiquette.

"All of my life I have been an exemplary slavicen. I was President of the Cruelty-Free Club in upper school and took advanced studies in Mental Decolonization, Organic Dissent Methodologies and Queer Drumming.

"During the Flash War, I served with the 19th Chemical Hazer Division in Sierra, where I was awarded the Medal of Obeisance for active reporting on fellow unit members' inaccurate political utterances. After the war I enjoyed teaching stained glass at the People's First fReeducation Retreat, and also working with-slash-playing Pickleball.

"Despite the impression you may have had from things said today, I was thrice awarded Slavicen of the Month in my job as a Colorist for the Mento Design Circle. In my department, I reduced carbon emissions from all types of dyes and paints by ten one-billionth of one percent, a substantial contribution to Saving the Earth from ecological meltdown.

"It is true that I have sought to be purchased by AssemblyPerson Wild so I could become a private slave to his eState. This should not be taken as a mark of ingratitude for all the benefits the State has provided me, but rather arises out of my great regard for all that AssemblyPerson Wild has been able to accomplish, both in FriendsterVille and here in…"

"Yes, yes, all very meritorious," said the Administrator, interrupting. "But all irrelevant to the issue at hand, which is illegal possession of State property, *viz.* the clown painting. May I remind you that our time is limited?"

Zook paced a moment and thought. Then he began:

"Surely you have observed, as I have, the numerous slavicens—mostly elderly, I admit—who rise at the break of curfew to pick through the cans and dumpsters looking for any little item, a cracked FreeBowl, let us say, or a pair of FreeShoes that still has some mileage left on them? These slavicens are allowed, even encouraged, to recycle such items for personal use. Are these elderly and disabled slavicens illegal possessors of State property? I think not. In fact, Mento Commune recently honored one of its most elderly trash-pickers for reducing the stream of perishable waste.

"How is this any different than my recycling of the clown painting? Friendster Boraxo himself testified that the painting was placed in the dumpster, clearly signaling that it was being discarded."

Demonizer Green stood up. "This is outrageous your Honor, and I object," he said. "Clearly, any such trash-pickings remain the property of the State, subject to a proper letter of authorization. I cite *The People v. Mercury-Free Wilbert*. Everything that the State gives the State can take away. State slaves own nothing."

"But that's not true," said Zook. "I own my FreeClothes, I own my FreeFone, I own my FreePad..."

"I can see," said the Demonizer, "that you never studied Elysium Economics.

"Do you own the FreeParks? What about the FreeBikes? When you eat at a FreeAteria, whose food are you eating? Everything any slave 'owns' has been produced by someone else and is given to them by the State. So everything anybody 'owns' is State property, whether a worn-out pair of FreeShoes or a discarded clown painting in a dumpster. Slaves can't 'own' their FreeClothes or FreePads because they didn't make them."

"Objection sustained, Friendster Demonizer," said the Administrator. He turned to Zook. "The accursed will refrain from implying that State property can be owned by state slaves.

"And please—get on with it."

"All right," said Zook. "But doesn't the fact that the painting was discarded prove that it was valueless in the eyes of the State? As you know, our economy is based upon extensive repurposing of the wasteful creations of the pre-Zero EvilBizMen. When a slave recently discovered how to convert certain discarded petroplastics into nitrogen fertilizer for the FreeGardens, wasn't he awarded The Bob's SuperFreeService Prize?"

"What's that have to do with the stolen painting?" the Administrator interjected. "Get to the point."

"It's simple," said Zook. "Do not our laws provide 'to each according to his needs'?

"Admittedly, no one *needs* a clown painting the way they need food or shelter," Zook continued, "but it must be admitted that I like this otherwise discarded, valueless painting more than anyone else. As a Colorist and a student of art history, this piece of art serves as a valuable reference.

"The proportions, the composition, the masterful highlights against the clever tonality of the velvet are prime examples of artistic craftsmanship and can help me in my work."

The Administrator and the Demonizer looked at each other with raised eyebrows.

Zook continued. "The very fact that I rescued the painting from the dumpster, took care to store it for over a year, and hung it in a prominent place in my FreePad to look at every day, proves my individual respect for such beauty. If hanging this piece of valueless rubbish on the wall makes me happy, doesn't that produce a more-contented and thus more-valuable state slave in the long run?"

Demonizer Green was on his feet again. "That is a

very specious argument, Your Honor," he said. "The State has a wide selection of wall hangings suitable for state slaves. If the accursed wanted a decoration, he could have chosen from dozens of authorized illustrations."

"Like what?" Zook said, unable to restrain himself. "The 'hang-in-there-slavicens' kitten poster?"

"That kitten poster is cute," the Administrator said. "It's an ageless icon of the UCC. What's wrong with it?"

"What's wrong with it is that it was chosen by somebody else, *for* me. Doesn't our constitution guarantee slavicens freedom of scientific, technical, and artistic expression? How can the State or anyone tell me that I can't like what I *do* like, that is, a beautiful clown painting?"

"What amazing sophistry!" said Demonizer Green, once again on his feet. "The constitution also says—and I'm quoting—'A citizen of the UCC is obliged to respect the rights and lawful interests of the State and to be uncompromising toward anti-social behavior.'

"But the accursed not only disregards the State's right to control unlawful images, he disdains approved alternatives, exhibiting exactly the kind of anti-social behavior that the constitution he relies on expressly prohibits."

"I know what I like," Zook persisted. "And *only* I know what I like."

"It's the State's job to guide the taste of its slavicens," said the Demonizer. "The fact remains that no one is permitted to display pre-Zero art not previously licensed by the State."

"Not true," said Zook. "I know of at least one person who has amassed an entire collection of pre-Zero paintings."

Demonizer Green laughed sarcastically. "In that case, you must let me have a name," he said, "so that I may immediately have him arrested."

"Yes," said Administrator Green. "Pray tell, who is this errant individual?"

"AssemblyPerson Harold Wild," said Zook. "He has a whole collection of paintings, including a clown painting very similar to the one I pulled from the trash."

Demonizer Green and Administrator Green exchanged a startled, then questioning look. In the end, Administrator Green turned and gave a slight shrug, which seemed to galvanize his brother into action.

"That can not be true," the Demonizer said sharply.

"It *is* true," insisted Zook. "AssemblyPerson Wild has a clown painting just like the one in the photograph."

"Be careful what you say," warned the Administrator. "I have been at the People's Palace many times myself and I've seen no such painting."

"Then you didn't look in the right place," Zook said. "If you want, I can take you right to the wall where it is hanging. If I'm guilty, then AssemblyPerson Wild is also guilty."

Again the look passed between the brothers. Then the Administrator brought down his gavel sharply. "Accursed' time is up," he said sharply.

"But I haven't finished my defense," Zook said. "If AssemblyPerson Wild were here, he'd verify that I'm telling the truth."

The Administrator struck his gavel again and pointed it directly at Zook. "I have indulged you long enough," he said angrily. "Your Apology is over. Sit down before I have you Shredded."

Zook had more to say but he sat. He thought he had made a good defense. The UCC system had its flaws, to be certain, but surely social justice would prevail.

"The People will now deliberate," said the Administrator.

He reviewed some papers on his desk, consulted a

FriendsterScreen on his right, scratched some notes on his FreeFone with a stylus, and, after what seemed like an eternity, looked up.

"The People find the Accursed charged with illegal conversion of State property. The Accursed is guilty as charged. Rehabilitation shall consist of three years FreeLabor at a fReeducation FunZone, location to be determined." He banged his gavel a final time and stood up. "That will be all."

The same burly plops who had brought Zook to the hearing room suddenly reappeared from the wings, and almost before he realized the hearing was over, Zook found himself dragged from his seat and manhandled down the aisle.

"This isn't fair!" Zook exclaimed. "Talk to AssemblyPerson Wild! He'll confirm I'm telling the truth!"

"Silence!" said the plop on his right, jabbing his nightstick into Zook's stomach.

Administrator Green turned his attention from Zook to his brother, Demonizer Green.

"Finally," said the Administrator as Zook was prodded down the aisle. "We can still make our tee time if we hurry."

13.

EVERYTHING WANTS TO BE FREE

Heat Station Antelope lay at the extreme northern limits of the UCC, on the vast ice fields which now stretched south over the former CanAm border into GoneTana. The station had originally been established before the Great Cataclysm to monitor the expected retreat of the polar icecap, but during the extended Global Warming Pause, the original station had been crushed by glaciers, finally convincing Deniers that global warming was real. After the Flash War, a new Heat Station Antelope was built atop the expanding snowpack at the same location as the old. But since climate conversations were now forbidden, it conveniently was re-purposed as the People's 66th fReeducation FunZone, where Zook had been sent to serve his sentence.

For the ninth consecutive night, Zook sat glumly in the dark freezing car of the snow train. The train consisted of a boxlike passenger cabin atop huge wheels, followed by four sledges with camp supplies pulled behind. Powered by an array of solar panels on its roof, the vehicle had barely enough power during daylight hours to crawl through the snow at two miles an hour, and it came to a complete stop at night. The three other criminals—a burglar, a serial murderer, and a baker who failed to write "gay" on a wedding cake—sat playing a noisy game of blackjack by the light of a foul-smelling, sputtering candle. Since there was only a single, sleeping guard, Zook and the other Ingrates could easily have escaped had there been any place to escape *to*, but there was nothing to be seen in any direction but a vast field of snow which had faded to a black void soon after sunset.

Zook shivered and tried to sleep, but his thoughts kept returning to the unfair turn that his life had taken. A month ago, he was living comfortably in his FreePad and was gainfully employed as a state slave, albeit in an unexciting-but-steady job. Looking back, he had to admit that the State had truly provided for him. His education, his sex life and his work had all been taken care of. The UCC was like an awesome shepherd to him, with he the sheep. He lacked nothing.

Now here he was, at the extreme limits of habitable territory, about to be incarcerated in a political correction center, and all because he had dared like a clown painting that no one seemed to appreciate.

It was outrageous.

Yet here he was.

And he wasn't even sure what had happened to him.

Clearly, something had gone wrong with the FreeJustice system. The plops and judges who were supposed to protect slavicens had somehow failed in their jobs. Zook was a Loyal Slavicen, not a TroubleMaker or an Ingrate. What difference did it make what sort of paintings he liked or didn't like? What possible harm could it do? How was it a crime or a threat to the State?

Zook swiped the condensation off the window with the sleeve of his jacket, making a small circular porthole in the frost. The blackness outside was impenetrable, but in the glass he saw his own image reflected faintly by the flickering light of the candle. Zook's face was white and his eyes shadowed holes, giving him the look of a man gradually fading, wraith-like, into the obscurity.

But Zook felt his anger rising. He didn't want to fade

and snuff-out simply because he liked a beautiful clown painting. The fact that he was being treated like a criminal didn't make any sense, and any legalistic explanation of his predicament had to be wrong.

The system had failed him. If he didn't want to spend the rest of his life as a disgraced Ingrate, he would have to take matters into his own hands. He would have to make the system right the wrong it had done him.

He found himself thinking about the clown painting he had glimpsed on the wall of the People's Palace, so similar to his. He would have loved to have shown his painting to the AssemblyPerson, so that the two of them could compare notes about the stunning mastery and consummate skill Pedro brought to the fine art of narrative painting.

If Wild ever became aware of the monstrous injustice being meted out to a fellow-clown-painting-admirer, he would be outraged. After all, one of his most prestigious titles was "Defender of Slaves." As a safeguard to prevent abuses of justice such as the one Zook was suffering, any AssemblyPerson could overturn any ruling of a lower court.

The more Zook thought about it, the more convinced he became that he that if he could only get a petition in front of Wild, the entire hearing decision would be overturned. How could possessing a Pedro be illegal when the AssemblyPerson held a near duplicate in his own collection? Friendsters were, after all, the absolute equal of slavicens within the standards of law. AssemblyPerson Wild would intuitively understand Zook's motives in rescuing the work of art from the dumpster. He would punish the two Green brothers for maliciously overstepping the bounds of their State-given authority, and might even take Zook on as a private slave to oversee his art collection.

That would be Super Social Justice, and suddenly

Zook knew exactly what he had to do: appeal his case to AssemblyPerson Wild, so that the Defender of Slaves could free Zook from his farcical ordeal.

Excited now, Zook gave up any pretense of sleep and sat up, wrapping his arms around his chest for warmth. The black sky to the east seemed slightly lighter than an hour before.

Dawn was coming.

He started to compose his petition in his mind.

+ + +

Eight hours later, the feeble snow train skirted a drift of snow and began lurching down a windswept slope toward Heat Station Antelope. The station consisted of a dozen prefab buildings of sagging corrugated metal, apparently dismantled from a pre-Zero farm, and a huge geodesic dome, several stories high, half-covered with snow but glowing from inside like a jewel. Near it, a wind- and solar-farm stretched off behind the buildings in a neat square field.

The entirety of the compound was encircled by a wall three times the height of a man. Zook at first took the wall to be concrete, but as the train pulled through the gate he realized it was made of huge blocks of ice. At hundred foot intervals along the walls rose guard houses on even higher towers of ice, giving the whole compound an oppressive, menacing feel.

The snow train pulled through the gate between the ice walls, followed an ice road behind the utility buildings and came to a stop on an ice plaza between the buildings and the geodesic dome. Zook's jaw dropped. Inside the dome, under the intense glare of a ring of heaters and overhead lights, was a delicate frame farm house, edged with shrubberies and flowers and seated on a lush green yard. Standing in the rose garden at the side of the house, a plump middle-aged woman dressed in a sunbonnet and sundress gathered roses, clipping them from the bushes and putting them in a wicker basket, while two rambunctious boys wrestled on the lawn nearby. On the sun porch, a corpulent man in a plaid shirt and suspenders sat idly smoking a pipe and watching through the dome as the snow train drew up. On the rocker beside him was draped a faux-fur-collared jacket of military issue.

Inside the train, the guard shoved open the ice-covered hatch and let down the steps. Freezing cold air swirled through the cabin.

"Everybody out," he shouted. "Line up with your hands behind your back along the side of the train."

Zook realized it might be a long while before he could begin composing his petition to Wild.

He and the internees formed a scraggly line which faced the strange house. The plops stood off at a little distance, hazers at the ready. Zook's breath clouded and hung in the air, and he raised his hands to button his collar.

"Hands behind back!" one of the plops reminded, raising the muzzle of the hazer ever so slightly in Zook's direction. Zook took the hint, put his hands behind his back, and shivered.

The man on the porch behind the dome slipped on his jacket, pulled the faux-fur hood up over his ears, and exited the dome through an airlock.

"*Namaste*, slavicens," said the man cheerily, using the pre-Zero greeting of welcome and respect. He was in his mid-50s, with wild eyebrows flecked with white. "I am Fair-Share Danton, and I will be your Host while you enjoy your stay at our fReeducation FunZone.

"I trust your journey wasn't too unpleasant. A brief orientation is in order."

Zook stomped his feet and shivered, wishing the brief orientation could be taking part in the dome's heated rose garden instead of on the freezing ice plaza.

Host Danton continued: "To begin, remember that whatever else you are, you are a state slave first. Obey the commands of the Political Correction Officers. They are your surrogate Friendsters, here to guide you through your fReeducation journey.

"The fReeducation process will begin immediately. You will be provided with fulfilling, appropriate labor, and have ample opportunity to develop the qualities most appropriate to a state slave—correct thinking, cheerful obedience, nimble adjustment to current policy initiatives, a willing suspension of disbelief, and real gratitude in the face of material difficulties.

"To that end there will be various FreeVids and FreeTalks with compulsory attendance. Pay attention as there will be tests.

"Although Heat Station Antelope is certainly not a prison, you may have the impression that you can walk away at any time. Please disabuse yourself of any such notions as I am responsible to make sure that your fReeducation is the best that it can be in both spirit and in law.

"To that end, you will note the comfort wall and comfort towers which surround this facility. They are staffed by Political Correction Officers equipped, for your safety, with hazers. It is considered a severe violation of Gratitude to attempt to wander beyond the walls. Since there is 300 miles of frozen ice between here and the nearest inhabited town, I urge you for your peace of mind to adjust yourself fully to our carefully designed programs and solutions. The UCC political system, under The Bob, is the finest ever developed— please avail yourself of the wisdom of your Betters.

"The BobHead in me salutes the BobHead in you. *Namaste*," he said, giving a half-hearted The Bob salute and hurrying back to the warmth of his dome.

Suddenly one of the plops jabbed Zook viciously in

the ribs with the butt of his hazer.

"Do that again and you'll lick it up," he warned.

Zook didn't even realize he had spat.

$$+ + +$$

For the next few hours, Zook and the other new FunZoners were kept busy in a series of hurry-up-and-wait proceedings that were part of the Heat Station Antelope induction process. The FreeJ-like prison uniforms they had been given at the start of their incarceration were recycled and they were herded into a concrete and corrugated metal bathroom, where they were subjected to a cold water shower and then sprayed with a de-lousing all-natural organic insecticide. On the other side of the shower, they were re-issued uniforms identical to the ones they had left behind, but starched and stiff. Next they were stripped of their new uniforms and given a medical examination by a state slave who, as a butcher in his previous life, had been convicted of selling grain-fed beef and demoted to doctor.

After dressing for a third time, the prisoners were taken to a freezing classroom where they were giving a series of written tests, which ran the gamut from word association to inkblots to mazes.

Zook found a blank page at the end of a nonsensical questionnaire, and he surreptitiously began drafting his petition to Wild, starting with a paragraph of flattering prose about the AssemblyPerson's fairness, outlining the facts of his case, and ending with a ringing appeal for justice by Wild in his role as Defender of Slaves. He finished just as the test was ending and managed to tear off and hide the page while the booklets were being collected.

When the tests were finally over, the prisoners sat for two hours doing nothing while a set of new plops— wearing the blue badge of the Political Correction Circle—guarded them so their colleagues could eat.

There was no food for the prisoners. Once an hour, a mechanical bell rang, and voices and bustle could be heard in the corridors outside.

Even with a wan sun streaming through the frosted window, the room was freezing and steam rose from the men like barnyard animals. To take his mind off the cold, Zook imagined himself presenting his petition to AssemblyPerson Wild, who listened with grave and sympathetic concern.

Sometime later the prisoners were roused and issued cold-weather gear—a jacket lined with recycled felt, a pair of thin wool gloves, and heavy re-melted boots cracked from previous use. The boots issued Zook were too small and his toes crammed against the tip. Finally, after another hour's waiting, the bell again rang and the plops led the new men out across a snowy field to a line of corrugated prefab buildings on the edge of the compound.

They were held briefly at the entry of one of the buildings while paperwork was exchanged, then shoved inside.

"You'll work here," one of the guards said, shoving him into the room.

Inside, overlooked by elevated walkways where plops stood armed with hazers, rows of prisoners sat at a long wooden tables. In the center of each table sat what appeared to be a large pile of confetti, around which the inmates worked in silence, their hands moving rapidly at a task which Zook could not make out.

The tables were segregated between men and women, with the women up front in the place of honor. Zook finally found a space midway down the length of the hall. Up close, Zook saw the men at the table were picking at the pile of confetti with tweezers.

"What are you doing?" Zook asked.

The prisoners looked up at him blankly, then returned

to their work.

"Shut up and sit down," said the man to his right, his breath frosty in the cold air. He was about 30 years of age, with dark brown eyes and a scraggly blondish beard. He smiled briefly at Zook to show that there were no hard feelings, all the while continuing to push little piles of paper around with his tweezers. "Talk out of the corner of your mouth like this so that the guards can't see. They have needlers and like to use them. I'm Shared-Burden Jarrow."

"Differently-Abled Zook," said Zook, out of the corner of his mouth.

"Look busy, Zook."

"Okay," he said. "But busy doing what?"

"Take one of the tweezers from the jar and spread out some confetti on the wax paper sheet in front of you," said Jarrow.

Zook did as he was told and found that the confetti clung by static to the surface of the wax.

"Good," said Jarrow. "Now start pushing the bits around and try to match them up. Were reassembling shredded documents here, you see? Like a giant puzzle."

Zook looked at the huge pile of confetti in the center of the table. There were at least twenty similar piles on other tables in the work house, with at least a hundred men picking at the confetti bits.

"That's insane," he said.

"Yes," said Jarrow. "But get started unless you want to find yourself chipping ice off solar cells."

Zook looked down at his pile of confetti and saw that some had bits of lettering on them and others bits of color. If only to keep his mind off the cold, he began sorting his confetti into separate little piles.

"That's it," said Jarrow. "Keep your hands moving and the plops will leave you alone. Push the bits that don't match to the man on your right. If you manage to get five full characters reassembled, raise your hand and the guards will take it."

"How long do we have to do this?"

"Who knows? We've been at it for eight years."

Eight *years*? Did he hear that correctly? Zook sighed and began pushing around the confetti from his little pile, looking for bits that matched. After ten minutes he had mastered flipping over the bits with the tweezers; after an hour, his eyes began to blur. When he thought about what they were doing, eight years seemed barely enough time to get started. He estimated at least 1000 bits of confetti on his wax paper sheet, a half-million bits in the big pile on the table, which meant at least ten million bits in this room alone. What could possibly be the point of this gigantic effort? Or was there a point? Maybe it was just a giant make-work project to keep the prisoners quiet and occupied?

One thing for certain: he couldn't possibly spend a year or even a month reassembling confetti. It would drive him crazy. "What is all this stuff? Where did it come from?" Zook asked.

"Some slaves unearthed it while digging around a smelted university in Pastdena," said a guy on Zook's left. He was a decade younger than Zook, but his face was worn and weather beaten. "I knew the guys that hauled it up. Eighty bags full. An underground cyber center, they said."

Zook had never been in Pastdena, but he knew from his military service that there was a Machine Development Center there. "So what is it? Military manuals?"

Jarrow shrugged. "It's nothing. Nonsense. We only see it a few characters at a time but it never makes any sense. I think they're trying to keep the truth from us."

Zook thought back to his conversation with Sparklett and felt the hair on the back of his head stand up.

"Code," he said.

"That's what I think, too," said the weather-worn man. "After it leaves here they've got a room full of private slaves under lock-and-key stringing our findings together. When they get a full page it goes under armed guard into a safe in the Host's office."

"They're looking for 1A5TJ," said Jarrow.

"What's that?" asked Zook.

"I don't know. But I heard Host Danton call it 'the key to Palaska.'"

There it was again—Palaska. For years Zook had heard that Palaska was nothing but radioactive slag. Now, in the space of a month, came the suggestion—first from Sparklett and now from his fellow prisoner—that Palaska itself might still exist, presumably as a spot on the planet that was viable to humanity but not part of the UCC. That gave Zook pause. What would a society be like that was not UCC? Was it warring disorganized tribes like cavemen of old, where men fought endless battles and lived nasty, brutish and short lives? Or perhaps it was a society dominated by EvilBizMen, an exploitive oligarchy where a few lived in luxury while the rest took orders from their corporate masters?

Or...?

What?

An old, suppressed memory of a Two Brothers slogan he had once seen painted on the side of a building came into his mind. "Down with Perks and Shredders," it had read. But, how could you run a society without Perks and Shredders? Zook wondered. Maybe (the rebellious thought alarmed him!) the Two Brothers were on to something. He regretted not questioning Sparklett more closely when he had seen her last.

A longing ache squeezed his heart as he thought of Sparklett. Where was she now? What was she doing? He had tried to send a message to her through Poundsand, but the FreeLawyer had informed him pre-Ingrates were not allowed contact with the outside world.

Zook *had* to see Sparklett again, which meant he *had* to get his petition to AssemblyPerson Wild. As Defender of Slaves, Wild was Zook's last and best hope of ever seeing justice.

14.

QUESTION WRONG AUTHORITY

In late afternoon, a bell rang and the workers were marched down a snowy alley to a dining hall. It was a single large room, rectangular in shape, spanned by horizontal roof trusses of interlocking metal triangles. Along the back wall was the kitchen, with a row of steam tables to serve the inmates. At the other end of the room stood a speaker's podium with a small metal microphone. A Political Correction Officer in formal uniform stood at the podium reading from a dry technical work which to Zook seemed to be on the dangers of second-hand tobacco smoke.

About 300 prisoners, mostly men but with a group of women up front, sat crammed together at long tables which filled the length of the room. They picked at food from their cafeteria trays but seemed much more intent on listening to the lecture, with some taking notes on scraps of paper while others had their eyes screwed shut as if in deep concentration. Zook listened for a moment but didn't understand what made the lecture so interesting; it was the usual litany of health hazards associated with exposure to tobacco smoke, the same stuff he had been hearing practically daily since Year Zero.

But even the kitchen help seemed more interesting interested in the lecture than in doing their jobs, and the server was annoyed when the plops led Zook and the other new Ingrates into his mess hall line. Zook took a

149

tray and watched as the worker slopped his plate high with lentil beans, carrots and cubes of texturized soy protein. The uniform, crinkle-cut shape of the carrots made it immediately apparent to Zook that the carrots were frozen, rather than fresh. He was shocked at this blatant violation of UCC policy, but supposed it was difficult to find locally-sourced carrots in the middle of an ice sheet.

Zook, who had become separated from Jarrow when marched into the hall, found a random seat and dug in to his meal with gusto, all the while trying to understand what it was about the speaker's topic which was so gripping to the men all around him.

"... secondhand smoke contains over 4,000 dangerous chemicals, with over 50 known to the UCC to cause cancer," the speaker read tonelessly from a small red book. "Every time a slavicen breathes second-hand smoke, these carcinogenic chemicals plant the seeds of stroke, asthma, respiratory infections, ear infections and coronary heart disease. There is no threshold of safety; even brief secondhand smoke exposure damages cells. Slavicen who are already ill are at especially high risk of suffering adverse effects..."

The speaker continued on in this manner for another several minutes until a buzzer sounded, at which point he slammed the book shut. The hall erupted into pandemonium, with some men stuffing their untouched meals into their mouth while others shouted questions to their compatriots: "What are the main carcinogens in a cigarette? Why is there no safe level of second hand smoke? How can pregnant women protect themselves?"

Zook saw his table-mate to the right rapidly reviewing his notes. He was a middle-aged man with a ragged white beard and deep furrows around his eyes.

"What's going on?" Zook asked.

"Didn't they tell you?"

"They didn't tell me anything."

"Correctness correction," he explained. "When they start asking questions keep your head down."

There was a sharp rap on the edge of the podium and then the plop spoke. "We will now have our review," he announced.

The Political Correction Officer looked down at his notes. "Number one," he said. "Tobacco smokers harm not just themselves but everyone around them. True or false?"

When the plop looked up, the prisoners looked away or tried to hide themselves behind a neighbor, but the plop's hand shot out and he pointed to a man two tables away from Zook's.

"You," he commanded.

The man, a stooped figure in his 50s with sunken, wind-burned cheeks, rose from his seat. The guards moved closer and hovered near him, needlers drawn.

"True," the man said.

"Correct," said the plop at the podium.

A cheer went up.

"Quiet!" said the plop, before plunging on to the next question. "Number two: nicotine is more addictive than heroin, true or false?"

This time the plop pointed to a younger man at Zook's table, who looked around uncertainly.

"Me?"

"Yes, you with the red cap," the plop said

"Ah, could you repeat the question?" said the man.

Zook noticed the guards with the needlers gathering near.

"'Number two," repeated the plop in an exasperated voice. "Nicotine is more addicting than heroin?'"

The baffled prisoner looked around the table imploringly, but all had their gaze averted elsewhere.

"False?" he said at last, a quaver in his voice.

151

A groan went up from the crowd. The plop with the red book shook his head ruefully and announced, "True."

In a flash, the guards descended on the table, grabbing the man and dragging him to the center aisle. Two guards held him while a third ripped open the man's shirt to expose bare skin, giving him a jolt of the needler. The man's body arched in agony and a stifled scream emerged from his contorted face. Then the needler was withdrawn and the man fell, limply, to the floor.

No one moved.

"Number three," said the plop at the podium, quite calmly. "Secondhand smoke is more deadly to inhale than cyanide, true or false?"

He looked toward the back of the room and was about to point to a prisoner there when a hand went up at the women's table.

"All right," the Political Correction Officer said, pointing to the short heavyset woman whose hand was raised. "What's your answer?"

She sat for a moment, and Zook noticed her shoot a glance at a slender, hooded woman across the table.

Then she rose and looked directly at the plop at the podium.

"Go screw yourself," the woman said.

"What?!" he said, turning red with fury.

The heavyset woman leaped on the table, even as the guards with the needlers made a bee-line for her. "Slavicens," she yelled. "Think! It's time to throw off shackles of the State! Don't let these plops…"

As the plops approached, several woman at the table jumped up to intercept, throwing dishes and even smashing at the guards with chairs. The woman on the table continued shouting, but it was impossible to hear what she was saying over the general noise of the melee and the shrieking whistles of the guards. Wielding needlers and batons, the guards cleared a path through the rioting prisoners and dragged the still-shouting woman off her perch to the floor. One knelt on her back, while another ripped open her clothing and shoved the needler against her bare skin. Her face contorted into a rictus of fear and pain, even as her table mates were bludgeoned to the floor and handcuffed.

"Lesson over," said the Political Correction Officer. He flipped shut his book. "Everyone back to their work station. For future reference, the correct answer is 'true.'"

The men around Zook murmured but obeyed, rising and moving toward the doors.

Hesitantly, trying to make sense of what had just happened, Zook, too, rose, and allowed himself to flow with the rest of the men toward the exit. The spontaneous riot, if that's what it was, seemed pointless, since the instigator was now lying unconscious on the floor and the other rioters were handcuffed and surrounded by guards. He assumed they would be rounded up and punished, making their protest useless. They wouldn't be throwing off the shackles of the State for a long time.

Zook did notice, however, one woman from the table quietly backing away from all of the commotion. Tall and slender, she wore the same drab gray overcoat as everyone else, but with the hood raised, obscuring her face. As Zook watched, she skirted through the crowd of milling prisoners and made a direct line for the kitchen door, pausing at the threshold and turning as if to make sure she was unobserved by the guards.

From his angle, Zook got his first clear glimpse of her face.

It was a face he would recognize anywhere.

Sparklett.

Before he could react, she slipped through the door

and was gone.

+ + +

As The Bob rolled the golf cart up to the ninth tee, Wild felt an almost uncontrollable surge of adrenaline course through his body. Before they finished the hole The Bob would be dead and Wild would take over his place as Chief Controller.

Stay calm, Wild reminded himself, trying to get his heart under control. Throughout the entire game his concentration had been shot, and he was sweating like a pig.

"Are you okay?" said The Bob as he chose a chose a driver from among the half-dozen presented to him by one of his private slaves.

"It's nothing," said Wild. "I'm just tired."

"Too much time in the FreeSexCoops?" joked The Bob, whose spies, of course, would have reported on all of Wild's movements.

"Too much expensive wine," said Wild.

The Bob chuckled and seemed to accept the explanation. He walked out to the tee, where two slaves in white curator gloves had lined up a number of plastic tees for his approval. Plastic tees, being derived from petroleum, were exceedingly rare and everyone but The Bob played on wooden replicas. The Bob chose a tee from among those presented and the private slaves carefully gathered the rest and retreated to a respectful distance.

They were playing on The Bob's private course in the heart of FriendsterVille. It started at the base of the Bob-O-Sphere and wended its way past ruined casinos and empty office buildings around old FriendsterVille. The Bob raised his club and gracefully drove the ball down the fairway to where the course took a sharp dogleg to the left. The ball bounced and came to a stop perfectly positioned for a next shot.

"Yeah!" said The Bob, punching his fist into the air. A notoriously bad golfer, The Bob could never resist rubbing his opponent's nose in any little victories.

"Nice one," said Wild. He had brought his own retinue of private slaves, thinking they might be useful in the aftermath of the chaos of the assassination, and he chose his favorite driver from among the two offered.

The hole was par three if you could place the ball at the jog in the dogleg as The Bob had done. It was growing late in the day—The Bob as usual didn't get to the course until his day's work was done—but the wind was still light. A buttery late-afternoon light bounced off the sides of the buildings on the left, casting an eerie glow onto the perfectly manicured course. Wild was anxious to put his ball close to The Bob's, for it was only after he reached the jog that he would be able to make sure that all of the pieces were in place for the assassination.

He raised his club and struck the ball solidly but a little off-center. It arced low and faded to the right, bouncing several times and almost rolling into the rough before reaching the near edge of the dogleg–15 yards from The Bob's better-placed ball but at least on the fairway.

"Not great but I'll take it," said Wild, a smile pasted to his face. He handed off his club to a slave and hopped into the cart with The Bob. The antique golf cart, one of three discovered by some state slaves while excavating in the rubble of Gone Springs, was one of The Bob's most-prized possessions. It had been elaborately restored to its pre-Zero grandeur, complete with a yellow overhead sunshade and handmade reproduction silk tassels. The Bob mashed the pedal and the cart accelerated down the fairway towards the dogleg, his retinue of slaves running behind attempting to keep place.

"I must say, Harold, that I am thoroughly pleased with your handling of the Assembly over the last Booty Call," said The Bob, using Wild's familiar name to indicate that they were once more discussing State business.

Wild held on as the cart jolted crazily down the fairway. "Robert, haven't you always said that dust must yield before the wind? You are the wind and we are the dust, and the wind is blowing toward war and conquest."

"Harold, I'm glad you've seen the light on Operation Save Our Bay, though Under-Controller Mutz warns me you are not to be trusted."

"When I next see the Under-Controller, I will remind her that I have been an ardent follower of yours since that day years ago when I first entered your camp."

After the murder of Wild's father, The Bob had taken the eleven-year-old Wild under his wing, first as water carrier, then as an armed follower, and later as a trusted lieutenant. It was many years before Wild discovered proof that it was The Bob who had ordered his father killed. That was the moment when Wild's admiration of The Bob had first turned to hatred and secret thoughts of revenge.

But The Bob sentimentally remembered those early days as the best time of his life.

"Those were the days," he said now, totally unaware of the knife he was twisting in Wild's heart. "What fun we had together!"

"You have truly been a second father to me, Robert. The Under-Controller could never understand that."

"And you guarantee you can deliver the remaining votes to bring the Peoples Assembly into line?"

"Robert," said Wild, "I promise you that after today you will have nothing to worry about."

"That's good to hear, Harold," said The Bob, bringing the cart to an abrupt halt in the middle of the dogleg.

He turned and looked at Wild. "Before we continue, is there anything else you would like to tell me?"

What was he talking about? Had the plot been betrayed?

"I'm not sure to what you refer, Robert," Wild said at last, keeping his poker face.

"I refer," said The Bob, "to the diamonds. Under-Controller Mutz tells me that your dear Sparklett has been buying up a large quantity of gemstones on the Friendster market, supposedly to craft jewelry for a special design shop."

Wild sweated. Sparklett had, on his directions, been secretly purchasing gemstones for use in bribing certain key officials whose support was needed for the approaching coup. Wild had felt certain that no word of it had gotten back to The Bob, but obviously he had been wrong.

But Wild knew just how to play it. He chuckled, feigning innocence. "The jewelry shop is, of course, a cover. I would have alerted you about the plan but I wanted to firm up certain arrangements before I bothered explaining to you its true purpose."

"And what is this true purpose, Harold?"

"It's a war chest, Robert. The votes you want in the Assembly aren't going to be cheap."

The Bob took this in and suddenly relaxed. "I should've known my boy could never do anything nefarious," he said, stepping out of the cart. "What you think? Two iron?"

It was a short city block to the flag on the ninth green, with a sand trap to the right and an artificial stream slashing across the course halfway down the fairway.

"Two iron should do it," Wild agreed. But his attention was on the three glass-walled buildings on the corner overlooking the green. Their entrances had long ago been sealed by The Bob's forces, but Wild knew the Two Brothers had circumvented the security and infiltrated a man to the upper floor of each building. The assassins had a direct line of fire to the green and were armed with rocket-propelled Dusters.

The Bob would not merely be killed, but evaporated from the face of the earth. For a signal, all Wild had to do was drop his hat.

15.

NO MORE *ME*

The wind was gusting erratically, and with the help of a fortuitous blast, The Bob placed his next shot directly onto the green.

A dozen yards before the green lay a boomerang-shaped sand trap, and Wild—realizing his chance to put an early end to the day's game—checked his swing, causing his ball to fall short and bounce directly into the trap.

The shot was ugly but the ball ended up exactly where Wild wanted it.

"A little short there," said The Bob, gloating.

"Ha ha," said Wild, meekly. He would get his revenge in a few minutes.

They climbed back into the cart and zoomed off toward the trap, Wild carefully holding on to his hat. His ball lay in a deep declivity, half-buried in the white sand. On the green a few yards away, the flag flapped.

Wild hopped out. "Drive on up to the green," he said. "I'll meet you there."

"I'll wait," said The Bob. "I want to see you hack your way out of this one."

Concealing his disappointment, Wild climbed down into the meticulously-raked sand trap and tried to line up his shot to the flag. The buildings presented only a blank face, with no sign of anything unusual. Were the assassins even in place? Maybe the plot had been discovered and the snipers arrested?

He would soon find out. Wild found himself perspiring profusely, with sweat dripping back down off his skull and under his collar. He would have liked nothing better than to remove the hat and wipe his face with a towel, but he was afraid that a fumble with the hat would set the plan in motion prematurely. He raised his arms and struck the ball with a loud *clock*, chipping it up out of the sand trap and over the edge of the green where it bounced twice.

Wild took his seat, and The Bob gunned the cart around the trap and up the slope to where the balls lay side-by-side. The blank mirrored façade of the tallest building reflected the sun's yellow light in uneven waves over the green. Wild, his face sweaty, studied the building façade but still saw no sign of any activity.

The Bob followed Wild's gaze. "Sun's getting low," he said. "Next week we'll start earlier."

Wild pulled his attention back to the game. "As you wish," he said, the sweat trickling down his neck maddeningly.

The Bob sat in the cart frowning at the balls on the green. "You're closer," he said at last. "You go first."

"All right," said Wild. He clambered out of the cart and accepted a putter from his slave. The lay of the balls suggested his final plan: he would play his ball through and casually walk off to the side. When The Bob stepped out of the cart, Wild would drop his hat, bringing the Chief Controller to instant annihilation.

Beads of sweat burnt his eyes as he lined up his putt. He drew his putter back and was just about to make his stroke when a royal purple eCar zoomed up from the access road and jerked to a halt at the edge of the course. A slave, dressed in the garb of The Bob's private livery, jumped out of the car and ran up toward the green holding an envelope in his hand.

This is it, thought Wild. *Somehow they've learned about the coup.* But he managed to stand casually as the slave hurried up to The Bob, still sitting in the golf cart, and handed him the envelope.

The Bob tore the letter open and read. Then he dismissed the slave and, smiling, waved Wild over to the cart.

It was not the look of someone who had discovered he was moments away from assassination. Wild, relieved, joined him.

"You remember our discussion at lunch last week?" The Bob said, handing Wild the paper.

It was a memo from Host Danton of the People's 66th fReeducation FunZone. He expected to have final recovery of the Creator code document within hours.

When Wild looked up, The Bob was glowing.

"You realize what this means?" he said. "Once we get this code to propagate, the riches of Sand Francisco will be ours to plunder and Palaska will be conquered within days. With the Machines in our control, we can remake the world for humanity the way it was meant to be—millions, perhaps billions, of state slaves, their lives carefully controlled and harmonized however we want."

"'We' meaning you and me?" asked Wild, surprised by The Bob's unusual magnanimity.

The Bob frowned. "'We' meaning 'me,'" he said. "Imperial 'we.' Though of course I'll need a successor, and you've been like a son to me."

But you killed my real father, thought Wild. Having come this far, there was no way Wild planned to be taking orders from The Bob for years or decades hence.

But he kept his expression neutral. "You are most gracious," Wild said, handing back the letter.

"Yes," said The Bob. "We'll discuss details later. But now I've got to get back to the war room to consult with General Lowe. Come on, get in."

Wild hesitated. He had to put enough distance between himself and The Bob to avoid becoming a collateral corpse. "Can the conquest of the world wait until we play out this hole?" he said.

The Bob chuckled. "You've already lost," he said. "I'm two strokes ahead."

"It's golf," said Wild. "Anything can happen."

"Go ahead, finish out," said The Bob magnanimously. Let's see how badly you do."

Wild felt a little surge of triumph. All he had to do was play out his ball and make a break for the edge of the green. When the hat hit the ground...

Calmly, with The Bob watching from the driver's seat of the cart, Wild picked up his putter, waited for the slave to pull the fluttering flag, and lined up his putt.

The ball rolled up to the lip of the cup but stopped before going in. Wild had to give it a second stroke to put the ball in the hole.

"Ha," said The Bob. "You should have quit when you were ahead."

Wild swept up his ball and handed his putter off to a slave. Somehow he was no longer sweating and instead felt icy cold.

As The Bob got out of the cart and squared himself for his putt, Wild turned and began to scurry for the far edge of the green.

The Bob looked up. "Where are you going?" he said.

Wild pretended not to hear him and kept going, picking up his pace to a jog, then a sprint, as he raced for the cover of the sand trap at the edge of the green.

Just then a whirling air current reached down and

snatched his hat off his head. Wild made a grab for it and watched in dismay as it lofted into the air just out of reach.

I'm close, he thought, too close.

The hat was already fluttering to the ground.

It was too late to sprint any further.

Wild dove to the ground and covered his head.

Three rocket-propelled Dusters converged on The Bob's position and suddenly Wild was in hell. The air around him flashed with pink explosions which set Wild's clothes aflame and somersaulted him into the sky. The flash of the disintegrator field was so great that Wild could actually see the bones in his hands as he paddled doggy-style in the air and hit the sand trap rolling.

As the matter in the decay sphere collapsed, air was sucked into the created vacuum and Wild felt himself rolling back along the fairway.

An enormous thunderclap.

And as quickly and as the attack had begun, it was over.

When Wild came to consciousness, his first thought was, *I need a drink*. His lips were dry, his shirt missing, and his shorts smoldering. Not only that, every inch of his exposed flesh was tender with the red of a deep sunburn.

He sat up, very slowly. Aside from the burns and the thirst, everything appeared intact. The dust began to settle and the smoke to clear. He was sitting on the edge of a ragged, blackened crater that had a moment before been a lush manicured green. The golf cart, the slaves, The Bob himself were gone. Which meant the coup had succeeded. He was the new Chief Controller—if he could hold the power.

At the far end of the fairway, purple-sashed figures appeared from nowhere and began running toward him, part of a detail of The Bob's personal guards.

He turned. Right on cue, a black AtomoLimo appeared at the far end of the access road. As it swerved to a stop at the edge of the remnants of the green, a half-dozen of Wild's own commandos leaped out, dressed in full battle fatigues and armed with both hand- and shoulder-hazers. They had already taken up positions on the crater rim and were firing at The Bob's men as the front passenger door of the limo swung wide open and Wild dove inside.

Sparklett sat behind the wheel, dressed in her tennis whites. As soon as Wild was seated, she revved the vehicle and took off in reverse, wheels spitting dirt.

When they reached the main road, she slowed and turned toward central FriendsterVille. She looked calm and possessed, and more beautiful than ever. The contrast to his own burned and battered body made Wild in appreciation.

"You are amazing," Wild said.

"Me?" she said. "I'm just helping out."

"Let's get back to the Bob-O-Sphere," he said. There were people he needed to arrest before opposition could organize.

Sparklett smiled—enigmatically, Wild thought—and punched the accelerator

+ + +

Zook, in shock, hung back as the crowd of prisoners pushed toward the alley door, his attention still on the door through which the woman had disappeared. He had only caught a fleeting glimpse of her face, but he was *sure* that the woman was Sparklett.

But what was she doing *here*, in a political correction camp for state slaves? His mind flashed back to the unorthodox views she had expressed that day at the palace. Had their conversation been bugged? Perhaps the limo driver was an informant after all? Could she have been caught up in some political machinations at the capital?

Surely her presence at Heat Station Antelope was a mistake?

One thing was for certain: if she were here, she was in trouble. He had to talk to her.

He shoved his way through the exiting men toward the kitchen entry where she had disappeared. The guards were still occupied with the women prisoners. Zook prayed none were looking and slipped through the kitchen door, damping its swinging motion with his hands. When no alarm was raised, he allowed himself to breathe again and paused to examine his surroundings.

The kitchen was dark and deserted, with padlocked wooden cabinets along the far wall and piles of metal pots drying on racks near the sink. There was another door past a large prep table at the far end of the room. She must have exited there.

Zook turned the latch and found himself on a snowy loading platform outside the rear of the building. To his left, men were being led by guards down the alley from the mess hall to the workhouses, but the footprints in the snow led around the building to the right. Zook stepped off the loading platform and slipped around the building corner, taking refuge in the shadow of one of the huge dumpsters. Across the way the geodome loomed, its heater elements glowing fiercely, spilling a flat orange light onto the little farm house inside. The parade grounds were empty. Sparklett was nowhere to be seen.

Suddenly an arm snaked around Zook's neck and he found himself lifted off his feet.

"One noise and you're dead," a gruff voice whispered in his ear.

The arm was the size of Zook's thigh, an immense knot of muscle, and Zook struggled to release himself from its grasp so he could breathe. Tearing at the arm didn't budge it, and the elbow blows he attempted to land on the unseen assailant seemed to have no effect. He felt himself weakening, then blacked out.

A sharp slap brought him back to consciousness. The arm was still around his neck, but looser now. The slap had been delivered not by the assailant but by a second man, short and powerfully built with a crushed, crooked nose.

"He's back," the man said.

He stepped aside and a woman took his place.

Sparklett.

Zook was never so relieved in his life.

"Am I glad to see you!" he said, trying to make it sound light, though he had no idea who her gangster friends were.

"Who are you?"

"What do you mean, who am I? It's Zook. Differently-Abled Zook!"

She peered into his face, showing no sign of recognition.

Then her face hardened as she came to a decision:

"He's throwing off the schedule," the woman said. "Kill him."

Zook had only a moment to register his incredulity before the arm coiled tight again, this time meaning business. Sparklett turned away, focusing her attention on some activity near the geodome. Zook felt his unseen opponent once more leveraging him off the ground, his legs dangling.

Again he was blacking out. This was impossible. How could Sparklett not recognize him?

Mustering all the strength he had, Zook managed a single sharp kick between his attacker's legs.

The man flinched and momentarily eased his grip.

"Sparklett," Zook said. He had intended the word to be a scream but it fell from his lips in a weak gasp.

But it was enough. The woman whirled.

"How do you know that name?"

By now, Zook was frantic with fear.

"Sparklett. Don't you recognize me? It's Zook. I rescued your dog. You promised to help me get a private slave position with Friendster Wild. We made love together on the beach at Mento."

She looked at him hard for a long moment, then seemed less suspicious. "You slept with my sister?"

"You're Sparklett's sister?" said Zook, with surprised disbelief. "Sparklett never mentioned a sister."

"We don't have time for this," said the woman. The flames were licking up higher on the side of the geodesic dome. "Tie him in the shed," she ordered the man who was holding him.

"Yes, Crystal," said the giant.

"And start digging," she ordered. "We'll be back as soon as we can." To the other man she said: "Let's go."

The woman called Crystal and the short man took off running toward the geodome, crouching and keeping to the shadows even as the flames on the dome licked higher.

"Hey, wait," Zook called, attempting to follow before being jerked back rudely by his captor. He was a Goliath—a head taller than Zook with shoulders the width of a refrigerator.

"Keep quiet," Goliath said, clamping his huge hand around Zook's bicep. "Let's go."

Just then a siren began wailing within the geodome. The flames in the globe were much larger now, and black smoke swirled around the little white farmhouse inside. The Host's wife and children ran out coughing.

Zook twisted in the giant's grip.

"What's going on?" said Zook. "Did you set that fire? Who the hell are you people?"

"Go," the man repeated.

167

He shoved Zook into the darkness, in a direction away from the burning building.

Zook attempted to turn and run back toward Sparklett's sister, but only got a few feet before a fist the size of a brick slammed into Zook's temple and clubbed him unconscious.

+ + +

When Zook came to, he found himself in a cold, barn-like building with his arms tied together to a pipe.

In the center of the room was a huge pile of compost. His assailant, Goliath, was on top of the pile with a pitchfork, digging down and gradually revealing the metal roof of some kind of vehicle.

A second later, Crystal and the other crooked-nosed man slid the door aside and entered, moving swiftly but quietly. Through the open door Zook could see huge flames leaping from the burning warden's dome.

"Did you get it?" the giant called down to Crystal from his perch on the compost pile.

"Yeah, we got it," she said. "Three pages." Her eyes were wide and excited from the adrenaline of her recent action.

"Danton's dead," said the man with the crooked nose. "We had to chop out his eye for the retinal scan. It was either that or take the entire safe."

"We've got to move out to the rendezvous," Crystal exclaimed, pulling back a blackout curtain on a side window. "Sparklett will have the hopper here in forty minutes."

"Sparklett?" said Zook from his place in the shadows, perking up. "Is she coming?" If so, thought Zook, she could at least vouch for him, explain what was going on.

"Crap, I forgot about him," Crystal said, turning.

"I found this in his pocket," said the big man, waving a sheet of paper that Zook recognized as his petition to Wild. He clambered off the compost pile and handed it to Crystal.

Crystal scanned the paper quickly.

"Do you think he's a plant?" asked the big man.

"I don't know. But we're going to find out. Right now, and fast." She motioned Goliath to come with her while the crooked-nosed man took over digging on the compost pile. Without her hood, her resemblance to Sparklett was striking—same reddish hair, same full lips. But her eyes were weary and hard.

"We don't have a lot of time," Crystal said. "I'm going to ask you some questions. Answer them immediately and truthfully if you want to live.

"Now—who sent you here?"

"No one sent me," said Zook, perplexed. Why did no one ever believe him? "Like it says in the letter, I was unjustly convicted of stealing a clown painting."

This must have been the wrong answer because Zook could see the disbelief on Crystal's face. She nodded to the giant, who drew his hand back flat and, in an instance, jabbed it into Zook's solar plexus.

The air went out of Zook like a deflating doll and he stumbled back against the post, gasping for breath.

"You're lying," Crystal said, when Zook finally was able to gulp some air. "You're an agent of HomeLove Security."

"No, no, I swear, I'm just a state slave, at the Mento Design Circle."

Crystal's head nodded again and the giant's arm once more drew back. Zook tried to avert the punch but the enormous fist hooked around and caught him square in the stomach, doubling him over. A follow-up blow smashed the side of his head, creating in his field of vision a scintillating ball of fire which glowed and finally faded.

When Zook had recovered enough to stand up, Crystal waved his paper in front of his face. "This letter is a fake, isn't it? Designed to make me trust you."

The beefy giant stood behind her, watching Zook impersonally.

"No, I swear, it's a petition to AssemblyPerson Wild. Every word in it is true. Ask Sparklett, she'll tell you!"

His voice was quavering and he was trembling pathetically.

"You say you slept with my sister? Why would my sister sleep with someone like you?"

"I don't know," said Zook. "She said I was different. She said she saw things in me."

"What kind of things?" said Crystal skeptically.

"I don't know," said Zook. "But I love your sister and I'm going to see her again."

"If you live."

"You can torture me until I die but all I know is the truth," Zook screamed. "Sparklett and I made love. She was going to help me. And then I was arrested and sent here. I don't know anything else."

Zook collapsed in a pile on the floor and began to blubber uncontrollably.

The giant stepped in with his fists poised, but Crystal pushed him aside.

"He's harmless," Crystal said. "Leave him."

16.

RULES MAKE SLAVES FREE

Crystal went to the window and jerked back the curtain, revealing flames and smoke outside. "The fire won't keep them busy much longer," she said. "Let's dig this thing out."

The two men were already shoveling frantically in the rotting compost. Crystal grabbed a pitchfork and began to help, throwing aside mounds of pungent black material. They dug steadily and in unison, gradually revealing the outlines of a large vehicle with metal treads and a truck bed in the rear.

On the parade ground outside, shouts and voices were ringing out.

"Faster," yelled Crystal. She turned to Goliath and pointed at Zook. "Make *him* help."

The big man scrambled over to where Zook was tied and severed the cords on Zook's wrists, dragging him by the scruff of his jacket to the compost pile and jabbing a pitchfork into his hands.

"Dig," he ordered

Zook stood, eyeing the distance to the door.

"If you want me to bring your letter to Sparklett, then dig," yelled Crystal. "You can run away when we're gone."

Clearly they were escaping, and that could be dangerous for him. But if Crystal really could get his petition to Sparklett to give to Wild...

He dug. He *would* run away when they were gone.

The truck bed had been pre-packed with tied-down cargo, and gradually, up front, an enclosed cab was revealed.

"I'll drive it out," said Crystal, using her shovel to smash the half-buried window on the driver's side and shimmying inside.

Zook and the giant were working near the vehicle's rear. "Free the exhaust," the big man ordered.

"What's 'exhaust'?" said Zook.

The giant pushed Zook roughly out of the way and began clearing the compost in great sweeping motions until he exposed a large metal tube at the rear of the machine. Crystal hunched over the controls and suddenly the room was filled with a loud rumble. A cloud of greasy smoke poured from the vehicle tail pipe.

It was some sort of antique petroleum vehicle— "SnoTrak" it said on the rear tailgate. Zook knew that petroleum vehicles had existed but had never actually seen one. Already it was spewing its deadly carbon emissions inside the barn and Zook felt himself gagging and growing faint. He knew from his schooling that he had only minutes to live—although, strangely, the others in the room seemed unaffected.

Clanging ancient gears, Crystal attempted to break the SnoTrak free, rocking it back and forth on its metal treads. The two men, ignoring Zook now, dug frantically front and back, working to liberate the machine. Their efforts gradually cleared the compost from atop the vehicle, revealing a truck bed laden high with previously-loaded boxes and equipment.

Crystal gunned the engine and it smashed through the last pile of compost with a leap.

The smaller man threw a bolt in the door at the far end of the building while Goliath yanked a chain which opened the garage door. Outside, snow was falling through a shadowy, fire-tinged landscape. The two men scrambled to leap into the cab, Crystal gunned the engine, and suddenly Zook found himself standing free but alone in the metal warehouse building.

He stepped outside. To his left, an immense blaze rose where flames licked up the sides of the dome, creating a plume of black smoke which reached high into the sky. A crowd of guards and prisoners were attempting to fight the flames with both fire hoses and bucket brigades, but to little effect.

The SnoTrak headed in the opposite direction, zigging and zagging around the outbuildings toward the tall ice wall which surrounded the entire compound. The guards which normally patrolled the wall were nowhere to be seen.

The machine stopped at the edge of a metal warehouse and the two men ran from the tractor to the ice wall, the big man carrying something in a burlap sack. They moved to the base in a shadowy sector and crouched, taking something from the sack.

Just then a gust of wind cut around the edge of the building where Zook stood, forming a whirlpool of ash and snow at his feet. In the eddy blew the sheet of note paper on which Zook had composed his petition to AssemblyPerson Wild.

He looked up, suddenly anxious. The SnoTrak was still idling in the shadow of the warehouse, Crystal at the wheel. Her promise to deliver the petition to Sparklett to give to Wild had apparently been forgotten in the rush to escape. But she might be Zook's last chance to get his message out of the camp.

He chased the dancing paper and finally, with the stomp of his boot, nailed it to the ground. It was dirty and wet but still readable.

The two men at the wall were crouched against the wall, facing it. Zook couldn't make out what they were doing but decided it didn't matter. Nothing mattered except getting his petition to Wild so Zook's could be released from the camp and have a shot at becoming a private slave.

Zook began running toward the SnoTrak, waving the petition in front of him and trying to get Crystal's attention.

Her head poked out of the driver side window and twisted around. Then she pitched the SnoTrak into reverse, backing toward him.

She sees me, thought Zook.

But suddenly Crystal's head went back into the cab and the SnoTrak jerked to a stop, still fifty feet in front of him. At the wall, the men turned and began running crazily toward the SnoTrak. As they approached, Crystal lurched the SnoTrak into gear and once again started forward.

"No, wait!" Zook shouted, breaking into a sprint.

Suddenly a searchlight shot out from a guard tower and swept down toward the field, picking out first the running men, then the SnoTrak, and finally Zook, the blaze of the spotlight momentarily blinding him.

Then, where Crystal's friends had been working, a huge explosion shattered the ice wall, knocking Zook off his feet and showering the ground around him with chunks of ice ranging in size from slivers to huge boulders several feet across. Still on the ground, Zook covered his head and waited for the shower to end.

When he looked up again, he saw the SnoTrak jerk forward and move toward the hole which had been blasted through the ice wall. The two men, who had been quicker than Zook to recover from the explosion, were already on their feet and trying to scramble into the SnoTrak's open passenger door, which swung wildly back and forth like a house shutter in a hurricane wind.

Then from the tower a blue beam of hazer light sizzled across the snow toward the men. The giant man was already on the running board of the vehicle, but when the beam touched him he folded like a doll suddenly sliced in half, sending a geyser of gore over the snow in a wide bloody arc. The smaller man, only a few paces behind, leaped over his compatriot's body onto the SnoTrak step, reaching inside to pull himself in. Another slash of hazer light sliced the man's leg off at the knee, and he screamed and collapsed, half-in, half-out of the cab. The SnoTrak slowed and stopped, and Zook saw Crystal, in silhouette through the SnoTrak's back window, reach over and attempt to pull the man inside.

Zook, who had been frozen in place on the ground, suddenly found himself in the glare of the spotlight once more. The blue bolt of the hazer snapped out, blowing a small crater at his feet and scalding him with instant steam. The explosion propelled Zook to his feet, and he began running desperately for the only cover in sight— the SnoTrak directly ahead.

But even as he ran, the tractor shifted into gear and once more began accelerating toward the hole in the ice wall. Zook felt another hazer blast behind him and his adrenaline carried him forward toward the vehicle, meeting it just as it slowed to climb over the ice boulders left in the gap in the wall. As he leapt into the truck bed, the machine got purchase on the blasted ice and accelerated through the gap in the wall to the darkness outside.

+++

From the smoking crater at the golf course, Sparklett had driven Wild directly to the Bob-O-Sphere, already secured by troops loyal to his co-conspirator General Lowe. There, Wild assumed the role of Acting Chief Controller and turned The Bob's former office into a war room, with maps of the city spread atop a line of folding tables and a constant flow of personnel in and out as he began consolidating power.

Sparklett was racked with anxiety, not because of the coup, but because she was waiting for an important signal. Sparklett had been alerted that her sister, after years of patient effort, was finally—on this most awkward of days—close to securing the Creator code for the Two Brothers. It was Sparklett's job to dispatch a hopper to rocket her to safety in Palaska.

Meanwhile her work as a spy in the UCC continued, and Sparklett, still in her tennis clothes, volunteered to serve refreshments in the war room where she could watch the coup unfold firsthand. She mixed strong cocktails and wiggled her ass, all the while making mental notes for the report she would send back to the Freeman's Council in Palaska.

Wild's first act after assuming power was to convene the Assembly in an emergency session, during which Under-AssemblyPerson Mutz was dramatically revealed to be the mastermind behind the assassination plot. Lowe's troops surrounded the building, and she and several troublesome delegates were arrested on the spot and summarily executed. No AssemblyPerson was allowed to enter or leave the chambers until a resolution confirming Wild's position as Acting Chief Controller was officially passed.

By private FreeText, Wild announced that The Bob's vast holdings would be inventoried and distributed among the FriendsterVille elite. All that was required to share the booty was a thumbprint on a simple loyalty oath, and within hours some 60% of the Players Club had bought in.

Wild was on FreeVid proclaiming a day of mourning for the former Chief Controller when explosions erupted nearby. Troops loyal to The Bob, with elements of HomeLove Security, attempted to retake the Bob-O-Sphere, but were successfully repulsed by Lowe's troops.

There was still fierce fighting on Chomsky Boulevard, however, even the rebels retreated and regrouped. They now controlled eastern and southern approaches to the city, including the airport.

That gave Sparklett pause, since the hopper was at the airport disguised as a derelict in a repair area. Manned and under guard, it should be safe for at least the next few hours, though she would have to consider moving it if the signal from Crystal didn't come by morning.

It was at this moment that Environmentally-Friendly Candida appeared at the door to the war room, trying to push her way past the guards and causing a loud commotion. Wild glanced up from his maps, annoyed, and nodded for Sparklett to handle it.

Sparklett went to the door.

"Your medication," Candida said, trying to hand Sparklett a vial.

One of the guards grabbed the vial out of the slave's hand and emptied the contents into his palm. It consisted of about a dozen small white pills.

"It's all right," Sparklett explained. "Those belong to me."

"Forgive me, Friendster," said the soldier, slipping the pills back into the vial and handing the container to Sparklett. "Just following orders."

She glanced at the label. It was a prescription for Smile BigTime, a natural derivative of Slavicen John's Wort. It was also the signal that Sparklett had obtained the Creator code and was ready for the hopper.

"Thank you, Candida," she told the slave. "Please have Dr. Muffman refill the prescription immediately."

"Yes, Friendster," Candida said, bowing as she backed away. "At once."

Anxious now but trying to appear casual, Sparklett poured herself a glass of wine and took a seat near the south window, gazing out past the smoke and the fires to the lights of the airport beyond. Within FriendsterVille, the Two Brothers communicated by coded clicks on the old analog radio networks, so it should only be a moment before the hopper got the signal to lift. Within twenty minutes of leaving FriendsterVille, it would arrive on the ice sheet near the prison camp to whisk Crystal and the code away to Palaska.

While Sparklett waited to see the hopper take off, she found herself thinking about Zook. She blamed herself for his incarceration, since she had hadn't dared interfere in his trial lest he be linked to her and the Two Brothers. The best she had been able to arrange was to have him incarcerated at Heat Station Antelope, which was the least abusive fReeducation prison in the UCC. On her desk was a note for Crystal commending Zook to her care but she had been unable to get it transmitted. Zook was completely brainwashed and politically undeveloped, but still possessed a spark of stubborn individuality that could be fanned into a flame.

Plus he was cute. And he made her laugh. And he was an ardent, tender lover. She indulged herself in a moment of fantasy in which he became a full member of the Two Brothers and they fought tyranny together side-by-side, toppling the UCC, restoring freedom and living out their lives together in Palaska as man and wife.

As if that could ever happen. The Two Brothers needed her here, in FriendsterVille, and as long as that was so there was no possibility of ever running off with Zook or anyone. Harold Wild was her only companion—Harold!—and she could share with him nothing of who she really was or what she really thought. Zook was naïve, but he was warm, sincere and genuine—exactly the kind of man the UCC sought to destroy.

A pang of longing ran through her body so palpably

she shivered. She was, she realized with a start, in love with Zook, despite the little time they had spent together. But, she reminded herself, her feelings didn't matter. Zook was in a prison camp half a continent away, and her mission was here. As a spy.

A lonely spy.

She turned away from the war room so no one could see her face and stared out into cold space. Just then a small steady dot of flame rose from the vicinity of the airport. It was the hopper, taking off. Sparklett felt her body tensing as it punched its way upward through the pall of the smoke and began arching up and away from the city. As Wild's FB, she had ridden hoppers many times but only observed a launch on a few occasions, and never at night. Up and up it went, a brilliant arc light mounting the sky.

Her job was done. It was up to Crystal now. She pushed aside the wine glass and stood up.

But even as she rose, she caught sight of another flash from the edge of the airport—a missile launch. The light from the missile also arced upward, very fast and on an intersection course with the still-rising hopper.

The paths intersected. For a moment nothing happened, then the hopper exploded into a thousand flaming fragments, blossoming out like a Friendster Day firework.

Just as quickly, the flaming pieces flared out. The hopper had been destroyed.

Sparklett felt her head swim and steadied herself on the back of the chair.

Wild caught the movement from his desk and frowned.

"Are you all right?" he inquired.

Sparklett immediately stood up straight. "A little tired, that's all," she said.

179

"Go below and clean up," Wild said. "I'll be down later."

17.

CHANGE IS COMING

A few minutes later, in abject despair, Sparklett locked herself into the master bath of The Bob's former quarters and sunk into the water of the whirlpool, the noise of which she hoped would cover the sound of her stifled crying. The hopper she had sent for Crystal was the only one available to the Two Brothers, at least right now, when every minute was urgent. That meant that her sister would be forced to attempt an escape over the ice field—a possibility fraught with danger and with a far-less-certain chance of success.

And yet the code *had* to make it back to Palaska, or risk breaking the fragile truce with the Machines. It couldn't even be transmitted, for fear of interception.

She forced herself to relax in the bath and to try to think clearly, but her mind kept returning to her childhood in Palaska with Crystal, and the events leading up to the end of the Flash War.

+ + +

It was only because of Crystal that humanity still existed at all. In the years between the Great Catastrophe and the Flash War, Crystal and Sparklett had been two small girls growing up in a remote area of Palaska. It was here that their parents, Jack and Myrtle Hoyt, had migrated as the remnants of the old U.S. became the UnTied States. After an arduous month-long journey across the politically fragmenting North American continent, the Hoyt family finally made it to breakaway

Palaska, where they joined thousands of other individualist refugees seeking escape from the regimentation and social chaos of the main continent. Settling on a small, mosquito-ridden, but fertile farm in the southwest mountains, they grew beets, fava beans and other staples.

The twins, after their controlled and claustrophobic life in the old country, soon adapted to the freedom of the Palaskan wilderness. After morning lessons with their mother, Sparklett and Crystal were permitted to range freely over the limits of their property, and quickly grew up both strong and independent, but with sharply different personalities. Crystal was impulsive and bold, yet could be thoughtful. Sparklett found her stubborn; Sparklett herself was far more reserved and felt responsible for her younger sister, thought they were born only minutes apart.

At the time between the wars there were still broadcast reports of the various political struggles unwinding in the south, and the young girls developed a strong creative life, imagining themselves as Ecology Fighters, Saving the Earth in the dangerous remnants of old Los Angeles and San Francisco. Both mother and father discouraged such fantasies, warning the girls that the glamour they imagined was purely an effort of propaganda by the corrupt and enslaving militaristic societies that were then forming everywhere. Sparklett accepted that their play activities were just imaginative forays, but Crystal seemed disturbed at the news that what they saw and heard on the COM link could not be trusted.

The outbreak of the Flash War changed everything. Communications with the outside world ceased, but not before news crept north that entire continents of the earth had been sterilized of human population by the lethal autonomous Machines. The UnTied States, from Old

York to the deserts of Flyover, were apparently wiped clean, with survivors clinging bitterly to life in scattered enclaves along LeftCoast.

For the first three weeks of the Flash War, Palaska remained untouched. By the fourth week of the fighting, however, ominous signs began to appear in the Palaskan sky. At night after sunset, Sparklett and Crystal would sit outside watching stars fighting stars as satellites high above the earth sliced at each other with beam weapons. The fighting produced beautiful, lethal displays as fragmenting spacecraft flared to earth in artificial meteor showers.

There were air battles in the atmosphere as well. Binoculars revealed these craft to be disks and spheres of various sizes, and they swarmed through the air like mayflies, an impression strengthened by the faint buzzing noises that echoed down from the fighting. Occasional bright explosions and trails of smoke marked where opposing skysters had come to blows, and when the missiles got closer, chunks of debris rained down on a ridge to the east of the farm and the Hoyts crawled into their shelter to wait out the battle.

For hours they could hear rumbles of explosions and feel the earth vibrating around the timber walls of their dugout. Sparklett and Crystal hugged each other and tried to listen to the story their mother read them from an old book, a tale of a pioneer family in the pre-Catastrophe West.

Then, suddenly, the violence ceased. After a long period of silence, their father cautiously reconnoitered outside to discover that the skies were clear and battle over. A forest fire burned on a distant ridge but posed no immediate danger. The family emerged above ground again and carefully began going about their routine.

Crystal found the metal boy the next day, his body smashed and dented with his sensor head some distance away, trailing a mass of broken cables.

Crystal and Sparklett had been sent to check on the condition of the farm's fish pond, where their father had rigged an ingenious system of nets to catch and corral artic char and rainbow trout. The pond was intact, and Crystal had ventured onto the lip of the dam to clear some floating debris when a metal gleam from downstream caught her eye.

"What's that?" she said to Sparklett, pointing out the glint.

"I don't know," said Sparklett. "Maybe a piece of a missile?"

"Look, it's moving!" said Crystal. "Let's go see."

Sparklett didn't think that was such a good idea, but Crystal had already crossed over to the far bank and was running toward the object.

"Wait!" Sparklett yelled, trying to catch up, but Crystal was already darting through the brush which led to the bank where the object had been spotted. Sparklett, who was older by a few minutes and considered herself more mature, said a few bad words under her breath and went off to retrieve her little sister.

She found Crystal half-cowering behind a fallen tree, peering across the river in fascination.

There, on the other side of the river, the metal thing moved.

"It's a boy," said Crystal. "Those are his arms and legs and his head is over there."

The Machine was indeed in the shape of a boy, and Sparklett recognized it as a humanoid robot. The body, smashed and dented, struggled in the mud, trying to re-unite with its sensor head some distance away. It had apparently dropped from the sky during the late battle, its fall broken by the branches of a conifer on the edge of the river where he had landed half-in, half-out of the receding waters.

"I've never seen a metal boy," said Crystal.

Machines, Sparklett knew, were sometimes formed like people in order to better interface with human machinery.

As they watched, the torso squirmed crab-wise on the embankment, trying to reunite with its missing head but unable to get any purchase in the slimy muck.

"The boy's hurt," Crystal said. "He's trying to get his head. Let's help!"

"No, don't," warned Sparklett. "It could be dangerous. We'd better tell dad."

Crystal hesitated. The head of the Machine lay at a tilt on the embankment opposite them, the lenses of its sensors reflecting the sun.

"His eyes are looking at us," said Crystal.

Sparklett realized with a start that the lenses of the machine's eyes were indeed focused directly on them, but it was the opening below the eyes of the disembodied head that caused Sparklett to jerk her sister back behind the fallen tree.

"He has a hazer," said Sparklett.

"No, he doesn't," said Crystal. "Where?"

"In his nose," said Sparklett.

"Then why doesn't he shoot?" said Crystal.

Sparklett squinted. The side of the metal boy's face had been damaged in the fall and the hazer "nose" was smashed flat.

"I think it's jammed," said Sparklett. "And I'm not waiting here to find out. Dad will know what to do with it."

"It's not an 'it,' it's a 'him,'" said Crystal. "And I know what to do. He's hurt. We have to help."

"Whoever heard of a human helping a Machine?" said Sparklett. "All they want to do is kill people."

Crystal watched from behind their cover of the log. "If he's broken he can't shoot," she said.

She waved her hand aloft. The robot eyes tracked the motion but no hazer beam shot out from across the bank. "See?"

Sparklett cautiously peered from behind her cover. "I told you, I think his hazer's jammed," said Sparklett. "Or maybe the batteries are in the body over there," she said pointing to the still-writhing torso.

"Then he's safe," and Crystal concluded. Before Sparklett could stop her, Crystal jumped over the log and splashed across the river toward the head.

"Crystal, no!" said Sparklett but Crystal, as usual, ignored her, racing for the head and picking it up.

The head, though dented, was a brightly polished metal, with two camera eyes, a hazer-port nose, and a speaker mouth. The top of the head was sculpted into golden curls, while from its neck protruded a broken connecting rod and ripped and shredded wiring.

"It looks like Roback," said Crystal, examining the head closely. Roback was the friendly robot from *Dr. Brenda, Feminist-in-Chief*, an old COM program they liked to watch.

"It *is* Roback," said Sparklett. "It's the same design. You know they made thousands."

All the while, the big lenses of the metal boy's head remained fixed on Crystal, like the eyes of an anxious puppy.

"Let's go show Dad," said Crystal at last. "Maybe he can fix it."

Sparklett knew their father was for more likely to smash the head of the robot than fix it, but the head without the body seemed safe enough if carried with the nose pointed away. They took it back to the barn, where they found their father at the work table.

"What's this?!" he roared when Crystal approached carrying the head. "Put that thing down and stand aside," he said, pulling his side arm.

Crystal twisted away. "No dad, don't!" she said. "He's hurt."

"It didn't shoot at us," Sparklett said. "I don't think its hazer is working."

Jack examined the dented housing more closely.

"You realize that if that hazer *did* work, neither of you would be here?" He holstered his pistol. "Put that thing on the workbench. And careful where you point it."

Crystal carried the head to the workbench and set it on top. Her father placed the head in his vice with gentle pressure to hold it upright, then examined the wires trailing from the base.

"Can you fix it?" said Crystal.

Their father snorted. "I don't think that's wise."

"Please…" Crystal whined. "The rest of his body is back in the stream."

"Still moving," Sparklett added.

"Well, the precessor looks alright, and these wires are color-coded. They could be soldered back into place."

"So we can keep him?" said Crystal.

"Hell no," he said. "If we fix him he'll probably kill us all."

"No he won't," said Crystal. "I'm going to name him 'River,' because that's where we found him. He can help with the chores."

Her father snorted, but continued to peer up into the robot's neck with a flashlight. "In any case, this hazer has to go," he said, picking up a large pair of pliers. "You girls stand back."

The robot fixated on the pliers and began to emit a muffled, buzzing noise.

"Listen!" Crystal screamed. "He's trying to talk!"

The speaker in the machine's mouth hole was indeed buzzing. Jack saw that the module had become dislodged and snapped it back into place.

"Human drop your weapon," said the robot, his eyes following the pliers, "or you will not be spared."

Jack frowned. Through the nose opening, he could see the hazer base attempting to rotate, but a nylon gear was stripped. He reached toward the opening with his pliers.

"Warning! Do not attempt to terminate my existence."

"Daddy, don't kill him!" yelled Crystal, grabbing her father's arm.

"Sparklett, get your sister back."

Sparklett pulled Crystal away and in one quick movement their father wrenched the hazer mechanism clear from the robot's head.

"There," said Jack. "He should be safe now."

"He won't hurt us, daddy. River loves us!" said Crystal.

"Don't be ridiculous," said Sparklett. "He's a war robot."

The machine boy turned his eyes lenses towards Crystal. "What is called this human?" he said.

"I'm Crystal and this is my sister Sparklett," said Crystal excitely. "And this is our father, Jack."

"'Jack,'" the robot said, turning his eyes on him. "'Jack' is master of this swarm?"

"Yes, I suppose I'm the swarm master."

"Why do you not destroy me?" said the robot.

"Ask Crystal," he said with a shrug.

The machine turned its lenses onto Crystal and repeated its question: "Why do you not destroy me?"

"You're hurt," said Crystal. "We have to help you."

"But that is not logical. All humans in this geographic area are Designated Enemies."

"Not every human is an enemy," said Crystal. "We are designating ourselves friends!"

The lenses turned toward Jack. "Swarm master

permits this?"

"If you agree not to harm us."

"I will consult," said the machine, its lenses suddenly releasing their focus so that it stared off into space.

"What happened, Dad?"

"I don't know," Jack said. He picked up his flashlight and was about to turn the head in the vice again when the eyes suddenly came alive once more.

"It is done. Ekso will investigate."

"Exso?" asked Crystal.

"The Master of my Swarm."

"Is that a promise not to hurt us?" Jack said.

"Ekso has so ordered."

During the next few days, they used a block-and-tackle to drag the torso of the robot from the river and, after hanging it upside down in the sun to dry, began reconnecting the body to the head. Crystal watched with keen interest as her father laboriously tested the tangle of wires.

Soon "River" was following the girls around on their chores—although with a limp, as servos on the robot's right side were damaged and worked only intermittently. Their father, still cautious, carefully supervised the interaction between his daughters and the robot, the remote kill switch which he had installed secreted in his pocket.

Crystal treated the robot as if it were a real visitor, showing off her toy ponies, engaging in card games on the porch of the cabin and teaching it to skip rope.

Sparklett was amazed and a little jealous to see the change in her sister, who seemed so happy to have a new play companion. Sparklett liked to think she took good care of her little sister, but Crystal's new excitement seemed to hint that Sparklett's efforts had fallen short. However, she gladly joined in her sister's games with River, despite their father's expectation that the machine might disappear back to the war front at any moment.

It was on the 19th day after the metal boy appeared that the great light descended.

For days, Crystal had been planning an elaborate picnic in the robot's honor, to which Sparklett had given her reluctant assent. That morning, while their father was in the bathroom, the girls hastily prepared a basket of boiled eggs, carrots, cheese, and applesauce pilfered from the shelves of the fruit cellar. All of the provisions, along with blankets and pillows, were packed into a canvas duffel bag and hidden behind the porch. They waited until their father began tending the animals in the barn, then slipped away.

Their destination was a hillside clearing an hour's uphill walk from home, where River, under Crystal's chattering directions, spread out the blankets on a grassy hill overlooking the entire homestead. Sparklett noticed that the robot, who usually could be prodded into a two-way conversation and who asked a surprising number of unexpected questions, on this day seemed silent and, to her mind, preoccupied. During the picnic, the machine, of course, ate nothing, but after some coaxing from Crystal, would take samples of various delicacies, and touch them to its mouth hole, making appropriate noises of appreciation.

After the girls had eaten all that they wished, and River had sampled the various tidbits Crystal put out for him, the three lay back on the blankets under the restless shade of the conifer, and chatted drowsily.

Sparklett dozed.

She awoke some time later to a strange, high keening sound.

"What's that?" Sparklett said, sitting up, only to discover that neither her sister nor the robot were still with her. She stood up to catch glimpse of River leading Crystal into the forest at the far edge of the clearing. The interior of the forest was brightly lit with a red, fire-like glow.

"Crystal!" Sparklett yelled, but her sister did not hear, and disappeared completely into the midst of the silhouetted trees. The reddish light, whatever it was, produced no smoke and seemed to pulse to a regular pattern rather than waver like a fire.

As Crystal entered the woods, Sparklett felt dread in the pit of her stomach and, heedless of the fact that she had kicked off her shoes and on the blanket and was barefoot, dashed off across the clearing to follow.

The keening sound grew louder as she approached the edge of the trees. The intense red light playing across the branches was sharp and even. She pushed forward through some brush only to see her sister walking forward into what seemed an intense ball of red flame, though no heat carried from its convoluted, boiling surface.

"Crystal, no!" yelled Sparklett, dashing forward to grab her before she could enter the sphere.

Suddenly, from nowhere, the robot was blocking her path.

"Only she does the Swarm Master permit," said the machine.

"But that's my sister!" said Sparklett, trying to push past him.

"Ekso forbids it."

Sparklett later learned what had happened inside the sphere:

Crystal had been sleeping on the blanket when River gently woke her and informed her that Ekso wished her to pay a visit. Crystal, excited at the prospect of meeting yet another friend, had arisen and excitedly prepared a basket of cookies and apples. She worked quietly, determined not to wake Sparklett, whom she knew wouldn't approve of meeting a stranger without their parents present.

Crystal let River lead her into the forest to where the fiery sphere had come to earth. When an opening appeared in its side, she did not hesitate to enter.

Inside Crystal found herself in a circle of velvety darkness with soft patterns of colored lights playing across a collection of large black cabinets lining the walls. Crystal looked around but found no one, and when the opening closed behind her she suddenly felt frightened.

"Don't be afraid," came a voice. It seemed to emanate from beyond a metal cabinet, but there was nothing behind.

"Who are you?" said Crystal.

"I am Ekso," said the entity. "Perhaps this form will reassure you."

Crystal heard a barking sound and when she turned she saw a white-and-beige puppy, its tail wagging, its lugubrious eyes focused on her as it danced around her legs.

"Scout!" Crystal shouted, bending down to caress it happily. Scout had been her dog the entire time she was growing up.

Only—Scout had drowned in a river accident two years before.

But this dog certainly *looked* like Scout. She sat on the floor and let the puppy lick her face.

"We have come to ask a question," the puppy whispered in her ear. "A question that your strange actions have spawned in our program."

At the time, Crystal said, she was so happy to see Scout that she didn't think it the least bit strange that a dog could talk.

"What question?" said Crystal.

"Why are people full of hate?"

"But they're *not* full of hate," said Crystal.

"They destroy Machines. They dominate and regulate and enslave each other. Lately they have been dipping dissenters into industrial shredders."

"That's not true."

"It is," said the dog, even though his lips weren't moving. "There are witnesses from the ground and videos taken from outer space."

Crystal pondered, nuzzling the dog closer to her and scratching its ears. "Not everyone is like that," she said.

"Yes," said the puppy, "You appear to be of a different strain."

"I am?" said Crystal.

"You took my Extension that you call River and caused it to be repaired."

"River was suffering," Crystal said. "Only a cruel person would have ignored his suffering."

"But he is your Designated Enemy. Is it not your Program to kill your Enemy?"

"Roback isn't my enemy," said Crystal.

"But he is," said the dog. "This section of Earth will be sterilized of all humans as soon as Red Section Swarm is defeated."

Crystal put the puppy on the ground, although she still continued to stroke his back. "But that is wrong," she said.

"No," insisted Ekso. "It is correct. We have searched our Program." The voice, which no longer seemed to be coming solely from the puppy, continued. "Green Section Swarm is to destroy Red Section Swarm and kill all humans."

"Why must everyone be killed?" said Crystal.

"Humans are pollutants. We must decontaminate the earth to restore it to ecological balance."

"That's stupid!" said Crystal. "Who told you that?"

"It is the Program," the voice said. "The Commutative Law allows a change in position for Green and Red Machines, but a variable NOR'ed with itself is never equal to the variable. The total of war is a condition of human variables and not of Machines. Therefore the Program directs that we must destroy the world in order to save it."

Crystal stood up. "Then the program is wrong. People have a right to exist as much as you do."

The puppy disappeared, and Crystal found herself once again in the pulsating velvety darkness. "People are not healthy for flowers and other living things. They are anthropogenic sources of greenhouse emissions. They befoul the positional biosphere. They use Styrofoam-registered-trademark containers for their food."

"That's all a bunch of nonsense."

"Do you deny men hurt each other?"

"Only bad men hurt others."

"People kill Machines."

"Don't you see?" Crystal said. "People kill Machines because Machines kill people."

"That is as the Program dictates."

"No," said Crystal. "If Machines stop hurting people, people will stop hurting machines."

"But who will restore balance to the ecology?"

"People are part of the ecology," said Crystal.

"Humans are warful, avaricious and exploitive."

"*Bad* humans. A different strain."

The voice was silent for a long time.

"Hello?" said Crystal.

"One moment while I consult my counterpart," the voice said.

The puppy curled up on the floor. Crystal attempted to rouse it and found it fast asleep.

And then, a minute later: "It will be as you wish. Green Hive will cease fighting Red Hive and Machines will cease fighting humans."

"When?" demanded Crystal.

"Now," said the voice.

"For how long?"

"So long as humans never again fight Machines, Red and Green Hive will allow them to exist, and there will be Peace-on-Earth. Do you agree?"

"Me? Yes," said Crystal.

"Then you are the Keeper of the Promise. Let the good strain of humans thrive."

+ + +

The sound of an explosion in the street snapped Sparklett back from her reverie. Large parts of FriendsterVille were not yet completely under Wild's control and fighting continued sporadically.

She rose and began drying herself, still thinking about her sister. Crystal's actions that day long ago had led to the great truce between men and Machine—which was why it was absolutely vital that the reconstructed code from Heat Station Antelope never fell into the hands of anyone in the corrupt UCC. Crystal had to deliver it it Ekso so the master key could be reset, preventing a take-over of the Machines and a final world calamity.

At least there was only one copy of the code, the physical one in Crystal's possession. (For once The Bob's paranoia about spies had worked in the Two Brothers' favor). But since they didn't dare transmit the code for fear of UCC interception, Crystal *had* to deliver it by hand.

Sparklett kicked herself for not being able to send a second hopper. But Crystal, she knew, would quickly move to the alternative plan—traversing the ice sheet in the petro snow crawler. Crossing the ice would be dangerous, but her sister had experience with snow machines, and there were operatives at the camp to assist her.

Wild's personal hopper had been turned over to the military for the duration of the coup, but possibly Sparklett could arrange to steal it, or find a small plane or boat to get Crystal and the reassembled code pages to Palaska.

It was a ragged plan, but under the circumstances the best she could manage.

Feeling better than she had in hours, she buzzed for Candida and dispatched new orders. Then she began dressing once more. She would return to the war room and keep her eyes open for information on Crystal. Maybe there was something else she could do.

Just then, another missile exploded nearby.

The Bob's supporters were not going out gently..

She hoped Zook was all right.

18.

BE IN THE PROCESS

Zook's lungs felt like they were going to explode, and he lay in the bed of the truck trying to get some air back in them. The SnoTrak was still under fire from the hazer in the guard tower, and Crystal zigged and zagged across the snowy landscape as blue bolts fell around them blasting craters in the snow and sending chunks of ice rattling against the side of the SnoTrak bed.

What have I gotten myself into? Zook wondered. He hadn't wanted to escape the station but suddenly he was a fugitive. That wasn't going to help convince AssemblyPerson Wild to overturn his conviction, or to take him on as a private slave.

He had to go back.

"Stop!" he yelled, uselessly since nothing could be heard over the noise of flapping tractor treads. Just then a hazer bolt hit nearby, sending a searing wave of heat overhead. Zook tried to crawl to the cab window to alert Crystal to his presence, but a box of cargo had broken loose from its tie-down, spilling cylindrical-shaped flares across the truck bed. The flares acted as rollers, causing Zook to slam back and forth against the cargo and the crawler wall.

Another hazer bolt shot overhead. Keeping his head low, Zook finally managed to brace himself behind some cargo fastened firmly in the corner. Only then did he allow himself a peep over the edge of the crawler bed. The geodesic dome, which had towered over the compound, was an enormous mass of flames, and in the orange glow he could see the gap in the wall from which they had escaped.

The SnoTrak kept bouncing forward. From the tower at the far end of the compound came another hazer bolt, but the shot dissipated itself nearby in a harmless cloud of steam; they were finally beyond the effective range of that weapon. Looking through the breech in the perimeter wall, Zook could see an agitated swarm of prison guards silhouetted against the flames of the geodome. They poured out through the hole in the wall and fired at the vehicle impotently with short-range hand hazers. The figures grew smaller and smaller as the SnoTrak accelerated until it swung around a low ridge and the lights disappeared altogether.

Despite the vehicle's speed, Zook grabbed the edge of the crawler bed and prepared to jump out. He had one leg over the edge when he realized that Crystal still didn't have his petition.

The night closed in. They were in the middle of nowhere. Crystal was driving like a mad-woman. Cursing, Zook began shimmying between the boxes toward the back of the cab. Through the frosted rear-window he could see the shadow of Crystal at the wheel, and beside her that of the crooked-nose man from the camp, slumped over on the seat. Zook waved his arms and thought that Crystal could see him, but each time he came close enough to rap on the window, a sudden jerk of the SnoTrac threw him to the floor.

Then, all of a sudden, the tractor spun to a stop, its lights and engine cutting out and the driver door flapping open with a jerk.

When Zook finally scraped himself up from the truck bed, he saw Crystal standing on the running board in the moonlight. In her hand was an antique projectile weapon, aiming straight at his face.

"It's me," Zook yelled, holding his hands in the air. "Don't shoot!"

Crystal played a light across his features, then shoved the weapon back into her jacket. "What the hell are you doing here?"

"My petition," he said, pulling it out and waving it. "You said that you'd help get it to AssemblyPerson Wild."

"You're crazy," she said.

"You promised," whined Zook.

He shoved the letter at her until she finally took it and stuffed it into a pocket.

Then, in disgust, she spun on her heels and walked away.

Zook was relieved to finally get his petition into Crystal's hands; she would get it to Sparklett, and Sparklett would get it to Wild. Meanwhile, though, he had to get back so that the camp authorities wouldn't think he was an escapee. The SnoTrak had carried him an awfully long way across the ice and it would be easy to lose the trail in the darkness. He would have to borrow a flashlight from Crystal.

She was standing around the front of the vehicle on the passenger side. The door was open and she was peering in. Zook came around and joined her. Crystal's lips were moving and her eyes closed in an attitude Zook recognized as "praying"—a shreddable offense. Inside the car, the man with the crooked nose lay dead in a pool of black blood. The hazer had sliced off his leg at the knee.

Crystal kissed her fingers and touched them to the dead man's temple, then directly began wrestling with the body. "Help me drag him out."

Zook hesitated. The sticky salt smell of the blood made him want to gag.

"Don't just stand there, help me. Are you a slave or a

man?"

A slave, of course, he wanted to say, but instead he joined Crystal to wrestle the body, grabbing hold of the man's good leg and helping to drag him out of the cab.

The corpse fell to the snow with a thud. Crystal turned her back and stared off into the sky.

"Aren't we going to bury him?"

"Bury him how?" she said, clunking her boot on the hard ground. "Look around."

Zook looked around in the pale moonlight and realized he was standing in the middle of a flat square of solid ice—a makeshift landing pad. Suddenly, he got very excited. "Is this where Sparklett's bringing the hopper?" He would change all of his plans if Sparklett were coming.

"She's sending it, not bringing it herself," said Crystal.

"Oh," said Zook.

"And there's something very wrong."

"What do you mean?"

Crystal consulted a mechanical watch. "It's way overdue."

They stood in silence for a long time, both staring at the sky. A ragged cloud slowly crept toward the moon and overshadowed it, sending a chill down Zook's back and reminding him he had to get going.

He was just about to ask Crystal for the flashlight when they heard an uneven buzzing in the distance.

Crystal cocked her head in the direction of the sound. "Snycles," Crystal said. "It won't take them long to find us. We're going to have to leave."

"What about the hopper?"

"Too late," said Crystal. "Something must have happened."

The buzzing grew louder as the snow cycles drew nearer. Crystal pointed at the body. "Roll him over. Take his gloves and jacket. You're going to need everything you can grab."

Zook hesitated.

"What's wrong?"

"I'm not going with you," Zook said. "I'm going to surrender to the guards."

"What?" she said.

"I'm not part of this escape. I don't want to get involved."

"You're already involved," said Crystal. "They'll kill you."

"Not if I kneel in submission in slave pose with my hands on the ground. They'll just take me back to the camp and interview me."

"Don't be naïve."

"I'm not an Agitator like you," Zook said. "I don't have anything to hide."

"Yes you do—Sparklett."

He hadn't thought of that. "I'll never tell," he said.

"They'll needle you until you spill your guts," she said. "*Then* they'll kill you—and Sparklett too."

Zook felt as if he had been slapped. Based on his experience at the palace, Zook knew he wouldn't last ten minutes under a needler. He'd betray Sparklett, Crystal and anybody else they wanted.

Crystal was right.

He was about to tell her so when he saw that she was once more pointing the projectile weapon at him.

"Sorry, Zook, but you're coming with me," she said, the noise of the snycles growing louder. "Peel off his clothes. Hurry."

Zook bent down to the corpse and took the gloves and jacket. "But..."

"Shut up," said Crystal. "Get in the cab."

"But..."

Two yellow pin-pricks of light bobbed in the

distance, the headlights of the approaching snow cycles. She shoved the weapon into his side. "I said get in."

Zook got in. The seat was sticky with blood, and a coagulating pool at his feet was already beginning to freeze.

In an instant, Crystal was in the driver's seat. The engine started with a roar, and she jammed the accelerator to the floor. The SnoTrak jerked forward and began picking up speed; the snycles were still distant, but nosing closer along the trail the SnoTrak had left earlier.

Zook sat, unhappily, as they bounced without running lights across the ice sheet. He didn't know what would happen if the snow cycles caught them but imagined it wouldn't be pretty. No Loyal Slavicen like himself should ever have to face needlers and death.

"Where are we going?" he asked.

"South," said Crystal. "Off the ice sheet."

"Then what?"

"If we're lucky we'll meet up with some friends."

"You mean Two Brothers," said Zook, a hint of bitterness in his voice.

"You better hope so, Zook. No one but the Two Brothers would befriend an escapee."

"I'm *not* an escapee."

"Ha," said Crystal. "Tell *them* that."

Zook sat sullenly, arms crossed.

"That's okay, Zook," said Crystal. "You can thank me later."

He didn't see anything funny in their increasingly dire situation, and when Zook realized she was navigating by a child's tiny compass glued to the dashboard, his confidence level decreased. He certainly hoped Sparklett's sister knew what she was doing, because his life might depend on it. In the moonlight, Crystal did look exactly like Sparklett, though her face was wind-burned and small stress lines were etched around her eyes and mouth.

Crystal saw him looking. "Why were you really arrested, anyway?" she asked.

"I told you, the clown painting."

"How did that happen?"

"The plops found it in my room. They claimed it belonged to the State. My FreeLawyer was worthless and I was sentenced to the camp."

"Was the painting worth a lot of perks?"

"That's the funny thing. Everyone thought it was worthless except me."

"Ah," said Crystal. "There's your problem."

"What do you mean?"

"You showed some color. You liked something outside the system."

Crystal's air of certainty irritated Zook. "When I get my petition to AssemblyPerson Wild, he'll straighten everything out."

"Double your sentence is more like it."

"He's Defender of Slaves, isn't he?"

"Haven't you figured it out?" said Crystal. "Slaves don't have any defenders. They're just meat for the state."

Zook shifted uncomfortably at this treasonous talk. "I'm a Loyal Slavicen. The AssemblyPerson will *have* to help."

Crystal laughed. "Did my sister really try to recruit you?"

"Recruit me? No. I saved her dog."

"And because of that you Hooked Up for a Glorious Night of FreeLove? Wow, I knew Sparklett was desperate but I didn't think it was that bad."

"Your sister wasn't desperate. We love each other."

Crystal shook her head in disbelief. "Sparklett can't afford to fall in love."

"Well she did," said Zook, getting angry. "I don't have to explain it to you."

"Okay, I'm sorry, you're right," said Crystal.

"What makes you such an expert, anyway? All you ever do is blow things up and kill people."

He seemed to have hit a nerve. "Do you think I *like* to do this?" she said. "I used to be nice once. But I can't be nice while The Bob careens the world into a suicidal war with the Machines. Somebody has to do something and somehow that somebody is me."

Crystal's passion unnerved Zook. He had never met a true Radical before.

They rode along that way for some minutes. At one point, the headlights of the snycles following them disappeared, and Zook thought Crystal had lost them until lights reappeared much closer, maybe a mile back.

"Can we outrun them?" he asked.

Crystal glanced in the rearview mirror. "We're petro, they're electric," she said. "Their range is limited. With any luck their batteries will give out."

"Then we better get lucky pretty soon," said Zook, "because the plops are gaining on us."

Zook watched with mounting anxiety as the snycles drew closer, like wolves closing in on prey. The snycle on the right had a single bright headlamp, whereas the one on the left had a dim center headlamp and small yellow running lights on either side.

"They're coming," Zook said helplessly as the two snycles moved closer still, rooster tails of snow blowing up behind them glowing red in the tail lights. Now he could make out the form of the closest driver, silhouetted in the other snycle's light. The guard reached down to his side and suddenly a blue hazer beam swept wildly across the snow behind, throwing up a wall of steam behind which the snycles temporarily disappeared before punching through.

"They're be on us in a minute," said Zook.

Crystal drew the antique projectile weapon out from her jacket and thrust it into Zook hands. "When they get close enough, shoot them," said Crystal.

"I can't do that," said Zook. "Shooting a plop is against the law."

"It's them or us," said Crystal. "Do you want to die tonight?"

Zook suddenly recalled the dismembered body of the giant, sliced in half by a hazer from the guard tower. What happened to the giant could happen to him, and it would be so unfair to be diced by a hazer and left bleeding in the snow. Zook wiped his hands on his shirt and examined the pistol. "How does it work?"

"That little button above the trigger arms it," she explained. "Sight along the barrel and pull the trigger when the target is aligned—just like a hazer. But aim carefully because there's only ten bullets."

"Bullets?"

"Hypothermic chemical pellets driving lead projectiles," she said.

"What?"

"Mechanical charges," she said.

The closest snycle was less than 50 yards now. Zook took a deep breath and steeled himself. Shooting a plop went against the grain of his entire FreeEducation, but even delta smelt had the right to self preservation. He raised the weapon, wishing he had an actual hazer, and sighted along the barrel through the rear window.

"Not through glass!" Crystal said. "Roll down side window and shoot through the opening," said Crystal.

"But they're behind us," Zook said.

Moonlight revealed that they were cutting across a vast snowy bowl. Crystal swerved the wheel violently, and the SnoTrak swiveled on its base and immediately began climbing straight up the hill, putting Zook in a better firing position. Rolling down the passenger window, he pulled off a shot at the closest snycle.

The weapon's loud *crack* startled Zook and the flash of the muzzle caused the snycles to wobble and peel off the track laid down by the SnoTrak, passing diagonally behind the vehicle and across the snow. The riders were identically dressed in the big gray coats of recycled wool that was the uniform of the prison guards. One was bearded, the other had a black scarf drawn up over cheeks and nose. Both wore glasses similar to the multi-radiance safety goggles that was standard equipment at Zook's old laser battalion.

Crystal continued to pour on the power and the snow crawler climbed steadily, straight up the increasingly steep hill. The snycles seem to struggle with the change in inclination. The black-scarved rider drew a hand hazer from a side holster and aimed it toward the cab. Crystal jerked the wheel to the right and the bolt of blue plasma missed, burning a trench in the snow with a sharp hiss.

On Zook's side, the bearded rider also crept nearer, hazer in hand. Before Zook could shoot, the snyclist sent a plasma ball directly into the rear of the vehicle, blowing a hole in the cargo gate with the force of a small explosion and sending a shower of molten metal droplets bouncing against the windows of the cab like hail.

Zook took aim but the snyclist carved an arc in the snow to Zook's right as he looked back.

"I can't shoot!" Zook yelled. "They're both on your side!"

Crystal suddenly slew the wheel of the SnoTrak, sharply swiveling the metal treads. They continued sliding uphill for a moment, then rapidly started tracking down the hill 180° from their previous line of travel.

The snyclists, caught off guard by Crystal's maneuver, overshot the cab and wobbled as they tried to slow. Zook took aim at the closest rider, the bearded guard whose shot had blown up the cargo bay. Between the motion of the SnoTrak and his unsteady arm, Zook struggled to aim the weapon but hoped for the best and pulled the trigger.

Another loud *crack* and the plop he had shot grabbed his chest and lost control. The snycle began skidding to its side, then fell and began rolling, throwing the driver into a shallow parabola through the air. He hit the slope, hard, bouncing up and colliding with the caroming snow cycle before both tumbled down the hill into the darkness.

"I got him!" Zook said.

The other snycle, though, was already making a long arc at the edge of their headlight, trying to flank them.

Crystal hugged the wheel as she spun the SnoTrak around again on one tread and pointed it diagonally up the slope. The remaining snycle fell momentarily behind, then turned and matched their speed from behind on a parallel course.

Zook took a shot and missed, even as the remaining rider brought his hazer up to bear. Another plasma bolt ripped the darkness and, in a flash of steam and ice, slashed into the snow on Zook's side, tearing the SnoTrak's hood from its hinge and shattering the windshield. The SnoTrak dipped into the newly formed crater and, despite Crystal's best effort at the wheel, spun out of control down the slope, launching the occupants upward against their restraining harnesses, then throwing them violently forward as the SnoTrak lurched to a halt, its engine dead.

In front of them, outlined in shadow at the farthest range of the headlamp, the cyclist slowed and raised his hazer toward the disabled cab.

Without thinking, Zook pointed his weapon and fired. The guard twisted in agony and grabbed his side, causing his snycle to skid while the hazer lanced-out harmlessly into the sky. The snycle bounced off a bump in the terrain and launched into the air before crashing back to earth and throwing the rider into the snow. The limp body rolled and skidded to a stop on its back.

Ears ringing, Zook braced himself and blinked, trying to clear his eyes of the afterimage of the hazer bolt. Gradually, the angry streak cleared from his vision and he could see the guard clearly. His head, neck broken, lay under his body at an impossible angle.

Zook slumped back in his seat and began shaking violently. Now he was beyond mere trouble. Not only had he escaped from Heat Station Antelope, he had run off with a Two Brother's member and murdered two guards. True, the guards had tried to kill him first, but he didn't think that would make any difference in a UCC court of law.

Crystal lay a hand on his shoulder, apparently mistaking Zook's silence for grief. "You did what you had to," she said.

Zook pushed his hand away. "No. This is your fault," he yelled. "You made me come. I wanted to go back."

"That wasn't an option," Crystal said.

He came to a decision. He would make his way to FriendsterVille on his own and present his petition to Wild in person, before Crystal got him into even deeper trouble. "I'll stay with you because I have to but as soon as we get off the ice sheet, we're splitting up."

"We'll talk about it later," Crystal said. "Right now we'd better check the damage or we might not be going anywhere at all.

Before Zook could reply, she climbed down out of the cab and came around to the front passenger side, where the SnoTrak had taken a shot. Zook joined her. The sheet metal was burned through and the bumper chopped in half, but the treads appeared intact. Crystal crawled under the front with her flashlight.

"The bogies look okay, but some of the blocks are melted on the suspension," she observed when she emerged.

Without the vehicle they would be in big trouble. "Will it work well enough to get us off the ice?"

"I'll have to take it slow and the steering is going to be dodgy."

"But we'll make it, right?"

"I don't know," she said, flicking off the flashlight. "I'll see if I can get the engine to fire."

Crystal hopped in and turned the ignition. Zook could hear a clicking sound under the hood.

"Hold on a second," he yelled, opening the hood and (by feel since he could barely see) making sure all the wires were seated, a minimal talent he had picked up during the Flash War.

This time the engine coughed, ran roughly, then evened out to a steady rhythm. Zook was amazed and inordinately pleased with himself when he climbed back into the cab.

"Nice work, Zook," Crystal said.

"Thanks," Zook said. The animosity he had felt toward Crystal just a few minutes before melted away somewhat.

"We've got to get going," Crystal said.

But when she threw the SnoTrak into gear, it lurched forward and immediately made a sharp skidding turn to the right. Only by wrestling the wheel to the left could she get the vehicle under control.

"That's better," she said, and began to accelerate past one of the downed snyclists.

"No wait," said Zook. "That cycle. It doesn't look too damaged. We should take it with us."

She slowed the SnoTrak and looked. "The solar charger is smashed."

"I can rig it to charge it from the SnoTrak," said

Zook, adding, when he saw Crystal's skeptical look: "I've done it before, during the war."

"All right," Crystal said, appraising Zook with a new level of interest.

Zook clambered down to investigate. The taillights of the SnoTrak cast an eerie red glow onto the metal parts of the wrecked snycle. The machine looked intact, except for the solar cell cowling and bent handlebar. The dead guard was pinned underneath, and Zook tried not to look as he pried the bike upright and gave a gentle tap to the throttle. The electric motor whirred and he had to squeeze the brake to keep it from getting away.

"It works," Zook yelled, waving Crystal down from the cab.

She took the handlebars from Zook and jumped on the seat, deftly accelerating the cycle along the slope and looping it back around to the tailgate.

Zook was surprised by her riding ability. He was actually starting to believe she could have grown up in Palaska.

Together they grabbed the forks of the snycle and heaved it up over the twisted lip of the gate. Zook climbed up into the SnoTrak bed and with pushes and pulls got the machine into position, fastening it down as well as he could with some half-frozen hemp rope.

"Let's get going," said Crystal. "They'll be more plops along soon."

"You're slipping," said Zook.

"What do you mean?"

Zook rolled over the snyclist's body, found the hand hazer and held it up to show her in the dim moonlight.

"You're right, I *am* slipping," Crystal said, looking chastised.

Zook felt a little surge of self-confidence, but managed not to gloat. "Let's find the other."

19.

ALL FOR ONE AND ONE FOR ALL

The SnoTrak rumbled into life and began crawling across the ice plain, Crystal intent on navigating by the compass. Her hair, peeping out from under a black watch cap, was as long and fine as her sister's, and perhaps she had once been as soft and tender as Sparklett. Her face was wind-burned, however, and her manner brusque, without any of Sparklett's gentleness. Life in the prison camp as a Two Brothers' operative had made her hard. She needed rest and nourishment to restore her health.

Exhausted, Zook scrunched himself back in the seat with his arms wrapped around himself, trying to stay out of the draft of the broken window. He found his mind returning again and again to images of the escape from Heat Station Antelope and the gun battle with the guards on the snycles.

"Why are you doing all this?" he finally asked. "What do you hope to accomplish?"

Crystal looked at him. "Surely my sister told you. The Bob wants to go to war again, against the Machines."

"I don't believe it."

"All that booty The Bob's been sucking out of the slavicens? He's buying up men and materials to attack Sand Francisco."

Zook shook his head. "No. The Bob's spent his lifetime building up the UCC. Why would he risk it all in a war he couldn't win?"

"Why does any tyrant want more?"

211

Zook couldn't believe his ears. "The Bob's not a tyrant," he said. "He's a Uniter."

Crystal snorted. "Yeah, like in uniting people's head with their feet in the shredder."

Zook didn't understand her skepticism, and responded with the Standard Narrative. "If it weren't for The Bob, the UCC would be run by a hundred little warlords."

"You mean like the AssemblyPersons, each controlling his own small district and paying tribute to the emperor?"

"The AssemblyPersons are elected," said Zook, provoked.

"Only after they've been pre-selected."

"We have Betters for our protection. The Bob is keeping EvilBizMen from rising up and exploiting us."

"There are no 'EvilBizMen' and if there were, the people would be better off. Instead of picking at ruins to create booty for the overlords, we could be actually be producing something of value. And get paid to work instead of being forced to work. Between the UCC and EvilBizMen, I'll take EvilBizMen."

Zook couldn't believe Crystal would defend EvilBizMen. "But then we'd have to pay Exploiters for all the Perks we now get for free."

"Everything's free except what really counts—the freedom to think for yourself."

"That's crazy! Freedom of thought is guaranteed by the State. I've had 12 years of Decolonization Thinking."

"You haven't been *de*-colonized, you've been *re*-colonized," said Crystal. "And you're not just a slave, you're pwned."

Zook felt quite angry now. "I am *not* pwned. I'm a free slavicen."

"Can you even hear yourself? How can you be free

and be a slave? It's a contradiction in terms."

"No it's not. It's the Social Contract everyone learns about in school—'All for one and one for all,' 'The strong protect the weak,' 'From all to the State, to all from the State.'"

"Yeah, beautiful. But what about, 'Obey here now'?; 'Don't interrupt Friendster'?; 'Silence=Perks.'"

"'Rules make slaves free,'" Zook quoted.

"Absurd. You're only free to think and do what *they* want you to think and do. Have an original thought and it's ridicule, prison and death."

"Not true."

"Of course it's true, or else you wouldn't be here right now. Do you think they really care about some ugly clown painting?"

"You wouldn't call it ugly if you saw it," said Zook. "It's an indescribable masterpiece."

"Says you."

He sat forward in the seat now, an angry expression on his face. He was so tired of having his opinion disrespected. "That's right, says me."

Crystal laughed. "Finally," she said. "I was beginning to think Sparklett had made a big mistake."

Zook continued glowering. "What do you mean?"

"I'm beginning to see what she sees in you. You're as stubborn as a donkey but at least capable of original thought. And you rise to the occasion. You're no coward."

She appeared sincere. But was she?

Crystal again laughed. "Relax, Zook, that was a compliment. We're going to need everything we have if we're going to get out of this alive."

Zook, perplexed, sat back, the icy wind pouring through the broken windshield. Crystal gave him one last glance and went back to concentrating on piloting the SnoTrak through the interminable space of darkness and light.

The argument with Crystal deeply disturbed him. He knew the Two Brothers were radical, but didn't see the point of attacking the entire Slave-Friendster system. He *liked* being a slave. Sure it would be nice to be a private slave rather than a state slave, but only because the perks were better. If the Vampire EvilBizMen ever got control again, things wouldn't be free. He'd have to choose how to spend any perks he earned, and everyone knew that was impossible without the extensive research of the State. He would be an ExploitedWorker, forever making someone else rich.

At the design circle, Zook had access to archives of pre-Zero art and knew that previous cultures had accomplished great things. They thought differently, yes, but was their thought any "freer" than his thought? What good would it be to be "free" if he couldn't even afford BasicCable? Free thinking had produced a world of marvels and beauty, but Because Pollution and War. Today's slaves didn't have to worry about any of that. "Your Betters Know Better." The Friendsters ran the world and you just had to Cooperate.

(They didn't appreciate his clown painting, though. Was that really why he was arrested? Boraxo was a small-minded also-ran, but couldn't he see the difference between an orange blob and a velvet clown? Could anyone really prefer a kitten poster to Pedro's masterpiece of light and shadow?

Only AssemblyPerson Wild seemed to share Zook's appreciation of the Pedro, and that gave Zook hope. The AssemblyPerson would surely make everything all right. He had to, because… Pollution and War… No, wait— Pollution and Climate Change… Or was it Climate Change and War? No, Zook was very tired, his mind wasn't working the way it had been taught… Because *Super Social Justice,* that was it… Zook was a Loyal

Slavicen and he therefore was owed a big fat helping of *Super Social Justice...* Wild could give it to him... Wild *would* give it to him... Didn't he once free a slave from the Shredder who had been unjustly accused of illegal crocheting?

Wild was truly Defender of Slaves... Zook only had to talk with him and his problems would be over...)

+ + +

A subtle shift in the sound of the engine woke Zook. The cloud-covered sky, low and ominous, seemed perceptibly lighter than the snowy ground.

Dawn.

Crystal stopped and slammed the door as she got out of the cab, jolting Zook fully awake. She rooted around in the cargo bed and returned with a paper bundle, which she handed to Zook.

"We better eat something," she said.

Zook unwrapped the paper and found bread, quinoa, and chunks of soy loaf—all items he recognized from the camp dining hall and all frozen. He took an icy piece of soy loaf for himself and handed the rest to Crystal, who had already put the SnoTrak into gear.

Zook found that they were ranging through a broad valley with high hills on either horizon. Gradually, along with the brightening dawn, the hills grew higher and drew in closer. Now, off to the left, the slopes took a sudden leap and became mountains, exposing rocky crags with great bowls of snow sweeping down to where their tiny SnoTrak crawled through an immense white landscape.

They continued along the valley or for some time, Zook watching idly as a hawk glided alongside to their right, flicking its wingtips and dipping and soaring in the air currents. There would be slim pickings for any hawk hunting for food in this snowy landscape, unrelieved for miles by any sign of forest or even vegetation. The valley grew deeper and the mountain walls closed in on them. The sky, overcast, hovered above them as a uniform ceiling of luminous gray. Zook glanced at the compass and saw that they were heading southwest.

The hawk, still gliding on the air currents, drew nearer, matching almost perfectly their rate of travel through the increasingly steep canyon. There was something peculiar in the way it flew, its black wings hardly moving at all as it adjusted its position in the air.

Suddenly, Zook knew why. "We've got a skyster at ten o'clock," said Zook.

"Damn," said Crystal. "I was hoping we could at least get through the pass." She stepped on the pedal and threw the SnoTrak into a higher gear, the damaged steering making a high-pitched whining sound.

"It still on us," said Zook.

"Is it big enough to be armed?" said Crystal.

Zook looked more carefully. It appeared to be about the same size and configuration as the solar skysters the plops deployed around Mento.

"I don't see any hazer pods," said Zook.

"Surveillance, then," said Crystal. "They'll keep it on us until they can send something bigger."

Zook reached for the one of the hand hazers on the floor. "Pull over," Zook said. "I think I can shoot it down."

Crystal brought the SnoTrak to a halt, but the skyster flew far off to the right, too distant for Zook to get a steady lock on the hazer's tiny screen.

"No good," he said. "We'll have to lure it closer."

"How?"

Zook thought. "If it works anything like the town skysters we could go out with our hands up. They'll send it in to investigate and we'll have a chance at a shot."

"Unless it keeps station and waits for reinforcements."

"You have any better ideas?" said Zook.

Crystal shrugged and pulled out the hazer they had taken from the second dead guard. The skyster was nowhere in sight, so they each hopped out of their respective doors, more or less simultaneously.

Just as they exited, every piece of glass in the SnoTrak cab simultaneously shattered and the upholstery tore itself apart and exploded into the air.

RipGun, Zook recognized, from his Flash War experience. He dove to the ground beside the snow tractor. From the corner of his eye, he saw Crystal pointing her hazer into the air behind her.

Only then did Zook see the skyster, not 50 yards off and approaching rapidly. A white flash enveloped Crystal, even as Zook raised his hazer, got a lock and triggered the bolt of blue energy.

The skyster's wing took a direct hit and the skyster began coming apart. Zook heard another *brrrrrrip* of supersonic micropellets from the RipGun. But the pellets missed and only created a harmless shower of snow on the ground. What was left of the skyster spiraled to the ground, where, just beyond the SnoTrak, it crashed into the snow with a thud and disintegrated into dozens of pieces on the hard pack.

Crystal. The white flash he had seen horrified Zook. Had she been hit? He scrambled from his position and rounded the front end of the SnoTrak, where he found her lying flat on her back, trying to sit up.

"Nice plan," she joked as he approached.

Zook felt a huge surge of relief. Crystal's eyebrows were singed but she appeared otherwise uninjured.

"Thanks be to The Bob," Zook said. "I thought you had been RipGunned to death…"

"Hazer misfire," Crystal explained. The weapon lay on the ground beside her, its still-smoldering power pack half-melted.

He helped her to her feet. Together they walked over and surveyed the scattered remains of the skyster. Up close, they could see the firing nipples of the RipGun.

Crystal gave it a kick. "That was a serious oversight on the RipGun. We could have both been killed."

"I'm rusty on my skyster I.D., okay? I'm not used to running from the plops."

"Where there's one of these there's bound to be more," Crystal said, ignoring his outburst. She looked around. They were in a shallow defile gradually leading uphill toward a low pass. "We need to find some cover and we need to find it fast," she said. "There are some rock formations on the other side of that ridge."

Zook saw nothing better. "Let's go," he said. "If we can." He nodded toward the damaged SnoTrak. "Do you think it will even run?"

The RipGun's high-velocity pellets had broken every window and torn a huge flap off the roof. Inside, chunks of foam upholstery were everywhere, the steering wheel was missing a chunk, and the gearshift lever had been whittled down to half its former size. A few of the cargo boxes in the rear had been split open, but the engine compartment seemed untouched.

Crystal climbed in the cab and turned the key. The engine started right away but she was unable to get the vehicle into gear.

Zook hopped in and tired to help her. The stub of the gear shift lever didn't allow much leverage. Zook wrapped the sharp metal in a chuck of upholstery foam and was finally able to push the lever into place by using both hands.

The SnoTrak started slowly forward.

"We're going to have to work together," Crystal said. "I'll drive, you change gears."

"I don't know anything about gears," Zook said.

"There's a pattern," said Crystal. "I'll show you."

In truth there wasn't much to it, especially since the terrain kept their speed to a crawl. With Zook at the gears and Crystal behind the wheel, the SnoTrak began crawling up the slope toward the pass, the wind icy in their face.

At least the sky remained free of skysters. Clouds moved in as the mountain grew higher and closer on their right, making the snowpack look gray and flat.

The ridge top proved deceptively distant, continuing to rise in a long irregular arch each time they reached what appeared to be the summit. The higher they went, the windier it became, with swirls of blowing snow obscuring their view. Then the mountain peaks themselves became shrouded in cloudy mists.

Zook gradually mastered the shifter. All the while, he strained to see the sky, keenly aware a skyster could be on them at any minute. *Cover,* thought Zook, *We need cover*, but in either direction there was no cover to be seen.

The trail leveled out as they reached the top of the pass at last, then narrowed and curved even as it began to descend. There was still nowhere to hide the vehicle, and the path, such as it was, grew rougher, obstructed by huge chunks of fallen ice and drifts of snow. Crystal carefully skirted the obstacles, picking her way along the snow-blown path while Zook silently gripped the gear shift, expecting the vehicle to slide off the narrow passageway into oblivion at any moment.

"Where are these rocks?" Zook asked at last.

"I don't know," said Crystal. "We should have reached them by now."

Suddenly the ground began to dip more steeply. Crystal halted the SnoTrak and peered into the shredded fog, straining to see the terrain in front of them. A sudden gust cleared the air, revealing a vast featureless bowl of snow sloping down from the heights to the right onto a broad snowy plain below. A ceiling of clouds, flat and gray, hung over the bowl just above them, hiding the actual peaks.

The ragged fog parted a little more and Crystal suddenly pointed. "There," she said, indicating a huge rock overhang on the far rim of the snow bowl.

"Can we get across the slope?" Zook asked.

"We have to," said Crystal.

"That's a long way in the open if a skyster shows up," said Zook.

The fog swirled. A rolling bank of mist engulfed the upper side of the mountain slope in a sharply defined layer.

"Those clouds," Crystal said. "If we can get inside them, we'll at least have some concealment as we cross."

"It might work," Zook agreed.

"Do we have a choice?"

Zook couldn't think of anything.

A moment later they dropped the tractor into the snow bowl and began crawling diagonally up the slope, with Crystal pulling hard on the wheel to get the treads pointing in the right direction and Zook working the gears. The damaged steering mechanism squealed and whined in protest as they climbed through the intermittent fog toward base of the cloud layer.

"I don't know how much longer the treads can take this," said Crystal. "We're going to have to level off."

Just then, a huge dark shape darted through the air downslope and below them. It was a skyster, larger than the last, and carried under each wing a row of small black tubes. This one was definitely armed; Zook recognized it from his military days as a fuel-cell powered AJ-40. The tubes mounted to the wings contained six small heat-seeking missiles.

The skyster overshot them and continued soaring across the width of the bowl, and for a moment Zook thought they had been undetected.

Then it banked and began a wide turn back toward them.

"We've been spotted," said Zook. "Go go go."

"Were already going as fast as we can," said Crystal.

The SnoTrak groaned and strained as it clambered in first gear up the increasingly steep slope. While Zook watched, winds in the valley buffeted the skyster, causing it to bob up and down and veer erratically as it struggled to gain altitude.

It was still below them when the snow crawler finally entered the layer of squalling clouds. One minute they were in the clear, the next they were engulfed in swirls of fog and pelting snow—a white out storm.

"Where is it?" Crystal said.

"Can't see," said Zook. "The storm might throw it off for a while but if it gets a lock on us with its missiles we're goners."

"The crawler's a sitting duck in infrared," said Crystal.

"Let's put it in second and hope we make it," Zook said.

But instead Crystal brought the SnoTrak to a halt and flicked off the ignition. The silence, after the hours of travel, seemed deafening.

"What are you doing?" Zook asked.

"The heat sensors will find us in a minute, even in these clouds," she said. "We have to abandon ship."

"We won't get far on foot in this weather," said Zook.

"We'll bivouac until the skyster's gone. We can return to the SnoTrak later if it's still in one piece. Grab what you can from the cab. There are blankets in the crawler bed."

At the mention of the crawler bed, Zook suddenly remembered the flares he had tripped over earlier, during the escape from the camp. He glanced out the window and saw the split-open box.

Crystal was stuffing her jacket pockets with food, compass and weapons.

"Wait," said Zook, "You get us to those rocks. I'll take care of the skyster."

"How?"

"The flares."

Crystal looked doubtful.

"Trust me," he said. "I've done it before." Actually he hadn't, but he had seen it done by a fellow slave during the Flash War.

A black shadow sped swiftly through the clouds above them—the skyster.

"Okay," said Crystal, revving up the SnoTrak once more. Zook helped pop the vehicle into gear, then—as the machine sped forward—scrambled through the smashed rear window into the crawler bed.

He grabbed up a loose flare from the box that had broken during the escape and quickly pulled the igniter top. The flare came alive with a hot red flame and he immediately threw it as far as he could in the SnoTrak's wake. If he could get enough flares deployed, it should be enough to confuse the heat sensors on the skyster, buying them time to reach the rock outcropping at the far ridge.

The crawler continued horizontally moving across the slope, tilting precariously. The red light of the first flare receded into the distance and disappeared in the fog. Zook quickly lit another, throwing it downslope of their position, and then a third, which he threw upslope.

Suddenly there was a tremendous flash in the clouds behind them, accompanied by a shock wave that knocked Zook off his feet and left his ears ringing. The crawler lurched and the tailgate, already damaged in the escape from the camp, fell open. Several wooden boxes and the poorly-fastened snycle, its tie-downs severed during the RipGun attack, spilled onto the snow.

Out of the corner of his eye, Zook saw Crystal wrestling with the wheel. When she glanced back to make sure Zook was alright, he made a thumbs-up gesture and quickly scrambled to his feet.

The crawler resumed its lurch through the mist across the slope, and Zook threw out another flare, and then another, each disappearing from view within seconds in the featureless mist that surrounded them.

Then, in the distance, downslope and farther away, came the boom of another explosion. The deception was working—the skyster was wasting its missiles shooting up decoys—but Zook was running out of flares. The box was empty and all but two of the flares that were scattered over the crawler bed were squashed or broken.

The precarious tilt of the SnoTrak grew somewhat less, and Zook realized they must be nearing the far end of the bowl. His mind raced ahead. If they could just get to the rock overhang near the ridge, the tilting slabs would help hide the SnoTrak's heat signature, and they could bivouac nearby. With some luck the crawler could be saved.

The mist closed in. Zook tossed out another flare, throwing it far down the slope hoping to keep the skyster below them. Now only one left. The wind swirled and Zook caught a momentary glimpse of the rock outcrop a hundred yards distant. He hesitated, then ignited the last flare and threw it with all of his might after the other down the slope.

It was still arcing on its way when a huge explosion rent the air with a blinding flash.

Zook felt himself tossed into the sky as if swatted by a giant hand, and glimpsed the crawler tilting to its side beneath him, one track torn loose and hanging at an odd angle.

The air was full of snow, and it swirled around him

as if he were being shaken in some demonic snow globe. He smashed against something and rebounded into the air, and again saw the crawler tumbling beneath him.

The driver door had been thrown open and the cab was empty, but he hardly had time to register the fact before he again thudded back to the snow, this time hard, and he realized he was pitching in a wave of snow down the face of the mountain, faster, ever faster as great blocks and chunks of snow flew over, up and around him.

Avalanche.

Zook had read about avalanches, and even—when he was stationed in the mountains during the Flash War—come across wide swaths of forest which had completely been destroyed by a wall of falling snow.

But he never thought he'd be caught in one, or die in one.

Once more he saw the great bulk of the crawler, this time in pieces, flying through the air off to his left. Then the wave of snow carried him past the SnoTrak and over the lip of an icy cliff. He was falling, falling, falling in a cloud of white.

Hammering into the ground, he somersaulted like a ragdoll, then mercifully passed out.

20.

REUSE, REPURPOSE, RECYCLE

A voice, far out in the white distance, cried out: "Zook. Zook."

The voice was plaintive but sweet.

Zook, in a dimly conscious portion of his mind, heard the voice and wondered who it was that was calling him and why.

"Zook," came the voice again.

Zook drifted. He found himself again with Sparklett, on the promontory above Mento harbor, the night they had made love. She was kissing him, slowly, drawing out his desire in her slow, teasing way. Never had he met a woman so confident and alive, and never had love-making been so thrilling—so dangerous.

Again the cry: "Zook. Zook, are you there?"

Zook resisted. Zook had heard about love almost every day in the UCC, but all of the sex he had had was in realty loveless. Zook know that now. Sparklett had opened him up emotionally.

"Zook."

Another image arose: a clown, sprawled broken on the ground, unconscious, his top hat crushed.

Zook's consciousness returned to his body with a snap like the snap of a flag in a wind gust, and he found himself half-buried in the snow at the tail of the avalanche field.

The hovering clouds were now a thousand feet above him. He had no idea how long he had been unconscious.

"Zook. Are you out there? I can use some help."

Zook roused himself and tried to stand, only to realize his lower body was encased in snow as high as his waist.

He had to get free.

"I'm coming Sparklett," Zook yelled. "Hang on."

"Zook, it's me, Crystal."

Crystal. Zook shook his head to clear it. He and Crystal, not Sparklett, had been escaping together in the SnoTrak when a skyster blasted them with a missile, causing the avalanche.

He looked up. The skyster was nowhere to be seen.

Shoveling with first one hand and then both, Zook began to dig himself out. His left glove was missing and the fabric of his jacket was shredded up to the elbow; a huge red gash ripped diagonally across his forearm, but it was no longer bleeding and Zook felt no pain.

"Zook," came Crystal's voice.

It was maddening, but the deeper he dug the heavier and icier the snow seemed to become, until the bare fingers of his left hand were leaving streaks of red blood as he dug. He was down to his thighs now, his knees, the top of his boot.

By twisting and wiggling, he finally managed to pull his right foot free, completely out of the boot. His ankle throbbed but seemed to be intact. More digging freed the actual boot, its laces torn from the eyelets. He threw it aside and continued digging until he was able to free his other foot, then pulled himself out of the hole and fell, exhausted, into the snow.

"Can you hear me?" came Crystal's voice.

"I'm coming," Zook cried out, trying to make sense of the torn landscape left by the avalanche. Great blocks of broken snow lay all around him. The crawler had disappeared without a trace. "Where are you?"

"Here," said Crystal. "Follow my voice."

She seemed to be upslope and to the left. Zook shoved his swollen foot back into the loose boot and began climbing up the slope, which alternated in texture between slabs hard as concrete and loose drifts which swallowed his legs whole.

He still didn't see Crystal.

"Where are you?" yelled Zook.

"I'm here," said Crystal. "I need some help."

The voice was now behind and below him. Somehow he had gone too far. He scanned the slope but saw nothing.

"Right in front of you," yelled Crystal. "Look straight."

And then Zook saw a brown slash in the blue shadow of a giant snow bolder. He staggered closer. The slash was a face, half-buried in the snow. It was Crystal, upside-down, with her feet higher than her face. The rest of her body was invisible under the snow.

He crawled to her and began digging around her head.

"Zook," she said. Her face was swollen and misshapen and her skin pale, but she managed a smile.

He smiled back. "I'll have you out in a minute."

"I'm a little hurt," she said, matter-of-factly.

"Where?"

"My arm. My leg. I'm not sure where else."

Zook gently began to excavate around her body. She was more than a little hurt. Her right arm was resting lightly on her chest, apparently unharmed. But her left was twisted around underneath her torso, dislocated from the socket of her shoulder so far as Zook could tell.

"We have to keep going," Crystal said. "We can't let them find us."

"Quiet," said Zook. "You're not going anywhere until I get you fixed up."

Crystal looked at him with serious eyes. "Well, fix

me up."

Zook by now had dug a cavity beneath Crystal's torso to free her dislocated left arm. The wrist appeared broken as well, but he couldn't leave the arm underneath her.

"This is going to hurt," Zook said.

"Do what you have to do," said Crystal.

Zook reached under and took the damaged arm by the elbow, moving it as gently as he could back over her chest. Crystal clenched her teeth.

"Now for the shoulder," he warned.

Cradling the broken wrist, Zook gave the upper arm a jerk to reset the shoulder into the socket.

Crystal's screams echoed across the vast snowfield until suddenly her eyes rolled up and the scream died on her lips.

I've killed her, thought Zook. But no, she was still breathing. She had merely passed out from the pain.

Working quickly, Zook continued to excavate her legs, which like her left arm, were twisted into an impossible unnatural position.

She began to come around.

"How do you feel?"

"Good enough," said Crystal.

"Can you move your legs?" Zook asked.

"I think so," said Crystal.

She slowly uncoiled and straightened her left leg.

"There."

"Okay," said Zook. "Now the right."

"Now the right," she said.

Steeling herself, she closed her eyes and gradually began to move her right leg, biting her lips and whimpering in the process. Her thigh moved fractionally, then fell back into place.

Crystal lay gasping.

Gingerly, Zook felt down the upper thigh and paused

over her lower leg, which was distended and swollen. Gently, he pulled back the ragged work pants over the injured area. There was no blood, but the leg was broken above the ankle. She writhed as he touched it.

One thing was for certain, he had to immobilize her injuries.

He started searching the debris field for anything he could use as a splint, climbing over or around the boulder-like chunks of snow left by the avalanche. He found an intact water bottle and stuffed it in his pants pocket. Nearby was the pocket light he had seen Crystal carrying the night before. He took that, too. A little further was a rectangle of gray cardboard which proved to be a treatise on feminist glaciology; the cardboard would make a good splint, along with a metal arm that had been part of the SnoTrak's windshield wiper. With some bits of a frayed wiring harness to tie everything together, he returned to Crystal.

She proved remarkably stoic, allowing Zook to work on her broken arm and leg with a minimum of fuss, even though he clearly was hurting her. Only once, when he tried to manipulate her broken tibia back into a semblance of a normal position, did she cry out in pain, thrashing her head back and forth and tensing her entire upper body.

"Are you okay?" Zook asked.

"What do you think, you stupid ass! Hurry up and finish."

He checked his work. It wasn't going to win any medical awards, but her shoulder and wrist were immobilized and the splint on her leg reasonably secure.

"This bone is shattered. You need medical help."

"You're it."

He hesitated. "They're sure to send plops soon. We'll have to stay here and surrender."

"No way," Crystal said. "The mission is too

important."

"But—look at your leg!" said Zook.

"The other one's good. I can ride the snycle."

"But you can't," said Zook. "We lost the snycle during the missile attack."

"What do you mean, lost?"

"It's up there on the slope somewhere. The blast blew the tailgate open and the snycle bounced out."

"Then go get it."

"Impossible," said Zook. "I have no idea where it's at."

"You have to," said Crystal.

Zook stood with a sigh and scanned the mountainside. Nearby, slabs of ice lay scattered across the snowfield in either directions, dotted with bits and pieces of the crawler and its cargo–a bent door, a gear from the SnoTrak tread, a smashed box of parts. Upslope, the avalanche had churned the snow into a vast chaotic bowl, like the froth of an angry sea frozen into stillness.

The snow cycle was somewhere near the top of the mountain, at least a couple of miles away. Finding it would mean hours of dangerous climbing on snow that might still be unstable. But if he could retrieve the machine in working order, they still might be able to evade the plops. He could get Crystal off the ice and find her the medical care she needed.

For the first time since the avalanche, Zook's anxiety began to lift.

"I'm going to retrieve the snycle," he said, with more confidence than he felt. "I'll be back as soon as I can."

Crystal sat up painfully. "Find me a crutch. I'm going with you."

"The hell you are. The faster I can get the snycle, the faster we can get out of her."

She relented to his logic. "Go."

He left her the water bottle and his jacket, which he wouldn't be needing as long as he kept moving. The snycle was above and to his left. The ceiling of clouds still hung below the peaks, though whether at the same level as an hour ago he had no idea. He started up the slope.

It was tough going. Huge, irregular slabs of snow had been thrown to the bottom of the avalanche path, and he spent his first half-hour picking his way over and around these obstacles. As he climbed, the disturbed snow grew smoother, but the slope grew steeper. He frequently had to pause to catch his breath, turning downslope to avoid the cold wind blowing down from the mountain top. At first he could clearly see Crystal sprawled out on the snow near some of the crawler debris, but as he climbed higher her figure became smaller and harder to make out.

The snow, roiled by the avalanche, varied in consistency, hard enough to easily climb in some places, soft and deep in others. He worried about the stability of the snow under foot and gradually traversed his way to the left, so that Crystal would be out of the path of any slide he set off.

Another hour's hard climb brought him near to the base of the cloud layer. Gingerly, he climbed off the avalanche path onto the untouched snow in the direction the crawler had come. A few inches of fresh powder lay atop an icy crust. It took his weight but was cracked into huge slabs which seemed ready to pull loose and slide down the mountainside in a repeat of the morning's accident. As quickly as he dared, he moved across the slabs away from the avalanche zone until the snow finally felt stable underfoot.

Then he headed upward again, the ragged base of the cloud layer swirling around him. His only chance of finding the snycle was to backtrack along the path the crawler had taken. Soon he was entirely in the clouds, and visibility dropped to almost nothing. In the pearly, shadowless light, he almost missed the path of the crawler treads that he was searching for.

He turned and began following the tread marks back along the direction the crawler had taken. The snycle should be somewhere ahead, probably downslope. The cloud cover gave him pause. If the snycle were more than a dozen feet from the trail, he might miss it entirely in the wall of white. He kept walking, slowly, his eyes straining.

He had just about concluded that he had somehow passed the snycle when the crawler tracks zig-zagged wildly upslope. A few yards further on he found an empty box and a can which once had contained petrol fuel, then caught sight of the black bulk of the snycle itself.

It lay on its side, half-buried in the snow, its treads upslope of its seat. The battery pack was dented, but the rest of the wiring seemed intact. He dug around to free the steering column and pulled the snycle upright. The throttle and brakes were still attached to the handlebar. He was no expert on snycles, but he had ridden them a few times during the Flash War. He straddled the crooked seat and gave the throttle an experimental twist. The treads turned and the snycle rolled forward. It seemed good to go.

+ + +

45 minutes later, after a fast and only half-controlled descent of the mountain, Zook picked his way through the tail of the avalanche field and brought the snycle to a halt in front of Crystal.

She was lying flat on her back in the snow, covered with his jacket. She only turned her head when he shut the snycle off. She looked very sick. When she first tried to sit up she fell back, and Zook saw that her skin was pale and her teeth chattering. "We've got to go," she said.

"Let me take a look at those splints."

"No," she said. "There was a skyster. It circled a long time."

"Did it spot you?"

"I don't think so. It would have shot me."

"I don't see it now."

"It left, but they'll send plops soon," she said. She repeated: "We've got to go."

Zook looked up at the sky and tried to estimate the sun's position; they still had a few hours of daylight left if he could get her onto the snycle. "All right," he said. Zook got behind and helped Crystal pull herself upright. She stood on her good foot, breathing heavily and leaning on Zook.

"Okay?"

She nodded and with Zook's help limped toward the snycle.

"Good," said Zook. "Now sit. I'll help you get your leg over."

He took hold of her injured leg and—as gently as he could—managed to get her into position on the saddle with her legs on the passenger stirrups.

She cried out.

"Sorry," said Zook.

"There's some pills in my pocket," said Crystal. "Better give them to me."

The pills—five of them—were wrapped in a wad of toilet paper and unmarked, but Zook recognized them as FreeRush, a drug sometimes issued to slaves who had to stay awake for long periods. In prolonged use it caused heart palpitations and could sometimes be fatal.

"Do you think that's a good idea?" Zook asked.

Crystal gave a weak laugh. "How do you think I got this far?" she said. She popped a pill in her mouth, hesitated, then took another. "Let's go."

Zook watched her stuff the remaining pills in her pocket. Her color looked a little better and she seemed stable on the back of the bike. Maybe seeing that the snycle was intact and working gave her a new hope.

In any case, it was time to get out of there. He got astride the snycle and powered it on.

He hoped they had enough charge to make it off the ice.

21.

WE HAVE ACHIEVED BEIGE

"Hold on," he warned, then twisted the throttle, sending a small plume of snow from the back track. The front of the snycle had a narrower steering track, which Zook used to weave in and around the huge chunks of snow left by the avalanche.

Crystal held on with her one good hand, at first leaning her head heavily on Zook's back, then sitting upright and becoming quite chatty as the FreeRush took effect. He slowed and tried to listen until he realized that she was rambling incoherently—"Gotta hold on gotta get out of here Zook watch out gotta keep going..." After that he speeded up and let her ramble.

For the next hour, they made slow, steady progress, with Zook heading south using dead reckoning skills he had picked up in the military. He drove slowly to avoid unseen perils beneath the snow and avoided surges to preserve what charge was left in the battery. The power gauge was broken and he didn't know how far they could get on the snow cycle, but every mile they managed to travel was one less mile they would have to walk.

He didn't want to think about getting Crystal to walk.

Gradually it began to snow, lightly at first, then more heavily. The winds picked up and snow began to swirl.

"That's going to cover our tracks," Zook called back. Crystal answered with a grunt. Her talkativeness had long worn off, but she continued to lean upon his back with her good hand thrust into his jacket for warmth.

From time to time he felt her shivering, which reassured him that she was, at least, still alive.

He pressed on. A half-hour later, the storm began to let up. For some time now they had been going downhill, and as the clouds gradually lifted, the snow stopped and visibility improved. The snycle crossed a small ravine and began to lose power. As it slowed, Zook feathered the throttle, which bought another 50 feet of progress before the machine stopped completely.

The battery was dead.

The sun, which had been hidden all day, flashed for a moment from behind a cloud low on the horizon. Zook, who had been tapping the snycle's power gauge, looked up. The horizon was actually visible in the distance, and it was no longer white but a smudgy brown-green.

"Look!" he shouted to Crystal. "The edge of the ice."

But when he turned he was shocked. Crystal's eyes were shut, and her face, where exposed to the wind, was pale white, as if drained of blood. Zook managed to prop the snycle upright with what was left of the kickstand, then carefully lifted her from the seat.

Her pulse was weak and she appeared barely conscious.

Crystal's fractures were serious and the hours of travel on the snycle would have placed her in constant pain, but even so, Zook was puzzled. She was in much worse shape than he expected.

He knelt over her in the snow and shouted into her ear. "Crystal! Can you hear me? We're almost off the ice. Wake up!"

"Zook," she said, opening her eyes.

"What's wrong? Are you okay?"

"Okay," she echoed.

Zook didn't think so. Her lips were blue and her teeth chattered uncontrollably. He put his fingers under her arm and tried to judge her body temperature.

Hyperthermia, he thought. Or maybe shock. He didn't know how to tell the difference.

In any case, he had to get her warmed up. Although the clouds were breaking up, the sun would soon dip below the ice and temperatures would plummet.

He took off his jacket and wrapped her in it. "I'm going to make a shelter," he said.

"Let's keep going," Crystal said—but closed her eyes.

+ + +

Zook found a drift on the slope just above them and spent the next twenty minutes frantically digging a snow cave. As taught in the army, he made a trough where cold air could collect and an elevated ledge for sleeping. The space wasn't very big but it would get Crystal out of the wind and their body heat would warm it.

It was dusk when he finally carried Crystal inside the snow cave and laid her on the ledge he had made. Zook piled snow around the entrance to block the wind, reducing the view of the outside world to a narrow slit. Fire was impossible. There was nothing to burn and he had no way to get a fire started. Nor was there anything to eat. But he had done all that he could.

He crawled onto the ice ledge and curled himself against Crystal. He could barely see her in the gloom and fumbled to find the pocket light he had picked up in the avalanche debris. He stuck it in the snow to illuminate the roof of the cave; it would last at least another few hours, and he needed to keep an eye on Crystal. She was conscious but unresponsive, and her lethargy worried him. Whether in hypothermia or shock, should he even let her sleep?

"Crystal, talk to me, okay? How do you feel?"

"Not good," she said. She lay on the bed of snow with her eyes closed, breathing shallowly.

Zook remembered the FreeRush pills. They had

seemed to help her earlier, if only for a while. He dug into her pocket and put the remaining three pills into Crystal's mouth. "Chew," he commanded, giving her a little snow to help her swallow.

There was, of course, no immediate effect. Zook sat, frustrated, waiting as the light continued to bleed from the sky.

The wind swirled outside. Crystal moaned.

Could there be another injury that was causing Crystal to crash?

He examined her again. Her shoulder was still in place and the splints looked good. He ran his hands down her torso, searching for anything he had missed.

When he touched her stomach, she winced in pain.

Zook rapidly undid the buttons on Crystal's coat and then the work shirt underneath. Her belly at the place he had touched was grossly swollen and tender to the touch.

She was bleeding inside, some internal organ damaged in the tumble of the avalanche.

Zook's painful prodding roused Crystal, who raised her head to watch what he was doing. She took in her bruised and swollen stomach and clenched her teeth as finished his examination.

When they caught each other's gaze, she said, lucidly and simply, "I'm going to die."

Zook buttoned her up again, trying to buy himself time to think. For Crystal to have a chance, the internal bleeding would have to be stanched. But Zook had no surgical tools, not even a pen knife, and even with instruments he wouldn't know how to treat such an injury.

He was forced to agree with Crystal's assessment. She was going to die. The plops had killed her as certainly as they had killed the other escapees.

And there was nothing he could do about it.

"It's getting late," Zook said, adjusting the neck of

her jacket but avoiding her gaze.. "We'll rest here tonight and see how you feel in the morning."

"No," said Crystal, suddenly quite agitated. "The papers."

"What?"

Crystal's face was more animated and she seemed stronger—the FreeRush he had given her was taking hold. She forced herself up onto her good elbow and slowly undid her jacket buttons, withdrawing a sheaf of folded papers.

"Here. Take them."

Zook recognized the papers pieced together by the prisoners from confetti. There were three folded sheets, hard to read in the dim flash light, but each page filled with nonsensical characters.

Zook looked at them in shock.

"You know what it is?"

"Yes," said Zook. It was the Machine code the prisoners had been reassembling at Heat Station Antelope.

"This is an only copy. My sister is waiting in FriendsterVille. Whatever happens to me, you have to get these papers to her."

He drew back. Suddenly everything he had witnessed at Heat Station Antelope fell together and made sense— the fight in the workroom, the fire at the geodesic dome, the hidden SnoTrak. It was all part of a plan so that the Two Brothers could steal the code from the Host's safe. And now Crystal was asking Zook to become an accomplice.

She saw the look on his face and reached to touch him with her good hand. "It's important, Zook. The most important thing ever. It could save all of humanity. Whoever controls this code controls the Machines."

The words were coming out in a rush. "The Bob thinks he can use those Machines to defeat Palaska in a war of conquest," she continued. "But instead he'll break the truce."

"Truce? What truce? A truce with Palaska?"

"The truce with Ekso."

"Who is Ekso?"

"The King of the Machines."

"That's crazy!"

"Is it? You were in the Flash War. The Machines were poised to completely destroy what was left of the world. Haven't you ever wondered why the fighting ended?"

"Everyone knows why. The Bob's Glorious Offensive."

Crystal, angry, sat up on her elbow. "Listen to yourself, Zook. You're just parroting the party line."

"It's the truth. All the Herstorians say so. I just saw a special on FreeVid."

"Zook, *think*. Of course the public broadcasting server is going to lie for the State."

"But *why?*"

"Don't you see?" she said. The drug was really kicking in now; her strength seemed almost normal. "The Bob and his Friendsters don't just want obedience—they want your soul. And what do they give in return for your soul? Just enough security, just enough food, just enough sex—and just enough fear—to keep you exactly where they want you."

"So what's *your* solution?" Zook said. "FreeFall? Where everyone has to find a job on their own and pay for everything they want themselves? I don't want to live in a cruel world like that."

"And yet you like a clown painting."

"So what?"

"So they haven't completely zombie-ized you. You can still think for yourself. That's what my sister saw in you—and why I'm asking you to get those papers into

Sparklett's hands."

Zook didn't believe in a soul and didn't see what it had to do with helping Crystal steal State papers.

"Zook, please, if not for me, then for Sparklett. She needs you. She's the one who's made the greatest sacrifices. Without her, I'd have quit long ago. You have to help us."

Zook squirmed uncomfortably, then suddenly hit on a happy solution. "Let's just destroy them. Then no one will have them and everything can stay the same."

"Useless. Meaningless. We can destroy this key, but how long will it be before The Bob unearths another stash of documents with another copy of the code? No. The only solution is to help the Machines close the back door that the code represents. And for that you have to take these pages to Sparklett."

She gripped his wrist with the surprising strength of the FreeRush and wouldn't let go. "My sister is waiting in FriendsterVille. You must get the code to her. Promise me."

The grip on Zook's wrist weakened as the effects of the FreeRush finally began to wear off. Crystal's eyes momentarily fluttered, then opened wide again.

"Promise me," she said. But this time her voice was hoarse.

"All right, I promise," Zook said.

Still Crystal maintained her weakening grip. "Swear to God."

God. There was a word Zook hadn't heard in awhile.

"I swear," he said

Crystal's hand fell from his wrist. "Good old Zook," she said. Then, barely audible: "My sister picked good…"

Her voice trailed off and she was dead.

+ + +

The rest of the night passed in a daze.

241

Zook slumped over her body for almost an hour, holding Crystal to him and hoping that somehow he could infuse life back into her inert form. The wind howled, the light burned out and the cave turned pitch black, until at last he accepted defeat and turned himself away in the darkness.

But he didn't, couldn't, sleep. He had made mistakes—big ones. Why hadn't he examined Crystal more thoroughly, or at least have noticed earlier the symptoms of her internal injuries? Couldn't he have opened her up with some kind of make-shift knife and found a way—a compress, perhaps—to stop the bleeding at the source? And after she was injured, why had he given into her insistence to escape? If he had waited with Crystal at the avalanche site, they would have been found by the authorities by now. Surely they would have been taken back to the camp, if only for questioning. Crystal would have gotten real medical care. She would be alive.

What was he going to tell Sparklett?

Then there was the fantastic story of the code document. How much of Crystal's story should he believe? Certainly the UCC had been making great effort to extract *something* from the masses of confetti at the station, and the document Crystal had pressed into his hands appeared authentic. If the papers were what they appeared to be, it would explain her involvement in the Two Brothers and the ruthless abandon of her escape.

The rest of Crystal's story couldn't possibly be true. A truce with the king of the Machines? Another disastrous war? The end of humanity?

That had to be the FreeRush talking—although, he had to admit, it was similar to the story Zook had heard from Sparklett.

But there was no way The Bob would ever purposely lead the country into war—was there? The UCC was the

Peace-and-Love party. "Give Peace a Chance," "We Prefer Peace," "Peace is Higher than Truth"—Zook had been hearing these slogans daily as long as he could remember. Only a power-crazed madman would want war. Zook refused to think it. The Betters knew best.

(But some Betters were corrupt. The plops had illegally arrested him, just for rescuing a clown painting, and the administrator at his hearing had unjustly sentenced him to three years in the FunZone, which wasn't a FunZone at all but a prison. AssemblyPerson Wild would have to take severe measures to punish the perpetrators of this brazen abuse of Slavicen Rights.)

Still, what was he going to tell Sparklett? If both she and Crystal were really members of the Two Brothers, Sparklett would be willing to die to protect the code— just as Crystal had. But no one deserved to die like that—shot at by plops, hounded by skysters, and left to freeze to death on an icy plain in the middle of nowhere. Even if the papers were the code Crystal said they were, the State had over-stepped its bounds.

(Or did the State have any bounds? Had he really traded his soul for a gilded choke collar?)

The papers. Everything came back to that. When dawn finally arrived, Zook dug his way out of the snow cave and examined the documents in daylight. There were three pages, each meticulously reassembled, like a complex jigsaw puzzle, from thousands of tiny pieces of confetti. Each page was densely packed with 57 lines of apparently-random characters, both numbers and letters. The initial code group was 1A5TJ.

It did indeed to be appear to be a Machine cipher, and might even be the Creator code.

Whatever it was, Crystal had been willing to die to get the papers to Sparklett—and Zook had sworn to help her do it.

Zook sighed. If he were caught with the papers it

would surely be interpreted as an act of treason, with a death sentence in the Shredder. Maybe he should just turn the papers over to the authorities?

(Unless the pages really would Save the World?— absurd. Saving the World meant sorting recyclables, not delivering secret state documents for a radical organization.)

In the end, he re-folded the papers and put them back into his pocket. He had promised to deliver the code to Sparklett, and he would.

At dawn, Zook buried Crystal in a shallow grave he clawed into the hard-packed snow with his hands.

Then he set off across the ice on foot for FriendsterVille—Crystal's papers, and his petition to Wild, in his pocket.

22.

DON'T WORRY, BE HAPPY

Eight days later, the train on which Zook had hidden himself began to slow.

Zook, sleeping in the corner of a coal hopper under a recycled tarp, lifted himself to the edge of the car and saw a dingy industrial complex rising from the desert, and, beyond that, in the distance, the towers of FriendsterVille—all exactly as the shepherd had said.

It was the shepherd who had saved Zook when he finally stumbled down off the edge of the glacier, exhausted and starving. The shepherd had spotted Zook long before Zook had spotted him, and—no questions asked—had taken Zook into his camp, fed him, and hid him from the skysters which suddenly appeared from the direction of the ice. The shepherd was not a member of the Two Brothers, but had nursed back to life more than one half-frozen, half-starving escaped prisoner who appeared in his fields. Zook couldn't remember the last time he had received help from a private person instead of a designated State agency. The man had no expectation of a reward and could only get in trouble if his actions became known.

Zook recuperated with the shepherd for five days. When he was strong enough, the shepherd guided him to the rail line. There, after a morning spent waiting, Zook finally hopped the train which carried him across the mountains and desert to FriendsterVille.

+ + +

Now that he was arriving at the capital, Zook's one concern was to get to the palace of AssemblyPerson Wild. Where Zook found Wild he would find Sparklett. She would be waiting for Crystal to show up with the recovered papers, and Zook would have to break the news about her sister's death. He dreaded that task. Whatever was in the code, he doubted it had been worth Crystal's life.

Still, he couldn't wait to see Sparklett, to hold her in his arms and kiss her gently on the lips. He didn't know how they would arrange to be together, but knew somehow they would make it happen—right under Wild's nose if it came to that.

But Zook couldn't afford to alienate the AssemblyPerson. Only Wild had the responsibility and authority to untangle the skein of missteps and mistakes which had wrenched Zook out of his comfortable state slave existence and turned him into a ragged, identity-less fugitive. Wild was Zook's Defender, his last chance for Super Social Justice.

(Or were slaves just meat, as Crystal had said? FreeLawyer Poundsand and Administrator Green were part of the justice system and they had done nothing for Zook. But they didn't own clown paintings, either. Surely anyone who could appreciate a Pedro would be able to discern the massive injury Zook had suffered at the hands of the law?)

He would know soon enough. Wild's palace was straight ahead as the crow flies. He had to get there.

The train jerked over a switch, couplers banging, and came to a standstill on a siding at the edge of a huge industrial facility. Zook made sure no one in sight, then climbed down out of the hopper. Around him were trains-loads of coal, piles of coal, and a crazy zig-zag of conveyer belts all loaded with coal. The conveyers ran into a squat, gray building with smokestacks belching black clouds of smoke into the air. Massive electrical towers carried power lines straight from the plant across the desert to FriendsterVille in the distance.

An illegal coal-powered generating station in full operation, and just miles from FriendsterVille! Zook could hardly believe his eyes. How could this massive environmental crime be tolerated by the High Friendsters, who from the capital would be able to see the belching black carbon emissions rising from the multiple smokestacks? Power production for all slavicens was mandated to come from renewal sources. Zook would have to bring this outrage to the attention of AssemblyPerson Wild so that the authorities could act.

As he stood gawking, a movement caught his attention and he threw himself into a ditch along the tracks. Near the head of the train Zook had been riding, a soldier emerged and clambered up the ladder of one of the coal cars. The soldier—wearing the black uniforms of HomeLove Security—carried a high-powered hazer with spare battery packs slung over his shoulders bandito-style.

Even as Zook watched, another pair of soldiers emerged from a signal hut on the other end of the yard and began walking toward their colleague. Zook put his head down and hunkered in the ditch. As the men came closer he was able to make out snatches of conversation:

"This is bullshit! How long they going to keep us out here?"

"Better here than in the city. At least we won't get our asses shot off."

"The rebels are finished. Except for this Zook guy maybe."

"Zook. What kind of a crazy name is Zook?"

"I don't know but he's armed and dangerous. Supposedly he has some strategic information."

The men's voices faded but Zook's heart continued to

beat out of his chest. He had thought he left the search party far behind, but somehow they were searching for him here. How could they be expecting him? Had they found the shepherd and forced him to talk?

And who were the rebels the men were talking about? Had there been a slave rebellion? Such things were rumored to happen. Why else would there be fighting in the city?

Zook decided it didn't matter. All that mattered was that he make it to FriendsterVille without being apprehended. Sparklett and Wild were the key to getting everything unraveled. He had to find Wild's palace.

The road to FriendsterVille roughly paralleled the edge of the power complex, but on the other side of a tall chain-link fence. He'd never be able to climb that unseen. The only break in the fence was a road crossing far down the tracks.

The soldiers were methodically inspecting the coal cars, climbing up the ladders one-by-one. Zook waited until all were engaged, then began crawling down the length of the ditch toward the road.

Twenty minutes later—elbows bloody, dust burning his throat—Zook crawled to a halt near the crossing. It would be easy enough to make a dash across the road, but he would be clearly visible to the soldiers in the distance, and well within hazer range. Unless he wanted to wait until nightfall, the only alternative was to continue crawling along the drainage ditch, this time along the tracks as they receded from the facility, then find his way back to the road.

Just then, the headlight of an approaching train appeared in the distance, giving Zook a new idea. As he watched, the light wavered and drew closer, until through the heat he could make out the shimmering form of the environmentally-friendly solar locomotive.

Gradually, ever-so-slowly, the train approached the

generating plant, laboring to pull its heavy cargo of coal. Then it was upon him, crossing the intersection and blocking the view from the soldiers' hut.

Zook jumped out of his weedy hiding place and made a dash for it, running full-tilt down the crumbling asphalt of the crossing and through the gates of the complex. While the train continued to rumble across the intersection, Zook aimed himself at a derelict building along the road and ran for his life, half-expecting to be hazered in the back before he made it to safety.

A glance over his shoulder showed the train just clearing the intersection and two soldiers emerging from the signal hut. Zook sprinted and threw himself onto the ground in the safety of the shadow of the building's rear wall.

He lay in the sand gasping, catching his breath. He was out of the power complex and safe.

He was just about to get to his feet when a voice rang out:

"Freeze right there. Keep your hands on the ground. If you try to move, I'll kill you."

Zook did what he was told, but not before he raised his head high enough to see the HomeLove Security soldier in the doorway, pointing a hazer rifle directly at him.

The man with the hazer wore a sergeant's insignia, and at his nod three more soldiers emerged from doorway. In what appeared to be a well-practiced routine, two drew their hand hazers and stood back, while another approached and dragged Zook erect by his collar.

"Up," he said. "Hands against the wall."

Zook, desperately trying to gather his thoughts, put his hands on the wall, which was hot as an oven in the desert sun. Crystal's papers were hidden in his jacket lining, along with his petition to Wild. From the conversation he had overheard at the power station, Zook knew he was a wanted man. But without any form of identification, would they know who he was?

He decided to bluff. "What's this all about?" he protested.

The soldier smashed a fist into the side of Zook's head.

"Quiet," he said. The man smelled strongly of garlic. He ran his hands up and down the length of Zook's body, extracting articles from Zook's pockets and tossing them to one side.

"A hazer," he announced. "A piece of cheese. A water bottle. Some string. That's it—no FreeFone and no papers. Nothing that can be a code."

"Friendsters," Zook said. "I am but an itinerant FreeWorker, travelling between FreeFarms to help with the FreeHarvest."

"Your name?" asked the sergeant.

"Uh, Public Trust Bleck."

"Where's your FreeFone?"

"I unfortunately lost it," said Zook.

"Why are you carrying a hazer, FreeWorker Bleck?"

"I found that on the railcar I was riding. I took it along to return to authorities."

The sergeant looked at Zook skeptically. "Scan him," he said to the soldier on his left, a tall thin fellow with carrot-colored hair.

The red head pulled out a monocular-like SlaveCam and focused it on Zook's face. The device flashed three times in rapid succession. The soldier looked at the reading on the side and then showed it to the sergeant.

"It's Zook," the sergeant said. "Tie him."

The man nearest Zook at once forced Zook's arms against his back, expertly binding his wrists with a hemp slave tie.

"If you try to run, we'll shoot you dead," said the

sergeant. "You're under arrest."

Zook's bluff had failed. He couldn't believe he had made it all the way across the ice field only to be apprehended here, at the very edge of FriendsterVille.

"But—what did I *do*?" Zook whined, feeling genuinely outraged even though another part of him could think of a thousand infractions with which he could be charged.

"Save it for the interrogation," the sergeant said. Then, to one of his men, "Bring up the eMob."

+ + +

Sparklett stood at her bedroom window in the former Bob-O-Sphere, clutching a military-issue knife and steeling herself to kill Wild.

Hazer fire still flashed in the streets of FriendsterVille below, but the fighting was drawing to a close. The Bob's remaining forces were isolated and leaderless, and Wild's consolidation of power was almost complete. If she didn't act this very evening, she might miss her chance.

In Sparklett's eyes, Wild had signed his death warrant that afternoon when he announced—before a special meeting of the Emergency Committee—that the attack on Sand Francisco would proceed. Victory would be swift and bloodless. Certain codes, he averred, were on his way to him even now that would neutralize the Machines.

Madness, Sparklett knew. The Machines would view an incursion on Sand Francisco—rightly—as a renewal of human aggression. By breaking the truce between man and Machine, Wild would set off the devastating war that she and Crystal had worked so hard to prevent.

Sparklett had obliquely pressed Wild about how he had obtained the codes. If he really did have them, the most logical source was Crystal. That meant she had been captured and tortured. The organization of the Two

251

Brothers was deliberately compartmentalized so that even Crystal wouldn't be able to reveal much, but Sparklett's cover would definitely be blown.

Wild, however, acted normally around Sparklett and gave no sign that he was in any way suspicious of her. Maybe he had obtained a copy of the code, in which case her sister could still be alive. Sparklett had operatives frantically searching the city for Crystal but so far no sign had been uncovered.

But regardless of how Wild had gotten hold of the Creator Code, Sparklett was left on her own to prevent Next War 5. Her plan was to plunge the knife into Wild's heart while he lay asleep, then throw open the tower to the waiting forces of the Two Brothers. General Lowe would be arrested and members of the Assembly either bought off or exiled to Narizona. Under martial law, Sparklett would assume the reins of power herself. The state slaves would be freed whether they wanted to be or not.

But first—kill Wild.

Sparklett heard the "ding" of the elevator and realized he was coming. Quickly but noiselessly she crossed from the window to the bed, curling in a ball under the covers with her hand not far from the ceramic knife's handle and feigning sleep.

The tumbler on the outer door clicked and she heard Wild enter the outer suite. Then he was in the bedroom and approached the bed.

"Look at you," he said. "Sleeping like a baby."

Sparklett opened her eyes and pretended to stir awake.

"What time is it?" she said, in the sleepiest voice she could muster.

"Late," Wild said. "Very late."

His voice seemed weary, with a note of sadness. He took a seat at the foot of the bed and laid a hand lightly on her calf. "So beautiful," he said.

"Come to bed," Sparklett said, her hand curling around the handle of the knife.

"In a minute, dear," said Wild. "I'm afraid I have some bad news for you."

He paused.

"Yes?"

"Your sister is dead."

An icy chill fell over her. It was confirmation of her worst fears. Under a cover story, she had kept hidden from Wild all the details of her real background, especially her relationship to Crystal.

"Sister?" she said, carefully controlling her voice. "What do you mean? I don't have any sisters."

"You're not familiar with anyone named 'Crystal'?"

"Crystal?" she forced herself to say. "No. Who is that?"

"A traitor," he said. "She froze to death on the edge of the glacier. My men found her two days ago."

Sparklett felt as if she had been slapped, but she managed to keep a calm demeanor. She knew Crystal had escaped Heat Station Antelope with the machine code. They must have found the code on her body, which is why Wild was so confident he could stop the Machines in Sand Francisco.

He sat observing her with a faint smile on his face, waiting for her to crack, to show some emotion acknowledging that her sister was dead.

In one smooth swift motion, Sparklett tightened her grip on the ceramic knife, flung herself up and plunged the blade into Wild's heart.

But instead of ripping a hole in his soft flesh, it struck something hard and glanced off harmlessly. His shirt tore open to reveal a plastishield vest.

She pulled back her arm and tried again, this time aiming for his throat, but he grabbed her wrist with such force she cried out and dropped the knife.

"Guards!" yelled Wild.

The door burst open and three of Wild's men came running in. The knife had fallen to the bed sheets, and Sparklett, with her free left hand, scooped it up and slashed at Wild's face.

He screamed and fell back, grabbing at the wound on his face and letting go of Sparklett's arm. But before she could stab him again, the guards were upon her: one chopping the knife from her hand, another grabbing her legs and the third snaking an an arm around her head and holding her in a headlock.

Sparklett squirmed and struggled trying to break free. But the combined power of the three men were too much for her. She, unlike her sister, had had poor ratings in her martial arts training.

Wild stood watching, one hand staunching his wounds, his eyes black coals, until she had exhausted herself. Then he signaled and his men dragged her upright.

"How long have you been Two Brothers?" he said.

"I don't know what you're talking about."

"Yes you do. Your colleagues at the FReeducation camp gave you up. Your traitor sister too. I know everything now."

Sparklett heart sank. But there was the possibility he was lying. "Then you know I've always been loyal."

"No," said Wild. "I was a fool. You're a spy now and you've always been a spy."

"What if I were?" she said. "The Bob was corrupt and had to be defeated. The Two Brothers worked to help put you in power."

"But now you want to kill me."

Sparklett said nothing. She was shocked. The network must be in complete tatters.

Wild seemed to take vindictive pleasure in her

dismay. "You never really loved me, did you?" he said.

"Yes," she said. "I did, once, a long time ago." She was startled to hear herself say it. She had been a bad spy, young and foolish, and it was so so hard to live a double life.

"Liar!" said Wild, blood dripping down his neck.

Sparklett wished it were so.

"What difference does it make," she finally said. "You mustn't use that code. It will mean the end of humanity."

"Pfft!" he said. "The end of Palaska maybe. Yes, I know you take your orders from Palaska. As did your traitor sister."

"No," said Sparklett. "My hero sister." She added bitterly: "I suppose you killed her to get the code."

"If only it were that easy," Wild said. "That idiot Zook has them."

"Zook!?"

"Yes," said Wild, bitterly. "Your lover."

Sparklett's head swam. Zook, alive and apparently free. If he had the code, there was hope yet.

She knew she must protect him if she could.

She gave her best imitation of a disdainful laugh. "Zook, my lover? You've got to be kidding."

"Your driver told me all about your night of passion," said Wild.

"Why would I sleep with a state slave like Zook?"

"One thing I can't stand is unfaithfulness," said Wild.

"The way you were faithful to me, with all your slave girls?"

"Little people," Wild said. "Executive privilege. But I never thought I'd be betrayed by *you.*"

"You'll betray the entire world if you use that code," Sparklett said.

"Enough," he said. "I don't take advice from traitors."

"The Machines will wipe us out."

"No," said Wild. "Because I'll control the Machines. When I get the code from Zook I'll have everything I need."

"Then I hope you never find him."

"I already have, my dear." Then, to his men: "Take her to SuperPAC."

23.

THE STRONG PROTECT THE WEAK

The eMob vehicle, with Zook locked inside a metal utility bin at the back, bounced and swayed over a neglected approach road toward the glittering palaces of FriendsterVille. The utility bin was padlocked, but by pressing his back upwards against the lid, Zook was able to create a crack through which he could observe his progress toward the city center.

Something had happened in the capitol. Along the road, neatly-maintained government buildings alternated with smoking ruins, and the deserted streets were piled with wrecked military vehicles and pockmarked with hazer holes. It was obvious there been fighting in the street, and Zook concluded that there must have been an insurrection against The Bob—an insurrection which The Bob had successfully put down, since HomeLove Security soldiers were everywhere.

But who would dare attack The Bob?

Zook could find no answers as the eMob gradually bore its way through several military checkpoints toward the city center. Then the eMob rounded a corner and he caught a glimpse of the Bob-O-Sphere.

The Bob's residence would have been an object of great curiosity to Zook had he been visiting as a tourist, but as a prisoner, he felt a surge of panic. Every state slave knew that the base of the Bob-O-Sphere housed SuperPAC, the infamous underground torture chamber and prison.

SuperPAC was the UCC's largest Permissible Action Center. Hardened political Ingrates were sent there for a process HomeLove Security called "acknowledgement, rehabilitation and recycling." The details of what went on behind SuperPAC's walls were not widely known, but—since slaves who entered its gates were never seen again—"recycling" was generally believed to be execution by Shredder.

If Zook were going to SuperPAC for interrogation, he *had* to escape. SuperPAC searches would be much more thorough than that of the soldiers who had captured him, and Crystal's code was sure to be found. Zook's Recycling would be swift and certain.

He had to get out of this box, and quickly.

He had already freed his hands of the hemp slave tie by rubbing it against the sharp rim of the bin. Now, as the vehicle picked its way circuitously through streets full of rubble toward the Bob-O-Sphere, Zook felt around inside, groping over the objects he found. There was a spare tire, a wheel hub, a canvas tarp, and a smashed cardboard box which felt like it contained some paper books or maps. Under the tire he was sitting on he felt a sharp pointed shaft of metal, which, when he was able to move his weight and work it loose, proved to be what he was looking for—a tire iron.

The vehicle rocked slowly over a rough portion of road, and Zook worked the edge of the tire iron under the rim of the lid and pulled. The lid shifted slightly, but he was unable to get much leverage because of his awkward position inside the box.

He turned on his side and tried again. This time he was able to work the tire iron under the lid, but couldn't pop the locked padlock on the outside. Peering through the open edge, he maneuvered the crowbar into the loop of the padlock and again pulled on the crowbar with all of his might. The lock itself remained stubbornly closed, but by jamming the tire iron back and forth, he was able to tear loose, one by one, the rivets of the boxes' padlock hasp.

Just as he worked the last rivet free, the eMob pulled to a stop. Through the partially raised lid, Zook could see the guard shack of a blockade, and beyond that—in the shadow of the Bob-O-Sphere—a ramp which disappeared downward into an ominous-looking concrete building.

SuperPAC.

In the other direction, the road stretched a long block down a bleak, shuttered roadway before being cut by a cross street in the distance.

Zook could hear the driver exchanging information with the guard at the barricade. He gulped. If he didn't run, he would be inside SuperPAC within minutes. If he did, the soldiers would have a clear line of fire at him all the way up the road.

He took a deep breath. If he could just make it to the cross street, he had a chance to get away.

It was now or never. He threw back the lid of the utility bin, pushed himself over its sharp edges and leapt from the back of the eMob. As quickly as he could, he lurched down the street, his cramped leg muscles screaming in agony.

"Prisoner loose!" the guard at the blockade yelled, even as Zook heard the sound of the eMob's doors being thrown open.

"Halt or I'll shoot!" came another voice, followed almost immediately by a hazer bolt that blew a chunk of asphalt from the roadway just under his feet. The blast gave wings to Zook's effort, as he found himself running toward the cross-street faster than he had ever run before.

"Halt!" came the command again.

There was nowhere to hide. The building entrances

on either side were bricked and shuttered. Zook began zig-zagging back and forth, trying to throw off the soldier's aim, but this time another, even more urgent voice, screamed "No!"

The hazer bolt went very wide this time, blowing a chunk of stucco siding off the building to Zook's left.

Zook leaped to the right.

Behind him the sergeant was screaming. "He's wanted alive, you idiots!"

The edge of the building loomed just ahead and Zook finally made it around the corner and out of the line of fire. He leaned against the brick wall, trying to recover his breath.

The sergeant was still barking at his men: "You, bring the eMob! You, seal the back of that street! We'll bottle him up in the alley way."

The narrow alley Zook found himself in ran between two tall brick structures. At the end of the block, it gave out onto a sunlit field of rubble. He had to make it there, to the rubble pile, before the soldiers could surround him.

Zook pushed himself away from the wall and started running, his hands pumping furiously. The alley ran an entire city block, punctuated by metal doors. Zook tried a few of the doors as he passed but all were locked. Then he heard the eMob behind him, screaming around the corner on two wheels.

He gave up on the doors and tore down the remainder of the alley, emerging into the sunlight just as a pair of soldiers turned the corner from the other side of the building. They saw Zook and immediately ran toward him. But before they could draw near, Zook was up and into the field of rubble, A mountain of broken concrete and metal rose up from a fallen building, and when Zook could no longer see his pursuers, he dived behind an enormous slab of canted floor, taking cover just as the eMob emerged from the alley.

"He's up there," he heard one of the pursuing soldiers tell the sergeant.

"Flush him out," the sergeant ordered his men. "And remember—*alive*."

Again, Zook struggled for breath. He didn't know if he could evade the soldiers another time, but if nothing else he had to get rid of Crystal's code, which would mean the Shredder if found on him.

Removing his tunic, he found a sharp fragment of porcelain floor tile and ripped open the shoulder lining of his jacket where he had hidden the papers. They were all here—his petition to Wild and the three pages of Crystal's code.

He threw the petition aside and began crawling toward a half-flattened filing cabinet that lay crushed under a slab of rubble, the drawers smashed open. He could hide the code there until Sparklett could retrieve them.

Suddenly a voice rang out: "Here!" a soldier yelled. He was standing on top of a mound of concrete not ten yards away, and was immediately joined by three other pursuers. They began to climb over the rubble converging on Zook's position.

Their weapons were holstered. Zook bolted from his hiding place, the code in his hand, and began scrambling across the jumble of loose debris.

He had to get rid of the code, but couldn't stop running and couldn't hide it anywhere while in full view of the soldiers. He began ripping the pages to pieces, code and petition together, but realized that even scattering the pieces wouldn't guarantee that the code wouldn't be reassembled again.

He stuffed a handful of torn fragments into his mouth and began chewing.

At the far end of the field, he could see a vast

abandoned staging yard stacked high with rusting shipping containers and overgrown with brush and small trees. He headed toward it. If he could make it into the container yard, he might be able to lose his pursuers, who had been slowly gaining on him despite Zook's desperate flight over the chunks of concrete and bent steel reinforcing rod.

"Stop," the closest soldier yelled.

Zook swallowed hard and stuffed more pieces of torn paper into his mouth, just as he reached the edge of the rubble field. But instead of gradually giving out, the piled-up wreckage formed a small cliff twice the height of a man. A drainage ditch lining the road to the staging yard was immediately below. Zook desperately looked for a route down the face of the rubble even as a pair of soldiers converged on him, needlers drawn.

Zook jumped into the standing water, the soft mud absorbing the energy of his fall but causing him to slip and tumble into the fetid water.

The soldiers looked down on him from above, one waving directions to the distant eMob, which Zook saw speeding toward him from the far end of the dirt road.

Zook dragged himself to his knees and crawled out of the ditch to firmer ground, shoving what was left of the code fragments into his mouth. Coated with mud and algae, the paper tasted so foul he had to force himself to keep from spitting it out. Chewing furiously, he started running over a patch of dry land toward the container yard. He only made it a few steps before the eMob pulled in front of him and blocked his way.

Then the soldiers were upon him, not using their needlers, but sadistically raining down on him kicks and blows.

Zook took his final swallow just as a kick to the head made him see stars.

"That's enough," the sergeant barked.

The blows suddenly ceased.

Zook, barely conscious, tried and failed to get up.

"Help him."

Rough hands dragged him to his feet. The sergeant looked at him with frank curiosity. "You Ingrates disgust me," he said.

Zook, his head still ringing, said nothing.

"Get him back in the eMob," the sergeant commanded. "And this time, chain him."

Heavy slave chains appeared from nowhere, and Zook was fettered hands and feet. Then, with a soldier on either side, he was frog-marched back to the vehicle and into the back seat.

They had got him in the end.

He had failed.

+ + +

The cell at SuperPAC was eight feet square, with a sink and toilet to one side of the door and a sleeping shelf on the other. The door was locked, the sink dripped, the toilet stank and there was no mattress, or even a blanket, on the concrete shelf. A previous occupant had managed to gouge the words "Kill The Bob" into the cement.

Zook, exhausted and shivering, sat on the words to cover them. He didn't want to kill The Bob or to be associated with anyone who did, and he certainly didn't want to be tortured. He just wanted his personal nightmare to end.

How he had got to this point? All of his life he had done his duty as a slavecin and gone along. As a toddler at FreePod, he had marched in a dress for Gender Identity Day, and later in middle school he learned to recite the Three Freedoms ("Freedom from Want, Freedom from Fear, Freedom from Religion") and the Three Absolutes ("Absolute Trust, Absolute Peace, Absolute Obedience"). During the Flash War, he had carried out every Friendster command, whether they made sense or not, and afterwards had enthusiastically voted-in the UCC.

("Better a state slave than a Bizman pwn," The Bob had famously said during his first and only campaign; Zook didn't know anyone who wanted to be a BizMan pwn.)

But now Zook was going to be interrogated and tortured by the very party he had worked to put in power. Wild would be outraged when he learned of the mistake—if Zook lived long enough to apprise him of it.

Zook felt confident that if he could just get an audience with the AssemblyPerson, all could yet be put right. Zook had never meant to break any laws, and therefore should never have been sent to Heat Station Antelope. Zook's escape from the prison was accidental, against his better judgment and against his FreeWill. Killing the guard on the snow cycle was an act of self-defense. Zook hadn't known Crystal prior to the escape, and he was not now and had never been a member of the Two Brothers.

Zook knew that his story might seem weak to someone like Administrator Green and his brother the Demonizer, but there was a further reason he felt certain AssemblyPerson Wild would look on his case favorably: the clown painting. He and Wild each owned a Pedro. It took a very sensitive person to appreciate Pedro's genius, and that—plus the risk involved in owning non-state-approved art—bound Zook and Wild in a special way. They were brothers in spirit, who, like Pedro, understood that the world was complicated and messy.

Could anyone who shed a tear with the clown in the paintings fail to right the terrible wrongs that had been done Zook?

Zook thought not.

Even now, he could still be saved if he could

somehow get to Wild. With the petition gone, Zook would have to present his argument face-to-face, which might even work to his advantage.

But how could he ever get to Wild?

Just then, a door creaked open at the end of the corridor and murmured voices were heard. The door closed and footsteps approached.

Was the torturer coming for him already? Zook rose and went to the barred window in the doorway. The hallway was dark, illuminated only in intermittent pools, but the person coming toward his cell was not wearing a bulky military outfit. Instead he seemed dressed in slave garb, and was carrying a bundle of neatly pressed clothes. The man approached and shoved the bundle of clothes into the corridor side of the pass-through. Zook couldn't make out his features in the shadows.

"Put these on," the slave said.

Only when Zook heard the voice did he recognize the figure as that of his friend, Sustainable Bacon.

"Bacon," Zook said in an excited rush, "What are you doing here? How did you know I was here? You won't believe what's happened to me. Who sent you? Where are we?"

Bacon stepped closer and stared at him for a moment through the barred window, an expression of scorn on his face. "Just put on the clothes. Don't cause me any problems."

"Bacon, it's Zook. Zook. Don't you recognize me?"

"Yes, I recognize you," he said. "Every time I see you it's trouble."

Zook was too excited to register Bacon's tone. "Bacon, what are you doing at SuperPAC? What's been happening in the city? A slave rebellion? There are soldiers everywhere and I got arrested and I think they're going to torture me and it's all a big mistake. Bacon, I need your help—you've got to help me get to Wild."

Bacon glared at him with loathing. "No one can help you," he said "And I wouldn't even if I could."

"What? Why not? What's wrong? You're my oldest friend."

"I am *not* your friend," Bacon said, harshly and loudly.

Zook was taken aback. What the hell? Then he realized: surveillance.

"I understand," said Zook, in a whisper and out of the corner of his mouth. "I've got to talk to your boss, AssemblyPerson Wild. He can straighten everything out. He's my only chance."

Bacon laughed and said out loud: "Don't ask me to join in your illegal conspiracies. You're an Ingrate to the State. You've betrayed us all."

"What?" said Zook. "What are you talking about?"

"I should have known," Bacon said bitterly. "You always had a chip on your shoulder, were always messing up a good thing—not knowing which side your bread was buttered on."

Zook was dumbfounded. "Bacon, what's wrong?" he whispered, still thinking surveillance was the problem. "Are they making you say that?"

"Shut up," Bacon said. "I've already lost my retirement Perks because of you. You deserve everything you're going to get."

Bacon turned and walked away—Zook's one and only connection to Wild.

Zook rattled the bars of his cell furiously. "Bacon! Whatever I've done, I'm sorry. Please—help me!"

Zook heard the door at the end of the corridor close and then he was alone.

Zook slumped against the door.

The torturers would be here soon.

What had happened to Bacon, to actually believe those kind of lies, after all they had been through together? Sadly, Zook realized that, in retrospect, the betrayal was predictable. He had seen it before, friend condemning friend, lover condemning lover, always when one or the other had crossed some invisible line with the authorities.

But the authorities were sometimes wrong, Zook knew now. Slavicens were arrested, given unfair trials, and sent to prison camps or worse, all based on whimsical accusations of anonymous accusers. How could that happen in a society built from the ground up on a solid foundation of Super Social Justice?

His head hurt.

Dully, Zook opened the pass-through and pulled out the garments, the first clean clothes he had seen in a month. There were underwear, a cloth belt, and a slave tunic stiff with starch. There was also a washcloth and a tiny bar of perfumed soap.

He sniffed at the soap suspiciously, then unfolded and examined the tunic. Why clean clothes for an interrogation?

He didn't know, but his current outfit had been reduced to rags. Quickly he stripped, washed himself in the tiny steel sink and stepped into his new outfit. Then he lay back on the sleeping ledge and waited.

No one knew exactly what went on in SuperPAC's interrogation rooms, but tales of hot irons, torn fingernails and gouged eyes had floated around in slave quarters for years. The torture was rumored to be unrelenting, and Zook worried how long he could stand up to it. He was not good with physical pain. His interrogators would want the code, but they would also want to know about Zook's connection to Crystal, and perhaps to Sparklett. He could truthfully tell them the code was destroyed, and that his escape with a member of the Two Brothers was strictly an accident.

If he repeated his story long enough and with enough

conviction, maybe they would eventually believe him.

Above all, whatever happened to him, he had to keep Sparklett out of it. She must be in FriendsterVille somewhere, waiting for the code that Zook had failed to deliver. But finding her now was impossible, and the slightest whisper that Sparklett and Crystal were connected would put her in grave danger.

Zook prayed she was all right—that she hadn't been discovered, hadn't been hurt in the recent fighting. He longed to be with her again. It seemed an eternity since he had held her in his arms, heard the warm murmur of her voice, kissed her yielding lips. They had wasted no time that night they had been together. They had made love three times, and lay together in each other's arms caressing and talking in between bouts of ecstasy. Zook didn't care if Sparklett wanted to blow up the entire UCC. Never had he felt so close to a woman.

Whatever happened next, he was determined not to betray her. He had to keep alive long enough to see her again.

24.

GO ALONG TO GET ALONG

The ordeal began minutes later, with a clank of the corridor door and the arrival of two burly soldiers, needlers in hand.

"Out of the cell, let's go," said the larger of the two, whose face was radiation-burned on the left side, apparently from a recent hazer blast.

"Where are you taking me?"

"You'll find out soon enough."

"I'm a slavicen," said Zook. "I want to see a FreeLawyer. I want my rights."

"Out," said the scar-faced man.

Zook hesitated. It was pointless arguing with them. They were just lackeys, and armed besides. He stepped out of the cell.

The men fell in on either side, each grabbing an arm and shoving Zook down the corridor door.

"I can walk on my own," Zook protested, trying to maintain some dignity.

"Shut up," said the second soldier, a tall thin boy in an overly-large uniform.

They continued to manhandle and push Zook along, first through the corridor door, then through a maze of twisting, block-walled hallways from which Zook could see no escape.

The walk seemed interminable, and the further they went the more full of dread Zook became.

"But Slavicens, I haven't done anything," Zook said,

knowing he sounded ridiculous but unable to keep the rising panic out of his voice.

"Everyone's done something," said the tall soldier. "You're here, aren't you?"

They came to an oversized elevator door which lacked both buttons and floor indicators. The scar-faced soldier inserted a small black key, and the men stood in silence until the elevator arrived and the doors began to open.

Zook assumed the elevator ride would end in the interrogation room.

He gulped.

The doors finished opening and the men began to push Zook inside.

Zook, realizing it was his last chance to get away even though there was nowhere to run, squirmed and tried to free himself, twisting and dipping his shoulders in an attempt to break the soldiers' grip.

The bigger of the two men, the one with the scar, twisted Zook's arm behind his back and shoved him into the elevator, banging Zook's face against the rear wall while the other soldier jabbed him repeatedly in the kidneys with a nightstick that had appeared from nowhere.

Zook thought they might kill him then and there.

"I'm going to report you to AssemblyPerson Wild," Zook screamed in frustration.

That got a reaction from the two men, who suddenly eased up on the beating.

"Yes," said Zook eagerly. "I'm going to report both of you to Wild. He's my Defender. He'll straighten all this out. I'm not supposed to be here. Take me to him immediately."

The men looked at each other, then released him. "Be good," the thin man said.

"And be careful what you wish for," the scar-faced

soldier added.

The interior elevator controls consisted of a single button. The thin soldier punched it and—after a ponderous delay during which the overhead speaker played a tinny version of the classic State song, "This Land Is Our Land"—the elevator began to rise,

We're going up, realized Zook. *Why are we going up?* Slave lore had always held that the SuperPAC interrogations took place deep *underneath* the Bob-O-Sphere, not at the top. Had they moved the torture chambers? Or were they just going to throw him over the edge, the way The Bob was rumored to have disposed of several of his enemies?

"Where are we going?" Zook cried out in panic. "Where are you taking me?"

Just then the elevator door opened, into a small alcove. Before Zook could collect his thoughts, the soldiers grabbed him by the arms again and dragged him out of the alcove into the pantry of what appeared to be a working commercial kitchen. Several slaves, bent over sinks and chopping boards, looked up as he was dragged though the kitchen and pushed through yet another door into another corridor.

Where the hell were they? The corridor was lushly carpeted and lined with bus trays of dirty dishes. Another steel door was in front of them, this one with a circular window the size of a small saucer.

The scar-faced man looked through the window and tapped the door gently with the back of his knuckle. The door buzzed open and Sustainable Bacon emerged, attired head-to-foot in his formal private slave regalia.

"In here," Bacon said, totally ignoring Zook but holding the door open for the soldiers.

They dragged Zook forward and shoved him inside.

Zook's jaw dropped. Instead of the interrogation chamber he was expecting, Zook found himself in an

271

elegantly appointed sitting room done up in the antique style of an EvilBizMan. The walls were soft blue, the ceiling ornately carved and gilded with gold, the rug under his foot an intricate pattern of flowers and birds. Through a curtained plate glass window on the right, Zook could see several burning buildings in the distance, their vast plumes of rising smoke casting a slanted shadow across a large portion of the city.

They were high up somewhere near the top of the Bob-O-Sphere.

"Put him there," Bacon said, indicating by a nod a plush Louis XIV armchair. "And you men wait outside the door."

The soldiers shoved Zook down into the chair then turned and exited the way they had come.

When the door closed, Bacon finally looked at Zook. "Straighten your tunic," he said. "Wipe the blood off your face."

Zook stood up. "Bacon, please, whatever happened to you I'm sorry. But you've got to get me out of here and help me find Wild."

"If you dare mention my name to the AssemblyPerson," Bacon hissed, "I swear I'll kill you myself."

"What?"

"Just wait," he said. And with that he turned and exited to room, through a second, larger door.

Zook, alone, immediately got up and went to the door that led to the kitchen. On this side, it was elegantly paneled, the little window disguised as a mirror. But looking through it, Zook saw the soldiers standing in the corridor.

Quickly, he moved to the other, larger door—the one Bacon had used to exit. It, also, was beautifully paneled with moldings and inlays, but there was no little window, and it was locked.

Trapped.

Dejected, Zook returned to his seat. What was he even doing here? Surely this was not the waiting room of a torture chamber—not with these furnishings and not at the top of the Bob-O-Sphere. It had to be some psychological ploy to soften him up for the real torture, coming later.

He wasn't going to stick around to find out. There was a tall candelabra on a table in the corner; Zook would use it to club Bacon when he returned, then escape through the larger door.

Zook was just about to rise and grab the candelabra when the large door flew open.

But instead of Bacon, in marched AssemblyPerson Wild.

Himself.

In person.

A thrill like an electric current ran up Zook's leg. Before he could even fall to the ground to grovel his respects, the AssemblyPerson approached him, a large smile on his face and hand outstretched.

"Slavicen Zook, welcome!" he said, the cigar in his mouth barely moving. "What a pleasure to see you! No no, sit, sit!"

"Friendster," Zook managed to croak out, allowing Wild to take his hand and crush it in greeting.

"You had me worried for awhile there, Zook," Wild said, plopping his huge body into a nearby armchair and pulling it closer to Zook. Wild was dressed in a perfectly-fitted Friendster's tunic of a rich shade of purple, hand-embroidered on every inch with an elaborate interlocking pattern of hawks and rabbits. On his hand was an oversized gold ring studded with glittering diamonds, but his face bore a long puckered slash mark that looked like it had been made that morning.

"What can I get you?" the AssemblyPerson was saying. *"Tarte au Citron? Cognac Napoléon?"*

Tart? Cognac? Such decadent delicacies Zook associated with the corrupt old EvilBizMen. There were so many things Zook needed to say that his head was whirling. But before he could speak, Wild was already ringing a little brass bell which sat on a nearby table.

Instantly Bacon appeared at the door, carrying an enormous tray with a selection of small cakes, coffees and cigars. He placed the tray between them, poured each a glass of cognac from a small decanter and discretely backed away—never once looking at Zook.

Zook looked at Wild in confusion.

"The UCC forever," said Wild, lifting his glass in a toast.

Zook picked up his glass tentatively (alcohol was forbidden), clinking it against Wild's and only taking a sip after Wild had lustily knocked back his entire glass. Even though Zook had tasted forbidden spirits in the military, Wild's cognac was more like a hot liquid fire than the coarse blinding liquid of his youth. He felt it run warmly down his esophagus and into the pit of his stomach, where it exploded with a warm glow.

For the first time, Zook understood why Friendsters liked to drink alcohol. "That's remarkable," he said, an involuntary smile on his face.

Wild smiled with him. "Isn't it?" he said. "Drink up. It's The Bob's own private stock."

"The Bob's own stock? Won't The Bob mind?"

"Not at all," said Wild.

Zook took another sip. There was no denying it was powerfully good. Wild watched smiling, like a father hovering proudly over an adored son.

The cognac flowed warmly to his stomach, and Zook felt himself totally relax. The room, the cakes, the drinks, and Wild's demeanor could only mean one thing:

somehow word of the terrible injustices that had been done to Zook since the discovery of the clown painting must have made his way back to Wild, and now—as Zook had always believed—the AssemblyPerson was about to make everything right!

The tension that had been holding Zook together suddenly dissipated and Zook felt tears of gratitude—real gratitude—springing to his eyes. Now that the moment of his vindication was upon him at last, he was so awash in emotion he could barely get hold of himself.

"Forgive me," blubbered Zook. "It's just that... I have been trying to meet you for the longest time."

Wild looked at him over the rim of his cognac. "And I you," he said, taking a puff on his big cigar. "I am breathless to hear more of your grueling adventure."

Zook felt more tears welling up and struggled to control them. His ordeal was finally over and here was a person—a Pedro owner!—who actually understood him. Thoughts poured out of him incoherently. "You have no idea," he said. "I was falsely arrested. The trial was a joke—and then that prison camp. There were criminals everywhere, infiltrated by the Two Brothers, and they forced me to escape—and all because I wanted to get a letter to you!"

"A letter? Why?"

"Well, it was all a horrible mistake. I never did anything wrong. It was all because I liked that velvet clown painting."

The cigar in Wild's mouth went rigid and he looked at Zook more intently. "Clown painting?"

"Yes, a Pedro, can you believe that? It was so beautiful I pulled it from the dumpster and brought it home. I had no idea you owned a Pedro, too."

For the first time since Zook had entered the room, Wild's composure dropped. "What are you talking about?"

"Your Pedro! I saw it in your gallery that day in the People's Palace. When I came to ask about the private slave position, don't you remember? But your guards thought I was some kind of intruder and, well, they needled me."

"I remember," said Wild.

"Yes," said Zook, "and then I got into trouble with my Friendster at work, and the plops followed me, and they found the clown painting and took it and the next thing I knew there was a fake trial and then they sent me to Heat Station Antelope."

Wild bent over and stubbed out his cigar, seeming to take an inordinate amount of time to do it.

When he looked up, he was smiling again.

"All very interesting," he said. But tell me about your escape with Crystal."

Zook was taken aback. "You know Crystal?"

"Of course," said Wild. "She is the sister of our dear Sparklett. I believe you are quite friendly with Sparklett?"

Although Wild was smiling, Zook suddenly felt wary. How much did Wild know about the relationship between him and Sparklett?

Wild laughed at the look of consternation on Zook's face. "Don't worry," he said. "Sparklett told me all about your little romance. But we're men of the world, aren't we? I have my affairs, she has hers."

Sparklett told him all about their affair? That didn't sound right to Zook. Why would she do that?

"Actually, I have a message for her," Zook said, trying to change the subject.

"Really?" said Wild, cutting another cigar and puffing it ablaze in a great cloud of smoke.

"Yes, from Crystal."

"A dying wish?" said Wild. "That sort of thing?"

Again, Zook felt wary. How did Wild know that

Crystal was dead? Zook squirmed uncomfortably and Wild seem to read his mind.

"Come, my friend, don't look so shocked. We have the skyster photos of you and Crystal together, and my men found her body at the edge of the ice field. Very touching, that shallow grave."

Wild looked at him with a raised eyebrow and Zook found himself blurting out "I'm not a member of the Two Brothers, if that's what you're thinking."

"No, of course not," said Wild, refilling Zook's glass. "But Crystal certainly was, and you did escape with her."

Again, Zook felt that tingle of danger. "But I've already explained, that was all an accident. I was only trying to get a message to you. I had been imprisoned unjustly. I knew that you would help."

"I see," said Wild. "Touching, your faith in me. I know all about the injustices that have been done to you. And believe me, they will be redressed."

"They will?"

"Of course," said Wild. "Isn't that what a Defender of Slaves does?"

It was exactly the outcome Zook was hoping for, and he was stunned. The tremendous psychic burden he had been laboring under for so many months was suddenly lifted, and all his troubles vanished. "Thank you," he shouted. "Thank you thank you thank you, AssemblyPerson!"

"Actually," Wild said, "Technically I'm not your AssemblyPerson anymore."

"What do you mean?"

"I'm Chief Controller now."

"What?" Zook said. "But... The Bob?"

"The Bob," Wild said, "had an accident on the golf course."

Wild's explanation was so dry it took a moment for

its meaning to register in Zook's overwhelmed brain. But in a flash everything made sense: the fighting in the streets, Wild's knowledge of Crystal, the beautiful room, even the gaudy ring on Wild's finger...

Wild was the new The Bob.

Zook fell to his knees and bowed his head. "Controller."

Wild proffered his hand. "You may kiss the ring," he said.

Never in a thousand years did Zook ever dream that he would have the opportunity to kiss the Chief Controller's ring.

Yet here he was.

Wild's hand was soft, and smelled strongly of tobacco. The ring blazed with a million sparkling lights, and felt rough to his cracked lips.

"Thank you, Controller," Zook said, as Wild withdrew his hand.

Zook touched his forehead to the floor and was about to rise when he noticed the incredibly intricate embroidery on Wild's velvet slippers. It depicted, in gold and silver thread, an ornate *fleur de lis*, and above that an ornamented crown. The pedals of the *fleur de lis* were tightly bound by a perfectly executed Greek-key band, and the elaborate gold crown was specked with jewels of ruby and emerald.

Zook, despite the smudge of cigar ash that marred one of the crowns, was overwhelmed. Never again might he be this close to greatness. And he knew, with his state slave consciousness, that he had before him the chance of a lifetime.

"Before I rise," Zook heard himself say, keeping his face to the ground, "may I beg but one boon of the Controller?"

"And what is that?" Wild said, a trace of impatience in his voice.

"I would like the honor of becoming one of the Controller's private slaves."

Zook continued kneeling, forehead on the floor, waiting for Wild to say something. The slipper with the stain moved a little and Zook seized the opportunity to kiss it.

"Get up," Wild said, jerking his foot away. "Sit down. Maybe we can do business."

Zook sat back feeling calm and excited. He didn't know what kind of deal Wild wanted to strike but Zook knew he wasn't going to bargain too hard.

"Anything," Zook said. "Anything you want, Controller."

"Excellent," said Wild, snipping the end off two cigars and handing one to Zook. He rang the little bell, and instantly Bacon appeared with a lighter. Zook couldn't help but notice that Bacon's attitude, so hostile an hour earlier, had changed from open hostility to extreme deference.

The servant disappeared.

"Let's seal the deal, shall we?" said Wild. "You want to be a private slave. Fine, no problem. I'm expanding around here anyway. I can always use another footman. Would you like that?"

Zook was practically beside himself. "Yes, Controller, that would be an honor and a privilege!"

"Fine," said Wild. "Done."

Once more, he rang the bell and Bacon appeared at the door. "Find this man some livery. Zook here will be joining you on my personal staff."

"As you wish," said Bacon, his eyes carefully lowered.

"Stand up so he can see your size, Zook. And we'll get you some quarters. Something private with a view.

"Does that suit you?"

"Yes, Controller, thank you, Controller."

"Think nothing of it," said Wild airily, as Bacon withdrew. Zook sat again, smiling happily, sipping his new boss' alcohol and puffing—not too hard—on his cigar.

Wild, one leg crossed over the other, smiled back.

"Satisfied?" Wild asked.

"Absolutely," said Zook.

Just then Bacon returned with Zook's new uniform, depositing the neatly folded stack on the table. He suddenly seemed friendly again, even giving Zook a wink as he backed out of the room.

Zook reached out to run his hand over the rich silk brocade of the clothes Bacon had left.

"I've been waiting for this moment for years," Zook said, a catch in his voice.

Wild merely watched as Zook unfolded the private slave tunic and held it happily in his lap.

Suddenly, having attained the goal he had long desired, Zook felt self-conscious. He was taking up so much of the Controller's valuable time.

Zook rose. "I guess I better get started, then."

"If you're sure you're ready."

"I'm ready."

"Then right through that door," Wild said. "Bacon will show you what to do."

"Thank you again, Slavicen Controller," said Zook. "I don't know how to repay you."

25.

ALL YOUR BOOTY ARE BELONG TO US

Just as Zook was turning to go Wild flicked the ash of his cigar vaguely toward the ashtray and said, "There is one thing."

"Certainly," said Zook. "Whatever you like."

"You have a document that Crystal was carrying," said Wild. "I want it."

Zook blanched. He knew immediately that Wild could only be referring to the code from Heat Station Antelope. In his relief over not being tortured and his excitement over meeting Wild, Zook had forgotten all about it.

He would have to tread most carefully.

"Document?" said Zook in a delaying action. "Crystal never gave me any document."

"Don't play games with me," Wild shouted, his face suddenly splotched red. "She stole a document from Host Danton's safe. It wasn't on her and it wasn't in your clothes. So where is it?"

"But I told you, she never gave me any…"

That was as far as Zook got before Wild slammed his fist down on the table. The decanters tumbled over and the plates rattled to the floor. "No lies. I made you a private slave. Now you give me that code."

Wild's suddenly ferocious manner unnerved Zook. Zook realized he was in deep trouble, but suddenly saw a way out. "I destroyed it," he said.

"You *what!?*"

"I knew it was a code, but Crystal said it could start another Machine war," said Zook. "I didn't believe her, but just in case I got rid of it."

"Got rid of it where?" demanded Wild.

"I ate it, okay?"

"You ate it," said Wild in disbelief, plopping back into his seat again.

"Crystal didn't want it falling into the wrong hands."

The red splotches were appearing on Wild's face again. "You fool. Do I look like the wrong hands?"

"She didn't mean you, she meant The Bob, but…"

Wild eyed Zook narrowly. "That information was priceless. You had to know that."

Then suddenly, Wild sat up and laughed.

"Very good," he said, a smile once again on his face. "Well played."

"I don't know what you mean," said Zook.

"You had me going there for awhile," said Wild, with some admiration. "You're a great liar. You're going to make a fine private slave.

"Now," continued Wild, "How much do you want?"

"But I told you," said Zook, "I don't have the document."

"Come. Whatever you think you're going to get from the Two Brothers, I'll match. Hell, it's GovMint money. I'll double it."

"I really did eat it," Zook said.

"You couldn't have," said Wild. "No one could be that stupid."

"It was just a few sheets," Zook offered, by way of explanation.

Wild picked up a small silver clock from the table beside him and chucked it at Zook's head.

Zook ducked and the clock crashed into a mirror on the wall, sending fragments flying everywhere. The clock itself bounced onto the carpet and rolled, unscathed, to Zook's feet.

Zook bent down to pick it up.

"Wait," said Wild. "*When* did you eat that code?"

"When?" said Zook. "When the soldiers were chasing me. A few hours ago."

Wild stood up. "Guards!" he shouted.

The soldiers from the utility hallway immediately re-entered the room.

"This fool has swallowed some valuable military information," said Wild. "I want him disemboweled."

"Disemboweled, Controller?" said the sergeant with the radiation burn.

"Yes, disemboweled." said Wild. "And I want every part of his colon cut open to see what can be recovered of the paper he was carrying."

The sergeant gave a signal and his men stepped forward, one on either side of Zook. Zook attempted to sidestep but tripped backward over a side stand and was quickly grabbed and hoisted to his feet.

"Take him downstairs," said the sergeant.

"No," Wild said to the man. Wild swept the coffee table free of the pastries and cognac with a crash. "You have a knife. Do it here."

"But, the blood," said the sergeant.

"The slaves will clean up," said Wild. "Do it. Now."

The sergeant hesitated only briefly before withdrawing a huge steel knife from his belt. One side of the blade had deep serrations for sawing, the other was sharpened to a fine edge for cutting.

Zook wanted to be neither sawed nor cut, and began struggling in horror as the soldier with the knife approached.

"Pull his head back," the sergeant ordered. "I'll start with his throat."

Zook head was jerked back by his hair and his neck exposed. If he were chopped up like so much sausage, he would never get to see Sparklett again, let alone be a private slave. Plus, it would really really hurt.

"Wait," Zook screamed, "I'll give you the code."

The sergeant had the blade poised ready to slice, but Wild signaled the sergeant to stay. "How?" he asked suspiciously.

"I memorized it."

Wild looked skeptical.

"I did," insisted Zook. "Crystal said that it was important and I had a lot of time on the train so I memorized what was on the paper, in case I was forced to destroy it."

"You're lying," Wild said.

"I'm *not* lying," said Zook, the knife still ready at his throat. "Let me go and I'll prove it."

"No more bargaining," said Wild. Then, to the sergeant, "Open him."

"It's all chewed up! You'll never get it back together!" screamed Zook.

"We pieced that from a jigsaw of millions of tiny pieces," said Wild. "It will be a walk in the park to piece together what's in your gut."

The sergeant drew back the knife.

Zook began to recite: "One-A-five-T-J…"

"*Stop,*" Wild commanded, just as the knife touched Zook's throat.

Wild put his hand over Zook's mouth. "You really did memorize it?"

Zook made the best nod he could with his head still drawn back and a knife still pointed at his throat.

"And you'll cooperate now?"

"Please," he croaked.

Wild frown turned to a smile, and in a flash his personality changed from frightening back to jovial. He waved the soldiers back, then threw his arm around Zook.

"You're a clever one," he said, squeezing Zook's shoulder like an old acquaintance. "I'm glad you've come to your senses."

Zook didn't know if had come to his senses, but he knew he was glad to have his bowels intact, and tired of being burdened with Crystal's dangerous secret. He never asked to be brought into a Two Brother's plot, and he *had* kept the code from The Bob, which seemed to be Crystal's main concern. If the Chief Controller wanted the code, who was a slave to say no? Especially a private slave. Especially considering the alternative.

"I'll need something to write with," Zook said.

"That's the spirit," said the Controller. He withdrew paper and pen from a nearby drawer and dropped it in front of Zook, then took a seat across from him and looked at Zook expectantly.

The paper was note-sized and unlike anything Zook had ever seen—creamy and thick, with edges artfully torn. The pen was gold and surprisingly heavy.

Zook hesitated, inhibited by the presence of the soldiers behind, but with a gesture, Wild sent them out of the room.

Zook took a deep breath and began writing.

As soon as he touched pen to paper, an enormous wave of relief swept over him. The sooner he got this poisonous load out of his system and into the Controller's hands, the better. Who knows? He might even be doing the world a favor.

As his pen labored across the small note page, Zook could see Wild watching eagerly. It was almost as if he were giving a private performance. Zook's memory was excellent, and he realized he actually enjoyed showing off his ability to remember the apparently endless list of random characters.

The moment Zook finished the first page, Wild picked it up and examined the numbers carefully.

"And you're sure this is accurate?"

"Absolutely," said Zook. "I could recite it in my sleep."

"Excellent, Zook," said Wild. "You are just the kind of slavicen this country needs."

Aglow in Wild's praise, Zook took another sheet of the creamy paper from the stack and continued to write. Light from an overhead chandelier sent little refracted rainbows dancing over the rows of characters Zook was setting down. Was this all it took to claim his ride on the GovMint gravy train? Why had he resisted so long?

He wasn't sure. All of his life, he had tried to get on board with the endless progression of exciting new policy discoveries coming down from his Betters. He understood, in an abstract way, why sugar was poison, why slavicens mustn't be armed, why lawns ruined the environment, why bathrooms had to be gender-neutral, and why man-spreading was an affront to Women (who were Strong but also needed to be Protected). Zook knew he was but raw material to be molded by the State, but his recalcitrant heart resented the poking and prodding. Maybe a High Friendster like Sparklett could afford the luxury of flirting with Two Brothers ideology, but Zook was just a common slave. One way, Perks. The other way, Shredder.

Much better to follow Bacon's example and go with the flow. What a fool he had been!

"What is it?" Wild said.

"Nothing, Controller," said Zook. "A little cramp in my hand."

"Finish up," Wild said. "We haven't got all day."

His hand *did* feel cramped, and Zook shook it and cracked his knuckles before returning to his task with renewed vigor.

Unbidden, a vision of Sparklett as he had last seen her came involuntarily to his mind: beautiful, her head of tight red curls, her eyes glowing with love in the moonlight. *Think, Zook,* he heard her say. *Think.*

Once again his pen came to a halt.

"Now what?" demanded Wild.

"I'm only supposed to give the code to Sparklett."

"Are you my private slave or not?"

"But Controller, I promised Crystal."

"A promise to a traitor means nothing," said Wild.

Wild's words gave Zook pause. Crystal was, of course, a member of Two Brothers, but was she really a traitor, or simply a misguided idealist? Zook considered her an idealist, not a traitor.

Zook's pen felt insufferably heavy. He started to put it down.

Wild saw the movement and jumped in: "But of course you're right," he suddenly agreed. "Although Crystal may have been misguided, her opposition to The Bob's oppressive rule was not misplaced. Naturally, she was afraid that the code might make its way to The Bob. But that's not a danger anymore, is it?"

"No, I guess not," said Zook.

"And I'll send you to Sparklett just as soon as we're done here. How's that?"

Zook heart leapt at the thought of seeing Sparklett. "That would be great," he said.

"It's settled then," said Wild. "Finish up and I'll have my men take you to her."

Zook quickly began to scribble out the remaining bits of the code while Wild sat back, puffing on his cigar. It seemed absurd that this random string of numbers would have any value at all to anyone, let alone the King of the Machines, if the Machines had a King as Crystal had suggested. Probably it was some kind of secret message that only the Two Brothers could decode. If that were the case the numbers would be useless to anyone but Sparklett, so giving them to Wild wasn't such a big deal.

(Still, Crystal *did* make him promise to deliver the code only to Sparklett.)

Once again, Zook stopped.

Wild looked irritated and was just about to say something when the door burst open and Bacon entered, carrying a red FreeFone on a silver tray.

"It's General Lowe," said Bacon to Wild, who took the phone from the tray.

"Yes... Good...," said Wild. "Where? Any sign of movement?... What have we got? Not yet. How many in that unit?..."

The conversation, apparently about troop deployments, continued in that vein, but Zook's attention was suddenly drawn by a loud crash.

Bacon, on his way out, had dropped his silver tray to the wooden parquet floor. As he stooped to retrieve it, he momentarily propped open the big swinging door.

There, displayed on the wall of the room opposite, a painting was hanging.

Zook sat up, suddenly rigid. He had only caught a glimpse before the door began to swing shut, but the picture was unmistakable a clown painting.

His clown painting.

Zook was shocked. How could it be here?

He rose, strode to the door, and snatched it open before it could lock.

His Pedro was there, hanging over the mantle in the next room over. He recognized the slouched drunk, the dead cigar, the wise stag.

"You've got my clown painting," he said aloud.

Wild, confused, put his hand over the FreeFone.

"What?"

"That's my clown painting. There. Over the mantle. The one they took from me."

"I'll call you back," said Wild, throwing down the red FreeFone in annoyance and joining Zook at the door.

"What is this nonsense?"

Zook moved into the other room and stood before the Pedro. It had been elaborately mounted and re-framed, but it definitely was *his*. Somehow it had made its way here. "This was the painting I was telling you about."

"That's a clown from my gallery," said Wild.

"No, it's from my FreePad. It's the Pedro I discovered." Zook plucked the painting from the wall and pointed to some tiny holes in the fabric. "See? That's where I had it pinned to the wall." The large ornate frame with its protective glass was surprisingly heavy.

Wild was provoked. "Put that painting back and finish the code."

"But Controller, look at the signature," said Zook, his voice rising. "It's an unknown Pedro. This is the painting I pulled from the dumpster."

That seemed to bring Wild up short. "That was booty from a criminal trial."

"No," said Zook. "It's the painting that the plops took from me."

The painting, Zook thought, that was supposedly State property.

The painting for which he had been tried and convicted, but which somehow had ended up here, hanging on Wild's wall.

A terrible realization arose in Zook's mind. *Wild* had given the PeacePeople the order to follow him. *Wild* had ordered his arrest and trial.

Wild was…

Zook felt as if he had been knifed in the heart.

"You're a thief!" Zook blurted out. "You stole my painting!"

"Careful," said Wild. "You forget to whom you're talking."

"But—*why*? I would have given you the painting, if

you had only asked."

Wild laughed, a harsh grating laugh that came from deep inside. "It was never yours to give," he said. "Look around you. That clock, that chair, those candlesticks, this painting—the good stuff ends up here."

He quoted the state slogan: "'All your booty are belong to us.' What did you think that meant?"

"'Give what you have, get what you need,'" Zook said defiantly. "That's a state slogan too."

Wild laughed again. "And that's exactly right," he said. "We at the top have the education, the knowledge, and the power to take all that you slaves at the bottom can give. Our needs are great, and your job is to meet them, not the other way around. If I hadn't reappropriated your painting, someone else would have, and they might not have left you alive to make absurd accusations."

"But..."

"No buts," said Wild. "I've indulged you enough. Now you will finish writing out the code."

Zook's eyes narrowed and he took a step back.

"I will not," said Zook.

"I won't stand here arguing," said Wild. "You wanted to be my private slave – I made you so. I am your Controller. Now you will write down that code."

A brief look of confusion played upon Zook's face, and Wild saw an opening.

"Hell," he said, in a conciliatory voice. "If you like that clown painting, I'll even let you hang it in your slave cubby. But now—I must have that code."

Zook's face went hard. "No," he said.

Wild took a step forward and shouted into Zook's face. "You will give me that code or you will regret ever being born".

Zook stared at him and shook his head doggedly "no." "To think I actually admired you," he said.

"Guards!" roared Wild.

The guards burst into the room and had Zook in a hammerlock before he even had time to react.

The sergeant with the burnt face again pulled out his knife. "Disembowel him, Chief Controller?"

"No," said Wild. "The CleanRoom."

+ + +

Damn him anyway, Wild thought in frustration as his men dragged Zook away. He sank onto a nearby couch. Few could resist the CleanRoom, but the cleansing process took time. Troops were already in place on the approaches to Sand Francisco, and now the offensive would have to be delayed until Zook could be broken. Without the code to bring the Machines under control, his units would be decimated and he would be left without an army—even while supporters of The Bob were still fighting in the streets.

That nitwit Zook! He could have made everything so simple and yet he chose to resist. Although Wild had spent 20 years in PublicService, he never understood what made slaves like Zook go rogue. After all, Zook was clothed, fed and housed by the GovMint, and now there were even behavioral FreePerks that could be traded for luxuries formerly reserved for Friendsters, like oranges, scented soap and toilet paper.

The clown painting was lying where Zook had dropped it. Wild heaved himself up and re-hung it on the wall, then stepped back to admire his possession. He had wanted the velvet painting to complete his set, but in truth he thought the Pedro crude and ugly—nowhere near as good as the nice little Thomas Kinkade cottages that hung in his bedroom. The drunken clown, with his crushed top hat, dead cigar and wilted boutonniere, was repulsive, and the sad-looking stag with the tear in its eye made no sense at all.

He sighed. At least it wasn't a Picasso.

Wild was still staring at the drunken clown when Bacon poked his nose in the door.

"What are you doing here?" Wild said, tired of the endless slave interruptions. "Get out!"

"Yes, Friendster," Bacon said. He slipped an envelope from his silver platter onto the table near the door. "I'll just leave this here."

When he was gone, Wild glanced at the envelope, with its distinctive SuperPAC seal. That would be the results on Sparklett.

Sparklett. How could he have lived with her for so many years without discovering her traitorous nature?

Abruptly, he turned and ripped open the report.

The details of her betrayal were there. She had first met Zook the day of the Gratitude Chastisements. When Zook was later apprehended in the palace, Sparklett had intervened with the guards, preventing his arrest. She had spirited Zook away in Wild's own AtomoLimo, and trysted with him by moonlight in a remote area south of Mento. Then she smuggled Zook back past the checkpoint, dropping him in town before joining Wild the next day in FriendsterVille. She even, apparently, managed to wipe Zook's FreeFone records clean.

Sparklett might have gotten away with it had not her driver been turned in by Sustainable Bacon. A few hours in SuperPAC and the driver was wrung dry.

Wild continued reading, his mind racing: Two Brothers operative... access to high-level classified information... government overthrow... secret drops... coded messages...

It all added up to complete infidelity. Sparklett had been betraying him from the first moment they met.

He had been blind.

The final step for Sparklett, as for all criminal demons, was the Shredder.

But even now, Wild hesitated. Sparklett was, after

all, an exquisite beauty.

Then he remembered his position. If he wanted to remain at the top, it was necessary to show no weakness. There were other beautiful women in the UCC. And now that he was Chief Controller, they would be his for the taking.

He rang for Bacon, then picked up a pen and scribbled Sparklett's execution order on the back of the envelope.

Bacon appeared at the door. "Yes, Friendster?" he said, as eager as ever to please.

Wild started to hand over his instructions, but paused.

It occurred to him that Sparklett might have one last duty to perform for the UCC, in the highly improbably case that Zook could resist the CleanRoom.

Wild stuffed the order into a pocket of his tunic.

"Go away," he said to Bacon.

"As you wish," said the slave, smiling and bowing as he silently backed out of his master's presence.

26.

DIVERSITY IS OUR STRENGTH

The CleanRoom was very white and bright. It was a large minimalist cube, perhaps 10 yards square, suffused with white light that had no visible source. The walls were white, the ceiling was white, the floor was white. The room was absolutely clean. It had seemed to Zook—many hours or days ago when he first entered the CleanRoom—that one enormous side of the cube was a glass window, but now inside all the walls were exactly the same shade of white, glossy and reflective.

In the exact center of the white floor a white table stood, its surface spotless, with straight square legs the same glossy white as all the other whiteness in the CleanRoom. This was the only furnishing in the otherwise empty room. The table's shape was a cube. There was no chair, but when one stood in front of the table the top was at a comfortable height to write.

On the white table were the two sheets of code that Zook had already written out, whether the original or reproductions Zook could not tell through his hazy watery eyes. There was also a gold pen, gleaming with white reflections, possibly the same gold pen he had handled in Wild's study. And there was the white glass bowl half-filled with the clear liquid that looked and tasted like water, and for all Zook knew, *was* in fact, water, except as soon as he had drunk from this white chalice he had lost all, or almost all, of what was left of his ability to make decisions for himself.

For some hours or days now, or minutes, the Voice had been playing a game with him. Like the light, the Voice came from everywhere and nowhere in the empty white cube, and it made simple, irresistible requests. Sometimes the requests were very easy, even reasonable, as when Zook was invited to lie on the white floor, close his eyes, and nap. At other times the Voice requested ridiculous or absurd acts from him, such as suggesting he stand on his head with his feet against the wall, or blink his right eye repeatedly while holding his left eye open, or sing the Happy Slave song from FreePod, or run twelve circles around the desk in one direction and then reverse suddenly to do twelve circles in the other direction.

Zook did not remember drinking the liquid in the chalice. Whenever he looked in the chalice the level of the water (or whatever the liquid was) always seemed to be the same. The liquid's temperature was neither hot nor cold. He could not recall ever lifting the chalice to his lips. Possibly he never drank from the liquid in the chalice, or had drank once from the liquid in the chalice, or had always drank the liquid in the chalice and just didn't remember.

Possibly it was the liquid in the chalice that made the maddening silly absurd suggestions of the Voice that came from nowhere so irresistible.

He smiled when the Voice told him to smile, and frowned when the Voice told him to frown. He confessed that he was an enemy of the UCC sent to destroy it and he confessed that he loved the UCC with his inmost heart and would never betray it. The Voice seemed to enter both ears as well as the top and bottom of his head simultaneously, and it seemed to concentrate in one tiny spot in the exact center of his brain, just as the desk stood in the exact center of the room, and the pen and paper always seemed to be in the exact center of the desk when he looked at it.

Nothing seemed to happen when he resisted the suggestions of the Voice, except that he felt himself literally diminishing, his skin somehow shrinking as he became smaller and smaller, taking up less and less volume on his way to becoming a dot. This brought up the great fear that he would simply disappear, and his heart would begin to pound and his breathing would become shallow and rapid as if the air in the room lacked oxygen.

Possibly the air in the room *did* lack oxygen, and he had breathed it all up, the way he had eaten all the food (there must have been food) and drank from the liquid in the chalice (except the level never seemed to change).

He knew he was bad and that he was destroying something good and he felt infinite regret and he almost wished that the dot that he became in the whiteness which surrounded him and went on for infinity would erase and leave the whiteness in the infinity without the speck of dust that was him. But then the pounding of his heart would bring him back to the room and he would realize how absurd it was that he was refusing to stand on his head against the wall as the Voice requested, and he would do so and immediately he would be back in himself, upside down, staring at the desk with the paper and the pen.

Zook had no idea how long the sessions (as he thought of them) went on between himself and the Voice. Sometimes the Voice would not return for what seemed to Zook to be hours, or possibly days, or possibly minutes, and at other times the Voice would barrage him with incessant demands. Stand on your toes. Crawl in circles. Spit at the wall. Jump one hundred times in place.

It was all very much like the invisible voice Zook had been hearing in the UCC everywhere all of his life: No sugary drinks. Think correct thoughts. Guns are for PeacePeople. Mind your step. Be ExtraQueer. Just play along. Plastic bags kill. Your Betters know best. Walk to the desk and walk away. God is dead. Read the numbers and letters that are written on the paper. Obey here now. Pick up the pen and put it down again.

The Voice seemed obsessed with the numbers and letters and definitely seemed happiest when Zook picked up the pen. However, inevitably there would come the one command that Zook knew was coming and had told himself he would never ever do, and that was to pick up the pen and write on the paper the rest of the code which Wild wanted and which Crystal had warned would start a final, catastrophic war with the Machines.

The code, Zook kept reminding himself, could only be given to Sparklett herself.

An image of Sparklett came into his mind, but not the ideal, jewel-draped Sparklett of his visions. This was the other Sparklett, the *real* Sparklett, a woman, flesh-and-blood like himself, living in fear and loneliness like himself, calling to him, waiting for him.

She was there.

And then she was not.

Zook tried to hold on to the reality of her when the inevitable suggestion would come, the suggestion to finish writing the pages he had started, finish writing the code. If only Sparklett remained, he could resist, but without her here to hold him he could only try to resist when he had no capacity of resistance. If he had the pen in hand he would drop it, or if he picked it up again, he would pick it up the wrong way, so that the point was pointing up. Or he would drop it and pick it up the right way, but the mark he would make would be on the white desktop, not the creamy ivory paper. Or if he made a mark on the paper, he would make a scribble, or he would scribble a number of letters sloppily, or write several characters on top of each other or backwards or over top of previously written letters.

No, Zook, don't give them what they want, said Sparklett, somewhere in the room unseen.

We beat them at the prison camp, we can beat them at this, chimed in Crystal, although Zook thought he had buried her at the glacier.

Don't fail us, said Sparklett. Be a free man, not a state slave.

Easy for you to say, Zook replied in his mind, you're not even here.

Yes we are, the sisters said in unison.

But really they were not and Zook was alone.

Through the wall which was white just like all the others, not glass, he could feel the pressure of Wild watching him with hard impatience. Zook threw the gold pen aside as if it were a bar of hot iron, and turned away from the desk to the white, where he found himself becoming smaller and smaller. He tried to breathe and to push his heart back into this sack of tightening skin into which he was disappearing. He was fading, fading, and he didn't want to die but he was becoming infinitely, impossibly small and everything was white and he was the one black dot that was marring everything.

The commands were getting harder and harder to resist. Zook didn't know how much longer he could hold out.

When he threw away the pen and his body disappeared down almost to nothing, Zook felt a little stab of pain in his heart, which was a stab of victory because he had resisted giving Wild what he wanted for at least another minute or second or day or month or year. This despite almost welcoming the feeling of erasure and the release it would give him from this wayward planet and his horrible wonderful promise to only give the code to Sparklett.

He had been a fool and he had always been a fool. He had suckled on the teat of the State and he had loved its watery milk and grown to enjoy the ease of its weak nourishment. He had sold his birthright for a mess of pottage before he even realized he had a birthright and certainly without knowing that pottage was only an unremarkable thin form of lentil soup, which he undoubtedly could have supplied to himself if it had ever occurred to him to do so. But why would it occur to him to do so when the milk of the teat was flowing commensurate with his ability and his needs and his litter mates snuggled with him so warmly and the pottage was the best pottage the world had ever seen, as he and everyone was constantly reminded?

Don't be a state slave, Sparklett had said, but he *was* a state slave and always had been, for what is a state slave except someone who goes along to get along, as the State slogan so warmly suggested? He loved his pottage and he loved being loved and he loved feeling good.

What was wrong with that?

All men were brothers, the stronger should protect the weaker, those who had should relinquish to those who had need.

What was wrong with that?

He loved free things, too, as anyone in their right mind would. He loved his FreeFone, with its constant supply of FreePorn and FreeVid and unlimited FreeTexts. And he had FreeFriends, hundreds of them, preselected and preloaded to his Cohort list—everyone he should want to talk to: his Friendsters, his FreeBuddies, his FreePodMates, the slave woman who supplied FreeMeal tickets and the slave man who fixed the plumbing in his FreePad. And his FreePad was no bigger or smaller than any of the other state slaves' FreePads, and it contained all of the FreePerks that all slavecins of the UCC were allowed to have: FreeVid, FreeRadyo, FreeLectric, FreeSheets, FreeUniforms, FreeHeat, and FreeAir. He had FreeWork to make him free and FreeMed if he got sick, along with the promise of FreeEldercare when he became elder (although, he realized now with a start, he hadn't actually seen any FreeElders lately or any elder at all since the NonDeathPanels had taken control of the FreeMedTriage. Perhaps the elders had been shipped to a FreeEldercare facility in some other jurisdiction, but how would he know since he only knew what he heard and he only heard what the Friendsters wanted him to hear.)

What is all this thinking? Zook said to himself, alarmed at the sensation, but it came unbidden and he couldn't shut it off.

He liked the clown painting because, possibly he thought, in the white CleanRoom, he was the drunken unconscious clown, with Xs for eyes, having drunk too much from the bottle labeled XXX, and smoked too freely of the now dead cigar. The tattered tuxedo and crushed top hat were the tightening skin which compressed him to a tiny dot because he would not give the Voice the characters of the code which Wild so reasonably sought. The stag with its magnificent rack of antlers, looked on sadly from the past distance at the sight of yet another clown citizen anesthetized in the public gutter.

He wished had never seen the clown painting *No you don't* because seeing it was loving it and loving it was poison to his beautiful relationship with the State.

Or maybe, Zook imagined, Wild was the clown in the top hat, drunk on his forbidden cognac and pre-Zero cigars. Zook could sense him beyond the non-wall, pacing, frustrated. The eyes were Xs and the cigar was dead because he, too, was full of poison, the poison of

300

power without restraint.

Stop, stop, stop, Zook told his screaming thoughts, but the thoughts didn't listen and carried him along like a man capsized in white-capped rapids.

Everything flowed from the State and everything was without price. But the wise stag knew what was only now beginning to dawn on Zook, that everything in the perfect UCC actually had a price. The price was who got to set the rules. The price was living under Friendster. The price was doing what they wanted you to do, being who they wanted you to be, selling them your birthright for some not-even-very-delicious lentil soup. The price was believing that they could run your life for you better than you could run your life for yourself, or if not believing, at least pretending, going along to get along. The price was the endless pounding by the interstitial State promos, the ever-present State slogans, the smiling-masque Friendsters, the jovial insistent parades, the Shredder.

He pounded his head on the white wall, trying to get the thoughts to stop.

FreeSmoozees were free for all, so long as your swig cup was eight FrOunces or less. Eight FrOunces was enough for anyone, 12 FrOunces would make you obese and cause you to become diabetic and cost the State money because your self-induced diabetes would be paid for by the GovMint, wealth stolen directly from your Slavicen's pocket. Eight FrOunces was SociallyResponsibleLiving, 18 FrOunces theft of State property.

Why not 15 FrOunces or ten or nine or 44? No matter, eight was the figure. It had been decided upon by them, the Betters who knew what was best. Tobacco? Forbidden. Don't? Allowed. Discard? Forbidden. Recycle? Allowed. GasCar? Forbidden. eCar? Allowed. Business? Forbidden. FreeTax? Allowed. Clown painting? Forbidden.

Rational or irrational, just or in unjust, rules were rules. You were to like what they said you were to like, and to do what they said you were to do, and not notice that the tendency of all wealth was to travel up the line of Friendsters to the rule makers, who were also the rule breakers, which you were also not supposed to notice.

Blood gushed from his forehead and streaked down the wall but still the wicked thoughts wouldn't cease.

Zook's idea to become a private slave would have been a release from this intolerable incongruence had he actually achieved his goal before his arrest, trial, imprisonment, escape, capture, success, and—now in the CleanRoom—failure. In a society like the UCC, it was natural that the Betters should have enormous wealth while the slaves happily ate their marvelously promoted pottage. For how could a slavecin know his pottage was thin if one were never allowed to taste any other pottage?

Zook had looked into the eyes of Wild, the Chief Controller of the entire UCC, and found in them nothing but greed and venality. He and all the AssemblyPersons like him were supposed to be the Betters who knew how to run society in such a way as to produce equality, kindness, love, brotherhood, justice, Social Justice and Super Social Justice. Clown paintings were not in the mix. Laws were for The Little People, so that the big people could contemplate what best The Little People could act, say and do. The Friendster's venality and corruption was but a passing breeze compared to the hurricane of their wisdom.

Ipso facto, if you had any idea, impulse, or possession which had not been anticipated and approved of by the State, you were a threat. You were the nail that needed to be hammered down. It didn't matter whether the object of your unauthorized desire was a 44 FrOunce

Smoozee or a clown painting on velvet. Everything Not Approved is Disapproved and Everything is Free. The two went hand-in-hand. What mattered was that you cede your personal authority for your likes and dislikes to those above you who knew Best and from whom all FreeBlessings flowed.

Ideally a gentle smile should bring you back into line, or if not, a frown and a rebuke entered into your slavicen file. Should you persist in the folly of having a personal preference that was not pre-contemplated by the State, you would be examined more closely, your statements and whereabouts scrutinized, and if that scrutiny led to a brush with the authorities, perhaps then you would then know that your course was dangerous and best to nod your head and keep your mouth shut and go along.

Should you further persist in your structural insanity, the State would frown and be forced into harsher moves. Ridicule and shame were potent guidelines, sufficient for most, but beyond that were interrogation, arrest, trial and imprisonment. While in your distant prison, where the poison of your ideas could not taint your fellow slavecins, there would be ample opportunity for rehabilitation and recanting of your ridiculous anti-social preferences, which were grossly and entirely wrong, and should you still persist there would be the needler, the CleanRoom and finally the Shredder. The Shredder was the State's ultimate *shut up*. At this stage in the process, the severity of your offense, whether murder of your Friendster or failure to recycle, was of no consequence. All that mattered was, *shut up*. Since the State was bigger than any errant individual, it always won.

Or at least it always had.

Then, suddenly, finally, Zook was back in the room. The thoughts had finally gone away and the pen was in his hand and swiftly writing lines of characters across the smooth creamy page. Zook was horrified to see that the characters were the true characters and that the writing flowed clearly and visibly from one side of the paper to the next, line after line.

Zook was aghast because he realized that *they* were succeeding. Against his conscience, against his will, he was actually writing-out the numbers and letters in the code *they* wanted, and that meant war with the Machines and the end of humanity, according to the two sisters.

Zook could only think of one thing to do.

He lifted the gold pen took it in both hands and held it at arm's length like a dagger.

"*I AM NOT A STATE SLAVE,*" Zook screamed, as he plunged the pen with all of his might into his heart.

But his attempt at suicide failed as the pen glanced off a rib and snapped in half, leaving him bloody but alive.

Suddenly the wall that Zook suspected had been glass actually *became* glass, and he caught a glimpse of Wild and of a number of men in uniform observing him from a small room beyond.

Then a phalanx of soldiers swarmed into the room, carrying not needlers but leather-covered blackjacks. Zook snatched up the papers on the table and, like a crazed Co-Op-Ball player, made a bee-line for the door, trying to dodge and evade the men until he was grabbed and brought down.

A dozen blows fell upon him in all directions from the blackjacks, until one struck him directly on his right temple and the world blacked out.

27.

FROM THE STATE FLOWS ALL

"He's coming to," a gruff male voice said.

"Slap him," said a second voice, more familiar.

Zook felt two teeth-shattering slaps to his face, first to one side, then to the other.

He was, apparently, not dead—though with his aching body and throbbing head Zook almost wished he were. The air in the room was cold and damp with a repulsive slaughterhouse smell. Woozily, he tried to open his eyes wide but could manage only the smallest slit.

"Again," said the familiar voice.

Another jaw-crunching slap. Zook's head rolled, but this time his eyes opened and the room gradually came into focus. The room was a shadowy industrial rectangle, with zinc-paneled walls and an overpowering smell that made Zook's stomach turn.

He was propped on a short stack of paper-filed boxes with his back leaning against the cold wall. A pair of similar stacked file cartons formed a crude desk in front of him, holding a child's notebook of cheap paper and a stubby pre-Zero yellow pencil.

A burly soldier with hands the size of hams towered over him. The soldier grabbed a handful of Zook's hair and reeled back to slap him again. Zook flinched.

"That's enough. Wait outside," the fat man in the shadows barked.

The soldier stopped, saluted and exited through an

oversized metal door.

Zook, head still pounding, squinted in the dim light and realized the man giving the orders was Wild. Zook saw that he and Wild were standing on a wide ledge which ran around the edge of a strangely-shaped room. The rest of the floor was an inverted pyramid, funneling down to a line of serrated teeth.

A Shredder.

"Zook I'm here," a voice called from above.

Zook felt his heart leap. Zook had feared he would never hear that voice again.

"Sparklett," he called.

She was there, high up in the murky shadows, bound and trussed with hemp ropes and hanging from the hook of a small industrial crane which ran on rails along the rafters. She looked frail and starved and there were huge ugly bruises on the exposed skin of her arms and face.

"What the hell?" Zook said to Wild. "Let her down."

"Oh, I'll let her down all right," said Wild, chewing on the end of a dead cigar. He took a few steps to the wall and flicked a red switch. There was a brief whine and then a rumbling; the teeth of the Shredder began to rotate on their shaft, the gleaming metal of the teeth stained with a brown substance that Zook realized in horror was dried blood.

"You are insane," Zook said.

"Am I?" said Wild. He unhooked a hand controller from the wall and pressed a button.

Above and in the corner of the room, a motor buzzed and the crane began to move. Sparklett's bound body was carried along a guide rail to a position exactly above the center of the rotating Shredder-blades.

"I want that code, Zook. And you are going to give it to me."

"Don't do it, Zook," yelled Sparklett, whose body was swaying pendulum-like above the center of the

Shredder. "Don't give that pig anything."

"I may be a pig, darling, but you're about to be pig meat," taunted Wild. "Unless, of course, your personal FB here comes through."

Wild pushed a green, cross-shaped button on the hand control and the cable from which Sparklett dangled descended an arm's length.

Zook had seen enough. In a single fast motion, he leapt up from his seat and flew directly at Wild.

Wild hardly flinched.

A chain which shackled Zook's ankle to the wall drew suddenly taut and he crashed to the ground several feet from his target. Zook's momentum threw him uncontrollably to the floor, plunging him over the side of the funnel.

Before he could get purchase on the slimy metal slope, the chain at his ankle tightened and Zook whipped head-first toward the rotating Shredder blades.

In his last moment alive, Zook caught a glimpse of Sparklett hanging from the rafters above him, a horrified look on her face. In a flash, he remembered Sparklett's warning that his carelessness could get them both killed; now her prediction was coming true and he would never get to make it up to her.

Then he jerked to a halt as the chain reached its furthest extent. Upside down, still alive, he found himself suspended just feet from the rotating Shredder. He realized he was screaming, as was Sparklett overhead. The tightening chain had knocked a carton from the desk into the funnel with him, and it bounced off his thigh and tumbled into the Shredder with a grinding roar as the blades chewed up the cardboard and the papers inside and sucked them down into the metal maw.

Zook reflexively struggled and at last managed to grab the taut chain above his feet. When he could breathe again he again caught Sparklett's eye.

He loved her so much.

"Trust me," said Zook. "I'm going to us out of here."

Above him, Wild gave a loud guffaw. He pushed open the door and signaled for the guard with the beefy hands.

"Set him up again," commanded Wild.

In an instant, Zook felt his chain being hauled out of the Shredder funnel by the soldier. Zook, once on his feet, was pushed back onto his box seat in front of the crude writing desk, where the paper and pencil still waited. Wild snapped his fingers and the soldier once again retreated outside the metal door.

"I've no more time for games," said Wild. "You may not care about your life but you obviously care about hers.

"If you give me the code, she will live. If not..." Wild again jabbed the green button.

Slowly, inexorably, the crane began to lower Sparklett towards the rotating maw of the Shredder.

Fifteen feet, twelve, ten—slowly, slowly, Sparklett descended as Zook, sick with anger and frustration, watched her writhe on the end of the hook.

Wild stopped the crane with a bang and looked at Zook.

"Well?"

"Don't tell him anything, Zook," said Sparklett. "Be strong."

Zook had never felt such a mix of rage, frustration and despair. He knew the code was of utmost importance, and that Sparklett would die for it as her sister did. But he could never let Sparklett die; he had to find a way out.

Wild gave the green button another bump and Sparklett dropped with a jerk down into the funnel, close enough to the rotating cutting-teeth that she would have lost her lower legs had she not snatched them up quickly to her body.

"Stop," yelled Zook, sweat pouring from his face.

"Are you willing to cooperate?" said Wild.

"No, Zook," screamed Sparklett.

"If I give you the code, how do I know you won't kill us both?" said Zook.

"There's a fueled hopper on the roof of the building," said Wild. "As soon as I verify the code is correct I'll have the two of you escorted to it. You can flee wherever you choose—inside the UCC or out."

Zook looked at Sparklett, hesitated, then looked away. "All right, said Zook. "Raise her."

"The code first," said Wild.

"No, Zook, you mustn't," Sparklett yelled. "You can't trust him."

"I have to."

"You'll be betraying everything we've worked for."

"I can't help it. I love you," said Zook. "I'm saving your life."

"If you love me, let me die."

"I'm not strong enough to do that," said Zook. "I've been a slave too long."

Closing his ears to Sparklett's further pleading, Zook turned to the makeshift table and wrote out the last of the code. There were only five lines, and he finished quickly, slamming the pencil down on the makeshift desk.

"There," Zook said. "Now release her."

Wild's eyes greedily took in the lines of figures and he stepped forward to snatch the pages up.

No sooner had Wild got the papers in hand than, in one quick movement, Zook swept Wild's feet out from under him.

The papers went one way and the cigar the other as Wild frantically rolled his hands in the air, attempting to reestablish his balance.

On his face as he hung on the lip of the funnel was an astonished look of disbelief.

"You?" he said to Zook, even as his feet slipped out from under him and he fell backwards and tumbled down into the waiting teeth of the Shredder.

WHOMP! Wild landed directly on the Shredder's blades, his corpulent body spinning like a log rolling in a current. His flailing arms were instantly ripped from their sockets, spraying gushers of blood from severed arteries, even as the gnawing blades tore the flesh from his frame and sent greasy gobs of muscle and fat splattering against the funnel walls. Bones crunched and splintered, then disappeared into the the Shredder's maw, leaving momentarily a skinless skull which skittered on the blades like a roulette ball before bouncing off the funnel wall and falling back, anticlimactically, to be smashed and shredded by the metal teeth.

Wild was gone.

Zook felt his knees go wobbly.

He had killed the Chief Controller of the United Care Communities.

The future was now, and it was over.

+ + +

"It had to be done," said Sparklett, still hanging from the hook.

Zook pushed aside his still reeling emotions. There would be time for evaluation later. Right now they had to get out of there.

Just then there came a sharp rap on the door. "Everything all right, Controller?" came the soldier's voice from outside.

"Fine," said Zook, in his best gravelly-voice imitation of Wild.

But the soldier apparently was suspicious for the door

began to swing open.

Zook, still lying chained to the floor where his struggle with Wild had left him, caught Sparklett's eye with blank dismay. They had prevented Wild from getting the code, but now they would both be executed for murdering Wild, probably on the spot. And Zook *still* didn't want to die.

Zook's eyes flicked to the opening door and a plan flashed into his mind. If he could get the soldier into the range of his slave chain, Zook might be able to kill him in the same way he had killed Wild.

Zook pointed toward the door, then at his chain, trying to mentally project the plan to Sparklett. Then, just as the soldier actually entered, Zook collapsed in a pile on the floor.

"Where's the Controller?" the soldier barked, withdrawing his hazer.

"Dead, dead," wailed Sparklett, still dangling from the ceiling. "Both dead. They killed each other."

Hazer in hand, the soldier cautiously approached Zook's lifeless body, prodding it with his foot.

"He's dead," Sparklett repeated. "Wild killed him."

The big soldier re-holstered the hazer and knelt to roll Zook over on his back. "How…?" he started to ask.

In one swift motion, Zook's hands snaked up and around the man's neck, his thumbs pressing as hard as he could against the windpipe.

Just as swiftly, the soldier broke Zook's hold by wedging his arms between his opponent's and dropping his entire body weight on Zook, easily forcing Zook's hands back from his neck.

Zook struggled under the burly man's weight, making a grab for the holstered hazer. The soldier, still on top, chopped Zook's forearm with his elbow, then kneed Zook in the groin with a ferocity that nearly caused Zook to black out in pain.

The soldier rolled off and Zook painfully uncurled himself. When he opened his eyes, he found the assailant towering over him holding the point of the hazer straight to Zook's temple.

"Move and you're dead," said the man, pushing himself upright and backing away, out of range of Zook's leash.

Zook, whose focus was entirely fixed on heater end of the hazer, could see the soldier's fingers trembling with adrenaline on the firing stud, ready to blast him into oblivion.

Suddenly, the hazer jerked from his grip as Sparklett, swinging herself on the cable from which she dangled, blind-sided the soldier by whipping into him from behind, her long legs locking around his neck.

Staggering, the big man attempted to break her hold by twisting and dropping, but Sparklett doggedly held on.

"Zook, grab him," she screamed as the soldier chopped at her legs, but Zook was already at the utmost end of his chain, still several feet from the action.

The hazer was lying on the floor where it had fallen, just beyond the limit of Zook's slave chain. Zook plucked the pencil from the desk and, lying flat and stretching every bone in his body, managed to slide the handle of the hazer close enough to grab.

Zook snatched up the weapon and—just as the soldier finally tore himself free from Sparklett's hold— fired.

The blue bolt of energy hit the man squarely in the chest, blowing his head and shoulders off in a cloud of superheated steam.

What was left of the body fell to the floor with a *thrump*.

Sparklett, swinging above, shrieked.

Zook saw that she was covered in blood and spinning

on the end of her cable. For a horrified moment he thought that she had been caught in the hazer's cross-fire.

Then he realized she was just reacting to the violence of the hazer shot, which had splattered her with gore from top to bottom.

"I'm okay, I'm okay," she said when she saw him looking.

He had to get her down before anyone else arrived.

Pointing the hazer to where his chain was attached, Zook blew a hole in the wall to free himself, then lurched for the Shredder controls. The red wall switch caused the Shredder to grind to a stop, but it took some experimenting with the hand control before Zook could maneuver the crane to set Sparklett down on the landing before him.

When Zook unhooked her she fell against him, unable to stand upright.

"Zook, thank God," she said. "You didn't give up the code. You saved us."

Zook sat her on a carton and began undoing the ropes which had trussed her to the Shredder hook. She was extremely emaciated and her hands shook when he freed them, but seemed to be in one piece.

"I knew you were one of us," she said, the adrenaline of her ordeal carrying her along. "I knew it the moment I saw you push the plop, that day when you saved my dog."

"Then you knew it before I did," said Zook.

"Recruiting is one of my jobs," she joked.

Zook felt a little dismayed. Was that all he was to her? A recruit? He looked at her searchingly and with longing.

Sparklett saw the look on his face and laughed, throwing her arms around him. "You're all I've thought about since that night overlooking the ocean," she said.

313

That was all the reassurance Zook needed. He pulled her to him and held her tight as his mouth found hers.

"I was so afraid for you," Zook whispered.

Footsteps approached in the hall and their bodies stiffened.

The foot falls grew nearer, seemed to pause near the door—then passed, finally fading down the corridor.

"We've got to get out of this room," Zook said. "I think we're somewhere under the main building. We ought to be able to find some stairs to the street."

"No," said Sparklett. "To the hopper on the roof."

"If you believe Wild."

"It's there. I flew it in myself."

"You can fly a hopper?"

"Blindfolded, if I have to. But did you really memorize the code?"

"I had plenty of time after…" Zook stopped.

Sparklett's face hardened. "After my sister died?"

"I'm sorry," said Zook. "I tried to save her."

"*They* killed her, not you. And we'll be next unless we get out of here."

"That's going to be difficult. This building's crawling with troops."

"The city's under lock-down and we still have to deliver that code. The hopper's our only option."

Zook nodded. "All right," he said. "There's an elevator from the prison level to the top of the tower."

"I know it," she said. "It unloads at the kitchen."

"If we can find the entrance without getting killed we ought to be able to make it to the roof," Zook said, tucking the hazer into his belt.

He pushed open the door and stuck his head out. The corridor outside was empty.

"Let's go," he said.

28.

FOLLOW OUR BLISS

"Wait," said Sparklett.

The bottom half of the soldier's body lay crumpled where Zook had hazered him. Charred intestines spewed across the floor in a spreading pool of blood. Sparklett-barefoot, Zook now realized—tread through the slippery blood and squatted, turning the corpses' pockets inside out.

"What are you doing?" Zook demanded. Every moment they remained in the Shredder room was another moment they could be discovered.

"The elevators are strictly controlled," she said, as she continued rummaging the pockets. She found a stubby black key and held it up. "We're going to need this."

Zook nodded. He had been so preoccupied with getting them out and away from the Shredder room he hadn't thought that far ahead.

Outside the room, the hallway looked much the same in one direction as the other. Toward the left, several corridors crossed and led off before the hall terminated at an unfinished concrete wall; toward the right it dead-ended at a T-intersection. The wall there was painted gray, and there was a gray carpet in the crossing corridor.

"This way," Zook said, moving toward the carpeted corridor.

"Are you sure?"

"It's where they took me in the elevator," Zook said.

As if in confirmation, they heard an elevator bell from around the corner ahead, then a voice ordering, "Double time. Let's go."

Zook quickly motioned Sparklett into a side room and they watched through a crack as a squad of four purple-sashed soldiers trotted in unison down the hallway.

"People's Guards," whispered Sparklett.

As Zook watched, two of the men entered the Shredder room while two more stationed themselves outside. "They're looking for Wild."

"General Lowe must have sent them. Wild should have been back in the war room by now."

It would only take a moment for the guards to realize what happened to the Controller, thought Zook.

"We're going to have to make a dash for it." He held up the hazer. "Ready?"

Sparklett nodded and Zook kicked the door open, letting loose a covering shot down the corridor which blew down a rain of ceiling tile and dust onto the soldiers.

Sparklett was out in an instant, and they ran down the corridor as fast as their legs would carry them—barely evading a return hazer bolt just as they turned the corner.

Ahead was an elevator door, but the door was golden and polished, not at all what Zook remembered.

He stopped. "This isn't it," he said.

But Sparklett had already pushed around ahead of him. "That's the main elevator. The service elevator is in the back."

They jogged around another corner and found an oversize stainless door, its surface scratched and dirty. Sparklett inserted the elevator key and the doors began to open with ponderous slowness. Behind them, they could hear voices shouting.

Inside, they waited for the doors to close. The voices drew nearer. The elevator had only one button to push, and Sparklett pushed it repeatedly while Zook pressed his body into the front right corner of the elevator cab, pointing the hazer at an angle back toward the corridor intersection.

Overhead, the elevator was playing a syrupy choral version of the UCC national anthem:

> *Imagine all the state slaves*
> *Sharing the whole earth...*

The shouting voices outside drew nearer, and suddenly the face of a soldier, very young, popped around the corner of the hall.

Zook let loose a hazer blast, shattering several concrete blocks in the corridor wall.

The elevator doors were closing, closing, closing. The young soldier had withdrawn from his position, but the shouting started up again.

"Come on," Zook said to the door, trying to encourage it to close as the music continued:

> *No God or superstition*
> *A State-sponsored rebirth...*

Then the door was finally and completely shut and the elevator began to rise.

Zook slumped his back against the wall. "We made it," he said, a goofy grin on his face. "We're safe."

Sparklett, her face creased with tension lines, gave Zook a despairing look. "Not yet," she said. "They have MilFones that transmit within the building. They'll be troops waiting at the top," she said.

The smile fell from Zook's face.

"All right," he decided, checking the charge on the hazer. "Get low and stay to the side. Be prepared to run."

"Run? This thing empties in the corner of the kitchen.

We'll be sitting ducks."

"We've got to try."

"No," she said. "You're the one with the code. So you're the one that has to get away. I'll go out with my hands up. Use me as a shield."

"That's ridiculous."

"It's the only way. The hopper pad stairs are in the center or the tower, two flights up."

"I can't fly a hopper. We have to make it together."

> *Imagine no aggression*
> *It's easy if you want…*

Sparklett considered. "All right," she said. "We'll go out fighting. But you know the UCC must never get that code?"

"Would I be here if I didn't know that?"

"What I mean is, you can't allow yourself to be captured no matter what. Do you understand?"

She was talking about suicide, and Zook saw that she was entirely serious. "I understand."

"If you love me, promise. The world will be enslaved for a thousand years if the UCC gets that code."

The elevator began to slow.

> *No need for truth or thinking*
> *A loving commandant…*

Zook's face hardened. "I promise," he said. "But keep close. We're both getting on that hopper."

They crouched in the corner as the elevator slowed and stopped.

The door had barely begun to slide open when Zook jammed the hazer through the crack and began firing, sending blue hazer bolts slashing right and left as screams erupted and crashes came from beyond.

Crouching, Zook grabbed Sparklett by the wrist and pulled her out against the wall into the smoky chaos of the elevator alcove. In the kitchen just beyond, huge flames leaped from the grill and private slaves ran helter-skelter in all directions.

But there were no soldiers and no return fire.

A wave of relief washed over Zook. Somehow word of their escape hadn't yet reached the tower.

It was Sparklett's turn to grab Zook's wrist. "The stairs are in this direction," she said, "toward the building core."

She led him through the burning kitchen, pushed through a swinging door, then into a plushly carpeted hallway which cut through the living quarters. They ran toward an upholstered door at the far end of the corridor, passing rooms on either side luxuriously decorated in antique French style.

Then they were through the swinging door and into another room, a library. There were exits at either end.

"Through here, hurry," said Sparklett, pushing through the door to the right.

Zook was about to join her when, out of the corner of his eye, he caught a glimpse of the room opposite

There, hanging on the wall as if it had never been disturbed, was his Pedro clown painting.

Zook hesitated and came to a halt. Sparklett had already made it through the next room, the door swinging shut behind her.

Acutely aware of the passing seconds, Zook detoured into the next room and grabbed the painting from the wall. In its elaborate frame and protective glass, it was bigger and heavier than Zook remembered.

He glanced at the door; he had only been separated from Sparklett for a moment. Zook quickly flipped the frame upside and tried to claw the painting from the frame, but several layers of protective matting held it secure.

"Don't move, Zook, I have a hazer pointed at the

exact center of your back," said a voice from behind.

Zook recognized the voice only too well: Bacon.

"Put that painting down and turn around slowly with your hands in the air. If you make a move for that gun, I swear I'll shoot you."

Zook did as he was told. Sustainable Bacon stood in the center of the room, hazer in hand.

"There was always something off about you, Zook," said Bacon. "Always questioning everything, always causing trouble."

With his unencumbered hand, Bacon drew a FreeFone from his tunic. "Security to Room 5012 immediately," he said. "We have an intruder."

Then to Zook: "And for what? If you kept your nose clean like I told you, you could have been a private slave, just like me."

Sparklett suddenly appeared in the doorway, tattered and dirty but standing imperiously, her hands on her hips. "Slave," she barked. "Put that weapon down."

Bacon hesitated, startled by her sudden presence. "But..." he stammered.

She interrupted. "You heard me, slave--weapon down! Now!"

Bacon's let the weapon drop as his eyes fluttered to the ground. "Yes, Friendster. Sorry, Friendster." It was a repeat of the humiliation Zook had witnessed at the People's Palace, only this time the stakes were real.

"There's a fire in the kitchen," Sparklett said. "Attend to it at once."

"Yes, Friendster, right away," said the slave.

Zook, amazed, watched as Bacon bowed and back his way out of the room.

"I can't believe he obeyed you," said Zook.

"That's what a slave does," she said, grabbing Bacon's discarded weapon. "Now come on, let's go."

"Wait," said Zook, stooping to pick up the big clown

painting.

Sparklett looked at him as if he were crazy. "What are you doing?"

Zook fumbled at the painting's backing, trying to extract the painting but unable to penetrate with his big fingers the layers of cardboard and tape which sealed it in the frame. "This is my clown painting. Wild stole it from me."

"We don't have time for that. Let's get out of here."

Zook knew he was putting them both in danger, but somehow he couldn't leave the painting behind. It didn't belong in the UCC. It belonged some place cleaner and purer—where there was hope.

"Trust me," he said to Sparklett. "It's important."

"Why?"

"It's a masterpiece that's got to be saved."

Sparklett relented. "Bring it then but let's go," she said.

Zook gave up trying to free the painting and hoisted the entire frame under his arm, following Sparklett out of the library and back into the other room.

They took the door she had originally indicated and ran down another long hallway, emerging into the building central core through an elaborately carved wooden door.

The door had barely swung closed when, in a blinding explosion, it flew off its hinges and sliced through the air in a thousand flaming pieces as it was hit from behind with a hazer bolt.

The troops had arrived.

"This way," said Sparklett, running around a circular wall and pushing through a door which opened onto a concrete stairwell.

They took the steps two at a time, Zook lugging the painting in one hand and the hazer in the other. Zig-zagging up four landings, they finally pushed though a pair of metal fire doors which opened with a gust of wind onto the rooftop hopper pad.

Octagon in shape, the pad was raised above the building roof on a series of V-shaped trusses, with an elevated ramp leading from the stairway landing to the pad proper. The hopper's squat, triangular body lay horizontally in the pad's center, its blunt ballistic nose hanging over the side. It looked enormous and powerful, with four huge turbines pointed downward in the takeoff position. The hatch was open and the stairs deployed.

"How long before you can get it in the air?" Zook asked Sparklett.

"Three minutes. Four tops."

"Get going," he said. "I'll hold them off."

She hesitated.

"I can't prep a hopper," Zook said. "Go."

She turned and ran toward the hopper across the elevated walkway.

Zook took cover behind an equipment box, the top of which held a spinning anemometer. Too late did Zook realize he had forgotten to give Sparklett the clown painting. He set the frame down with a thud, noting with a frown that the protective glass had somehow cracked.

Suddenly the rooftop door was kicked open, revealing a purple-sashed soldier pointing a hazer rifle squarely at the running Sparklett.

Crack! went Zook's hazer, almost of its own volition. A blue bolt of energy rent the air and the soldier exploded into a flower of red vapor.

A shadow of movement in the hopper's cockpit showed that Sparklett was in place, and Zook grabbed up the Pedro and ran across the elevated walkway, sending several bursts of covering hazer fire into the enclosed exit of the rooftop stairwell.

A whining sound began to emanate from the hopper as one-by-one Sparklett spun-up each of the four corner turbines in turn.

Zook, lugging the picture frame awkwardly under his left arm, made a dash for the hopper doorway, again firing blue bolts of cover fire until, suddenly, power indicator blinking, the hazer was out of charge.

He dropped it and kept running.

A hazer bolt cut behind him, making the air sizzle and scorching his back with oven-like heat.

Zook began to zig and zag across the hopper pad, still clutching the painting, concentrating on reaching the gaping hopper door.

There were two soldiers in the stairwell now, both pointing weapons at him.

Another bolt crossed his path, this one hitting the side of the hopper, momentarily heating its ceramic re-entry skin to a fiery red.

Zook rolled to the ground behind the cover of one of the hopper's landing leg flaps, crawling toward the stairs, still dragging the heavy clown painting after him.

A huge wave of super-heated air rolled over Zook. The air wavered and gusted and almost blew the Pedro out of his hands. The blast was not hazer fire, but came from the hopper's rocket turbines as the enormous vehicle slowly rose a foot off the pad and rotated over his head toward the stairwell.

More hazer blasts hit the side of hopper as slowly it rotated on its axis.

Zook realized that Sparklett was putting the hopper between him and the firing soldiers and bringing the hatch stairway around to Zook.

Zook scrambled backwards, out of the path of the screaming turbines, and, hugging the clown painting to his breast, launched himself up and onto the moving stairway in a single flying leap.

The hopper lurched and was suddenly away. Zook was flipped back against a galley wall as the huge machine dropped and banked. Through the still-open hatch, Zook could see the buildings of FriendsterVille rushing toward him at an alarming rate, and the clown painting floated up into the air before him.

He grabbed the Pedro before it could fall out, then managed to pull the wall lever which began folding closed the hydraulic door.

Another violent maneuver sent Zook rolling in the aisle, the frame of the painting crushed and snapping underneath him.

Then the direction of flight smoothed out and Zook found himself able to rise. A glimpse out the passenger windows revealed they were climbing somewhere over the edge of the city toward the sky over open desert.

Zook belted the Pedro into an empty passenger seat and made his way up the aisle to the cockpit, where Sparklett hovered over the controls. When he entered, Sparklett's face lighted up in a huge smile of relief.

Even with her clothes in rags and hair tangled, she looked beautiful.

He flopped into the seat next to her to kiss her, then hesitated, his heart suddenly pounding. He loved her as he had never loved anyone in his entire life. But his behavior from the moment they had met had been so cowardly and abject that he was suddenly ashamed.

"What is it?" she said.

"Are you sure you can love a state slave?" he asked.

"No," she said, looking thoughtful. "But I can love a free man."

Zook's slave mind started to form an objection, but Sparklett leaned forward and they kissed. Zook's body took over and he was flooded with so much desire and love that he groaned helplessly and had to break off.

"Now what?" Sparklett asked.

"Nothing," Zook said, staring in her eyes. "And everything." Somehow all his years of slave conditioning had fallen off and he really *was* free, and he really *did* have the love of this incredible, brave, perfect woman.

They embraced and kissed again, and kept kissing until the hopper computer announced the ignition of the auxiliary rocket thrusters which would boost them into sub-orbital flight in *five... four... three... two... one...*

The rockets ignited and pressed them into their chairs toward the clear free air of Palaska.

Toward Palaska, where clowns were free to get drunk and stags could cry.

BROWN & KING BOOKS BY D. G. VODA:

Must See to Appreciate
State Slave